W9-DDJ-104

WITHDRAWN

A SINNERS SERIES

HUNTED

ABI KETNER & MISSY KALICICKI

Month9Books

Donated by

SAN RAMON LIBRARY FOUNDATION
100 Montgomery • San Ramon • California 94583

This book is a work of fiction. Names, characters, places, and incidents are either products of the author's imagination or are used fictitiously. Any resemblance to actual persons, living or dead, business establishments, events, or locales is entirely coincidental. The author makes no claims to, but instead acknowledges the trademarked status and trademark owners of the word marks mentioned in this work of fiction.

Copyright © 2015 Abi Ketner and Missy Kalicicki

HUNTED by Abi Ketner and Missy Kalicicki
All rights reserved. Published in the United States of America by Month9Books, LLC.
No part of this book may be used or reproduced in any manner whatsoever without written permission of the publisher, except in the case of brief quotations embodied in critical articles and reviews.

Published by Month9Books for Georgia McBride Media Group
Cover by Kimberly Marsot
Typography and title design by Regina Wamba of Mai I Design
Cover Copyright © 2015 Month9Books

Month9Books

PRAISE FOR BRANDED

"Dark, intense, dangerous. We fell head over heels with the forbidden romance between brave heroine Lexi and swoon-worthy hero Cole. And Zeus? Best dog EVER. A must read for fans of the adrenaline intensity of *Shatter Me* and the totally hot guys of Jen Armentrout." **— Justine Magazine**

"A riveting and exciting dystopian read that will have you at the edge of your seat. I could not put it down and was entranced by this dark and unique world!" **— Ben Alderson, Booktuber at BenjaminofTomes**

"*Branded* is a fast paced, heart pounding, and swoon-worthy read that will make you fall in love with this dark and twisted world." **— Sasha Alsberg, Booktuber at ABookUtopia**

"It was page-turning, intense, emotional, and so much more! This is one dystopian filled with so much you just want and need in a book! I loved that Ketner & Kalicicki had me hooked from the start making me climb more and more into this book with each page. I really felt like I was taking to a whole other world and sometime got lost in what was going on around me!" **— Bella, Blogger at Paranormal Book Club**

"The concept of this book was amazing. From the very first page, I was on edge. I read this book in one day, it just wouldn't stop being exciting." **— Amy, Blogger at Reading Teen**

"I just can't stress how much I love this book! *Branded* will DEFINITELY go into my TOP FIVE FAVORITE BOOKS OF ALL TIMES!!! If you haven't read *Branded*, then stop what you're doing NOW and READ IT!!!!" — **Alicia, Blogger at Addicted Readers**

"Wow! What a story! What a set of characters! What an ending! Now I'm ready for the next book!" — **Lisa, Blogger at A Life Bound By Books**

"WOW! I want more. And I want it now. There are several revelations at the end of the story that leaves the reader hungry for more. Take it from me, you will enjoy this book so much, that you won't be able to it out of your head. It's just an amazing story that will blow you away." — **Savannah, Blogger at Books With Bite**

"This story is emotional and scary. This book literally brought the saying 'on the edge of my' seat to life. My heart was pounding with almost every chapter. I loved that feeling! I haven't read a book in a long time that left me feeling nervous and twitchy. I was dying to know how things would go for Lexi in the HOLE. And the ending was O-M-G! — **Damaris, Blogger at Good Choice Reading**

"Fast paced and fun, *Branded* has something everyone will love. Abi Ketner and Missy Kalicicki have created a unique dystopian romance that's sure to stand out in today's market!" — **Lindsay Cummings, Author of *The Murder Complex***

"I read until my eyes shut, and couldn't wait to get back to find out what was going to happen next. The battle scenes were AMAZING!!! It was a story beautifully told, and described, and has you straight front-and-center with the characters. All I can say is…add this to your lists!!! You won't be sorry!!! Oh… and HURRY WITH BOOK #2, Abi and Missy!!!" — **Cameo Renae, bestselling author of the HIDDEN WINGS Series**

"I LOVED this book! I went back and forth between biting my nails and swooning. Yes, quite the combination of emotions but it was awesome! This is one messed up society that I just couldn't get enough of. And the romance, oh man oh man oh man. Cole is something else, ladies. RAWR." — **Celeste, Blogger at The Book Hookup**

"It isn't often that a book can completely engage me from the start but right from the very first paragraph this book held me within its pages and did not release me from its clutches until the very last word. BOOM! I highly recommend this book to anyone that loves a nail biting read with constant twists and turns, a lead kick-ass female that you would gladly call your friend and a lead male that you want spider monkey because he is that amazing." — **Nancy, Blogger at Tales of A Ravenous Reader**

"The writing was strong, I fell in love with the characters and was totally wrapped up in the world. There was a swoon-worthy hero, a strong heroine, a forbidden romance (and I mean REALLY forbidden) and a super evil bad guy. Now, I don't normally read Dystopians but this one had me HOOKED!!!" — **Aesta, Blogger at Aestas's Book Blog**

Abi
My mom, Lisa.
My second mom, Sally.
My Mamie, June.

Missy
My mom, Jennifer.
My mom, Denise, gone too soon.

.

"The air is thick with dust and death." — Lexi Hamilton

A SINNERS SERIES

HUNTED

ABI KETNER & MISSY KALICICKI

CHAPTER 1

The rusted gray car is a luxury we haven't had in some time. I smooth its faded red upholstery and sink into Cole's body beside me as the chatter of the 2044 engine lulls me deep into thought.

A breeze blows through the window, whipping my hair around my face. I indulge myself in a smile, enjoying the smell of ocean spray, forgetting where I am momentarily. To imagine sun-kissed beaches, long summer days, and happier times. But something inside won't quite let me be.

I know this road like I know the curves and edged places of Cole's body. The dark gravel lines of the road, fading into smooth sand with occasional palm trees dotting the horizon, reminds me of the few photos my mother possessed in her bureau. It's familiar, comforting, and makes me smile as I close my eyes, trying to shake the uneasy feeling.

I remember how it looked years ago when my parents used to vacation here. Vibrant, full of laughter and life with rows of waterfront houses, people, and clear blue water as far as the eye can see. Now, it's empty, desolate, a shell of its former self, and half-covered by sand. Neglected and abandoned by people who know better than to return. I sit up and rest my elbow on the window ledge, while inhaling deeply. Despite the wars, there's an inherent beauty here, one I refuse to let go of.

Cole's right hand moves to my knee, and I tense under his warm touch. He squeezes, forcing me to jump as a giggle escapes from my lips.

"You okay?" He steals a glance and then returns his eyes to the road.

"Just thinking about how much has happened in the past few months," I say, feeling my face heat up as I turn toward him.

"Everything that's happened?" I see the corners of his mouth curving upward. His dimples make me lightheaded. I can't stop the blush that spreads over my cheeks.

"Not just that. I mean, we've been through so much in the past few months. I couldn't even hold a gun when we first met, let alone shoot one."

"Or boost a car."

"And what kind of person can sleep standing up?" I half-expect him to respond, but when he doesn't, I continue on. "It shouldn't have to be this way." My voice trails off, worried I may have ruined the moment. "Cole?"

He doesn't acknowledge me right away. His eyes are distant, focused on the horizon. Maybe he can feel it too, the dread in the pit of my stomach. That feeling you get when you know the moment won't last. I stretch out my left arm, wrapping it around his neck while I gently kiss his jawline. "You're amazing." Immediately, I feel his body relax. He turns his head, and the same gorgeous smile plays at his lips.

"You're pretty amazing yourself. A total badass with a gun *and* a great kisser." Cole's intense look is somewhere between satisfied and troubled. Holding his gaze, I smile back, hoping he can't see how sad and lost I feel.

Compliments are hard to come by nowadays, so when Cole offers one, I savor it. I want him to be proud of how much I've changed, how well I can handle myself. I need him to see that I'm not the same girl he rescued from the Hole.

Hair gets caught in my mouth. I push it away from my face and look out the window, watching the sand dunes flip past. Anything's better than the Hole. I can't go back to that place. I won't.

Now we rely on Sutton's underground resistance members to shelter, feed, and hide us. On occasions like this, we might almost get a break from living like animals, if we can determine whether a possible safe house is actually safe. But even if this safe house turns out to be useful, we can never let our guard down, get too comfortable.

The face of a former revolt member named Molly flashes through my memory as I grip the handle of the car door, turning my knuckles white. At nineteen and only a year older than me, Molly survived being branded orange and living in the Hole for two years on her own, only to be murdered in a safe house that wasn't secure. When one of her friends found us, he told us she had failed to clear one closet in the house, the only time she'd ever missed one, and was promptly shot by

3

a guard hiding inside. So despite riding in a car with beautiful and soft upholstery, snuggling up to Cole, I cannot become complacent. Complacency can get you killed.

I exhale, letting my thoughts drift away as I examine Cole's newly buzzed head, glistening from sweat. Just last night, he asked me to chop off his long, dark, greasy hair, grown out of control without the aid of a razor. Now, he looks like the Cole I met on my first day in the Hole—minus the spotless uniform and bossy attitude. *But he's still just as intense.*

"I miss Zeus, even though he can be a royal pain in my ass," he says, raising an eyebrow in my direction before planting a kiss on my cheek.

"How can you say that about Zeus? He was protecting me."

"I miss him, but it'll be good for us to be alone without any interruptions, don't you think?" Cole chuckles and squeezes my leg again, quickly taking a moment to look me over.

"What's so funny?"

"I just pictured him, sitting next to our bed, resting his head on the mattress, with his head cocked staring at us." He leans back into his seat with that mouth-watering dimple dented in his cheek.

I feel my face warm. My mind replays the night before, when Zeus interrupted us by licking Cole's back in the middle of a highly charged make-out session. *Yes, time alone will be good.* I laugh to myself.

I give Cole a coy smile, but he doesn't notice. He's turned his attention back to the road.

After a check of the rearview mirror, his lips seal into a thin line. He squints to get a better look and tightens his grip on the steering wheel.

4

"Damn it." His body tenses. "We've got company."

The hair on my neck rises. "What?" I glance behind us. A fast-moving, sleek, black vehicle trails a mile or so behind. One day, I'll learn to trust my instincts. I knew this was too good to last. I flip back around and face Cole.

"I'm gonna grab the guns." I can feel my heart begin galloping as adrenaline starts to pour into my veins.

"Yeah, we're gonna need 'em," he says.

I pull out his Glock and my SIG Sauer P229 compact that one of the resistance members gave me. Sweat trickles down my back as I place the guns on my lap and wipe my clammy hands on my pants.

"Hold tight. Don't shoot till I say." His voice is low and calm, but his rigid posture tells me he is just as nervous as me. *Fear makes us better fighters*, Keegan used to say. "Get ready." He checks the rearview again.

Cole slams the gas pedal into the floor. My head jerks back, hitting the headrest. The car bucks against his demand, protesting his urgency with an engine that has seen better days.

I grip the guns, willing myself to be calm and breathe like he taught me. *Here we go.*

Cole clenches his jaw. "Crap."

"What?" I glance over my shoulder again.

"They're gaining on us!" He unbuckles his seatbelt.

The speedometer ticks up past eighty, but it feels like we're moving at a snail's pace compared to the approaching car. I shake my head. I check Cole's Glock one last time, cocking it before handing it to him. Then I unbuckle my seatbelt too.

Cole raises an eyebrow at me, and I nod while pushing the seatbelt off to my right.

"Let's do this," I say.

"Remember, shoot to kill, don't hesitate, not even for a second."

"Got it."

I scan my own hand, wrapped around my two-toned silver and black SIG. I double-check the extra magazines I have strapped around my waist. It amazes me that just before he died, Keegan showed me how to use a gun. Now he's gone, and handling guns feels like second nature. *I've become a killer.*

My eyes focus on the vehicle closing in, though thoughts of Keegan bring me to tears.

The pounding in my chest gets louder. Just then, the sun disappears, and dark clouds, pregnant with rain, loom over us. I exhale while fingering the trigger of the cold metal weapon in my lap. I lick my dry lips and bite down in anticipation.

I hope we're ready for them.

"Holy sh—" Cole yells.

I grasp the door handle as a dark Charger swings onto the road with a flash of black paint.

Cole swerves left, narrowly missing the oncoming car by a hair. Gunfire erupts from the other car. We're so close I can see the green eyes of the driver and the black uniform he's wearing.

"Ahhhhh!" I scream as the passenger side window behind me shatters into the backseat. *They're shooting at us.*

Adrenaline bursts through me like fire, burning my veins. I lean out my open window and fire, pummeling the driver's door with puncture holes. "All right, bastards. Let's see what you got."

The guard steers his car into ours, slamming us into the left-hand shoulder. Our car thumps over God knows what along the edge, bouncing me all over the place. I struggle to hold on. Cole's shouting. Squealing tires and torrents of gunfire echo all around me as I'm thrown into him.

"Dammit!" I scream as I struggle back up and fire more rounds.

Click.

I'm empty. I eject the empty mag and slam another one in. Gripping the inside of the car with one hand, I try to aim with my right. But everything's going too fast. My hair blows in front of my face, and my hand slips off the ledge. A knife of panic slices through me as I try to brace myself back up.

Cole's cussing becomes background noise as he fights to keep the car on the road. "Shoot out their tires!" he yells. "Now!"

"I'm trying." It comes out whinier than I expected.

Cole keeps swerving the car, making it impossible to get a shot off. I don't want to waste bullets if I don't have to. *This is damn near impossible.*

"Shoot, Lexi." Cole jerks the wheel right, bashing our car into the guard's door. I don't think I'm even breathing as I take a few more shots. My ears are ringing, and my body's on overdrive.

The cars are locked together in a mass of spraying bullets. All around me, glass is exploding. I feel it slice across my face in a million little pieces, and I blink furiously as pain jabs my eyes like miniature needles. My hands fiddle for another magazine, and as I slam it in, I focus through the watery film of my eyes and meet the gaze of the guard. His neck's corded.

He's screaming something at me. But I can't focus on his mouth. And I can't hear anything he's saying to me. All that matters is putting him away.

He raises his gun at the same time. And as we're staring down one another's barrels, he flinches, and without hesitation, I squeeze a shot off.

Blood gushes from his face as his body slumps over the wheel. Abruptly, his car banks right and slows down. A cloud of dust rises as it rolls off the road into an embankment. I watch as it rebounds over the sand dunes and smashes to a stop.

Cole brings our beater back onto the road. His chest's heaving up and down, and he glances over at me.

"You were unbelievable."

Just as I start to respond, the other vehicle rams us from the back. *Crash!* Crunching metal and more shots split the air as I slam into the dashboard. I throw my elbows up to block my head. Beside me, I see Cole's head snap back into his headrest.

"What the hell!" he's shouting.

I grip the dashboard and try getting up, but my hands are slick with sweat. Cole floors it again, and this time, there's nothing. My head feels like someone took a mallet to it. I crawl halfway onto my seat, looking in the rear windshield before I realize what's about to happen. A black Charger has backed off, but suddenly, it zooms onto our bumper.

"Brace yourself for another hit, Lexi."

It rams us from behind again. A horrific crunching reaches my ears as I slam forward into the dashboard and slither onto the floor. For a moment, I'm disoriented. Warm liquid drips down my face. *Blood.* All I hear is the groaning, straining engine of our car. I'm wiggling my fingers in front of me, trying to focus, when I hear a thump.

"Lexi, are you all right? Come on, get up. Please." Cole's panicked voice rips through my fog.

I grip my head as splitting pain pulses through every nerve ending in my body. I've got to pull myself together. Dropping my hands, I move slowly up and onto the seat, looking for my gun. *Oh crap, where the hell is it?* I panic when the guard leaps onto the trunk of our car, threatening to get inside.

Cole fishtails, trying to throw the guard off, but instead of getting rid of the guard, it shakes me up even more. My blood burns in my veins, and fear builds in my chest. *Where is my damn gun?* I'm almost on my knees, shaking and frantically searching for my weapon.

Bingo.

I pick it up just as a shadow falls over the backseat.

I lift my eyes.

The guard's right hand pulls inside the frame of the blown-out back window. I notice his bulging muscles through his sweaty uniform shirt and know we don't stand a chance if he gets all the way inside. He looks like he could swallow me up. I raise my gun, trying to hold it steady, its metal parts rattling as I point it in his general direction.

But he's too quick.

He slides in and manages to grab Cole's neck. Cole grips the wheel with his left hand as he gasps for air. He's making gurgling noises, and I know I've got to act. With his right hand, he feels along the seat for his gun. I'm frozen in place, watching this nightmare unfold. *It's really over this time.*

Suddenly, I hear Cole wheeze. "Do some ... thing."

A flash of silver catches my eye, and as the guard pulls out a knife, everything clicks into place.

"Get off him!"

The guard's maniacal gaze turns to me, but I'm faster this time. I press my gun to his head, and without hesitation, I fire at point-blank range.

Bang.

Everything's amplified in the car, and I drop my gun to the floor and grab my ears. My head's ringing. The splatter of blood and brains makes me scream. *He's dead.* I must remember to breathe. Everything's tinged crimson, and my throat's dry like I've gargled with rocks.

Cole grunts and gasps for air. We're covered in blood and brain bits when he reaches out, cups my face in his hand, and whispers my name. But the body's strewn across the backseat, and the smell of blood makes me want to vomit.

"There's more!" Cole says in a hoarse voice. But I barely register his words.

I glance back and catch a flash of another vehicle. *Don't they ever give up?* Almost as if in answer to my question, another sleek Charger pulls up beside us. I see the driver's body tighten when his eyes meet mine. He must know what happened.

The black car drops back, and I brace myself for the worst.

"Oh sh—" Cole's cut off.

The Charger rams into our car, and we fly off the road and into a ditch.

Bodies, glass, blood, guns, and supplies collide. I squeeze my eyes closed, unable to focus on the melee surrounding me. I think I hear screaming. It sounds vaguely like my own voice. I grasp for anything to hang on to before we come to a rest upside down. The loud noise of an airbag inflating accentuates the madness.

Am I alive?

I inhale and wait for the blinding light people talk about seeing when they're near death. I close my eyes and then open them again. I see nothing but the dingy red of the car intermingled with stark silence.

I reach out, feeling around for anything familiar. My hands hurt from the glass as I attempt to pull myself out from the wreckage. My vision's cloudy, and every limb is marked with gashes. I stop and pick an inch-long piece of glass from my elbow, gritting my teeth as I pluck it out. All our stuff, backpacks, food, everything, is splayed out like a trail leading to us. I wince as I army crawl through the melee, unsure of where I am. My head feels thick with liquid, like it needs to be drained so I can remember who I am again. *Cole? Where the hell is Cole?*

I force myself to crawl away from the car and sit up. I glance around, looking left, looking right, and then left again. I see the guard's dead body, half hanging out the back of our upside down car, but not Cole.

Where is he? *God, please don't take him from me.* I wring my hair with my bloodied hands as I scan the area back and forth. He can't be far. Sweat's dribbling down my forehead, stinging my eyes, and I wipe it away. That's when I catch a glimpse of his dark blue t-shirt.

He's lying in the reeds, face down. I crawl closer to him. He's motionless. *No. Please no.* Overwhelming fear jabs me like knives. I reach out to check his pulse.

Crunch. Crunch. Crunch.

11

What is that?

"Don't move," a voice commands from behind me, instantly freezing my veins.

I swallow hard. My finger's a breath away from Cole's neck, but I have to pull back. I turn and face the guard, who points his gun at my head. His face hardens at the sight of me.

"Ah, jackpot." I clench my jaw and narrow my eyes at him. "You're gonna make me a very, very rich man." He reaches with his left hand and grabs an old radio from his waist. "I've got a revolt member here. Branded blue. No doubt, it's Lexi Hamilton." He pauses as he examines me.

A female voice crackles back. "Have you interrogated her yet?"

"No, ma'am. I'm going to question her when I've got her in custody."

I tighten every muscle in my body. *I can't let him take me. I won't go back to the Hole. I can't leave Cole.* I glance between the guard and Cole's motionless body, trying to form a plan, and fast.

"Are there any others with her?" she asks.

"Just one other, but he's already dead. I'll throw his body in the trunk."

"What about Patton?" she asks with hesitance. The guard pauses, takes a deep breath while his Adam's apple bobs up and down.

"This isn't news you should hear over the com." He pauses again. "But neither he nor any of the others survived the chase. I'm so sorry; I know how much you loved him." At first, there's no response, and the line seems dead. Then I hear it crackle loudly, and a female voice cries in the background as a

12

new male voice speaks.

"Bring that whore in."

"Yes, sir."

I shake my head. *No.* The guard squints at me and lowers his radio while keeping his gun trained on my head.

"All this time on the run for what? You're going home now, Lexi Hamilton. It's time to go back home."

In that split second, Cole rolls over and shoots the guard in the chest twice. A thick, dark red liquid begins to saturate the guard's uniform shirt, and he drops to the ground, crumbling into a heap. The radio clatters next to his feet with static pouring out before Cole crawls over and turns it off.

I'm not sure what I'm more relieved about: Cole waking up or Cole waking up and killing that guard who was about to take me back to the Hole. Tears burst from my eyes, pouring over my cheekbones and onto my bloody, sweaty, disgusting shirt.

"I thought you were dead." Cole grabs my face with both hands and kisses me.

"I thought I made it clear, I'm not gonna leave you. Ever!"

His desperate lips meet mine with force, as if reassuring me that he's real and he's alive. Then he wraps his arms around me and crushes me to his chest while we're on our knees.

"I'm so sorry."

"For what?" He kisses my forehead.

"Back there, I hesitated—"

His hands cup my face in an instant. "You have *nothing* to be sorry about. You saved us." He exhales and extends a hand to me while getting up. "Let's get the hell out of here." I grasp it, feel my knees crack as I straighten them, and wobble momentarily against his chest before stepping away.

"Wait," I say. "We can take his car." I motion to the side of the road where the last black vehicle sits with the driver's side door open.

"But then we'd have to find somewhere to ditch it." He looks at me thoughtfully as he scratches his head.

"We will." I examine his cuts, his bloodied clothing, and the sand peppered on his skin. He winces when I touch his right shoulder and his neck.

"Are you sure you're all right?" I ask with concern.

"Yeah. You okay?" he asks, his voice ticking upward, his hands hesitant to leave my shoulders.

"Never better." I pick a tiny piece of glass from his cheek as he cringes away from my hand. "Let's go."

We grab whatever we can salvage from the wreckage and slowly climb into the guard's Charger, hoping that they don't track us to the safe house in Lexington Bay.

CHAPTER 2

"Pull over," I say. Cole's head flicks toward me, one eye swollen almost completely closed, the color purple settling in. "Just do it."

He guides the car to a spot thickly overgrown with reeds and palm trees, and I quickly shove my door open, groaning, as every muscle in my body stiffens.

"And what are we doing exactly?" he asks.

"Hurry, follow me." I don't bother closing the door behind me and stumble into the reeds. My feet sink into the damp ground as water brims over into my shoes. He trails along, the uneven sound of sloshing boots tracking my every step. Cole arrives next to me.

"Let's make this quick." I bend over, palming a handful of water and then splash my face with it. A million knives could be stabbing me right now, and it'd still feel better than this.

Water slips down my hands, over my wrists, and washes away the rusty-smelling blood from my skin.

Cole stumbles left.

"Holy shit," he says. His hands shoot out in an attempt to balance himself.

"Oh my God, Cole." I straighten, trying not to hurt him when reaching for his arm. His jaw tightens as he grabs hold of his side.

"It's okay. Just probably bruised." He winces again.

"Here, let me help you," I insist.

"It's nothing. I'm fine," he says, almost breathless. He's so proud, never wants to appear like he might actually need my help with anything.

I carefully wash his face. His teeth grind together, and his hand grips my forearm, his fingers leaving marks.

"Here, I have to take off your shirt," I say, tugging at its hem.

"Lexi, I'm okay," he says. But even as he tries to push me away, his face contorts into a troubling grimace. Sweat trickles down his forehead.

"You're a terrible liar," I say. "I'll be gentle, just try to hold still." He exhales as I lift the shredded, bloodied shirt over his head, revealing a torso full of bluish, purple bruises.

"Oh, not good. That has to be wrapped. If any of your ribs are broken, the pressure will help."

"They're not broken."

"It'll only take a few seconds." I put his shirt in the water, squeezing it out with all the strength I have left to rinse away the blood and bits of glass embedded in it. Then I reach around his waist. He groans and slowly raises his arms above his head.

I tie the material as best I can, my hands shaking by the end of the process.

"It will do for now."

"Thank you," he says, breathing heavily. "We've got to go."

I rub my head, feeling woozy. He reaches for me as exhaustion, pain, and the weight of what just happened overtakes me.

"I'm all right ... " I say, but the words trail off.

He blinks his good eye, the area around his other eye swelling by the minute. "We'll do this together," he says.

I turn toward him, draping his arm over my shoulder and wrapping mine around his waist. "Now, let's hide the car and find that safe house. Maybe they'll have ice there ... or something." He snorts and then winces with the next step. "If we're lucky, we'll find extra clothes and something decent to eat."

"Don't get your hopes up," he says, the slightest smile on his face.

We drive the car into a ditch and do our best to hide it beneath reeds, sand, and whatever else we can find. By the end, Cole's leaning against the vehicle, barely able to stand up straight without grimacing.

"Here, let me finish," I say.

"Uh, I think not. You're hurt too," he says.

"I'm faster than you right now."

He mashes his teeth together as he lowers himself to sit. A thick sheen of sweat covers him, and I know he hates showing weakness.

"Almost done," I say, checking to see if the car is adequately hidden.

A few minutes later, Cole grabs his temples, closes his eye, and grits his teeth. His breathing is even more labored.

It feels like I'm moving in slow motion as I throw a few more handfuls of sand and grab a couple more fronds to place on the vehicle. Then I rub my hands together, feeling the grit exfoliate my palms, while examining our work.

"Well, it's not exactly the best cover-up, but it'll have to do."

Cole drops his hands and shakes his head. "Why do I get the feeling our luck's about to run out? Those people were serious. They wanted to take us back to the Hole even if they had to die trying."

A flick of wetness lands on my face, and I glance upward. It looks like someone took a brush and painted a fresco of rolling black and gray clouds.

"Yeah, luck hates us, royally."

Steadily, the rain picks up until it's pounding us with a fury. We watch hopelessly as Mother Nature completely destroys our efforts to hide the car.

"Well," Cole says, "there goes that."

His black eyes still manage to render me speechless. On his face is every emotion of the last few minutes—fear, anger, sadness, relief. I don't know what to say.

When I was younger, there was a movie where the guy

grabs the girl and kisses her in the rain. I remember wishing back then that I was her. Yet, here I am, with the man of my dreams, and while this could be a total romantic chick flick moment, killing two people and crashing our car has kind of spoiled the mood. I'm shivering, injured, and nauseous. All I really want is an electric blanket, some hot soup, and a safe place for Cole and me to cuddle up for the night.

He looks as if he's about to say something profound. But when he opens his mouth, all he says is, "We can't waste any more time out here."

"What about the car?"

"Forget the car." He pushes himself up, links his fingers in mine, and guides me away from the scene.

By now, the rain's slowed to a gentle pitter-pattering around us. Unfortunately, it does nothing to quell my ice-cold, wet toes or the water sloshing inside my boots. I hate walking in slushy shoes, but this is the least of things I've had to endure the past few months.

While walking, I slip on something slick—a "Wanted" poster. Seems Wilson wants me alive, and the reward for my capture is an extravagant one million dollars. Sutton, the leader of the revolt, will see his captor get paid an outrageous sum of seven hundred and fifty thousand dollars. But Cole's reward is more than mine and Sutton's combined. He not only broke rank and escaped, but he helped me escape and executed the Commander. And, if he is captured—dead or alive—Wilson will pay one lucky person two million dollars. My mind is blown.

"Our faces are everywhere. Can you believe Wilson wants us captured that badly?" My wet fingers struggle to keep the dripping poster from tearing in two as I examine it. "I thought, at least, down here, I wouldn't see these ... "

A black and white photo of myself at seventeen looks back at me. That girl looks so different. She's clean, well fed, dressed in the latest fashions of that time, and would not be caught dead looking like the me I am now.

The photo was taken at school the year before I was accused, dragged off to the Hole, and branded. I wipe water from my eyes. Still, I looked so unhappy, even then. I shrug and tear the poster into pieces, stomping it into the sand before moving on. *If I didn't know myself, I'd turn me in. That's a lot of money. A person could start a completely new life somewhere else, where no one knew them and no one cared what they had done in the past.*

"Even with your face everywhere, have they found you?" Cole asks. "No."

"Maybe we won't be so lucky next time," I say.

He turns around and kisses the top of my head. "You don't need luck. You have me."

"I will always need you, Cole."

"You already know, Lexi. As amazing as you are, and with all the new skills you've gained, I'll never truly be comfortable letting go. I know you can take care of yourself ... that if something happened to me, that ... " He pauses, a pained expression covering his face. Cole takes a deep breath and grabs at his side again before continuing. "When those jackasses were shooting at you, I was not okay with that." Cole's grip on my hand tightens almost painfully. "I was not okay with that at all." He turns away from me, averting his eyes.

"You think I enjoyed watching you being shot at, nearly run off the road, and choked? When our car tipped over and I couldn't find you, I thought I had lost everything." I swallow hard while wiping tears from my eyes. He turns back toward me, his lashes dripping with water, and his lips pursed.

"No matter how good you become at all of this"—Cole gestures to the area around us—"I'll always protect you. I love you, Lexi, and I protect what I love." I open my mouth, and then close it. Sometimes, hearing him say things like that confounds me. That he would put his own life before mine still baffles me.

He doesn't wait for my response, as if the matter is settled. He just takes my hand again and leads me in the direction of the safe house, which I hope is close by. Because I'm unable to move my toes at this point.

"I can't go back there."

"I won't let that happen. As bad as it was, it's even worse now. Sutton said Wilson executed pretty much all of the revolt members who didn't make it out and kept a few hundred people around to make examples out of for anyone thinking about joining. He shut down hospital access and medical care for everyone except his men."

"What's left? Some of those people were just like me, falsely accused. They don't deserve to be there. Wilson sounds as bad as the Commander. Maybe even worse," I say.

"And on top of that, he's still branding Sinners and sending them to the Hole. Nothing has changed."

I suck in a breath and keep moving forward, feeling pity for those we didn't free. I don't bother to mention how I really feel. Keegan died for nothing. My dad died for nothing. Every time I

21

see Sutton, I can tell he also carries the burden of those deaths.

Cole grips my hand tighter. "It can't stay this way forever. There are too many people fighting. I refuse to believe this is how we're going to spend the rest of our lives."

I cringe knowing I may never see my mom again, never be able to give Keegan a proper burial. "What if it is? We never thought anyone could be as bad as the Commander, right? What if things never get better?"

Cole stops abruptly. He stoops low to the ground and pulls me next to him. I look from left to right and crouch beside him. I wipe my face and force myself to focus, even as my nerve endings scream.

He motions to me with two fingers, pointing at his eyes and then forward. I follow his fingers through the tall reeds to the faded pinks, whites, and yellows of the beach houses on stilts. Wooden slats are missing in some places, and the windows are all boarded up. The only potential sign of life is a food wrapper wafting in the breeze, caught on some reeds near a rusted car that looks like it hasn't been touched in years.

Slate-gray waves crash against the beach, capped in white foam, making the bay look angry and forcing the water almost to the front steps of the houses. We need to get inside.

Just as I begin to stand, I see them, two figures in dark uniforms patrolling up the beach. They comb the perimeter, looking for trouble. *Looking for us.*

I point at one of the guards. Cole nods, and we both slink back from the edge. I press myself flat against the sand, pulling my gun out and struggling to hold it steady. Sand grinds against my arms. I grit my teeth in pain. Particles of sand crunch in my mouth. If I could somehow melt into the ground, I would.

22

The dark figures come closer as my shoulders tighten, and my breaths burst in and out. The rain stops, and they begin walking toward the edge, where the beach meets the dunes. One of them is short and stocky with tanned skin. The other, almost his polar opposite. I'm guessing he's just over six foot. The tall one's mouth is caught in a sneer as he trudges, barely lifting his feet from the beach. The closer they get, the more I resist the urge to run. Instead, I press my face into the sand, willing myself to disappear.

"Man, talk about a waste of time," the short one says. His voice comes out like a low growl. "Today makes it, what? Three days since we found a Sinner—I'm about to start shooting trees."

"Shut the hell up, and stop your bitching. Four more checkpoints. Then we'll head back," the tall one says, an M16 hanging over his shoulder. He looks up at the sky, which has grown ever darker. "Let's split up. I want out of here before this storm hits." His feet stop at the edge where the beach meets the reeds, and it becomes quiet.

"You really think we'll find anything?" the short one asks.

"Doubtful, but I don't want to be the one answering to Clayton when he asks," the tall one says with a snort. "That's all you."

"That guy's a real dick sometimes," the short one says. He shuffles from one foot to the other. "And nothing exciting's happened around here in fifty years … at least not since the last war." He kicks the sand with his boot.

"Oh right, like when they bombed the shit out of everything," the tall one says with a laugh. His partner chuckles, but then they both turn silent.

23

"All right, well, I'll comb that end of the beach, and you can take this area." Their feet move in different directions. "Let's get this over with."

When I lock eyes with Cole, his jaw twitches. He mouths to me, "Don't move."

My body freezes in place. I swear the beating of my heart can be heard for miles. I close my eyes and pull in cool, salty air as I wait for the guards to discover us. My finger tenses beside the trigger of my handgun.

When I open my eyes, I notice they haven't moved very far, and one is still dangerously close. Cole aims his pistol at the one closest to us. His finger's only a quick flick away from the trigger. His face looks rigid. I move the other guard into my line of sight, shifting slightly away from Cole.

Any second now, they'll discover us, and once again, it'll be a blood bath.

Two feet.

My pulse echoes in my ear, drowning out the sounds of the ocean. Just then, I hear the static charge of a guard's radio. My breath catches in my throat. He pulls it from his waist and holds it up. The other guard, hearing the static from his position, meanders back toward us.

"Ten twenty-four, go ahead. I'm listening," he says.

"All units: Code red. Code red. Lexi Hamilton sighted in the vicinity of Lexington Bay, Key Largo. Four men down. Possibly escaped with a male. Units in the area, please respond." The voice cuts off.

Now, I really wish we could dig holes into the ground.

"Ten twenty-four, responding to your Code Red for Lexi Hamilton," the guard says. "I'm in the area." His partner's eyes enlarge.

"Sinner is armed and dangerous," the voice on the radio says. Pause. "Thought to have killed four men. Use extreme caution, and call for backup if discovered."

"Affirmative."

The guard lowers his radio, and both men stare at each other in disbelief. "Well hot damn. Looks like we've got ourselves some action for a change. Maybe she's closer than we thought."

"Once we catch that whore, I'm taking a vacation to Italy," the growly voice says, excitement ringing through his voice. He steps even closer as he jumps around. I could probably touch the tip of his boot if I wanted to, but I don't dare make a noise as he pivots.

"You still there, ten twenty-four?" The voice from the radio cuts through the static.

The guard raises the radio to his mouth and faces his partner. "Ten twenty-four, still here."

"Their getaway car has been found. I repeat: Their getaway car has been found."

I knew it'd come back to haunt us. My blood feels like ice.

"Report back to quarters immediately," the voice commands.

"Ten-four." The guard clips his radio to his waist and shrugs while looking at his buddy. "They're going to mount a search I'm betting."

"Oh, I feel it in my bones. We've got her this time," the other says.

As they walk away, I can scarcely blink without fear of discovery. I can't relax. They know we're here. They know where the car is. It won't be long before they find us again. It's only a matter of time. Thunder crawls across the sky, vibrating the earth beneath me.

"Hey, breathe," Cole says into my ear. "I'm right here."

I turn my head, and his face is an inch away from mine. I relax a little, releasing the air trapped in my lungs. His warm breath on my neck comforts me as thunder reverberates again, followed by a beautiful display of lightning.

"The rain should've washed away our tracks, so let's hope they'll assume we've taken off running." He gives me a reassuring touch on the shoulder. "We'll be all right as long as they don't have dogs."

I chew on his words for a minute before deciding he's probably right. Slowly, my grip relaxes on my gun, and I swallow the lump in my throat.

"We have to stick to the plan. Get to the safe house, make contact with Sutton."

"Okay then, which one is it?" I ask, motioning to the houses in front of us.

"The pink one on the end." He wraps his hand around my forearm, and we take off across the open expanse between the reeds and the houses, fighting pain and fatigue. The wind kicks up spray in our faces. Any minute, it looks like the clouds are going to burst.

We reach the houses in silence. Cole quickly moves alongside them and beneath the stilts, making sure it's clear. Trash cans line the side of the house, half of them blown over by the wind. The garage has no door, and inside it, spare auto parts litter the floor. They rattle just enough to send prickles up my arms.

Then Cole rounds the front of the house, where the water

26

butts up against a rickety wooden staircase. *Some safe house.*

I know every move Cole's going to make and cover him with my gun drawn, ready. He runs up the steps, and I guard behind him with my gun cocked. He slowly twists the knob and enters the house while scanning the inside.

"Clear," he whispers as the musty smell hits my nose. I close the door and bolt it shut, double-checking the locks before turning around. We take turns clearing each room. It's a small house, not much wider than a three-car garage, so it's not long until we confirm it's empty.

Satisfied, we holster our guns, and then ransack the place, looking for food and medical supplies. Once that's done, I look around the living room with its chipping baby-blue walls and outdated wicker furniture. The ceilings are about eight feet high. Two chairs and a couch sit across from each other, and a brass lamp stands by the door. From the living room, I make my way to the open kitchen where the faded wallpaper, pine cabinets, and countertop remind me of pea soup. My stomach growls.

There's no dining table, just a bar with two black stools separating the kitchen from the living room. I make my way down a narrow hallway that leads to two bedrooms and a bathroom. I turn into the first bedroom and collapse on the mattress, letting out a sigh of complete exhaustion. Just then, I hear thunder crack outside as rain assaults the rooftop. It's enough to lull me to sleep.

Cole lowers himself to the bed and leans over me as my heavy eyelids slam shut. "Oh no you don't. You, my girl, need a hot shower."

I open my eyes, ready to protest, but stop when I see his

27

lips half-parted an inch from my face. I feel the fight go out of me. All I want is for him to melt into me, but he's right. I'm freezing, and I stink.

He hesitates before kissing my forehead, then my lips, and when he lowers himself onto me to kiss my neck, my breath quickens. Part of me still cannot believe he's mine. After getting our start in the Hole, he as my guard and me as his prisoner, who would have ever believed we could end up together? My lips quiver beneath his, and warmth begins surging through me. Somehow, I find the strength to push his face back and hold it with both hands. His eyes search mine, eager and vulnerable.

"Didn't you promise you'd never leave my side?" I ask.

"Yeah, why?"

"Then I guess you're showering with me?" I give him a sly smile.

He grabs my hand, a smile playing at the edge of his lips as he leads me across the hallway.

Once inside the bathroom, he closes the door behind us and gently sets me down on the edge of the bathtub. He kneels in front of me and removes my boots and socks, tossing them aside. He looks up at me and runs his hand over his head.

"There's something I need to say."

"Okay," I say, pulling on my belt. "I'm all ears."

I notice his lower lip shake, and when he realizes it, he presses his lips together before speaking.

"The last thing I ever want to do … is hurt you." He scratches his neck and looks at the wall behind me, seemingly unsure of exactly where to look.

"Hurt me? How could you possibly hurt me?" I run my

fingers down the side of his face, tracing his jawline. My fingers tingle at the touch of his skin.

"Well, if you left me … that would kill me." He reaches up and takes my hands in his. It feels as if something heavy is weighing on him. Something more than nearly getting killed before. Something he hasn't been able to say. Something that has hung in the air between us ever since our first kiss.

"Cole, I could never leave you."

He releases my hands.

"What's wrong? Tell me."

"It's everything. It's how we met. Where we ended up. Where we are now. What kind of life is this? What kind of future can we have?" I feel my legs starting to shake so I press my feet harder to the ground. How did we go from almost taking a shower together to not even being able to look at one another in the span of one minute?

"Will you please look at me?" I ask, placing my hand under his chin. I tilt his face up to mine. "For the first time in my life, I'm proud of who I am. There's no more shame, guilt, or disgust. I'm satisfied with the person I am today, and you're a huge part of that. I had to leave my normal life and be sent to the Hole to find out who I really am. You did that for me. And as crappy as life in the Hole was, I wouldn't change anything that happened because it led me to you."

Cole's face relaxes, and he blinks a few times before he reaches up and wraps his fingers around mine. When he tilts his head to the right and gives me his dimpled smile, I can't help but need him.

"Come here," he says.

I stand while looking into his eyes. Holding my gaze,

29

he slowly tugs at the edge of my shirt and slides his hands up my back. As if a train runs up my spine, my body shakes uncontrollably.

"I think it's time we get warmed up."

"Sounds like heaven to me."

He turns the shower on. It doesn't take long before steam fills the room. The warmth just adds to the moment, heating up my already burning flesh.

"Mind if I help you with your shirt?"

I manage to nod as I raise my arms toward the ceiling. Cole lifts my shirt over my head, and I watch it fall to the floor. His eyes, still locked on mine, burn through me as he steps forward, closing the few inches left between us, and unhooks my bra in one quick motion. The straps slide off my shoulders, and it joins my shirt on the tile floor.

"You're so beautiful," he says, soaking me up with eager eyes. His cheeks flush, and his dimples are so cute I want to kiss each of them.

"I look like a lion with a wild mane."

But he just shakes his head at me. He brushes my hair away from my face and tucks it behind my ears. Then he kisses my neck slowly and gently, running his soft lips up and down the right side of my neck.

I moan.

He chuckles, and it vibrates against my skin. "You have a huge scrape here. Am I hurting you?" He traces around the tender part of my neck that was injured during the car's tumble down the embankment.

"No."

"Are you sure? Because you have bruising on both sides

of your neck."

"It's okay. They don't hurt."

I allow my eyes to fall closed and tilt my head back as his hands make their way to the button on my pants, fiddling to get it undone. Once he succeeds, he pulls them toward the floor. One foot at a time, I step out of them. I can't take it any longer. I reach down and take his head in my hands, urging him back up to me.

"What?" he asks, desire coating his voice.

"Your wrap, mind if I help you? I'll do my best not to hurt you."

"Don't worry, not gonna happen. When I'm with you like this, all I can feel is you."

"Is that so?" I ask in a flirtatious tone.

My hands shake as I loosen the cloth binding his ribs, and my eyes settle on the road rash and bruises that cover his skin. Without hesitation, my lips lightly touch his wounds. Inch by inch, I brush my kisses over each spot. He runs his hands run through my hair as his breathing quickens with each kiss.

I smile at him, and then he presses his lips to mine with such urgency and desperation my head spins. His lips are so warm and so soft, and I can taste the sweetness of his breath. Our lips part, and our tongues meet, and we kiss in unison like our mouths were meant for one another. He cups my face as I wrap my arms around his waist and press my fingers into his back. Our breaths quicken as our kisses become deeper. For a moment, everything is as it should be. I am lost in him.

We continue to kiss. I feel a drip of what I think is sweat down my back—or maybe it's the steam. Whatever it is, my flesh burns with desire.

Smoothing my hair away from my face again, Cole drops his lips to mine, and our breathing goes haywire. I open my mouth slightly, inviting his tongue to graze mine, and as soon as our tongues touch, I shiver. He groans. It's a connection I can't explain, but instantly, it sends electricity through my veins and burns me to the core. His kisses become eager and harder. I wrap my arms around his neck as he pushes me up against the wall, overpowering me, which only sends my craving for him into overdrive.

"Cole," I say, almost breathless. "We should take this into the shower."

"Good idea." He removes the rest of his clothing in a matter of seconds.

We both get into the shower, and a few seconds pass before he wraps his arms around me and leans in, trapping me between him and the wall, again.

I know I should be enjoying myself, relaxing and allowing myself to feel every single touch, every amazing kiss. But in the warmth of the shower and Cole's body, I'm worried I might faint. *Why am I so nervous?*

"You feel incredible," he says between kisses.

His lips leave mine, and he kisses my cheek, my chin, and down the trail of my neck, across my collarbone, and back up my neck. It's nearly impossible to steady my breathing. Next, he sucks my bottom lip into his mouth, caressing it with his tongue, and I let him. Of course I let him. I crave him.

We've been deprived of closeness for so long. I run my fingers down his back, and he presses me harder against the wall. He licks away the water from my mouth and kisses my lips with urgency. Suddenly, I can't remember where I am. I

32

can't recall my name.

I can hardly hold myself upright any longer, and I start to slip.

"Easy, girl, I got you."

Cole holds me up and hands me a bar of soap that smells like roses and an orange washrag that looks like it's been through the shredder. And in that moment, I have everything I need.

"We better hurry," he says. "The water's already getting cooler."

I respond with a shiver and rush to clean the grimy layers off my skin, hardly able to focus with Cole standing so close. We switch places, and I wash his back, putting the soap in its small dish on the shower tiles.

As he reaches up, a tiny, wiggling object drops in front of my face, its eight legs unmistakably searching for a landing spot.

A scream escapes my lips, and my hands search for a shower handle as my feet slide out from beneath me. Darkness clouds my vision, and then nothing.

CHAPTER 3

When I open my eyes, I'm lying in the bed with my knees to my chest. The faint glow of a half-melted candle sits next to the bed. My breathing is steady. I feel Cole's warm arms wrapped around me, my back up against him. His fingers lightly stroke my hair, and I know I'm safe.

"I'm so sorry," I manage to say.

"Don't," he says. "Please, don't apologize." He squeezes me tight. "I'm right here, like I promised I'd be."

"I ruined—"

"Nothing, you've ruined nothing." He kisses the back of my head. "The spider's to blame, not you, but don't worry, he paid for it. Nasty bugger was huge. You should've heard the noise when I squashed—"

"Cole!"

"I know, but seriously, he was the size of my fist."

"Stop it."

"Okay, I'm done." He tucks my hair behind my left ear and whispers, "Any chance you'd be able to sleep? Blacking out doesn't exactly count."

I turn my head to the left to glimpse him out of the corner of my eye. The flickering candle gives off just enough light for my eyes to settle on his face. My heart sinks. He's beautiful. There's no denying that. "Maybe, if you hold me tight. Really, really tight. I should be able to."

He kisses my check. "Go to sleep then, I'll be right here when you wake up."

His words comfort my soul, so I give in to exhaustion and drift off to sleep.

The sun peeks through holes in the slats covering the windows, casting slivers of light across the bed, and I blink away the crust sealing my eyes. *It's gotta be around 7:30.* The candle next to the bed has burned into a lump of white wax. A yawn escapes my lips as I arch my back and stretch. My hair falls down my back in brown, curly waves. I reach for Cole, but he's gone. Panic bolts through me as I sit straight up, searching the room for any sign of him.

"Morning." Cole stands in the doorway looking handsome in his boxer-briefs.

"Morning." I smile briefly, feeling cautiously relieved. He sits next to me and hands me a bowl of something hot. It feels

35

almost normal sitting in bed with Cole serving me breakfast. Well, more normal than hiding in abandoned buildings and scrounging for food.

"It's not gourmet, but it'll do." He winks at me as I examine it with a skeptical face.

"Mmmmm. Canned chili for breakfast." I smile and look down at the steaming bowl. My stomach growls loudly, right on cue. It has been so long since we had hot food, and I feel bad about complaining. So I close my eyes and imagine steak and eggs.

Cole dips a piece of bread into my chili and eats it. "See? It's not so bad." But it doesn't go down so easily. He grabs the water on the windowsill and chokes it down.

Ever since we escaped the Hole, we've been optimistic and hopeful. But the longer we run, the more we get shot at and chased, the harder it is to keep that hope going. Even now, despite everything we've just been through, Cole tries to keep things light. But underneath his cool exterior, I know a storm is brewing inside him. Right now, he is quietly calculating how much food we have left, how many paces there are from here to the window in case we need a quick escape.

Still, here in this safe house without surveillance, we're free to be together, and for now, that's enough. We don't talk about the fact that we both wake up in the middle of the night screaming and sweating from nightmares. We don't talk about how, when, or if we will ever truly be free. We focus on the now, the moment, and these precious few glimpses of freedom we steal.

Someone once told me that hope was a luxury we couldn't afford. That determination was a much better option and one that would likely keep me alive. But hope is my motivation, my strength. Hope that humanity has a chance to redeem itself. Hope that what's left of this broken-down country can be saved and people will be free again, the way it was before the last war and the rise of the Commander.

"Do you think we can make a difference? I mean, we made it out. Do you think we can free others?" I slosh the chili around in the bowl and wait for Cole to respond. When he doesn't right away, I add, "You've seen some of those people in the Hole. Their eyes are dead. They've given up. They have no fight left. I was lucky. I got out. And even though I lost Keegan, my mom, and my dad, you and Sutton are my family now. But what about those who have no one? No one and nothing to live for? Who is going to save them?"

"I gotta believe this hasn't all been for nothing," he says, then takes another sip of water. "I'd like to think we might have inspired some people."

"Do you think we should go back? Help them?" My voice lowers as I lift my eyes to his. The thought of voluntarily going back to the Hole brings a sudden stinging pain to my chest. *I can't go back.*

"No, I don't. How can you even think about going back there?" Cole runs his free hand over his head as if he cannot believe the words coming out of my mouth. He rests his head against the wall and exhales. "You ever hear stories, growing up, about the world outside our country?"

I move the bowl from hand to hand nervously, unsure of where this conversation is going. Cole stares at me incredulously. No one ever talks about the *before*. "It was never discussed in school," I say. "The only reason I know

37

some of what it was like before the Commander is because my parents talked about it."

His eyes search mine, and he nods. "Yeah, school's a joke; the curriculum's pretty much just propaganda for the Commander. You know damn well the government doesn't want us to have hope."

"I remember the fourth and fifth wars were started by terrorism and that other countries refused to challenge those sheltering the terrorists who were responsible ... " I take a spoonful of chili, chewing slowly. "And that our country bore the brunt of everything ... bombings, attacks, financial ramifications."

"Do you know what happened out west?" he asks.

"That it used to be populated? My dad made mention of it long ago."

"It used to be one of the centers for technological development. Weapons, computers, everything." His eyes harden, and his voice becomes bitter. "But the United Powers had it destroyed, sending us back into the Dark Ages."

"The United Powers? Why would they do that?" I scrunch up my face as I prepare to take another bite of food.

"Who knows? I guess they thought it would eliminate weapons and bring peace. Some ambassadors of world peace they turned out to be," he says.

"But I thought we were part of the United Powers?"

"We are, but only after they united against our country and forced us to pay damages for World War Five, which crippled any chance our country had of rebuilding. That's why the first Commander was voted in. He pledged to rebuild, pledged to keep us out of war, and he talked a pretty good game." Cole exhales long and hard. "But here we are, barely surviving while the United Powers turn a blind eye to the desecration of what was once a great country. The rest of the world continues living as though nothing happened here. It doesn't affect them."

"No wonder people loved the Commander," I say.

He looks at me with a skeptical face. "Why is that?"

"Because they believed in him. Don't you get it? He made promises. He told them what they wanted to hear. What they needed in order to move on. He gave them hope. And when he didn't deliver, they forgave him because they wanted to believe in something and he was all they had."

"And it was a recipe for exactly what we have now. And Wilson, he's insane. He is hardly going to deliver on the promise of the first Commander. He's just as lost and so mad with power that he will do anything to keep things exactly the way they are. Please tell me you aren't feeling sorry for him." Cole raises an eyebrow.

"Definitely not. I don't know what I feel. Part of me thinks we can maybe change things. Get things moving in the right direction again. I mean, we got out. And the other part of me thinks the thought of it is insane and that we're going to die out here. Then again, my dad couldn't do it alone, so what hope do we have?" Unspoken words hang in the air between us as Cole shifts his weight from one leg to the other. "If only you could have met him. He was an amazing man. And I know he would've adored you."

Cole's silence makes me uneasy. He just stares for what feels like minutes.

"Lexi." The way he says my name causes the hair on my neck to stand. I can't bear what he might say next.

"I wasn't suggesting we should go back to the Hole. I'm not that crazy. I was just thinking out loud."

I suddenly have no desire to continue this conversation, so I shovel a spoonful of the spicy chili into my mouth. It's too much, and I gag. Cole doesn't even address my last comment, so I set the bowl aside and get dressed. I feel his eyes on me, following my every move. It makes me strangely uncomfortable, so I hurry and cover up.

"You do realize I've seen you naked," he says. "Several times."

No matter how many times he's seen me naked, I still feel self-conscious. When I'm done, I turn and offer him a shy smile.

"Feel better now?" He winks and clears his throat. A mischievous smile crosses his face. He claps his hands and heads toward me.

I'm about to take him into my arms for a kiss when we hear a strange grinding sound from somewhere in the house. Cole's eyebrows bunch up, and he freezes.

"Maybe it's just the wind," I say, trying to convince myself, heart pounding.

Beneath us, the trash cans bang around suddenly. Cole pulls back from me and heads toward the door.

"Maybe you should put some pants on first?" I suggest, only half-joking.

He quickly pulls his pants off the heater they lay drying on. *Please let it be the wind. Please let it be the wind. Please let it be the wind.* I rummage around for my boots, and by the time I get them on, Cole has his gun out and is handing me mine. I listen for more disturbances while Cole peeks through

40

a small hole in a window slat. *I wish Zeus were here.*

The front door handle jiggles, twists, and then I hear the grinding of pieces, searching for the magic click at the end. *It's not the wind.* My blood freezes, and my body becomes steel.

Click.

My stomach's one big knot. I want to scream.

Cole's eyes flick to mine. They're wide with fear as he whispers, "Stay here."

"No way. I'm coming with you."

"Damn it, Lexi." He clenches his jaw and tightens his shoulders.

I motion him forward with my free hand. He turns and carefully hugs the hallway with his body. His gun is raised in front of him as he checks the spare bedroom across the hall. Nothing.

He checks the bathroom, but nothing's there.

A loud clanging of metal echoes down the hall. I can think of nothing else that would make that noise except the lamp by the front door. I blink rapidly and mimic every move Cole makes, backing him up.

Footsteps. Pause. Whispers. More footsteps.

I put any other thoughts out of my mind as I focus on the sounds. I listen for how heavy or soft the foot placement is, the raising or lowering of the vocal tones of the whispers. I motion to Cole with two fingers, and I see it register in his eyes. He stops right before the living room. I can feel the tension rolling off him as the muscles in his neck tighten. Cole motions his move forward. I follow.

He rounds the corner.

Cole moves quickly. I follow him. Shouts, screams, and

bullets zing through the air, hitting the ceiling and windows. I hear them cutting through the fabric of the couch, slicing through the wood on the floors, ricocheting off the refrigerator door.

Just around the corner, I engage a female guard. She's small, fast, and she fires at me.

"Ahhhh!" The bullet burns as warm liquid trickles down my face.

I return fire, but she reaches for my arm. The bullet misses, going over her head.

She lunges at me with a knife. I jump back, stumbling over the wicker couch and flipping it onto its back. I land on my butt. She comes barreling over me with slashes and flashes of sharp steel. My gun skids away. I catch her hand with the tip of the knife poised above my chest. She's too strong. I clench my jaw, trying to force the knife away. It touches right above my heart.

"Cole!" I scream with everything I have. The guard sneers at me, knowing full well I have no fight left. I'm drifting. I can feel the energy leaving me. I'm getting weaker. I'm going to die. *I am going to die.*

Gripping the woman's hand, I clench my jaw and strain every muscle and tendon in my body, holding her back. I faintly hear Cole yelling in the background.

The guard's eyes squint as she pushes the knife farther down. Her sweat's dripping onto my face, and I know I can't hold on much longer. My arms burn from straining. I'm losing it. The knife pierces me. I close my eyes. *This is it.* Then I hear a loud, dull thump. Blood trails from the top of the guard's head, down and over my skin.

Her body goes rigid. Her eyes go blank, and her body relaxes as it shuts down. I feel her weight bearing down on me in its entirety. Her hands loosen on the knife, and it becomes lodged between our bodies.

I'm shaking as I kick her off the couch, rip the knife away from between us, and roll to my left. I'm barely able to catch my breath. A knife is lodged in the back of her head. Her blood gushes onto the floor, staining it in pools of crimson.

I scramble onto the floor, searching for my gun. Overturned furniture and blood-covered fluff from the cushions covers the wooden planks. The lampstand lies on its side surrounded by shattered glass. *Where the hell did it go?*

Cole struggles with a dark figure in the kitchen.

"Is that all you got? I've been waiting months to take you down, traitor. There's a special place in hell for people like you. Protecting Sinners. Turning against your own," the guard says with his hands wrapped around Cole's neck. They smash into pots and pans on the counter while fighting for control.

"Nothing's worse than covering your sorry ass. Or have you forgotten how I covered for you? You've always been pathetic," Cole says.

"You're gonna die, asshole. I already called Clayton. He's gonna rain hell on you when he gets here."

I can't take it. I rip the knife out of the dead guard's head. Then, with a grunt, I chuck it at Cole's opposition, just as his back turns toward me. It clatters to the floor. I missed.

Both men jump at the weapon. I clench my fists, trying to think of my next move. But they're wrestling on the ground, backed into a corner, and I don't see how I can get there without getting in Cole's way and jeopardizing his position.

43

They wrangle for control, choking and throwing elbows. Cole stabs the guard in the chest. I hear his skin and muscles tear open when Cole drags the knife down his abdomen. I swallow the bile in my throat.

The man continues wrestling Cole, all the while gagging on his own blood. He spits it out between his teeth as he grabs for Cole. The kitchen floor fills with smears of red before the guard falters. Cole pushes him away, surveys the scene. Blood splatter covers Cole's face and clothes.

"How'd they find us?" I rush to him, but he seems to be already plotting our next move, hardly looking at me.

"Not now! We gotta get the hell out of here!" He runs to the front door and pushes his shoulder against it. *Like that matters now.*

His chest heaves for air, and sweat pours down his forehead. He checks the rounds left in his gun. Once he's satisfied, he presses his lips together and stares out the front window next to the door.

I step over the bodies, retrieve my gun, and kneel below the front window, beside the broken lamp.

"You're freaking me out," I say. I peek through a bullet hole in the window and see a guard run around the front of the house.

"Promise me something," Cole says.

Out of the corner of my eye, I see the dark figure of a guard poised outside the front staircase. I keep my hand on the board, scanning for more while I listen to Cole.

"I don't like where you're going with this … "

He slides down the wall so he's on my level. "If I don't make it out, promise me you'll run."

My heart thunders in my ears.

"No, I won't do that," I say. He shakes his head fast. "I won't leave you."

"You have to survive. Promise me." His eyes plead with me. I grit my teeth and then let out a big sigh. I'm exhausted and hurt and terrified.

"I'm not going anywhere without you."

His mouth opens, but before he can say anything, the front door blasts open, throwing Cole back onto the floor.

Another guard storms in.

The new guard is taller than Cole, his shoulders broad like a wrestler. His muscles protrude from every inch of his body. His forearms are as thick as my neck and his neck as thick as my thigh. I realize it's over. We can't survive this. In his huge hands is an equally huge gun pointed at Cole's head.

"Don't move," I say, trying my best to sound tough.

Cole looks like a deer in headlights.

The guard sneers and says, "Drop it, honey." He laughs, never taking his eyes off Cole. He places the metal of the gun to Cole's temple. "You try anything, and I'll blow him to oblivion."

"Clayton, never thought I'd see your ugly face again," Cole says.

I can't think straight. I bite my lower lip to keep from screaming. I want to run.

"Well then today's your lucky day," Clayton says. "You got to see me one last time before I kill you."

"Not if I kill you first," Cole says.

"I hope after all your heroic gestures you at least got in her pants."

Cole remains silent. I can almost feel the rage rolling off his skin.

"You ignorant scumbag!" I shout, narrowing my eyes at Clayton. My stomach cramps, and I know that's what they all must think—that Cole is only in it for the benefits. "If you even flinch, I'll shoot."

"I'm guessing that's a no. She seems entirely too uptight," Clayton says through gritted teeth. If he wasn't pointing his gun at Cole's head, I'd have shot him already.

"What do you want from us?" I ask.

"It's simple, really. Wilson wants you alive." He nods toward me without taking his eyes off his target. "But he wants your boyfriend here in a body bag."

"I'm not going back to the Hole."

"You really are a stupid whore," Clayton says with a devilish smile, his eyes still trained on Cole.

"Shut up," Cole says. "You know nothing about her."

"Oh, I know some things," Clayton says. My eyes quickly turn to slits as I stare at him down the barrel of my gun. "I know she'd be interested to know that after you left Keegan's body to rot, it was strung up on a scaffold, for all the Hole to see. Just in case anyone was having thoughts about trying to flee as well." I feel my face heat up.

"You did what to my brother?" I ask.

"Lexi, don't believe a word he says," Cole pleads, but I can't get the image of Keegan's rotting body being displayed in that way out of my head.

"I didn't leave him there—" Cole protests.

"Sure you did," Clayton says, before Cole can finish his thought. "Anyway, while I'm enjoying this reunion, I'm afraid

46

our time's up." He brings his finger to the trigger.

No! With no other defense, I launch myself at him. But he's too fast so I only manage to grab a tiny corner of his shirtsleeve before he smacks me to the floor.

I land on my side, my gun skittering across the floor. Clayton's face pulses red as he kneels beside me, pulls my head up by my hair, and places his gun to my head.

I clench my teeth as he yanks me by my hair once more. It's over. He's going to kill me. But seconds pass, and all I hear is the sound of heavy breathing. Suddenly, the pressure eases up, and my face crashes into the floor. Cole and Clayton grunt, swear, and fight for control.

"Lexi, run!" Cole shouts as he pins Clayton like a pro wrestler.

I shake my head, scrambling to my feet. "Over my dead body."

"Run," he demands. He wrenches the gun from Clayton somehow, but Clayton uses his mammoth muscles to fight back beneath Cole.

Clayton gives up on the gun and whips out a knife from his knee pocket. He takes the hilt and smashes it across Cole's face.

My heart stops. My clammy hands wrench into fists.

Cole loses his composure long enough for Clayton to gain the upper hand.

Next thing I know, Clayton has the knife at Cole's neck.

I am frozen with fear, shame, and the promise of unrealized dreams.

"Please," Cole says. "Go." Blood spurts from his lip.

"I won't."

"Are you sure you want to watch him die like you did Keegan? If not, I suggest you close your eyes." Clayton presses his knife against the skin of Cole's throat.

Cole begs with his eyes—the eyes of the man who stole my heart. The eyes of the one who guarded me against his will and offered up his life for mine several times. I feel my jaw clenching as I try to think of a way we can both get out of this alive.

"Wait!" I shout. Clayton's eyes flick to me. "Don't you want to know where Sutton is? We can take you to him. But if Cole loses so much as a hair on his head, you get nothing. No Sutton. No Lexi. Nothing."

Despite my shaky voice, I keep talking, gradually taking control of it. Clayton bends his head back down, ready to slit Cole's throat.

"Cole's been keeping it a secret. Even from me," I say fast. Almost too quickly. But Clayton can't help himself. He pauses, interest flickering through his eyes.

"What's this now?" Clayton asks. "Our Cole does like to keep his secrets. Did he tell you the one about your father?"

"What about him?" I ask, worried about the look on Cole's face.

"Tsk. Tsk. Shame on you, Cole. You haven't told your little princess about her sweet daddy."

He's screwing with my head.

"Of course he's told me," I lie, trying not to alter my expression. *What the hell is he talking about?*

Cole's pained face reads my expression, and he has to know I'm trying to stall Clayton.

Keep talking.

I slowly inch my feet forward.

"Take another step, and I'll slit his throat." Clayton jabs Cole's skin, and a small stream of blood races down Cole's neck.

I can't let on that Clayton's getting to me or that Cole hasn't told me a thing about my dad. I can't look at Cole, vulnerable and bleeding.

"Go right ahead, then my secret dies with me," Cole says.

"Then tell that bitch to stay where she is."

"Don't move, all right?" Cole strains against the knife.

"All right." I lock my feet in place, feeling the sweat drip down my back.

"Put your hands in the air where I can see them!" Clayton commands.

"Get your knife off his throat," I say. "And we'll go with you willingly. Think about it. Wilson will have no choice but to promote you if you deliver me, Cole, and Sutton."

"You're lying. The minute I let my guard down, the two of you will be all over me. Do you think I'm stupid?"

"Find Sutton, and you find the key to the resistance," Cole says between gasps.

"My orders are my orders. Screw you, and screw Sutton."

"No!" I scream. In one fluid move, I yank a knife from my waist and whip it across the room at Clayton's head.

Please, let me throw true this time.

Time passes in slow motion.

The knife spins end over end, flying toward Clayton's ruddy face.

Before he has time to react, it strikes him right in his left eye. He grabs at the knife and his head and moans in agonizing pain. Blood swallows the hilt and trickles over Cole's head.

Cole falls forward on all fours, breathing heavy. Clayton falls to the floor, wrenching and screaming. For a moment, I think he might try to pull the knife out of his eye and stab Cole with it.

I crawl to Cole and pull him into a quick embrace. I swear he's crying. Or maybe it's me. But we kneel, covered in blood and holding each other tight. Blood from Clayton surrounds us on the floor, and I know he doesn't have long.

Cole shakes his head at the sight of Clayton who lies bleeding out and dying on the floor. Cole turns to me and kisses me with desperation and understanding. We've earned that kiss.

"Let's go," he says, dragging my nearly spent body into a standing position. He gathers our weapons from the floor and says, "More will follow."

Out of the corner of my eye, a shadow crosses the window.

Before I can think, we're sprinting out the front door and into the sand dunes behind the beach house. I look over my shoulder and see the guards jumping out of a car, aiming their guns at us.

"Follow me!" Cole screams.

I snap my head forward and run zigzag. We finally hit the tall grass, and we're out of their sights.

Everything is a blur.

But I've got to keep going.

I run, unsure of how my legs continue to hold me up. My eyes burn; I blink hard, but there's no relief. I can barely catch my breath. I don't even know where I'm going. I'm just following Cole's bloody figure as it scales the terrain in front of me.

That was too close.

CHAPTER 4

*M*om and Dad embrace on the front porch. Mom's dark hair spills down her back. As she pulls away, Dad's hand gets caught in a wave, causing Mom to tilt her head back and laugh. Dad leans in, kisses the side of her neck, and places his hands on her lower back. I hop over the railing, smiling. Dad's eyes seem to glow as his smile stretches across his face. I love seeing my parents this way. Even Keegan, who's working on his beat-up, fire engine-red car in the driveway, pauses to watch them. When they're finished saying their good-byes, Dad hefts his briefcase into his car, blows us kisses, and drives away. I notice how Mom's shoulders tense as soon as his vehicle disappears down the driveway.

I pad over and wrap my arm through hers. She looks at me, and a thin smile plays at the corner of her mouth. Worry lines etch across her forehead, but I know she's trying to cover up *her feelings. She's a strong woman, and I admire her for that. I can only hope someday I'll be like her.*

"When will Dad come home again?" I ask.

"In a few days," she says. She brings my hand to her lips and kisses it. "Maybe longer."

I frown. "I hate when he leaves us."

She pulls me in for a hug. Even now, the memory of her rose and honey perfume and the warmth of her flannel shirt comfort me. "I know, honey. Me too. It's hard on all of us." She sighs. "But he always comes back, and when he does, everything will be fine." Yet, she doesn't make eye contact with me.

"Mom?"

"Yes, dear?" she whispers, tucking a stray curl behind my ear.

"Is Dad the love of your life?"

She pulls away and looks me in the eyes. I watch as a smile, a real smile, creeps onto her lips. "Without a doubt."

"So, how did you know he was the one?"

She sits on the top step and pulls me close to her side. "Your father is the most kind, honest, and hard-working man alive." She turns toward me. "He swept me off my feet with his smile and his easygoing nature. He's smart, but doesn't treat others less. But you know that already because you're so much like him." She winks.

"But how did you know for sure?"

She raises an eyebrow and sighs deep. "I just knew; the way I felt when I was around him ... It's hard to explain. But one day, you'll meet the one, and you'll understand what I mean." She kisses my cheek and hugs me tighter. I can hear the steadiness of her heart and the calm breaths moving in and out of her mouth "Lexi, you're beautiful, so I've got no doubt you'll meet lots of young men who will want to date you. But the right man for you is the one who makes you stronger." She grabs my hand. "He'll be kind. He'll love you whether you're having a good day or bad day. He'll treat you like a lady, yet trust you to make your own decisions. Some will break your heart, but that's part of learning the pain of what loving someone can bring. But the pain will lessen, and you'll love again. And when that special guy comes into your life ... you'll be thankful for the ones who hurt you. Because the real guy will mend all the slashes your heart has endured." She smiles. "That is exactly the kind of man your father is. He filled my heart with the greatest love there is. Honesty and trust."

I lean my head against her shoulder and watch Keegan as he slides under his car. I hear him tinkering with something and occasionally cussing. I can't help giggling over the words he strings together, even though I know they're completely inappropriate. And Mom wouldn't approve, but if she heard them, she doesn't let on. A cool breeze ruffles the trees around our house. I breathe in the fresh smell of cut grass and impending rain. The porch creaks as I shift my position and face my mom again. I can see from the faraway expression on her face that she's thinking of my dad. I squeeze her hand.

"Dad really is the best, isn't he?"

"He sure is, darling, he sure is."

My eyes snap open. I've been clenching my jaw so hard it's sore. Remembering my mom that way seems weird now. I'd almost forgotten the sweet times we had before my dad passed. *Maybe it's better if I don't reminisce too much.*

I rub my face with both hands, wondering how long we've

been lying in this sandy ditch. Cole's head rests against my shoulder, his eyes closed and mouth slack. His clothing's completely stuck to him, and he smells like rust and saltwater. We're in desperate need of a change of clothes. I let my gaze run over his sand-caked skin, neat buzz cut, and long, brown lashes, which flutter occasionally in his sleep. *He can't be comfortable with his neck shanked that way.* I brush his cheek with my hand, and his eyes open. He sits up ramrod straight.

"What's wrong?"

"Nothing's wrong," I tell him. "I'm sorry I woke you."

"No, it's fine. I'm glad you did," he says. "How long was I out?"

"Not sure," I whisper. I pick at the blood built up underneath my fingernails. *Disgusting.*

"Do you think Sutton's looking for us yet?" Cole cracks his neck and rubs his biceps.

"Why would he? He's not expecting us to be back for another two days."

"True, but with all the connections that man has, he had to have gotten wind of something. He has to know the safe house didn't work out and we're on the run."

"I hope you're right."

He touches my hand, and I fight my emotions. I will not cry in front of him. Not now.

The sound of a roaring engine drowns out the hammering of my heart against my chest. It sounds close. Slowly lifting my head above the ditch, I squint through bleary eyes to try to make out the vehicle. Cole smashes himself against the embankment and rests next to me, an intense gaze on his face. As I look him over, I wonder if we will ever stop running, if

54

we will ever be able to just sleep and dream and muse.

Cole's gun is cocked and ready.

I turn my attention back to the road.

It's another black Jeep. My heart stops, nerves on edge. I just don't know if I have any strength left to run.

Then I see him.

Hanging out of the back driver's side window is Zeus, his ears perked and tongue hanging out to one side, slobber flying in the air. It's the most beautiful sight I've seen in a long time.

Instantly, a squeal of joy rushes out of me as I pull myself out of the ditch, and Zeus sees me. I practically run into the road.

Cole grabs my arm, but I shake him off. The Jeep slows down, but before it stops, Zeus hurls out and races toward us.

"Zeus!"

He runs into Cole's open arms and knocks him onto his back. After a brief moment, he turns his attention toward me, pouncing on me, knocking me onto the ground. He smells like mud, and his warm slobber coats my face. I let him lick me as much as he wants because his love is unconditional and his presence warms my soul. If anyone had ever told me it was possible to love a dog this much, I would've laughed. I can't imagine not having Zeus.

Two doors slam one after the other as Bruno and Grace exit the vehicle. Bruno's face is painted with concern; his mouth drops open and his eyes widen ... but I'm sure one look at Cole and me would do that to anyone.

"My God, guys ... what happened to you?" Grace asks, her forehead scrunching up.

"Zeus, move." Bruno pulls him away, but Zeus just parks

his butt right next to us, licking his hand. "Are you hurt?" I watch Bruno's eyes. He squints as he scans our blood-spattered clothes and our broken faces.

Cole and I lock eyes, unsure of what to say. Am I physically hurt? Sure, I've got some bumps and bruises, but nothing like in the Hole. Am I scared out of my mind? Yes, most definitely.

"We're in one piece, no limbs missing."

"That's always a plus. Because you're going to need them," Bruno says as he pushes me forward. "Guards are everywhere, like the nasty roaches they are."

I can't help but raise an eyebrow, being that he used to be a guard. Thankfully, they're not all evil.

"Hey, girl," Grace says to me. "Boy am I glad to see your face."

"Likewise," I say. There's something about Grace that puts me at ease. Besides Alyssa, she's the one person I've met since this whole thing started who I feel I could become close friends with, if we ever get a chance.

Grace wraps a blanket around me and ushers me into the backseat of the Jeep before sliding in next to me. Of course, Zeus lays across our laps, his head in mine and his butt in Grace's. I nestle my hands in his fur as I lean my head against the window and watch my breath fog it up. Zeus whines, and I kiss his head, right between his ears.

"How'd you find us?" Cole asks Bruno.

"Why, I used the incredible tracking skills I honed as a guard," Bruno says with sarcasm. He turns the key in the ignition and pulls a U-turn. Grace exhales.

"Oh please, more like you used Zeus," Grace says. Bruno laughs.

"Well, he helped, that's for sure. That dog was hell-bent on finding you. His ridiculous barking was so loud I was half tempted to shoot him." I raise an eyebrow at Bruno, who's eyeing me in the rearview. "I'm kidding."

"So what happened at the safe house?" Grace asks.

"Damn thing, it was compromised," Cole says sharply. Bruno shifts in his seat.

"But how did they know you were going to be there? It doesn't make any sense," Bruno asks in a higher pitch.

"Your guess is as good as mine," Cole says.

"How many were there?" Bruno's brows furrow together.

"Quite a few," Cole says shortly. From his silence, I can tell Bruno's processing something.

"Did you know any of them?" Bruno asks in a lower tone.

I wish I could block the entire conversation out. I don't want to relive the massacre or the way Cole looked with a knife to his neck.

Grace reaches over and wraps her hand around mine. I look toward her, and she smiles. I do my best to smile back.

"Clayton was one. And I recognized the other one, but I don't remember his name," Cole says quietly.

"Guy's a maniac, a total animal," Bruno says. "You're lucky you didn't get yourselves killed." I feel Bruno's eyes rest on me from the rearview mirror, but I refuse to look at him. "Did he say anything?"

"Clayton told her Wilson wants her alive."

"For what?" Grace asks. She leans forward in her seat while still holding on to me.

"Oh man ... " Bruno shakes his head and quickly glances in Cole's direction. "Well, she does carry a lofty reward. After

57

all, her dad built this thing. And Keegan was a revolt leader. They probably think she knows something important."

Hearing Keegan's name mentioned, even casually, feels like a searing hot knife through my heart. I can't help wondering if Clayton's words were true. Was I a threat to the regime? Had Dad or Keegan left me clues or told me something of significance?

Cole turns to me, his eyes raking mine, but he glances quickly away. "You think that's it?"

"Sure," Bruno says. "Why else would they want her alive?"

I'm silent. I can't really think of any other reason. Nor do I want to think about it; my head's so full of what-ifs that I'm unable to form a cohesive opinion on the matter.

"Oh, and get this: I've heard they want Sutton alive too, but the rest of us? We're wanted dead or alive, preferably dead," Bruno says as he squints and glances at Cole quickly.

"We have to protect Sutton," I say.

"Of course we will," Cole says before he turns to Bruno. "Man, what the hell's going on?"

"We both know Wilson's a sociopath. He thrives on having control over who dies and lives. And whatever he's up to, it's bad, really freaking bad."

"The wanted posters are all over the place, even in the bay," Grace says. "How long can we hide?"

"Till this ends, till Wilson's dead and the Hole's destroyed," Cole says.

I watch as Grace lowers her eyes and gazes out the window. She lets go of me, and from the way she twiddles her hands, I'm guessing Bruno didn't tell her he was wanted dead until now.

"This is my fault," I say. "The situation we're in, all of your lives on the line."

"It's not your fault, Lexi," Cole says. "Everyone here made their decision without your influence. We've made our peace with it."

Bruno turns off the paved road and onto sand. We all grab our door handles to keep from bouncing around. A slight breeze shifts the sand, blowing it over the hood. After a few minutes, Bruno turns onto another road, one blanketed in darkness, as he turns off the headlights.

"Where're you taking us?" I ask.

"To a safe house," Grace says in a quiet voice. "Sutton's waiting for us. He's pretty panicked right now."

"How soon till we get there?" Cole asks.

"We're already here," Bruno says in a clipped voice.

Next thing I know, Bruno slams on the breaks, and the Jeep skids to a stop. When I look up, Sutton's standing in front of a dimly lit cottage, staring at us all.

After we jump out of the Jeep, I make a beeline for his open arms.

"Oh thank God you're alive," he says as he wraps me into a strong embrace. Then he lets go and pulls Cole into a hug as well. "Come in, please. I want to know everything." He steps back and motions us inside.

Once inside, I notice his red-rimmed eyes and the hollows beneath them. His hair's flying in several directions. He takes a deep breath and places a hand on the wall, surveying everyone's expressions.

Except Zeus, because he's disappeared.

"Tell me exactly what happened," he says.

"We were ambushed," Cole says, "by three guards." His hand wraps around my shoulder. "We took care of them, but there will be more, make no mistake about that."

Sutton wipes sweat from his forehead and exhales. "What matters is you're alive. I admit, I feared the worst." He pauses as his words sink in. "The owner of this house was gracious enough to let us borrow it, but his family returns tomorrow. We don't have much time ... but there's something else I need to share with all of you ... something important that I've been working on." My head snaps up. "It's time to show you." He digs into the side pocket of his coat, pulling out an envelope. His hands shake as he produces a piece of paper from inside. "Read this." He hands it to me, and I read it out loud.

UNITED STATES COMMANDER INVESTIGATED FOR HUMAN RIGHTS ABUSES

In a surprise move today, the United Powers announced an investigation into the allegations of mass genocide in the United States, stemming from the rise of the Commander fifty years ago. Recently obtained footage shows the Hole, an expansive prison for those known as Sinners. The Hole's purpose is being questioned by the United Powers, investigating claims that innocent people are being branded, imprisoned, abused, and even murdered without a fair trial.

The United Powers announced its decision to send in a team of international monitors to

look into and validate these claims. A findings
report, followed by a committee inquest, is
expected within the coming months.

My hands shake as I let Cole take the paper from me. "What exactly does this all mean?"

"It means what I've been working so hard for is finally happening, and hopefully, they'll follow through," Sutton says.

I watch as Cole's eyes widen with each sentence, and I hold my breath, waiting for him to speak. Is it possible? Could all of this be over soon? Will the regime finally be questioned, exposed, brought to justice?

"How'd you manage to do it?" I ask.

"My connections in the Hole helped me assemble footage from the cameras and smuggle it out during the revolt. Now we have irrefutable proof. It's not just speculation anymore. Not just conjecture. Now, we have living, breathing, undeniable proof."

Sutton sounds so convincing that I hate to doubt him. I want to believe whole-heartedly. I want to grab on to the idea of freedom and never let it go. But something isn't right.

"And you didn't inform us of this because ... ?" Cole asks with his hands in the air.

"Because information makes you even more vulnerable. And I wasn't about to risk that in light of everything else," Sutton says, eyeing Cole suspiciously.

"So why risk telling us now?" Bruno asks what we are all thinking.

Sutton straightens. "Because now the timing is right. Each of you will be called on to tell your side of the story. You have already escaped. You have no fear of retribution from Wilson or the guards."

More silence.

"What is the United Powers?" Grace asks in a soft voice.

"More importantly, what can they do?" I ask.

Sutton's head turns toward me, a sigh escaping his lips. "They're a coalition of international leaders formed after the fifth World War. Their main purpose is to prevent another outbreak of wars. Everyone's still reeling from the damage of the last one." He makes a circle motion with his hands. "The entire east coast is pretty much destroyed. They have laws written in their mandate that are supposed to protect people from genocide. And crime? There's still such a thing as due process. Or at least there's supposed to be." When his eyes meet mine, I have to pull up my lower jaw to keep from standing with my mouth wide open. "You probably weren't taught much, if anything, about them in school. But there are other powerful countries in the world that still exist, and their interests would be best served by intervening here."

"What sort of time line are we looking at here?" Bruno asks, lowering the paper. He passes it to an eager Grace.

"Wait just a second." Cole motions with a hand out in front of him. "So all of this has been going on for over fifty years, and no one in the rest of the world knew about it? How could that be?" Cole pauses, glances at Bruno, Grace, and me, and then focuses on Sutton. He seems to be challenging him.

"There was a time when that would not have been possible. At one time, our technology was so advanced that we could see what was happening in other parts of the world on a daily basis. But after World War Five, everything changed. Most of the technology that connected nations was destroyed, partially as a way of isolating themselves from the conflict." Sutton looks tired as he tries to explain the history of the world to us.

He turns to Bruno and offers a slight smile. "The monitors should be arriving in High Society within the week. I've contacted some underground members to arrange a meeting before they enter the Hole. I want to make sure they get the full picture before going in."

"Are you sure you can trust these people?" I ask. "I mean, how can they even question what they've seen in the footage already? Why would they need to come and see for themselves?"

"Nothing beats the conviction of eye-witness accounts," Sutton says. "Besides, some of the people in the Hole deserve to be there. They did exactly what they were accused of to earn a place there. Some became criminals doing what they had to do to survive once there. But criminal or not, this is not how we're supposed to treat people. We're capable of much more, and the rest of the world will hold us to a moral standard we seem to have forgotten long ago."

"Good thing, because Wilson would probably wine and dine them to death," Cole says. "He'd make a big show of it, making himself out to be a hero rather than the monster that he really is."

"Without a doubt," Sutton says. "I'm just hoping they stick to their agreement. That they truly and thoroughly investigate, question, and hold Wilson and his regime accountable for their crimes against humanity."

"Why wouldn't they? What motivation would they have to turn their back on us?" I ask.

"Because a weak United States makes everyone else's position stronger," Sutton says, twisting his hands together.

We are all silent as that sinks in.

"So you trust them or you don't?" Bruno asks, pacing.

"I trust they'll do their job once they're here," he says. "They know they have some atoning to do since the last World War."

"Then that's all that matters. I'll do whatever you ask of me," I say.

Sutton's sympathetic eyes rest on my face.

"Lexi, it's our only chance." Sutton takes the paper back from Grace and tucks it away in the pocket of his coat. "It must be done. We need their support. We can't do this alone. But if we hesitate even for a moment, we may never get another opportunity."

"How long do you think the investigation will take?" I ask.

"There's no way of telling. All we can do is pray the monitors get their jobs done and the United Powers will care enough to step in afterward." Sutton sighs while looking at me. "So please do your best to hold it together for just a little while longer. In the meantime, I need to get back, get all of my documents in order."

"When will you go?"

"I'll be leaving in an hour."

"Why so soon?" I ask, but he doesn't answer me. He motions in Cole's direction.

"Cole. Bruno. I'd like to have a word with you," he says. Bruno and Cole follow him into the kitchen and remain there for a few minutes while I agonize over his impending departure. When he returns, he smoothes over his eyebrows with his fingers and glances at me.

"Come with me," he says. I raise my head. "We need to talk in private."

He guides me into the hallway and through the small kitchen at the end. Then he opens the deadbolts and leads me to the back porch. He sits on a peeling, white bench and pats the spot next to him. "Sit."

I sit beside him, lean back, and fold my hands in my lap. My nerves are already on edge from the excitement and promise of his news. My heart races as adrenaline moves through me.

"There's something you should know." He sighs, and I feel my shoulders slump. "There are things I should've told you a long time ago, but the right opportunity never presented itself. So please listen carefully to what I have to say."

"I'm listening," I whisper.

"Your father and I met when we were young boys. We lived just down the road from one another. And even though my brother was five years older, he still played street hockey with us all the time." Sutton forms a thin smile. "But the first Commander began drafting more guards each year, and my older brother was chosen. It wasn't long before he started to change. At first, it was little things like no longer having the time or interest in playing with us. Soon, he became impatient, almost angry, stomping and slamming doors when he was home. Every night at dinner, all he'd talk about was the guards and the latest Sinner in the neighborhood—how all Sinners deserved death. If anyone tried to change the subject, he'd become agitated and claim we didn't care enough about our country." I put my hand on his, suppressing my own strange mix of emotions. "My parents tried to talk sense into him, but my brother was immune to any punishment or any wisdom they offered. He eventually began yelling orders at my father, taking over his role in the home, and that was the moment we knew."

"Knew what?" My brain is foggy from the overload of emotion and exhaustion.

"We found proof that my brother wasn't just recruited to join the guards. He was being groomed for more than that. My brother was *chosen* to be the next Commander. But we also found something more disturbing." Sutton gulps loudly.

"Do I really want to know?" The revelation that Wilson was chosen to lead this regime and that my father knew was already a lot to absorb.

Sutton squeezes my hand before continuing. "My brother was collaborating with Wilson to develop experiments on Sinners. In the Hole." I nearly jump out of my skin, vaguely flashing back to the conversation I overheard my father having in the kitchen a few years ago.

"Experiments?"

"Yes, but that's all we knew. We had no idea what the nature of the experiments were. We just knew we had to stop them. So, I made the choice to go to medical school, and your father took a very different path. He founded the resistance movement." Sutton crosses his right leg over his left. "When my brother became Commander, I knew he'd continue the experiments. Any semblance of the boy he used to be, the one who played with us, was gone." Sutton's troubled eyes stare into the distance.

My head is reeling. I realize I've been gripping the bench with my free hand. "Why are you telling me this now?" I stand and face him.

"Because you need to know what we're up against. And

66

I want you to have all the facts this time." Sutton stands and grabs my arms, stopping just short of answering the question I am about to ask. "You deserve it."

I'm trembling, but I need to know. "Did they experiment on everyone in the Hole?" My voice is timid.

Sutton drops his hands and starts pacing. "We aren't sure."

"How would I know? I mean, what should I be looking for?" Panic coats my voice as the tears start to fall.

Sutton turns to me, and the look on his face contradicts his words. "You're going to be okay, Lexi. I'll make sure of it." He stops and holds my arms again. "I won't let anything happen to you."

I collapse in his arms, allowing him to comfort me. He's the closest thing I have to a dad right now. *Why do I feel like he's saying good-bye to me?*

"One last thing ... I'm so sorry about Keegan." Sutton pats my shoulder then pulls away so I can see his face. "Hurt reminds us we're human, and we all bleed when we're wounded. But wounds heal, slowly, not all at once. We must mend our wounds well ... to make sure they don't tear back open because infections can be deadly. Do you understand what I'm trying to say?"

"Yes, I do."

"Are you going to be okay?"

"I have to be." I don't want to tell him that his leaving leaves me with another wound, so I dry my tears on my shirt and smile. He seems satisfied.

"Now go. Get showered and changed. And remember, Lexi: you can overcome anything. And I mean anything ... short of death."

CHAPTER 5

I'd never really given thought to Sutton's past or the sacrifices he must have made. I don't know if he ever married, and he's never mentioned children. Looking at him now with his bloodshot green eyes and forced smile, I see a man who has dedicated his adult life to helping others with hardly a thought for himself. I wonder what his life could've been like if we'd lived in a different place, if the Commander had never come to rule. The thought makes my heart ache.

"It's time." Sutton emerges from the kitchen, shuffling his things, and pulls me into a strong hug. "Remember what I said: focus on the tasks at hand, and take care of yourself." He holds his breath for a brief second and then exhales. "Blood or not, you're my daughter, and I love you."

I press my cheek against his chest, and his heart races in my ear. I grip his shirt in my fists and choke out, "I love you, too."

He quickly moves to Grace and offers her a hug. I am too wrapped up in my own thoughts to hear their exchange, but I know he must be offering her words of encouragement. That's just the way he is.

Sutton swallows hard before walking over to hug Cole. He pats Zeus on the head. My throat tightens as the tears are closer to surging.

Bruno and Sutton wave one last time before they exit the cottage, get into the vehicle, and speed away.

I am overcome with emotion. It feels like something is sucking the life out of me, and all I can do to stop the pain of it is to run. I don't think. I bolt out the door and down the driveway. My feet pound the gravel harder than I expected and I feel my leg muscles starting to cramp. When I reach the road, I hear Cole and Grace behind me, yelling at me to stop. I keep going.

He needs to know!

Panic rises into my chest, threatening to suffocate me as I crash onto the pavement, exhausted. As a charley horse grips the back of my right thigh, I scream out in agony.

Sutton's gone, and I don't know when I'll see him again. I'm heaving, crying out in pain, and dizzy. When Cole catches up to me, his eyes search mine for a sign, a reason, logic.

I should have hugged Sutton one more time. I shouldn't have let him go without telling him how much he means to me. I had only just realized it, and now it's too late. This selfless man has been a father to me when my father couldn't.

I curl my arms around myself as I wrestle with my emotions, pain, and embarrassment. *Without Sutton, once again, I'm an orphan.*

Grace arrives and puts her arm around me. I turn into her, wrapping my arms around her waist. As Cole leans in and wraps an arm around us both, I realize there's nothing we can do but hope and pray for Sutton and Bruno's safe return.

They help me stand and walk. My leg is still sore from the cramp, and my back feels like fire is shooting up the middle. We head up the driveway in silence.

Midway to the cottage, Grace almost chokes on her words. "We'll see them soon, I pray."

Cole clears his throat and tightens his grip around my waist.

Grace and I release each other.

"I think Sutton's plan is going to work, and we'll all be together again real soon," Cole adds.

No one responds. Everything is silent except the waves against the beach and the seagulls overhead. Cole's words hang in the air like the smell of stale bread.

Inside, everything is quiet and amplified at the same time. The boards creak beneath my feet. Zeus has somehow made his way back into the house without anyone noticing. The couch squeaks when he jumps onto it. Grace takes a position by the back door.

"I'm going to make us something to eat before we head out to find another safe house," Cole says. "Why don't you wash up and get changed."

"Into what?"

"Sutton left us clothes. He said they're in the bathroom."

I look over at Grace, who nods in approval. I stink.

"Okay."

I examine my shredded shirt and blood-soaked clothes.

I had completely forgotten how I looked in the midst of everything. *And Sutton still hugged me despite it.*

"Make sure to leave us some hot water," Cole says. He smiles and rubs my back before going into the kitchen.

I pull myself up the stairs and into the tiny bathroom, where the toilet is so close to the shower I can barely sit on it without my knees touching tile. Sure enough, clothing sits on the sink in several piles.

I turn on the water, and after waiting for it to warm up, I step inside. Dried blood swirls down the drain, turning pinker by the minute. When finished, I pull on a small, black cotton t-shirt with dark green cargo pants in my exact size. The socks are what bring me the most pleasure though. As I slide them on, my feet celebrate their warmth and cushiness.

"Much better," Cole says when I reach the first floor.

"Except for the bags under my eyes."

"God, I hate seeing you so exhausted."

"I'm gonna try to eat something. Maybe that will help."

Cole playfully smacks my ass as he passes me going up the staircase. "I'm gonna jump in the shower. But if Zeus starts acting up, come get me."

"I will," I say. "Hey, let's not leave him behind anymore."

"We're not," he says. "He's the best weapon we have." Cole takes the steps two at a time and disappears after the landing.

In the living room, Zeus sprawls out on the couch, sound asleep. He snorts, sneezes, and then rolls onto his back with his legs straight up.

I pick up a plate of canned beans, canned hot dogs, and canned peaches Cole prepared for me. When I lived in High

Society, we always ate well. On the run, you eat what you can find—things you may never have considered eating before.

"Wake up," he says. I hear him laughing through the fog of my head. "Only you."

"Few more minutes," I mumble, turning my head away from his voice.

"I'm afraid if you sleep any longer, those beans stuck on your forehead won't come off."

"Ew, what?"

"You face-planted in your plate." He wipes a damp cloth over my face, and I sit up. Food tumbles into my lap. I give Cole a dirty look, and he laughs.

"I'm glad you don't have a camera."

"Oh, but I've got a great photographic memory."

"Of course you do." I lean into him, and he gives me a sweet kiss on my lips. Now, I'm awake.

"Why didn't you just lie down with Zeus?"

"Have you seen him? He's a bed hog, and wasn't it obvious I preferred my plate?"

"And you've got hot dog up your nose," he says with a twinkle in his eyes. He bends down to kiss my head.

"Shut up. I do not." But of course, I feel my nose, making sure he's just playing with me. I snatch his napkin and wipe my face just as I notice the dim lighting. "How long was I asleep? Where is Grace?" I look around.

"You've been out for two hours. Grace is outside patrolling

the perimeter."

"And you let me sleep in my food?"

"I tried to pick you up, but you kept smacking me. So yes, I left you there," he says. "Any sleep is better than none, right?" But he's smiling as he says it.

I groan as I stand up and stretch. The muscles in my neck feel like one tight knot.

Without warning, Zeus hops off the couch and begins pacing the room. He whines, and the hair on my neck rises.

"Maybe he's gotta poop," Cole says, but I know he doesn't really think that. He raises an eyebrow.

"When was he let out last?" I ask.

"A half an hour ago."

But Zeus's whining grows louder and more restless. The fur on his back shoots up, making a dark track down his back. My insides jump.

"Nope, that's not it," Cole says. His jaw's clenched, and I grit my teeth.

I run to the window. Cole grabs his gun, and I tug the blinds an inch to the left so I can see outside.

Just then, Grace comes tearing into the living room, gun drawn. Her eyes are wide with fear. "Someone's coming," she says.

"How many?" Cole asks. He presses himself along the wall next to me. "How far?"

"One car, and not far enough," Grace says.

"Okay," Cole says. "You guard the back door. Lexi and I will take the front."

"Got it," she says. I watch as she sprints down the hallway, and then I lock eyes with Cole. He presses his body against

73

mine so he can whisper in my ear. "You and me, remember?"

I nod.

My body's shaking, so I attempt to clamp down on my fear by glancing around the room and thinking up a plan. Nothing. I look out the tiny slit in the window. Time's up.

Headlights rip through the darkness. I watch as Cole's posture turns rigid. He slowly steps alongside the front door and holds his gun ready.

I slowly inch forward, but Zeus charges the front door, snarling and growling. "Zeus, halt," Cole says in a commanding voice. Zeus immediately sits in place, anxious and ready for the next command. My head's on a swivel between Cole and Zeus sitting at the door, his teeth bared.

The headlights flick off. A door slams. Footsteps come fast. My heart's racing. The front door vibrates with three forceful knocks. My breath catches as I hear a muffled male voice shouting. I clench my jaw as Cole peeks out the window. I watch as his white knuckles give way to a slight headshake.

"Something's wrong," Cole says, rubbing the back of his head with his left hand.

"Who is it?" I tilt my head toward him.

"It's Bruno ... " His voice trails off. He narrows his eyes and glances around as if looking for answers. "Why did he come back?" He looks at me, and his eyebrows squish together.

"Oh my God, then where's Sutton?" I ask.

Bruno pounds even harder on the door this time. "Open the door!" He's screaming and his voice is hoarse.

Suddenly, I run toward the door with Zeus at my heels and reach for the lock. "We have to let him in!" I say.

The door swings open. Cole grabs Bruno by the shirt and

pulls him into the house as I close the door and lock it.

"Where is he?" I yell.

Bruno's harried and wild appearance terrifies me. He doesn't speak at first. He bends over, places his hands on his knees, and coughs. He's sweating and trembling and ... *Is that blood?*

"Bruno, where's Sutton?" Cole asks in a low voice, glancing at me quickly, then turning back to him. Bruno stands up straight and looks directly at me and then at Cole.

"They took him."

CHAPTER 6

Panic sets in my chest like a bomb about to explode. Bruno's panicked eyes lock with mine, and everything in the room becomes a blur.

"Who? Who has Sutton?" Cole asks, his voice rising with each word.

"Guards. At least twenty or so," Bruno pants.

"How?"

Grace comes running into the room, nearly knocking me over, pushing past me, and taking Bruno into her arms.

"It happened so fast," he says, looking at Cole and hugging Grace. "We were headed toward one of the checkpoints, so I tried finding a way around. Everything was going smoothly, when all of a sudden they came out of nowhere. They forced me off the road, surrounded us." Bruno pulls away from Grace and wipes sweat from his forehead. Grace leads him over to take a seat on the couch.

"Here, sit down before you pass out," Grace says as she takes a seat next to him. Cole and I sit on the loveseat facing them, and Zeus remains by the door.

"They yanked Sutton from the car and threw him on the ground. Sutton yelled at me to run. I didn't want to, but I had no choice. I slammed my foot down on the gas and got the hell out of there." He lowers his eyes. "I would've never made it if I hadn't."

"Where are they taking him?" Cole asks.

"Where do you think?"

"No. Please, God, no." In a rage, I jump from the couch and without thinking, punch a hole in the wall, watching the drywall crumble into pieces just like my heart. But I'm too angry to cry, and my hand hurts like crazy.

"Let's go, we're wasting time." Cole moves quickly toward the door, and I'm a step behind him. Bruno steps in Cole's way, waking Zeus, who'd fallen asleep in front of the door. "What are you doing? Get out of my way."

"Man, we don't have a chance in hell."

"Screw that, we're going," Cole says in a threatening tone.

Grace is suddenly by Bruno's side, trying to get us to think rationally. "And even if we did find them ... which we won't ... then what? Nothing. Because we'd all end up dead."

"You don't know that." Cole starts pacing the room, and I cover my face with my hands because I know what Grace's saying is true.

"I'm sorry, but I'm not throwing my wife out there to get murdered. And what about Lexi? You're willing to sacrifice her for the cause?"

77

Cole's entire body goes rigid, and his hands are in tight fists. "Of course not," he says through gritted teeth.

"So what are you saying?" I ask. "Just let Wilson do what he wants with him while we sit back and allow it to happen?" I have to do something. I cannot sit around and let them kill Sutton too! It's hard to breathe. My pulse is racing. I reach for the wall to steady myself.

"Hey ... calm down. Breathe. You need to breathe." Cole's arms wrap around me, and it feels like the room is spinning.

Just when I was starting to think maybe there was hope. This can't be happening ... everything's backward and upside down.

"Man, she's turning white," Bruno says.

I hear him, but his voice sounds muffled as I grip Cole's shirt. I shake my head into his chest, and I can't believe the words that are about to come out of my mouth. I take a deep breath and try to calm myself.

"We have to"—I swallow hard, forcing the terror back down my throat—"go back in."

"No way. You're not going back to the Hole," Cole says.

I push off his chest and scoot back against the wall. "That's not your choice to make."

Cole stews silently, his jaw tight with tension.

"This isn't about you or me; this is about doing what's right. What I need to do. What I have to do. I refuse to let Sutton rot in there. So it's your choice ... you can come or not, but either way, I'm going after him."

He relaxes just enough that I can tell he really is concerned. He isn't just being pig-headed. "You swore to me you'd never go back."

"You're right. I did. But now things have changed. And if we don't man up and go after Sutton, no one will."

Cole's face hardens again, and he shakes his head. But seconds pass, and his expression changes. He's knows I'm right. He knows I have to do this.

"All right." Cole drops his eyes to the floor. "We'll go together."

"Thank you," I say. "Look, I know it's going to be hard. But we can do this. It'll be different this time. We have the upper hand. No one would believe we'd have the guts to go back."

"It won't be that simple," Cole says. "Guards still patrol the Hole. And do you realize how large it is? It could take years to find him."

"And you're the only one who's branded," Grace says to me.

"That's not an issue. Children who are born in the Hole, they're not branded ... just forced to live in the Hole with their parents," Bruno says.

"Lexi," Cole says, "do you realize how hard—"

"I didn't say it'd be easy," I cut him off. "But we have to at least try. We can't just leave him there to rot."

"Have you considered the possibility we might never get out?" Cole asks. "Just because we were lucky enough to get out last time, doesn't mean we'd be so lucky now. And let's not forget, not all of us made it out."

"You don't think I know that?" I face him, my body rigid and heated. How could he think I've forgotten about Keegan and the others who died trying to get us out? "But had it been us, he wouldn't give it a thought. He'd do the same and more."

"So then what?" Cole asks. "What are we going to do?"

"We'll live in the Hole."

"What? Do you even hear what you're saying?"

"We did it before, and I have to believe we can do it again. But if Sutton's in there, then he can't follow through on his plan, and then we really won't have any hope of ever being free. Don't you see? This is the only way."

"Dude, this sucks monkey balls," Bruno says. "The Hole sucks. Wilson sucks. This entire situation sucks."

"If Lexi, of all people, is willing to go back, shouldn't we be supporting her? I mean, she's right. Sutton wouldn't hesitate if it was one of us," Grace says.

"Yeah, babe. It's just, you have no idea what it's like in there. It's hell. Everywhere you turn, there's some kind of danger," Bruno says.

But I'm not paying attention to them as much as I'm watching Cole's face. From the way he strokes his chin, I can tell he's contemplating it. His eyes harden, and he takes a short, quick breath.

"Okay. How would this work?" He turns to Bruno.

"Well, before we do anything, we have to get Grace to her family. She's not going to the Hole, man. Once we get her settled, we can figure out a plan on how we're gonna get in."

"Oh no you don't," Grace says. "I'm going too."

"Absolutely not. You're going home."

"Bruno. I refuse to be that wife who sits around waiting every second of every day, wondering when or if her husband's coming back. I've made my choice. I'm coming, and you'll just have to deal with it!"

Wow! I didn't see that coming. Go, Grace!

80

Bruno storms off into the kitchen. I hear him open the refrigerator door and slam it shut before he comes back in with a drink.

"Feel better?" Cole says to him.

"No."

"Yeah, didn't think so."

"Okay, so we're all going?" I ask.

"Seems that way. Four is better than two," Cole says.

"Five. You forgot Zeus."

"Oh, praise the Lord, now we're saved!" Bruno says with sarcasm, and Zeus looks up from the blanket he's been tearing apart and growls at him. "What's with him and shredding stuff?"

"Stress reliever," Cole says. "Better the blanket than your leg."

While they're conversing about Zeus, my mind wanders, trying to think about others who might want to help us.

"We need to get help," I say.

"Huh?" Bruno asks. He looks at Cole.

"I'm talking about the monitors. They were expecting to meet Sutton. If we tell them he's been abducted, maybe then they'll have even more reason to believe us." My knuckles turn white as I clench my hands. "Sutton told us ... we have to find them."

"We don't know anything about them other than that Sutton was going to meet with them," Bruno says. "We don't know where the meeting was or with who."

"For heaven's sake, Sutton didn't tell you?" Grace asks in a high-pitched voice.

"I kinda got the impression he wanted to keep details to

himself." Bruno rubs his temples.

"You mean the entire time you guys were in the car he never mentioned it? You didn't ask?" Cole shakes his head.

Bruno's eyes brighten. "He did mention the monitors would get to High Society within the week. But from there, who the hell knows."

"So then what?" Grace asks.

"Just depends on how aggressive the United Powers wants to be and if they can get enough backing from their members," Bruno says. "If it's bad enough, maybe they'll intervene or something."

"And when Sutton's not there to greet them, they might become even more suspicious," I say. Cole searches my eyes with his. "Hopefully they'll head straight to the Hole."

"That's possible," he says. "But if we find them first, we'll tell them about Sutton and hope they'll care enough to want to find him."

"Exactly what I was thinking." I nod at him.

"Well … we have a plan," Bruno says. "Plans are good. If they work."

"So let's do this," I say, jumping to my feet.

"Whoa, hold on there, hot pants," Bruno says. "Preparation first. We need to grab all the food, water, and supplies we can and stuff it into our packs."

When the realization settles in that we're really going back to the Hole, I can't move. The truth is, I'm scared out of my mind.

CHAPTER 7

I sit on the doorstep with a fully loaded backpack and listen to the waves against the beach. Zeus nuzzles my hand, and I plant a kiss on his nose. Part of me wishes I could stay here forever. But I know it's not realistic. I sigh.

My life has been a constant flow of seemingly insurmountable obstacles. And now, as I prepare for perhaps the biggest one I have ever had to face, I wonder if I have the strength to overcome. Before, we were just surviving from one day to the next. If we go back to the Hole, we will have to do more than just survive. We will have to triumph.

"We're ready to go," Cole says, squeezing through the door and letting it squeal closed behind him. Zeus is up and attentive at once.

I pull myself up, put my arm through the straps of my backpack, throw its weight behind me, and push my other arm through the second strap. Cole's lips part slightly, and he leans closer to me.

"You all right?"

"Sure." I bend over, wiping my palms on my jeans. I could never hide the truth from him.

"Then we've got a train to catch." He picks up a pack and steps off the porch.

Bruno, Zeus, Grace, and I follow him as he treks down the winding driveway, along the cliff, and toward the main road. My stomach tightens into a fist the closer we get. I don't need to guess how vulnerable we are out here. I already know it. And I feel naked. Stripped of everything but our hope.

It's black out here. I mean, really black. But the darkness hides us, and the temperature drops. I cross my arms over my chest, silently thanking Sutton for giving me clean, dry clothes. Inevitably, sand fills my boots, my socks, and my hair. I lick my dry and cracking lips.

We're glad for the cover of night, but even in the daytime, there isn't much to see of Lexington Beach anymore. The ravages of war reach even out here, making it just another former paradise where abandoned houses rest upon splintered stilts along the beach. The citizens who remain choose to live silent lives, off the grid and away from the rule of the Commander. Like mice, they scatter when guards come around.

We tread miles and miles of sand and nothingness until headlights bathe the road in light. I have to squint to see Cole jumping into a ditch. Zeus pushes my knees with his nose, almost nudging me into the spot where the others already wait. We're breathing heavy as the sound of the oncoming engine gets louder. My pulse quickens as I smash myself against the side of the ditch, and sand trickles down my shoulders causing me to shiver.

The car passes. I wonder who's inside the vehicle, a guard or citizen. Then my mind wanders to Sutton and whether he's being tortured right this very second. Cole gently touches my shoulder, and I push myself up onto the road.

"Only two miles to go," he whispers. "Be on your guard."

"Already am." *Who is he kidding?*

"Then what?" Grace stutters as she takes a sip of water then passes the thermos to Bruno.

"We find a way to get on that train," Cole says in a lower voice, grabbing a sip when Bruno passes it.

Focus and get on the train ... alive.

I shake my head, refusing the drink. I'm too wound up to put anything into my body right now.

We keep going, and soon, I see the dim lights of a train yard. The barbed-wire fence rises around it, and the flickering light gives it a grainy, almost black and white appearance as if in an old photograph. I notice the large bodies of the passenger cars resting in lines. One guard tower sits at the far end, with the dark silhouette of a guard against the light. I exhale, slowly ... and try to take it all in. It's so quiet, I'm afraid one false step will alert them to our presence. And yet, as we move closer, the place seems like almost an afterthought compared to other guard bases I've seen. It doesn't even look like anyone's patrolling the perimeter.

When I lived in the country, there wasn't a lot of guard activity, only rumors about it from my dad and his contacts. But when we moved to High Society, they were around all the time. Every week, someone was hauled away screaming, and the people would turn their heads and act like they didn't know them. No one wanted to be mistaken for a sympathizer, or worse, a co-conspirator.

"How the cracker are we going to get in there?" Grace asks, her voice squeaking at the end. I look in her direction. Her eyes are wide with speculation.

A chuckle escapes me. "Cracker?"

Cole looks at me like he knows exactly what she was saying.

"Yeah, cracker. I know it's ridiculous, but Grace won't swear so she says cracker instead," Bruno says. The whites of his eyes are a stark contrast against the darkness. "Damn waste of a word, if you ask me."

Grace rolls her eyes at Bruno.

"Anyway," Grace says. "Back to my question: how are we getting in?"

"Very, very carefully," Cole whispers. I watch as he scans the yard, his eyes moving back and forth quickly. "From what I can see, it seems like it's a slow, quiet night."

"Yeah. There are three guards up there"—Bruno points to the tower—"with their eyes glued to the TV." We all turn our heads toward the tower. "I imagine two of them are supposed to be guarding the main gate."

"You think there's only the three of them?" I ask.

"This is an old train yard. I don't think they would waste guard resources on it." Cole readjusts his belt and backpack.

"I don't have a good feeling about this … seems way too easy," I say.

"Well, it's too late to chicken out now," Grace says.

Zeus snorts beside me.

"I'll lead, you guys follow," Cole says. "You know the drill." I fall in line behind him, Grace and then Bruno behind me. Cole pulls out his gun, and I notice it has a suppressor on it.

"Where'd you get that?" I whisper and draw my gun.

"Sutton gave it to me."

I nod and take a deep, cleansing breath. Next thing, I'm chasing after Cole through the reeds and sand, listening to the sounds of our heavy breathing and footsteps. The cool air bites at my cheeks. I push thoughts of our loosely made plans and what could go wrong out of my head.

Cole motions for us to stop. He jerks to a halt and franticly signals toward the fence. I follow his hand to a hole big enough for a child to fit through. My eyes lock with Cole's.

Every instinct I have is telling me that it's too easy as the hair rises on the back of my neck.

"Feels like a trap," I say to Cole. "We should look for another way."

"There is no other way. Go." He sounds impatient. But when he motions toward the jagged entry again, I shake my head. It's too late though; Zeus has already dug his way underneath and come up on the other side with his tongue hanging out of his mouth, staring at us like we're idiots.

"Damn it," I mutter under my breath. Now, we've got no choice. My gut screams as Cole holds the fencing up so I can squeeze just below the sharp points.

"Stay close to me," Cole says as I shimmy under.

"I will."

Once on the other side, I hunch down, staring back at Cole,

Bruno, and Grace through the gridded wiring. I'm afraid if I move too much, my feet will disturb the gravel, alerting the guards to our location.

Bruno barely slides underneath. Grace follows, and then Cole slides through last, carefully replacing the fencing. The scraping sound of it snapping back into place gives me the jitters. It sounds ten times louder than I'm sure it is, but I can't help my paranoia. *People have been caught for dumber reasons than this.*

Cole shrugs as if saying, "I told you so."

That's when I hear the low, familiar growl.

My head snaps to the left. Zeus's head is low, ears back and teeth bared. His fur is ruffled, and his eyes are gleaming. Bruno shoves Grace behind him and begins to back away. But she stumbles and falls before she has a chance to get her footing. That's when the figure comes into view.

My jaw drops.

Zeus charges toward the figure in full-on bark-and-attack mode. "Zeus! Don't!" I rush to stop him, but Cole holds me back.

"Zeus. Stop!" Cole is forceful, firm.

Zeus stops immediately, dirt kicking up as he slides into place. He assumes a guarded stance, and his growl becomes deeper, fiercer. That growl is returned by one equally as deep and savage.

A black Doberman with pointy ears, ferocious white canines, and a gigantic chain around his neck faces Zeus, growling and barking. With the saliva dripping down his mouth, it feels like he's just waiting for the command to eat us. The muscular creature licks his foaming lips. If he doesn't shut up, the guards will know we're here.

"Cole, shoot it!" I demand, drawing attention to myself.

The dog lunges in my direction.

"Lexi, move!"

Zeus jumps in front of me, snarling and snapping viciously, and then both dogs lock together in a mass of spit, fur, and violence. I can't stop myself from screaming, watching Zeus be bitten and attacked like that. From somewhere in the compound, I hear others, but all I can think about is what's unfolding in front of me.

I aim my gun. *He can't die!*

I tighten my grip, ready, but they're moving too fast. There's no possible shot. Sweat beads on my forehead and drips, burning my eyes. Blood and saliva fling out into the air as the dogs continue their assault on one another. Deep down I know, only one can win this fight.

Cole steps forward and points his gun, his body completely tense and his jaw clenched. He closes one eye and slowly pulls back the trigger.

God, please … don't let him miss.

Grace has grabbed my wrist by now, but I'm rigid, frozen in shock. Bruno's yelling at her to get away, to follow him.

Cole shoots.

My breath hitches.

Everything moves in slow motion.

One of the dogs staggers, then moves slowly away.

The other collapses to the ground.

I cover my ears to drown out the sound of my own screams.

It's Zeus. Oh God. Zeus.

I shove my gun into its holster and rush toward him. He

saved us. *He saved me.* He's swerving this way and that, losing his balance. I wrap him in my arms. "It's okay, boy. You're going to be okay."

Zeus's breathing is labored, his eyes are starting to gloss over. Cole looks wounded, crushed.

"Go! I'll carry him," Cole says. He pushes me gently away and lifts a whimpering Zeus into his arms. From this vantage point, Zeus's torn flesh is more evident.

The other dog sounds just as bad; his crying and whimpering hits a soft spot in my heart.

"Hold on," I say. The other dog shakes his head. "He's suffering."

"Look away," Bruno says as he aims his gun at the poor dog. I turn away, close my eyes, and cover my ears. I can't watch. Grace does the same. When Bruno fires, the dog makes one last yelp, and it makes me jump. I open my eyes and uncover my ears when I feel Bruno's hand lightly pat my back. "Now he feels nothing. Now run!"

The guards are coming. Their shouts and the sound of their feet tromping on stones give away their position. They're close.

We run alongside the long, sleek body of a newly polished railcar as the alarm blares, disorienting us. I dart between cars, hop over tracks, and check every door. My breaths are bursting in and out of my chest, and adrenaline pushes me to keep going. *Please, let us find an open car.*

Finally, I reach a long passenger car used to transport Sinners, and I dig my fingers into the door handle, managing to slide the heavy door open. My hands shake as I hold it open for Bruno and Grace.

Suddenly, the train creaks to life, jerking beneath my feet. I grab on to the doorframe, panic ripping through me. *Where are Cole and Zeus?* My shoulders tighten. Gunshots rebound around us, coupled with the whirring of wheels. I lean out the doorway, my hair flying in my face, obstructing my view.

"Where's Cole?" Bruno asks.

The train picks up pace, clicking along the track.

"Damn it, I don't know."

Pulling my hair away and gritting my teeth, I'm about to scream when Cole rounds the corner with a lethargic-looking Zeus in his arms.

Cole's knees look like they're about to buckle from the way he's staggering. His eyes lift to mine, desperation crossing his face.

"Come on," I say. He stumbles, almost dropping Zeus. "Cole, push yourself. You've got to get on."

I glance ahead of the train, as the barbed-wire fencing comes into view, knowing we'll soon be out of the rail yard. Focusing back on Cole, I notice guards following him, guns drawn. They fire at him, but somehow he finds the strength to run.

I reach out my hand, but he's just beyond my fingertips. Sweat pours off his forehead; Zeus lies limp in his arms.

"Hand him over," Bruno says. He moves behind me, reaching out his corded arms.

Cole's boots stomp to keep up, his face turning red and veins popping out of his neck as he struggles to keep up with the train.

"Come on man, a little closer," Bruno says. By now, Grace stands at his side, her hand on his shoulder for support.

Cole lifts Zeus up, his limbs dangling and kicking at the air awkwardly. One paw hits Cole in the face, but he just clenches his jaw and scrunches his forehead with determination.

"Grab him," he says breathlessly.

"I got him," Bruno says. He pulls Zeus into the train car just as the train picks up speed.

Cole just barely touches the ledge where I stand, his legs struggling to keep up. I lean out, my fingertips catching his. They brush each other, then air separates us.

"Cole!" I scream. "Get on the train!"

Bullets skim off the metal of the car, forcing me back for a minute. The black fencing surrounding the rail yard enters my peripheral vision. Then the door starts sliding closed.

"Cole!" I put my body in front of the door to block it. "Someone help!"

Grace pushes her way beside me and braces herself. "Grab him," she shouts. "I'll hold it."

I grit my teeth and jump for his hands.

They catch mine, and with Grace bracing the door, I pull Cole onto the steps. He lands on his stomach, heaving for air as he sprawls across the threshold.

The door slams closed with a hollow bang.

We all smash ourselves against the cold, metal flooring. My nose crinkles from the smell of sweat, bodily fluids, and old blood. *This is definitely a transport car for Sinners.* I can still hear the alarms ringing and guards' voices. My chest heaves as I roll toward Zeus to inspect him. He doesn't look good. He's losing a lot of blood.

"Hurry, I need something, anything, to stop the bleeding," I say. Bruno rummages through his bag and tosses a t-shirt at me. I tear it into strips. My hands shake, but I wrap Zeus's wounds as he whimpers.

"It's okay, Zeus," Cole says in a raspy voice. "It's okay. I'm here." He crawls over to us, still trying to catch his breath as he examines Zeus. "Everything's going to be just fine."

Tears sting my eyes. I know how much this dog means to Cole. He tries not to let on, but I know his heart is breaking.

"He has four gashes," I say. "They're not that deep, and the muscle's not torn, but he may need stitches if the bleeding doesn't stop." Suddenly, my thoughts turn to Sutton's medical bag. If he were here, he could help. He could save him.

"He'll pull through. He always does. He's had injuries worse than this." Cole gently touches my shoulders, and I lean back into him. My back rests against his chest, and he curls his arms around me. His reassuring tone calms me. So I fight my resistance and allow myself to be here for him.

Grace lies in Bruno's arms with her eyes squeezed shut. Her hands grip the side of her head, as if she's trying to block out the sirens. He encircles her in his giant biceps and squeezes. I can't help thinking she looks so small in his lap.

I twist around to look at Cole.

"I should've listened to you," Cole says. "I should've trusted your instinct. The fence was a trap ... and you knew it."

"No." I shake my head, taking his fingers into mine. "There was no other way. There'll never be an easy way for us."

The sirens stop, and I freeze in the gray light. I don't hear any more voices. The sounds of shouting, guns firing, and loose gravel under boots subsided as the train left the rail yard, passing the large, black fence surrounding it. Now, it's deathly silent except for the whirring of the wheels as the train kicks into high gear. I hold my breath, waiting for something to go wrong.

But nothing happens.

My lids grow heavy with exhaustion. There's nothing more tiring than the feeling you get after the adrenaline leaves your veins. Even though I ache from my head to my toes, I manage to keep applying pressure to Zeus's bleeding wounds and praying for a miracle.

There's no turning back. We're on our way to the Hole.

CHAPTER 8

Flashes of early-morning sunlight wake me from my slumber. It flits through the slits at the top of the railcar. The gentle humming of the train assures me we're still moving. I sit up and run my fingers through my tangled hair. No one else appears to be awake. I hear Cole's soft snoring behind me and see Bruno and Grace asleep in each other's arms. And it reminds me that love is the only blanket of warmth from this frigid world.

Zeus! I snap my head toward him and reach over to check his wounds. He's woofing in his sleep, and his paws twitch. I touch his bloodstained fur, and it feels stiff. Pulling my hand away, I glance at my fingers, rub them together, and realize they're dry. His bleeding has stopped, and I rejoice for that small gift. I peer closer. His wounds don't seem as deep as they did in last night's darkness and chaos. A deep sigh escapes my lips. My eyes drift to the opening at the top of the wall and the light filtering through. Pulling my knees to my chest, I close my eyes, because there's someone I need to talk to. In a whisper, I begin.

"Dad, I hope you can hear me because there're some things I need to say." *Ugh, this is harder than I thought it was going to be. And it's not like he'll respond.* I swallow hard and find myself proceeding anyway. "Okay, I'm just going to spit this out, so here goes nothing. I know your dream for me was to fight for the freedom of our society, but I can't, Dad. How can I possibly do that, when my heart is pulling me elsewhere? Trust me, I realize going after Sutton is pretty much a death sentence. But it's a risk I have to take, because leaving him there to die isn't something I can live with. And I'm pretty sure you'd do the same thing, because I know the kind of man you were. This world is one messed up place. It's a war I can't win on my own. And now, I have a smaller battle to fight, and I'm praying. Gosh, I'm praying so hard you'll understand. I love Sutton, and I know you do too, so I need to do this for me, for us. And no matter what the outcome is, I hope you'll be proud of me." Tears flood my eyes; I blink, and they spill out. I feel the warm streams sliding down my cheeks, and I lick the corner of my mouth, tasting salt.

"Why aren't you here, guiding me? You should be here; I need you. I need you so much it hurts to breathe." I bite down on my quivering lower lip.

I take a slow, deep breath and release it. "Okay, Dad, Keegan … I need your strength more than ever." The pain of their absence is everywhere, and it eats at my flesh every second of every day. "I love you both so much … and I'm going to do whatever it takes to carry on your legacy, to make sure you didn't die in vain. Please, watch over me. Please watch over all of us." I lay back, and Cole's arms surround me.

"I'm right here," Cole says. "I'll hold you, always. You're my strength, Lexi. So allow me to be yours."

I turn to meet his eyes. "Oh, sorry. I didn't realize you were listening," I say, tilting my head back into the crook of his neck. "What if I let them down? What if I'm doing the wrong thing?"

"I'm sure they're extremely proud of you," Cole says. I whip around and face him, while wiping my tears away. "But maybe you should focus on who's here for you now. Right here. Right in front of you."

"You're right, I shouldn't worry about what I can't control. Ugh."

"What?"

"Why are you always right?"

"Ha. That's far from the truth. Lexi, I've been wrong so many times in my life. We all have. But I think the only option we have is to accept our mess-ups and move on." He runs his thumb across my lips before leaning in and kissing me. "And knowing the kind of man you say your father was, I think he'd be doing exactly the same thing."

"I hope I make the right choices when … " My voice trails off.

"Hey, it'll be okay. Promise," Cole says. I rest my head on his chest and inhale the faint smell of sweat mixed with soap. "Zeus seems better."

"Yeah. His wounds aren't bleeding anymore, and they're not as deep as I thought. Which is a very good thing," I say. "As long as we keep his cuts clean, he should be fine. It would've killed me if he'd died."

"I know. You've really become attached to Zeus. That means a lot to me," he says.

"Cole?"

"Yeah?"

"Are you scared? Because, to be completely honest ... I'm petrified."

"We're all scared. We wouldn't been human if we weren't." He links his fingers with mine, pulls my hand to his mouth, and then kisses it. "And remember, our mission is to save Sutton so he can get to the monitors. We aren't trying to save the world."

"Without a doubt."

Bruno stirs.

"Man. What the hell? How long have we been asleep?" he asks, scratching his head. Bruno and Grace squint against the light. "Sleeping on the way to the Hole ... Who does that?"

"Apparently we do," Cole says with a light chuckle. It's nice hearing him laugh.

"How long before we arrive?" Grace asks.

"There's only one more stop before the Hole," Bruno says. I watch as he digs around in his bag. He swigs some water, then hands it to Grace.

"I'm afraid to ask, but how exactly do you know that?" Grace asks, before taking a drink.

"My first assignment was in the rail yard, before I became a rock-star guard inside the Hole."

More silence follows as the seriousness of what we are about to do sinks in.

I wrestle with my bag, searching for a bottle of water, when

Zeus flops onto his belly and shoves his head into my lap as if asking for water too. The heat inside this railcar is suffocating; I imagine it must be even worse for Zeus.

My stomach rumbles, and my neck muscles tighten at the thought of trying to pass another station before getting to the Hole. This is what my nightmares are made of.

We travel for the next ten minutes or so in silence.

The gentle thumping of the wheels grind to a halt.

We all freeze, staring at each other, not knowing what to expect.

Cole and Bruno immediately jump up, checking their weapons and gathering their wits. We hear noises from outside, voices yelling. I can almost smell the blood that might shed any second. My hair stands tall on my arms as I scramble to get my bag, Zeus, and my weapons secured. Shouting and crying catch my attention. Even through the walls, I can sense their fear.

"Are we here?" I ask Bruno. His attention is fixed on the door, his jaw's locked, and his eyes are narrowed.

"It's the last stop. That's all you need to know," he says in a tight voice.

I imagine the desperation of Sinners at the last stop. Their last breath of freedom before losing their freedom forever.

"Stay hidden and we won't have trouble," Bruno says.

Yeah, okay.

A glimmer of light reflects off my ring. It's been so long since I've looked at it. I find myself reading it again.

"You can overcome anything, short of death."

You're right, Dad. I sure as hell can. But how many times?

Suddenly, a loud squealing sound echoes throughout the

metal car we're in, and the door begins to slide open. Grace and I take positions behind Cole and Bruno. At first, nothing happens. I hear Zeus let out a low, menacing growl, and I put one hand on his neck to break his fixation on the door. My heart's getting ready to explode out of my chest.

And we wait.

The guards shout orders as Sinners respond with cursing and cries. I'm frozen in position, holding my breath ... waiting for something. Anything.

And we wait some more.

Anxiety gnaws at my insides. I clench my teeth as a single droplet of sweat travels over my brow.

"Form lines!" a loudspeaker blares over the din. "Sinners will no longer be allowed to work outside the Hole. If any of you try anything, try to leave, you will be shot."

Why can't Sinners work outside the Hole anymore? Why keep them locked up when they are needed for work? Now, getting back out is going to be harder than I thought.

Bruno slowly slides toward the door, peeking outside quickly and then snatching himself back. My eyes widen, waiting for him to signal to us.

"How many?" Cole asks in a whisper.

"Too many," Bruno responds. *Please don't let them find us.*

"Okay, let's get this car loaded," a voice says from beyond the door. He's close. Too close.

I hear footsteps resembling those of an army and brace myself. First, a dirt-covered hand appears. Then, slowly, a shoe appears through the doorway, and a person enters the car. Neither Cole nor Bruno move. Grace tenses behind me, and I'm a ball of nerves and adrenaline.

She doesn't see us yet. I pinch Zeus's neck, like Cole taught me, to quiet him.

The moment her eyes flick up, they bulge with terror. I motion her to move further into the car and allow others on, so she doesn't arouse suspicion. To my surprise, she steps forward. Upon seeing Zeus, who stands beside me with his ears perked up at full attention, she stops in her tracks. Her eyes flit from Zeus to me, and back. When she begins to back away, I pull Zeus away from her. She finds a spot in the corner and cowers, curling into the fetal position.

Next, a man enters. Then more people file in, their eyes surprised, but their mouths sealed. It's almost like a comradery between us. We won't hurt anyone, if they stay quiet.

"Move faster!" I hear the loudspeaker shout.

People begin shoving in, piling in until there's only standing room. Bruno and Grace are separated from Cole, Zeus, and I. I'm starting to feel claustrophobic. By now, I've lowered my gun. Zeus is getting restless. Every time he moves, he steps on someone or something and they groan.

Bang!

The gunshot ignites panic in the car. The accused shriek, cry, and step over one another to get on. I'm pressed against the wall, looking around frantically for the others. *Where's Grace?* She's too short to spot among the throng of Sinners. Bruno is easy to spot. He sticks out like a sore thumb.

"Anyone else want to try to pull that stunt?" the voice on the loudspeaker screams.

My stomach plummets when I think about the day I was brought to the Hole, and I imagine how these people must feel. I wonder if they are all guilty of the crimes they've been accused of, or if they could possibly be like me, wrongfully accused. Soon, we're all packed in like sardines. Shoulders to shoulders, backs to backs, and I'm breathing someone else's spent air. Beside me, a girl who looks like she can't be more than twelve years old stares back, terror but also hope crossing her face. I reach in my bag and offer her my water.

"It's going to be okay. Here, take this."

A small and timid hand meets mine as she takes the water from my grasp. I can't look at her too long. My heart is breaking from this little gesture.

I feel lightheaded, and my clothes are almost completely soaked through with sweat. I focus on the vein pulsing in Cole's forehead next to me.

"Guards! Seal the doors."

I bite down on my cheek and duck my head, hoping to blend in to the crowd. But we aren't home free yet.

Zeus lets out a low growl, but stays in place.

"It'll be okay," I whisper. I link my hand with his collar, for extra insurance.

A guard at the door fixes his glance in our direction. He stops and probes the packed car with his eyes. I move backward, accidently stepping on Zeus's paw. He lets out a loud, sharp bark.

"Zeus, stop it," Cole says, not realizing what happened. The guard's eyes zero in on Zeus, and I consider putting myself between him and the dog. My breath catches as he lifts his gun. "No!" I scream, and then everything seems to happen in slow motion.

Cole is up, gun drawn, pointing at the guard.

I shove Zeus behind me and see the girl I gave the water to

back away from me. She's afraid of me!

I quickly turn back to the guard. He has a sick, sadistic smile plastered across his face. He recognizes me. I reach up and try to cover my brand.

His barrel's now aimed at my chest.

"Lexi, get down!" Cole says.

Bruno shoves people aside like he's swimming. When the guard pauses, Bruno grabs him. He gets his giant arms around the guard in what looks like a hug. Then, in a motion of sheer power, he violently twists his head. I hear a sickening snap as the body crumbles to the platform. Bruno kicks it away from the train, then whips his gun out from his waistband.

The people around him gasp.

"Excuse me, excuse me. I gotta get through." Cole makes his way toward Bruno.

Sinners clear a narrow path for Cole while I shield the young girl from the gruesome sight unfolding.

For a moment, I think maybe we will get away with it. No one has noticed.

And then automatic fire sprays our railcar. Bodies hit the floor. Everyone's fighting to get down, piling on top of each other. Bullets whip through the air around us, puncturing the walls. I manage to look up and see the door's still open. Bruno and Cole are standing, firing back. Another man grabs a gun off Cole's waist and begins firing.

The car begins to move. The sudden jolt puts everyone off balance. Zeus yelps.

For a moment, I sway left. But Cole's figure in the doorway fuels me. *Please don't let this be it. I can't let him die.*

To my relief, the automatic door begins sliding closed.

With a loud bang, Bruno and Cole relax, pressing their backs against the wall and trying to catch their breaths as the train picks up speed. I hunch over; my chest's heaving for oxygen. Everyone's screaming around me. My ears ring. My head's pounding like a drum. All of a sudden, Cole's at my side grabbing my face and inspecting it.

"You're hit," Cole says. He touches my cheek.

"It just grazed me. I'm fine," I say. "How about you, you good?" I run my hands across his chest and then back.

"Yeah, I'm good." Cole's breathing is jagged. He looks past me.

I want to collapse, but instead, I survey the damage. People are piled on top of each other for protection. The floor's slick with blood, and I smell vomit and feces. A soft, wet tongue licks my fingers, and I look down to see Zeus bleeding. It hurts like hell to inhale. I scan him. His wounds from last night have opened up again, but this time, he's really bleeding badly.

"Cole, get me something, anything. He's bleeding again."

Cole frantically looks around, but a man next to him pulls his shirt over his head and hands it to him.

"Thank you," Cole says. It's the guy who helped Cole and Bruno fight back. He hands Cole his gun and nods his head.

I drop down next to Zeus and immediately apply pressure to the wound that's bleeding the most. He lets out a cry.

"Will you stop trying to be such a tough guy? You have to heal, you dork," I say to Zeus. His big, brown eyes look at me, and if I didn't know better, I'd say he was sad. My head snaps up. I know Bruno's all right, but where's Grace?

"Grace!" I call out, looking around the car. "Where's Grace?"

"Right here," she says. I breathe a sigh of relief when I see her arms around Bruno. Her face looks bloodless.

"Phew. We're all here; we're all okay."

As people around us pick up the pieces, collect themselves, and assess the scene, Grace, who's been quiet the entire time, decides to speak.

"Why do you suppose they let us go?" Grace asks. "They could've stopped the train."

"Because they know where we're headed." Cole's face grows serious. "They'll be ready for us."

CHAPTER 9

An injured woman lies flat on her back, arms at her sides and legs still. Fiery red hair is matted to her face and neck. Her light blue eyes stare blankly. I kneel beside her. She moans, and a man quickly grabs her hand. Her face has already turned ashen, and her breathing is labored. Beside her is a pool of blood. The man presses a hand against her stomach wound as blood seeps through his fingers. He leans forward and kisses her forehead. I watch him as he stares at her, skin bunching around his eyes. His eyes harden the instant he notices me watching.

"This is your fault. They were after you," he says, pointing to the brand around my neck. "She's going to die because of you."

He's right. And suddenly I'm sinking in my own skin; this is my fault, because they were after me. My hands shake as I pull my hair over my shoulders in an effort to hide my brand.

"She'll be at peace soon." I say the only thing I can think of. "Talk to her … tell her it's okay to let go." A sick feeling hits the pit of my stomach.

He stares at me like I just said the craziest thing.

"I know this won't account for much, but where she's going … at least she'll be safe," I say to the man. "Trust me." He nods.

The woman moans again, and blood dribbles over her lips. I can't watch her die knowing I'm the cause of the bullet that's killing her. *How many others are going to die because of me?*

I stand too quickly and then stumble backward when the image of Keegan's death flashes in my mind. My vision blurs.

"Whoa, I got you," Cole says, catching me just before I fall. "Come on, you need to sit down."

The man looks up at me, and I swear I see pity in his eyes.

"I'm okay. I just … I just got lightheaded, that's all." How can I be thinking about myself at a time like this?

"Come sit with me," Cole says. "That old man is grieving, but he's wrong. This isn't your fault, Lexi. None of this is on you."

Yes it is.

The light wanes, and everything is quiet except for the occasional shallow cough and the purring of the train on the tracks. I press my head against the frigid, cold metal of the train car. Bruno and Cole join others, moving dead bodies to the other side of the car and piling them up. It's a gruesome task, and I have to look away. At my feet, Zeus woofs in his sleep. *Probably chasing cats or something.* His wounds have stopped bleeding, but his fur's still smeared with blood. The dim lights of the car flicker, giving off an eerie glow. It's like we're being transported to space or something. *Space would be better.*

Cole slides down the wall and covers his face with his bloody, dirty hands.

"How many dead?" I ask.

"Six." He drops his hands and looks at me. "You've been pretty quiet. What's on your mind?"

I shake my head because I don't want to hear myself say these words.

"Hey, talk to me." He waits patiently for my response.

"I don't want to die, I don't want anyone else to die."

"If we stick to our plan, no one else will have to die. And if they do, that's on Wilson. We have to stay focused. We didn't start this, Lexi. But we sure as hell are going to find Sutton and finish it."

I say nothing. He smiles his crooked smile and kisses me.

Bruno and Grace settle next to us in the cramped car.

"All right, lovebirds," Bruno says to Cole. "What are we gonna do when that door opens again?"

"Unfortunately, since these people recognize us," Cole says, "they're a huge liability."

"We can't kill them," I say.

"Lexi!" Grace scolds, a look of horror on her sweet face.

"We need them on our side. We need them to help us blend

in," Cole says.

"We could move to another car, hide there until this one clears," Grace says.

"Yeah, then once they realize we're gone, maybe that'll be it," Bruno adds, a proud smile across his face.

"That's not going to work," Cole says. "Wilson would slaughter every single one of them before he would give up his search for us. He knows we aren't stupid. He knows we wouldn't give up that easily."

"Oh, that's reassuring," Grace says.

Seconds pass, and no one speaks. The only sounds come from a young boy crying in the back of the car and a woman speaking in Spanish to her elderly companion.

"I can get us in, if we can get past the guards waiting at the station," Cole says finally.

"Okay. Let's say, by some miracle, we make it past the firing squad after the doors open. Once we're in, then what?" I ask.

"I know a place where we can hide out, at least for a little while. Then we go in search of the monitors," Bruno says. He rubs the back of his neck.

"Whoa, hold on a minute. What about Sutton?" I ask. "We have to find him."

"Our first mission's to find the monitors and help them retrieve the information they need to end this."

"Wait, what?" I ask, as my stomach plummets to the floor. "Why would we do that?"

"Think about it. You know Sutton better than all of us, and this is what he's worked so hard for. If we don't help the monitors succeed, nothing changes. We can't hang the future

109

on saving one man. We get to the monitors first, then save Sutton."

I clench my fists and release them, allowing the anger to escape my fingers. I know they're right, that it's what needs to be done. I unclench my jaw and relax my shoulders.

"All right, but once we find them—"

"Lexi, one day at a time," Cole says. "This isn't going to happen overnight. There are only five of us. We're up against hundreds of guards and thousands upon thousands of Sinners."

"You're right," I say. "Don't worry, I can do this."

"I know you can." Cole pulls me into a hug, and I soak in his warmth.

Bruno begins banging on the wall opposite the door, drawing people's attention. "Aha, got you, bugger," he says.

Grace gives him a funny look. "Bruno, what are you—"

Just then Bruno uses the heel of his boot and kicks through the wall, shattering glass and revealing a brightly painted red handle in a hidden compartment.

"Just a little trick I learned when I worked at the station." He smiles. "Only a few know there's an emergency door release. All I have to do is pull it when we get close, and we can jump out before the guards show up."

"You're a genius," Cole says.

"Yeah, let's just hope this sucker still works," Bruno says. He sits down next to it, bringing Grace to his side. "When we slow enough to jump without breaking our legs, I'll hit it, and the engineer won't see the alarm in time to stop us."

"All right then, tell us when," Cole says, leaning his head back against the wall.

I lean against him, but I can't rest. I can't relax. Something is eating away at me. *Aside from the fact that we're heading into the lion's den.*

My attention's drawn to the end of the railcar, where someone's coughing. The rasping reminds me of holding Alyssa as she passed away in my arms. I place my hands over my aching heart, missing my friend. The figure's body wracks and then goes silent. I let my eyes be drawn to the thin aisle separating slumbering bodies, and that's when it hits me.

The small country church has only six pews on each side, all of which are empty. It's night time, and it feels like someone threw a thick, black blanket over us. I can feel something's not right when I see Keegan standing, empty-handed and shell-shocked, at the front of the church. The pastor's kneeling down with Mom at the altar. My feet stop, and my breath catches. I subconsciously reach out to hold the pew next to me, and the smooth wood meets my fingers. I'm afraid to go any farther.

I watch as Keegan gently folds up the piece of paper he's reading and motions for me. He's not smiling. He's not even cursing, for a change. His eyes look like two giant pieces of coal lodged in a pale face, and I step back.

"Lexi, Mom needs to tell you something," he says with a broken voice. I don't know what's wrong with him. Or me. He's whispering, but it feels like he's shouting.

"Where's Dad?" I ask, hesitantly moving away.

My mom's head snaps up, her makeup smeared and eyes swollen. Terror begins washing over me, and cool sweat trickles down my forehead. Mom slowly stands, letting go of the pastor's hands. She gives me a thin smile, but it brings me no comfort. Next thing I know, she's standing before me, and she looks even worse up close. Her lower lip trembles, and she

111

stops to take a breath.

"Daddy's not coming home ... " she whispers.

"What do you mean? You told me he'd be home by the weekend." I feel my voice come out sharp as a razor. I miss him. I want him home so I can swing with him and read stories with him before bed.

Mom grabs me, wrapping me in her arms, and I feel her shaking against me. "Lexi, I'm sorry, sweetie, but ... he's never coming home." Keegan hugs her, enveloping me at the same time. His lank body smashes us all together.

I still don't understand what she's saying, and I'm fighting against them with my body, trying to be released.

"Lexi, your daddy always did what was right," Mom says. "Even if it meant it would cost him everything. I want you to know that in the end, he made the right choice." She's wiping her face with a tissue, smudging more mascara beneath her eyes. "Because of that, he made some discoveries ... that cost him his life."

"What? What does that mean?" I push her away, but Keegan wraps his arms around my shoulders.

"I don't think we'll ever know." It's then that my mom, my usually composed, graceful, elegant mom, bursts into hysterics. Her hands shake, and her tears form a deluge of pain on her face.

What isn't she telling me? How does she know that in the end, he chose losing his life over coming home to his daughter? His family?

Something dies inside of me. My dad isn't coming home. Ever.

I remember the deluge of condolence cards from people all

over the country. They were piled up in a huge box, unopened for the longest time before my mom felt strong enough to read them. One in particular always made me curious: the one from my stepfather and former Commander. It's hard for me to understand how she could grieve so deeply for my father, and only a few years later, send me to the very place he abhorred: the Hole.

"Lexi, snap out of it!" Bruno slams down the red handle, and I hold my breath as the door releases, opening an inch.

Cole shouts as he shoves the door the rest of the way open. "Go!" He practically pushes me out of the moving railcar, and I fall in a heap on the dusty ground below. Zeus nudges me with his head, but I'm still trying to shake those memories from my head.

"Come on." Cole's in my face, dust and sweat streaking down his cheekbones, his eyes wide as he shakes me. "You all right?"

"Fine," I say, even though I'm disoriented and scared out of my mind.

I fall in behind him, whipping my gun out from my waistband. I feel the whoosh of the train pass us and realize what's happening. We're weaving through roiling clouds of dust. The kind that gets into your pores, your hair, and your mouth. It makes me cough so I lower my head to keep from inhaling more. I can smell the familiar stench of the Hole from here, and bile fills my throat.

I slam into something unexpectedly. It's Zeus. He barely budges when we make contact, but I bounce backward a bit. *I've got to get my head in the game.* Cole taps me on the shoulder and signals for me to move forward.

The train squeals quickly to a halt. The engineer doesn't seem too worried about his cargo, that's for sure. Sinners are the lowest forms of life in this country.

Then it's silent. The dust fades, and I see the silver gleam of the last car just in front of Bruno. He's sprinting like a madman, so I up my pace. The train lets out a sigh; maybe it's tired of transporting Sinners to and from the Hole.

Our feet thump through the dirt. My heart's bursting. I take one glance to my right, and I see the sharp outline of the wall against the sky. The sight alone brings me into focus. Sinners are jumping out of the car we were riding in, trying to escape. Their premature exit garners shouts from the guards. The rest of the doors slide open, and one by one, other Sinners exit from the right side of the train. Bruno waves us on.

That's when the sirens begin.

God help us. It's straight from my nightmares.

But Bruno keeps going, so we keep moving forward, hunched down, along the railcars. I wonder about the young girl from our car, and my heart aches. My feet burn, and my breaths come quick. Even though we have yet to be spotted, I feel so exposed.

I hear a resounding bang, unfamiliar to my ears.

I stop in my tracks. I grab Zeus's collar and pull him to me. The ground quakes under my feet. Cole jerks to a halt behind me. Bruno keeps running. Grace looks back, worry plastered on her face, but she keeps pace with him.

"Run!" Bruno yells over his shoulder.

Adrenaline surges from my feet to my brain. We sprint to catch up, separated by about fifty yards.

Boom! Something explodes behind us. A plume of smoke

114

rises from the dust. The earth vibrates beneath my feet.

I hear it fire again from the direction of the walls. *What the hell is that?* We're one car past the one we jumped out of.

Boom!

A few feet behind us, a thunderous explosion radiates, propelling all of us onto our faces. Burning, ripping heat feels like it's melting my skin. *Am I alive?* I've landed on my chest. My hands are curled into balls. My pack's gone. My gun's gone. Everything's dusty, blurry, charred metal and jagged edges. I open my hand and feel fur. A tongue works its way up my arm. Zeus is okay. A hand hooks under my arm and pulls me to my feet. In the haze, Cole's mouth is moving, but my ears are ringing so loudly I can't hear him.

Moments pass. "Go!" he's yelling. I try to focus on his face. Behind him is a burning ball of metal and carnage, and I can't seem to tear my eyes away. I want to cry and scream and kick. I want to fight back. I want to crawl into a ball. I want to go home.

Cole screams and points in the direction of the train. There's an enormous hole in the side of the railcar; shredded metal peels outward like the petals of a blackened flower in bloom. I stagger, the realization weighting me down. They just blew up the car we were in, all those other people. Cole shoves me forward, then drags me along at a cripplingly slow pace.

So much for needing me alive.

I struggle to keep up as my legs betray me, my knees wobble, and my hands tremor. *Where is Bruno? Grace?* Thick smoke, flames, and dust hide them from my view. Feeling around my waist, I remember my gun has been lost in the blast. Up ahead is hell, and we are running straight into it. My dad's words echo in my head. *You can survive anything, short of death.*

We're almost in the main rail yard. Its overarching, dark green metal beams and roof make it stand out on the horizon. Inside, it looks dark. For once, I welcome the darkness. I whisper a prayer as I run on lead feet. *Please let Bruno and Grace be alive. Please let Sutton survive long enough for us to reach him. And for the love of all that's holy, please help us stay alive.*

Cole makes his way over the tracks. I can tell his familiarity with the Hole has kicked in because his movements seem to come with ease. He looks so natural weaving in and out and over the tracks that brought us here, almost like he belongs. I push these dark thoughts to the back of my mind and try to focus. The rail yard is dark, but the sun blazes over our heads, slicing through the haze that threatens to drown us. I ignore the sweat trickling down my skin.

It's insane that I never noticed any of this when he drove me to the Hole the first time. I was so fixated on the walls and the commander's quarters that I completely missed the intricate setup of the rail system right outside the main entrance. And because I was never assigned a job outside the Hole, like many of the other Sinners, I never had occasion to take it all in. Until now.

"Umph!" Air rushes from Cole's lips as a guard hits him from the right side, out of nowhere, knocking him to the ground. My breath catches in my throat. They struggle for control, writhing around in the dirt. Zeus jumps to Cole's aid, snarling ferociously and biting the guard's leg.

Without a second thought to my own safety, I whip out my

116

knife and move forward. And then I feel the hard, metal barrel of a gun pinned at the side of my head. *Holy hell! Where'd that come from?*

"Hands in the air where I can see them," a voice says in a demanding tone. I slowly begin raising my hands, wondering if he's seen my knife. I need to move fast. I close my eyes briefly, listening to the melee.

"Faster," he says. He pushes the gun harder against my temple. I grimace. "Hey, drop the—" Before he can finish, I position my right arm behind his gun and slam it forward.

The gun fires an inch away from my face. It burns. My head vibrates with a horribly loud and unbearable ringing. But then my training kicks in. With lightning speed, I elbow him in the face. He drops his gun, stumbles a few steps back, and lets out a groan. Blood runs across and down his lips. When he raises his hands to his nose, I stomp on his foot. He buckles forward. Then, just before he has a chance to dive for his gun, I shove the knife into his gut, deep, past the layers of his bulletproof vest.

The sickening sound of puncturing human flesh makes my stomach roil. But I had no other choice; it was either him or me. As I push his bumbling body away from me, his face registers shock. His eyes loosely focus on mine and start to glaze over. He slowly loses consciousness and falls to the ground with a thud at the same time a single shot is fired from where Cole and the guard wrestle. And then silence. I can't hear anything. And for a moment, I don't know if Cole is alive.

I franticly move in his direction, disoriented. I follow the blood-splatter pattern, silently praying that he's okay. That Zeus is okay.

When I lay eyes on him, he's winded, standing, and wiping his hands on his clothing. Blood smears the fabric of his shirt and pants as his chest heaves rapidly up and down. He picks up his gun and that of the guard who lies at his feet.

"Oh my God, I thought you were dead ... I couldn't see you."

"Nope, like I told you before, I'm not going to die," Cole says, pulling me into a quick hug. He picks up his shredded pack and then pets Zeus on the head. "Thanks, buddy. I owe you one." Cole turns his attention back to the supplies that have fallen out. I quickly join him in picking up whatever I can save. Zeus sniffs at the dead bodies, and I call him away.

Cole takes my hand. "Run," he says, releasing my hand again as if to free me.

"I'm right behind you. Go," I say.

His veins pop out of his forearms, and his sweat stains his shirt. He checks over his shoulder before running.

I take off as instructed, barely noticing the bodies lying in the dirt, following behind him and Zeus. It feels like time is playing games with us, extending the path to the rail yard every time I look up. One minute, it seems right there. The next, it looks like five hundred feet. But we're vulnerable out here in the open. So we keep going.

I continue willing my legs to move, one step and then another. The gunfire has died down, and I'm afraid to admit that I'm feeling better, maybe even hopeful that we just might make it back into the Hole. Just then, Zeus begins growling, and the hair on his back shoots up. My heart jumps. I see Cole tense briefly, then follow his gaze, left to right, behind us, ahead of us, and into the train we're now running alongside.

Zeus bares his teeth. He barks once. Cole raises his gun, eyes roaming.

A figure appears out of the darkness. I still. Seconds pass, and Cole doesn't move.

Zeus bolts forward, and Cole runs after him.

"Man, took you long enough," Bruno says. "Hurry up; I got us a ride."

"How'd you manage that? Bruno, we don't have any money," Cole says.

"Doesn't matter. She's an old friend who owes me a favor, let's just leave it at that."

"Why am I not surprised," Cole says with sarcasm.

"And check this shit out—the monitors are already here."

CHAPTER 10

We follow Bruno into the black of the building. As my eyes adjust to the lighting, they water and burn. That feeling in the pit of my stomach, the one that has been gnawing away at me since I decided to return, churns. I'm nauseous.

Grace jumps out of the shadows and hugs me. She squeezes the air out of me, and it takes me off balance. She's covered in a fine layer of gray, but the relief in her eyes when she steps back warms my heart.

"Guys, hurry it up," Bruno hisses. "And keep your heads down."

Cole glances at me, raises an eyebrow, and strides forward.

We jog past the giant turntable where multiple engines and railcars are parked. Behind each parked engine is a workroom, but none of them have lights on. My heart jumps in my chest as we pass the engines. Their large, silent frames remind me of hearses, empty and silent, waiting for the dead to ride in them. I shake the nightmarish image from my mind and fix my eyes on Cole's back.

"The monitors are already here?" Cole asks, barely raising his voice above a whisper.

"Yeah, she told me they're going in as we speak," Bruno says, turning around.

"Who's your source?" I ask. "And how can you know for sure you can trust her?"

"Let's just say she's an old friend ... a guard. She's agreed to help us," Bruno says. I raise my eyebrows and glance at Cole then Grace.

"Well, hey, this is good news ... for once," Grace says. She shrugs at the mention of Bruno's contact, so I let it slide.

"They showed up, unannounced, like Sutton said they might. And they're taking a convoy in. Wilson has no choice but to allow it," Bruno says. He waits for it all to sink in. "Just say it—you know I'm a damn genius."

"More like pure luck," I say, even though we've been back all of five minutes and Bruno has already gotten us a ride and useful intel.

"You just don't want to admit I'm awesome." Bruno laughs. "Now, be quiet. She has no idea what kind of cargo I just convinced her to take in." Cole and I lock eyes. I roll mine. Bruno is anything but modest.

"How long until your secret contact gets here?" The sarcasm in Cole's voice cannot be ignored. I chuckle.

"Soon. Just relax. And shut that useless mini horse up."

Zeus has been whining the entire time we've been inside, but I hardly noticed until now.

"What about the blown up train? Won't the monitors notice that?" I ask, thinking back to the wreckage at the entrance.

"I'm sure Wilson will have a lie up his sleeve, as he always does," Bruno says. "He's good at playing mind games."

"Anyone who believes him is insane," Grace says.

A shuffling noise comes from behind us.

Bruno flinches and then waves us toward an engine workroom. We're all trying to be quiet, and I hope the gravel under our feet hasn't given us away. I hear footsteps not far behind us just as Bruno twists the doorknob to the dark workroom. I cringe when the metal knob grinds against the metal door, as if to say, *Here they are! Come and shoot them!*

No one breathes as we creep inside, and then we don't dare move an inch. Even Zeus is stone-still. We're crouched in the corner, in position behind the industrial workstation with guns drawn.

"They're in here somewhere," a voice says from the other side of the door. The sound of loose stones under their boots gives away their position.

I hear a door slam open, and my skin crawls as I listen to them clear a room not far away from where we hide. Bruno moves along the wall, using a hand to search for a way out.

"Hurry," Grace whispers with a shaky voice.

Another door slamming open echoes from the turntable room. They're coming closer. My stomach clenches into one big knot.

"Bingo," Bruno says.

He turns a knob and a door in the back of the room swings open with a loud squealing noise, revealing a hallway. Behind us, the guards' shadows stop outside our door to the turntable.

"Go, go, go," Cole says.

We jump to our feet just as the door blasts open. Immediately, they begin firing at us. The sound of the bullets ricocheting off the metal surfaces echoes in my ears.

Bruno grabs Grace and shoves her into the hallway and then I follow, ducking low to protect myself. Cole commands Zeus to go with me, and then he returns fire until he and Bruno scramble through last.

Once in the hallway, Cole slams the door closed behind us. He clenches his jaw and breathes steady and calm. He ejects his magazine and slams in another, nodding his head when ready.

"Follow me," Bruno says. He takes off, his boots clomping on the cement floor of the hallway.

We sprint past several doors. Fluorescent lights alternate with ceiling tiles like checkers on the ceiling. It casts an eerie pall over everyone's faces. I'm breathing hard, feeling out of practice. Or maybe it's just the dust. It seems to creep everywhere. Bruno reaches for a rusted door on the right and twists the handle. It doesn't move.

The door to the room we just vacated slams open with gunfire and loud voices. Cole fires off a barrage of shots, attempting to hold them at bay. I look at Bruno. Sweat's rolling down his face. His hands keep slipping off the knob.

"Come on! Open it!" I say.

"I'm trying! The piece of crap's stuck," he yells back.

He lowers his shoulder and barges into the door, but it doesn't budge. The guards are coming down the hall. I hear the clicking of their boots. Their guns are raised. I make eye contact with one of them. He smiles and then lowers his gun.

"It's her. Hold your fire," he says.

Cole stands rigid, his gun pointed at them. Zeus is planted at his side, snarling. We're outnumbered and outgunned. For a minute, everyone's at a standstill.

Pop! I turn in the direction of the sound, then back to the guards. *They won't shoot us. Not like this. They aren't animals.*

Just like that, the door slides open, and Bruno disappears through it. Grace follows, light on her feet. Cole backs away, slowly, pushing me toward the open door. Already, I smell burning trash, salty, sweaty skin, and sulfur wafting into the hall. I keep my eyes focused on the guards, and I can tell by the way they look from Cole, to me, and then to the door, that they have no idea what do now.

"Don't fire at her; we can't take the risk. Wilson wants her alive."

My shaky knees move me backward, one inch at a time, staying behind Cole. If they shoot him, they'll hit me too, and I'm hoping they'll judge it's not worth the risk. Finally, I feel the edge where the hallway meets the outside. My fingers grasp the doorframe. I take one last look at the guard, whose lips are pressed together in a tight straight line. With a deep breath, I step through the door.

The minute Cole, Zeus, and I are through, we push the door closed, using our bodies to keep it that way. Then one of the guards says, "We can't just let them go."

There's a brief silence before another says, "They won't get far. We got them now."

His chilling words echo in my ear and send a chill up my spine.

"Help me barricade the door," Cole says. He uses his gun to point to a dumpster a few feet away, and Bruno nods. They grunt, sweat, and curse the entire time but manage to push the rancid-smelling orange dumpster in front of the door. "Just in case." And for the first time in a long time, Cole's words do not comfort me. But I don't have too long to dwell on that.

Our ride screeches to a halt in front of us. I see the silhouette of a woman in the front seat. I feel her eyes on us. On me. The tinted window of the truck rolls down.

"Bruno, what the hell have you gotten me into?" she asks, her voice arching upward with every word. "You can't pay me enough for this shit!"

"Oh, shut your lid, and put your big-girl panties on," Bruno says.

When he gives us the nod to move, our feet make mini tornadoes in the dust as we run. I glance at the woman glaring at me. Ahead of her truck, in the distance, is a line of black vehicles making a neat, stately procession. A multitude of international flags sit at the corners of their hoods. Beyond that, the walls stand ominous in their majestic terror.

Bruno opens the tailgate. "Get in," he commands.

"This wasn't what I agreed to. And a freaking dog?" the woman yells out her window.

"Dammit, woman, this is a done deal," Bruno shouts as he motions us to get in. "You don't get us in safely, you won't see a cent." He gives me a fleeting grin and winks. Grace rolls her eyes.

"You're crazy," I say. "You do know that, right?"

"Miss Lexi, I've got mad skills. You should be thankful."

I'm doing everything possible to be calm and relax. This is my last taste of near-normalcy before I voluntarily go back to the Hole. The place that killed my father and my brother. The same place that made me estranged from my own mother. The place where I first met Cole.

My pulse quickens, and my mouth goes dry. Cole grabs my hand. Of course, it doesn't help that the driver's yelling at Bruno. She doesn't want us here any more than we want to be here. The emotions are overwhelming. Coming back here. Seeing the wall. Knowing that we may not make it back out. My stomach is doing flip-flops. With every thrust of the guards on the other side of the door, the dumpster vibrates, inching forward from its position.

Bang! Shots ring out, echoing off the metal of the door.

We're all smashed into the back against one another, trying to be as small and quiet as possible. Bruno quickly covers us with a blanket and a tarp. Next, he piles heavy pieces of something on top of us. *Whatever keeps us from being caught.*

"Sorry, guys. It's the best I can do. Let's pray it works." He shuts the tailgate and locks the rear window of the cab. I hear him run around the truck and get into the passenger side.

"Why's he sitting up front?" I ask.

"He's going to make sure she follows through." And when I hear the sadness in Grace's voice, I feel a sudden urge to punch the driver in the face.

I know I'm missing something, but I'm too distracted to ask for more details. I feel like I'm suffocating. Not only is it pitch-black, but it's hot. And there's Zeus's breath. It smells like rotting corpses, and I can't stop myself from thinking about what other bodies might have been in here before. I'm biting my lip so hard, I'm sure it's almost completely gone.

"Lexi," Cole whispers from my left side. "Hang in there. It'll be over soon." He grasps my hand in an effort to calm my racing heart. I squeeze his hand as hard as I can, and he strokes

126

his thumb over my skin. But hell, it's not working. What the hell are we waiting for? We may as well have a neon sign on our car that says, "Fugitives inside."

The engine kicks to life, and we're soon a jostling, bumping, bruised group of exhausted and wounded people in the back. I try to imagine anything but what we're doing—the beaches of Lexington Bay, my dad's smile, when Cole kissed me the first time. But my mind inevitably returns to the Hole. And that's when I know that somehow, deep inside, it was inevitable that I would return. My heart stops when I feel the truck's engine slow to idling.

"ID papers," a muffled voice commands.

There's a pause. I assume the papers are being handed over.

"You're part of the convoy?"

"Yes," the girl says in a soft voice, much different than her yelling at Bruno before.

More deafening silence. Then, a tap on the passenger side. I've seen them do this before. One guard questions the driver as the other inspects the passenger side and trunk. I think they call it a "walk-around." If the guard on the passenger side gets suspicious, he taps the car with his flashlight to signal a search should be done.

"I need to inspect all cargo coming in today," he says.

Oh, this is not good.

I'm sure the driver answers, but I can't hear it. My body's frozen. *Please don't let them find us.*

Cole's gripping my hand so hard, I feel like my fingers are going to snap. Zeus growls, so I swallow my panic and pull his head toward me, hoping the blanket dampens the sound.

I hear the guards unlock the window behind us. My palms

are sweating now, my muscles tense. As they get closer, I can clearly hear them talking.

The tailgate slams down, and I feel things being moved around at the edge of the truck bed. *We're going to be discovered.* The grim reality of our situation sucks all hope from my bones.

"Can you hurry it up?" asks a third voice. "The line's almost a mile long, and we've got all these cars to check."

It feels like time has stopped. But really, probably only a few silent minutes pass.

"You're clear to go," the first voice says. All at once, the three of us exhale in complete unison. "When you're done with your delivery, come by my place."

"Sure thing," our driver says.

I close my eyes as sweat seeps into them. The truck lurches forward as we presumably rattle through the main gate and back into the Hole.

An oppressive, eerie silence greets us, not like the first time I arrived, when hordes of people smashed against our vehicle and tried to drag me off. No, this time, under the cover of twilight and a political motorcade, no one is around to notice. It's just us and the shifting of the engine as it snakes along.

I gradually loosen my grip on Zeus's neck and feel him relax. The objects Bruno placed on us shift around as we begin to move more freely throughout the truck bed. I hear Grace groan.

"Hey, you okay over there?" I ask. I can't see or touch her because of Zeus's hulking body.

"Fine, except for the giant furball next to me forcing all the pipes to smash my back," she says with an edge in her voice.

"Zeus, come here." I try pulling him back to me to give her

128

some relief, but he's gigantic and wobbling all over, trying to push the covers off.

That's when we hit a massive pothole in the road. The right side of the truck sinks down into it. The metal pipes covering us fly into the air and smash back down on us. I grunt as the truck returns to even footing.

We hit another rough patch, and the truck spins its tires. And then it feels like we're slowing to a crawl. I swallow my fears, shove away the tarp, and sit up. The metal pipes are sprawled all over the bed. Zeus whines as he pulls himself out next to me, using his front paws to creep out from under the tarp as if to ask, "Is it okay?"

"It's okay, boy. Come to me," I say.

"Judas," Cole says to Zeus with a smirk on his face.

"Thanks a lot, doofus," Grace half-whispers. "Almost squashing me wasn't enough for you? Now you feel the need to step all over me?" As Zeus moves away from her, she moans and begins to uncover herself. Her tight curls peek out first, then I see the whites of her eyes as she slides upward against the cab. She pulls her right hand to her chest, opening and shutting it, with a grimace on her face. "Crap. I think my hand's broken," she says.

Excellent. "Can you move it?"

"I can, it just hurts when I do."

"I can take a look at it when we get settled," I say. "Try not to use it much."

"Lexi, we're in the Hole. I'd be willing to bet I can't make that promise."

"That's true. Well, at least it's still attached, right?"

"That's a brighter way of looking at it, yes."

129

The truck speeds up suddenly. It swings a wide and frantic turn, and the momentum hurls us all to the left and then across the bed to the right. We're all trying to keep still, to resist being thrown from side to side and back to front. My chest's pinned against the frame, and the nausea hits me again. Then we're thrown opposite again. What the hell is going on?

"She's going to kill us," I say through gritted teeth. Zeus tries to stand, but steps on a pipe and crashes down. His face registers shock, his brown eyes wide. And yet, he keeps trying.

We rattle along in silence. The road becomes more even. No one speaks as we travel further into the Hole. I imagine no one knows what exactly to say. My body betrays me, and I don't know how much longer I can continue to swallow down the bile that keeps coming up into my throat.

Our driver shifts into lower gears, and we rumble along, slow and steady. The metal piping continues to rattle, the tarp tangled around our bodies.

And then it begins—the sharp, whizzing sound of a bullet piercing metal as it zips over my shoulder. Then more. I count one, two, three holes before it registers in my brain.

"Get down!" Cole shouts as he yanks Zeus and me down with him. A look of horror and fatigue crosses Grace's face as she too hits the floor.

Metallic zinging echoes over my head. Our vehicle stops. I struggle to gather my bearings, but the tailgate slams open and moist air rushes in. I'm relieved to breathe in even this air.

"Out!" Bruno shouts. At first I don't hear him over the commotion outside. "Move!"

Cole moves first, ducking his head and jumping out the back. Zeus follows him, and I find myself pulling Grace behind me. I don't even look at her, I just grab her wrist and yank. We both tumble out the back and land in a mix of dust and gravel. A small poof envelopes us. But that doesn't give me comfort. From the chattering of guns, I know we've landed in the middle of a firefight. Cole grabs me around my waist, helping me back onto my feet.

"Now we run like hell!" Cole takes my arm and leads me.

I grab Grace at the same time and force her to follow me. Tracers light up the sky around me, illuminating the labyrinth of the Hole. Frameless windows stare back at me with black, abandoned faces. I'm afraid. More than I thought I would be. I see the silhouettes of figures on the rooftops amidst the battle, their heat signatures making them targets for any trained sniper. The whole convoy's been broken up. Vehicles have stopped in the middle of the street, car doors open, abandoned. People are running everywhere, diving for cover. Screams and cries reverberate off the walls of the buildings. My heart rate is off the charts as adrenaline flows to every inch of my body, and I sprint after Cole.

He crosses to the side of the street. I stumble, fall onto my knees, and quickly get back up. But only after I spot a small, broken flag from one of the vehicles lying in the road. I grab it. The red and white are covered in dirt. It's weird the things that strike you as important in the middle of a fight.

"Come on!" Grace shouts at me. She grabs my wrist, and we run together.

We're hoofing it down an alley, weaving through broken glass and the remains of overturned and broken furniture. I hear a deluge of shooting behind us, some hammering automatic fire and some more carefully chosen. *Pock! Pock! Pock!*

131

I imagine it hitting my heels. My breaths come fast. I let go of Grace and climb over a pile of old tires. My nose wrinkles when I smell the burned, charred rubber mixed with gun smoke. I struggle to hold it in, but the heavy air settles on me, and soon I'm heaving alongside a cracked, cement wall.

"Go! Go!" Cole yells to Grace and Bruno. He turns and grabs my elbow. "Lexi. We gotta go." I wipe my face on my sleeve and run with him, dizzy and on borrowed time.

The maze feels never-ending. Pretty soon, the battle sounds muted, like they weren't gunning for us. I can't relax though. My shoulders tense up, and my jaws hurt from clenching. I finally catch up with Bruno, Grace, and Zeus. They've stopped in a row alongside a familiar-looking building while Bruno surveys the street in front of us. Grace bends over and places her hands on her knees, panting. Bruno checks her for injuries, and when he sees she's okay, plants a kiss on her nose. I can see the love she holds for him mirrored in her eyes.

"Come on, you guys. We gotta keep moving," Bruno says. We barely catch our breath before Bruno takes off again. His colossal figure runs across the street and around the corner. Cole and Zeus follow closely behind, and it's my turn.

I buy myself some time, still suffering from the lack of water and oppressive humidity. I pat Grace's shoulder and nod for her to go before me. I mentally prepare myself for the energy it will take to make this next run. I don't have it. As I make an effort to move one foot in front of the other, it dawns on me.

Squinting in the dark, I lay eyes on it—rising from the ground, rusty old fence strewn into the street, the guard checkpoint half-manned.

My old building.

CHAPTER 11

My eyes are drawn up the building, stopping only to focus on the windowless frame of my old quarters. "Quarters" sounds as if I had a say in the matter, like I wasn't dragged from my home, branded, brought here, and kept under twenty-four hour surveillance.

It feels like it was forever ago that I lived there. Yet, here I am, back by my own choice, only three months after escaping. My hands clench, and my jaw tightens. I didn't think it was possible for things to be even worse than they were when I was held captive here. But now, Sutton has been kidnapped, and the monitors have been slaughtered. Wilson is an animal, worse than any other Commander in history.

My body feels lead-heavy and weighted down. The only hope we had has just been completely destroyed. I rub my eyes. Crying won't do me any good.

The black scarring of bombs and destruction left by bullets is evident, even at night. The courtyard outside the building no longer teems with Sinners bartering goods. Hairs prickle up on my arms. The guard checkpoint booth remains, but it's empty. The barriers still form a narrow pathway for oncoming cars, and the spotlights mounted above the checkpoint have yet to be turned on.

My heart rate picks up as I dart across the street. No matter how hard I try to keep my mind in the present, the flood of memories from a few months ago comes rushing in. Alyssa was still alive. Keegan, who fought to free us, didn't make it out alive. And Sutton. Oh God. Sutton. What will Wilson do to him? I shrug away fear and doubt. If we give up, or if we die ... who will save Sutton?

I come to a barrier and grasp the side, using my legs to push me over. Glass crunches beneath my feet when I land on the other side. Strips of rubber, from what used to be tires, lie in the street. Out of habit, I look both ways, but there are no cars. It's as if I'm looking down a black hole. I heft myself up over the next barrier and make for the darkness and safety of the buildings.

Once I get to the alleyway between my old building and the next, I'm enveloped by the shadows. The only things I hear are my steady breaths and the dull sound of clumping feet on cement. As I catch up to Grace, she stops dead in front of me. I almost trip before skidding to a halt, my hands grazing her taut back. She wavers just slightly forward on her toes. I place my hand on her shoulder, but she doesn't even acknowledge me. I step around her. Her jaw drops open, and she stares straight ahead.

"Grace, what's wron—"

She points in front of her.

I step back slightly, eyes wide with shock. The stench of stagnant blood, bodily waste, and decomposing bodies hits me like lightning. I bury my face in my elbow and try to block it. Without a doubt, it's a smell I can never get accustomed to. The shrouded shantytown is three times larger than I remember. I used to be able to see where the huts stopped, but now it's endless. Glancing to my left, I notice Cole taking it all in as well. His lips are slightly parted, and his eyes gleam with some unspeakable emotion. I swallow hard.

"What's happened?" I ask Cole.

"We'll find out," he says in a low voice. His jaw twitches, and he doesn't meet my eyes.

Torn fabric covers tin and crudely constructed huts that seem to run into one another. By the looks of it, they might even be holding each other up. An endless expanse of gray, tan, brown, and crimson cloaked with poverty greets us. The narrow pathways are covered in dirt and filled with glass, garbage, bodily fluids, and some with words of discouragement written in blood. Sinners walk around with visible injuries. Some have ragged clothing and some only wear underwear. Their hair's greasy, and a thick layer of filth covers them. One looks toward me, her eyes empty and almost lifeless. She holds her arms against herself, scratching at already bloody sores. Blood slips down her arms like dark red streams of paint.

Oh my God, my cell was a hotel compared to this. At least I was fed. Guilt overtakes me. Even when I saw the center of the Hole before, it never seemed this expansive. There were never this many starving people wandering around aimlessly.

135

My throat closes up as I struggle for words. I walk to Cole and reach for his arm. I cannot speak. Instead, I pray silently to wake up from this nightmare.

Dead bodies are piled on top of each other in a pit to the right of us. I watch as a man tosses the next body toward the pile. When the corpse lands, bones clank together, breaking and tearing through skin. The body's nothing more than a skeleton. Most of the dead are all the same, severely malnourished and stiff, thrown away like garbage.

Life is precious, but in the Hole … it's a curse.

Two women stand together at the edge of the pit, their hands clasped together. They're crying, and I want to cry for them. Cole shivers next to me, but I don't think he's cold. He remains silent, and even when I grab his hand, he doesn't look at me.

Others moan, cry, and some scream, their cries piercing my ears, making me unsure of whether I want to drop to my knees or pick up a gun. My entire body heats with fury. Wilson just lit another flame under me. He must pay for this. One way or another, he's going to pay.

"Take a deep breath, guys. Breathe through your mouth, and wipe the shock off your faces," Bruno says from out of nowhere. "Remember, we need to blend."

Like that's possible. We're probably the healthiest people in here.

We move deeper into the rows of shacks. Sinners lie on the floor, some asleep and some rocking back and forth with nothing but blank stares. It's almost like they're in a trance or something. Many have scars across their faces and on their arms; they look so diseased. We swat flies away from our faces as we continue to move slowly and deeper into the Hole.

"No please; it's all I got," a woman's voice calls from over my shoulder. Cole and I turn around.

A man shoves a frail and sickly woman to the ground and kicks her in the stomach. The woman lets out a groan, and before she falls, the man grabs her bag then takes off running.

"Zeus, attack," Cole says, his fists clenched at his sides.

Zeus charges, catching the man in seconds. As Zeus pounces on the thief's back with his front legs, the man plummets to the ground, and Zeus ferociously rips apart his clothes.

"I'll check on the lady," I tell Cole.

Cole takes off running toward the man, and I sprint to the girl who's curled up into a ball. Dropping to my knees, I place my hand on her back. She recoils from my touch.

"Hey, I'm not going to hurt you; I promise."

She runs a thin hand through her matted black hair. She's shaking. I can feel her ribs through the threadbare shirt she wears, and it reminds me of Alyssa. This woman's older, I'm guessing in her thirties. The smell of stagnant urine lingers in the air. People in the shantytown have nowhere to cleanse themselves. And the living conditions are far worse now than they were when I lived in the Hole just a few months ago.

"Are you okay?" I ask.

"Uh-huh," is all she manages to mutter back to me. I glance up, and Cole's hovering over the man who just beat her.

"Zeus, that's enough."

Zeus makes this awful hacking sound as he spits out a chunk of the thief's clothing. I can only imagine what that must've tasted like.

"What's wrong with you?" Cole asks the thief in a stern

137

tone. "Stealing from a helpless woman, and then you go and kick her? Really?"

"She's already half-dead. And I'm starving, asshole."

Cole punches him across the jaw, and the man's head whips to the left. He recovers, eyeing Cole up and down, his pride surely bruised as much as his face will be. "Give it to me."

"No," the man says. He turns and spits blood on the ground.

"Zeus, get it," Cole says.

Zeus sniffs the man and forces him onto his back. Then he bites down on his right wrist.

"Ahhhh!" The man screams, releasing the bag.

Cole yanks it away and signals to Zeus to release the hand.

"See? That wasn't so hard now was it?" Cole asks.

"Wait a minute. Where have I seen you before?" The man looks Cole over once more. "Oh … I see now. A guard, of all people. You do know every single one of you sticks out like a sore thumb? Your stance, the way you hold your head high, like you're all above us dirtbags down here. You've got more blood on your hands than any man in here. You self-righteous son of a bitch. But go, tell yourself you're a better person now for saving that lady. You are just as bad as the Commander, if not worse."

I can't tell what bothers Cole more, the man's words or the fact that he recognizes Cole. I catch his eye, then look over at Bruno. They both look from side to side, then all around the immediate area. Grace has tears in her eyes, and it hits me. Cole cannot risk anyone knowing he's here.

Bruno makes his way to Cole, and Grace joins me.

"Will she be all right?" Grace's voice is soft.

"I'm not sure. But we gotta find shelter soon, and we can't

risk anyone giving us up," I whisper in her ear.

"What about her?" Grace whispers back, thumbing her finger at the woman.

"I don't know. Just look the other way."

"I'll block you," Bruno says. "Hurry up and do it."

Grace and I turn away as Cole grabs the man around the head and prepares to do away with the threat to our safety. Then we hear the snap.

We turn around to see the boys throw the dead man into a hut. Zeus trots over to us, then sniffs and licks the woman's face. She opens her eyes. There is only one word to describe what happens next. Terror. The woman scrunches back and away from us. Her scream reminds me of the alarms from earlier. Grace reaches over and covers her mouth with her hand. The woman continues to scream, gurgling through muffled fear. Her eyes are as big as quarters.

She wriggles away from Grace, who plunges forward to catch her. She can't get away. I dive for her, but she smacks me.

"Please, we aren't trying to hurt you," Grace says.

"What'd you do that for?" I raise a hand to my stinging face, regretting trying to help her.

She stops screaming but continues heaving and breathing heavily. "What is that?" she asks in a weak voice.

"He's a dog. He's just a very big dog," I say.

"A dog. Looks like a horse." She chuckles. Then begins to cough. "I thought he was going to eat me."

I stifle a laugh, remembering the first time I laid eyes on Zeus. I'm grateful she's breathing and talking again.

Bruno and Cole arrive at our sides.

"Here, let me carry her," Bruno says, and he crouches down. "Would it be all right if I carry you to your hut?"

"I'd appreciate that, sir, thank you."

"Are you okay?" Grace asks him, but he just shakes off her concern.

He gently puts his right arm under the woman's legs and with his left arm, he cradles her back. He's gentle, like he would be with a child. Grace is so lucky. He'll make a great father, if he makes it out of here alive.

"Where's your hut?" he asks.

"The one with the blue curtains." She laughs. The laugh is long, hoarse, and full of mucus. Her sense of humor is unnerving.

Looking around, I see the hut she's referring to. It's just a few feet away, and I motion for Bruno, Cole, and Grace to follow me.

When we arrive, I grab the thin fabric covering the door, pulling it to the side. It feels as thin as tissue paper. Bruno ducks his head and carries the woman inside. Grace and Cole follow. There's nothing but a yellow sheet covering the dirt floor, and it has holes everywhere. We barely all fit inside, and suddenly I feel claustrophobic.

"Just put me down on the floor," she says, a soft, nearly toothless smile lighting up her face. Slowly, Bruno lowers her to the floor, and she moans.

"Are you hurt?" Cole asks. He joins Bruno in helping the woman move.

"I always hurt; I'm in constant pain." She looks around her home, as if checking to be sure everything is still there.

"Why? What's wrong?" I ask.

140

"I wish I knew," she says.

"If you're sick, why haven't they been treating you?" Grace asks.

"Because that costs money, and Wilson stopped all medical treatment, except for the guards, after the revolt. I guess he feels it's a waste of his precious dollars."

My stomach gets caught in my throat.

"Do you know how you got sick?" I ask, while bending forward, and all of a sudden, the room's spinning around me.

"Some say the vaccine we received wasn't effective. That we didn't receive it in time, and so the ones who were already exposed have fallen ill."

"A vaccine for what?"

"The virus," she says. "A lot of people are getting sick. More and more every day."

"Have we been exposed?"

"Don't worry, they said it only spreads through blood." She rubs her neck, and I feel guilty for being grateful that it was Bruno who carried her and not Cole.

That's when I notice she's branded with lust, just like me, and I wonder what she did to get here. *Is she innocent too?*

"I'm so sorry," I say. "I wish we could do something for you."

"Oh, honey, you already have. You showed me kindness and got my bag back. That's more than anyone has ever done for me."

On cue, Cole hands over the bag he took from the man he killed.

"Thank you," the woman says. She opens it and pulls out a piece of stale, moldy bread and a small vial.

141

"What is that?" I ask. "In the vial?"

"Our water for the day."

"That's all they give you to drink?" Grace asks.

"Yes. Enough to keep us alive."

We are all silent. I don't think any of us know what to say.

"Please don't feel sorry for me," she says. "Honestly, I don't want to live anymore, not like this. I know this might sound crazy, but at least dying … will set me free."

Her words crush my soul.

You can overcome anything short of death, I tell myself.

"We better go," Bruno says. "Is there anything you need before we leave?"

"No, I'm fine." She pauses and looks as if she is about to say something. She smiles and says, "Thank you again."

"It would really be great if you didn't tell anyone we were here," Bruno says in a stern voice.

"Don't worry. I know how to keep my mouth shut." The woman winks, and I realize we have no idea what her name is. There's a part of me that wants to stay with her and comfort her somehow, but I know it's not possible. It kills me to have to leave her here all alone. But we aren't here to make friends.

We say our good-byes and make our way out of her hut. We walk in silence, alert but pensive. We take turns searching for a place to settle.

Cole gives me a strange look. Bruno shakes his head and begins pushing into the next hut. Two blankets lie on the ground. There's no furniture. There's no water or eating utensils. He moves on.

It's like a city of huts, tents, and cement blocks. Every avenue is filled with something, whether it's trash or cement

142

blocks or bodies. There's no grid of streets, just zigzag alleyways and narrow paths between propped-up shelters. In the darkness, it feels haunted.

I can almost sense the lost souls inhabiting the black pits of every crevice. I glance upward. The moon hangs in the sky with its white body illuminating the corrugated metal roofing of some of the houses. My mouth feels like sandpaper. My body shakes as my adrenaline slows down.

Pretty soon, it's hard to pick up my feet. My boots weigh them down, and it's like I'm walking through quicksand. I can barely hold my eyes open. Even Zeus stumbles along beside me. His tongue dangles from his mouth, and his tail droops.

"Let's stop," Cole says. Bruno turns around. In the pale light, his usually smooth skin looks wrinkled and tired. "I think we're in far enough, and I'm about to fall over."

Bruno's broad shoulders disappear into a hut and then he re-emerges. "Found a vacant one," he says.

Zeus sniffs the cloth of the curtain before taking off into our temporary new home. Inside, I hear him sneeze twice. No, three times.

"So much for subtlety," Cole mutters under his breath.

The others enter the tiny, rundown shack before I do. I get halfway through the door when the familiar scent of decaying flesh hits me. Nausea creeps up my insides as I look around. A thin, dirt-streaked blanket lies on the floor to my right. An empty metal bowl sits on top of a crudely made stand behind it. Zeus's tail whips past it, and it topples sideways. Next thing, I'm scrambling to catch it so it doesn't clatter to the ground. The bowl lands perfectly in my hands, but unfortunately, I can't keep my balance, and I stumble and fall forward with a whoosh.

"Nice save," Cole says quietly. He takes the bowl from my hands and helps me up.

"Do you think that woman has the same thing Alyssa had?" I wipe the sweat off the back of my neck and then wipe my hands on my pants.

"Doubtful," Bruno says.

"Then what's killing her?"

"Could be a million different things. You heard her … Sinners no longer get medical care."

"Yeah, I guess you're right," I say with sadness.

"I'm always right, Miss Lexi," Bruno says with an exaggerated bow.

"Oh please," Grace says, giving Bruno a look of annoyance. "Does anyone have water?"

"Not me; my pack's gone," I say.

"I've got a little left," Bruno says, holding out a bottle. "I guess I'll share it with you." He winks at Grace, who takes it from him. Her hands are so small compared to his.

"Glad to see chivalry isn't dead," she says. She glances at the bottle and shakes it, raising an eyebrow. "There's not a lot left. Are you sure? You need your strength too."

"You know me, I can go for days," he says.

"Oh, Lord," I say. "TMI."

Grace laughs and raises the bottle to her lips, allowing the water to pass over them. She lowers it and holds it out for Bruno. "Take the rest."

"Did you get enough?" His eyebrows stretch up to his hairline.

"Just take it," she says in a firm voice.

He drinks the rest of the water. Then he tosses the bottle

144

and plants a huge kiss on Grace's mouth unexpectedly.

"You always take good care of me; that's why I love you, woman," he says. His bear hug lifts her slightly off the ground before he lets her toes touch back down.

I turn toward Cole, who lowers his backpack and digs his water out.

He twists around and gives me his last bottle. "Here," he says. "I have a bottle left. Just make sure Zeus gets some." He wipes sweat from his face with a hand towel from the safe house and says, "All right, so let's set up a perimeter for now. Once we rest, we'll focus on finding supplies."

"Roger that," Bruno says, letting go of Grace.

I gulp the water down like it's air, allowing it to dribble over my chin. I'm beyond caring about how I appear. I wipe my face with my forearm and hand it back.

Cole takes a sip, then gives Zeus the last bit to slobber over. When Zeus is done, Cole smashes the bottle between his hands and tosses it on the ground.

Grace seems disturbed. She's looking around the small space as if she can't imagine how this will work out.

"This place is as good as we're gonna get," Bruno says, a hand on her back.

"Meaning?" Grace asks.

"We've got something resembling shelter," Cole says. He touches a flap of the hut and lets it slide between his fingers. "It's a large area. The guards'll have a harder time finding us."

"But it's contaminated with something," I say. Cole scrunches up his face at me. "People don't die in numbers like that unless someone's either shooting at them or they're sick with something ... bad." Cole tilts his head.

145

"Now there's a pleasant thought," Bruno says.

We all go silent. I don't know if any of us thought things would be so bad here.

I feel like I've got the heebie-jeebies, and I itch all over. After I scratch my skin red, I remember the woman from earlier whose skin looked like she had scratched it to shreds.

I don't have what she has.

CHAPTER 12

"Cole!" I shoot up into a sitting position, clothes clinging to me like a latex glove while I tremble.

"Hey, I'm here, you're safe." He pulls me into his arms, securing me against his chest, and rocks me. "Deep breaths. Breathe."

"You were gone, I couldn't find you," I say and try to steady my breaths as my lip quivers. "You left me ... and I ran everywhere and you were just ... gone." My lungs gasp for air, and he places his hand over my heart.

"It was just a nightmare, Lexi," he says with a voice so familiar, so strong, and so loving. He holds me tighter, but it's not tight enough.

Finding his hand, I lace my fingers with his, kiss the top of his hand, and then press it against my clammy cheek. Perspiration has gathered above my lips, and I use my forearm to wipe it away. It might have been just a nightmare, but it felt so real. My chest aches, my heart pounds, and anxiety crushes me. I squeeze my eyes shut and allow Cole's arms to comfort me.

"Promise me," I say in a shaky voice. "Please … promise you'll never leave me, because without you … "

"Shhhh, stop." I feel his heart beating against me. "Try to relax."

"But in my nightmare, you left me because I'm a Sinner, and I am, and you'll never be able to change that—"

"Lexi. I need you to listen to me for a minute. Can you do that?"

I nod.

"Good." He gives me his crooked smile. "Guards are trained to suppress their feelings, show no remorse, and be intimidating. You do as you're told. Nothing more. Nothing less. I watched as friends of mine were shot point-blank in the head. One of them for shedding a tear, another for carrying a Sinner to the hospital because she couldn't walk, and another one because he handed his drink to a little girl who was dying of dehydration." He clears his throat. I cringe. "If you show any sign of weakness, you're executed. You have no idea what I went through to prove to the Commander that truly, my heart was made of stone. He used to call me 'the rock.' And I was a rock; I was full of hatred and angry all the time." Cole pauses; a strange look crosses his face. "Even when I killed people, I felt nothing." He lowers his head, and I think I see sadness and regret on his face.

"Oh my gosh … that's terrible. I'm so sorry, Cole."

"So now, can you understand why I couldn't let myself

care about you?"

"Yes," I say, resting my head on his arm.

"My life depended on it, but it didn't matter. I failed miserably. And I fought like hell to stop myself from having any kind of feelings for you at all. Believe me; I did. I was furious with myself for a long time. Furious because feelings make you weak, and I'm not weak. Being around you ... made me feel. That terrified me. My only option was to get away from you. So I filled out the transfer paperwork and was getting ready to hand it in on the day you came to me about Alyssa, begging and pleading with me to let you help her." He sighs. "I made a promise to myself that after she died, I would leave you." He tucks his face into the crook of my neck, tickling my ear with his breath. "But being around you was like being stuck in quicksand, the more I tried to get away, the deeper I sank."

"And now you're stuck?" I smile.

"Something like that. You're my quicksand. Before I met you, my life was work and allegiance to the Commander. Before you, I had no idea people could care about one another like you cared for Alyssa, like I was starting to care for you." He takes a deep breath. "When we had our little date, she called me out on my bullshit. She said it was obvious how much I cared for you. And of course, I told her I didn't, because at the time, I truly believed that. But then she said something to me. Something that changed everything."

I scrunch my eyebrows and ask, "What did she say?" My stomach flutters with anticipation.

"She said, 'Maybe you should think about this: how would you feel if Lexi was assigned a new guard?'"

"She said that?"

"Yeah."

"Wow."

"Tell me about it. And it was the strangest thing; it was as if she knew what I had planned. But there's no way she could have. She was just an amazing little girl, perceptive and way smarter than most people three times her age."

"She was such a beautiful, amazing little soul. Much too young to die."

"But it's what she said next that brought it home for me. She told me to close my eyes and picture you with someone else." He kisses my neck and rubs my arm. "And when I did, instantly, I felt a knife slice my heart open. Jealously and rage shot through me. It was then I realized that being away from you would kill me. So, that night, I shredded my transfer papers and made the decision that my life was now mine, not theirs."

I picture tiny, sickly Alyssa putting Cole on notice, and it makes me smile. A tear drops down my cheek. I wish she were here so I could hug her and tell her again how much she changed my life. Our lives.

"I cared about her too, you know," he says. "And the day before she died, she made me promise her something … and it's a promise I'll never break."

He doesn't even have to say the words; I already know what she asked of him, because it's who Alyssa was, a caring and loving little girl. No matter what, she could always see the good in everyone, even when others couldn't see it in themselves.

"You promised her … you would never leave me." The words just roll of my tongue, and I bite my lip.

"Of course I did." He kisses my head. "But even if she hadn't asked me, I wouldn't have anyway. Because, at that point, I was protecting you for myself, not because I was ordered to."

"I had no idea, Cole. I really thought you hated me."

"Sit up so I can see you," he says. His voice is lower.

I swing my body around, sit on his thighs, and wrap my legs around his back. He takes my face between his hands and uses his thumbs to wipe away my tears. He brushes my hair from my face and tucks the loose strands behind my ears. He gently traces an invisible line on my face with his fingers, and then runs them gently over my lips. He smells of sweat and blood and dirt. Even still, he smells like my Cole. He takes a deep breath and brings my forehead to his, and for a moment, we just stare at one another. I feel the hair rise on my arms and neck as my heart starts to flutter. We have a connection I can't explain. But being with him just feels right and safe.

"Wait. Where are Grace and Bruno?" I look around the hut frantically.

Cole lets out a small laugh. "They left to find some privacy just after you fell asleep."

"Oh," I say, embarrassed.

Cole pulls me back into an embrace. "Lexi, I'm scared." He trails his fingers lightly up and down my back, awakening a need in me.

"About what?" I moan against his lips.

"Of the man I once was." He kisses me softly. "Of the things I did in my past." He kisses me softly again. "The innocent lives I took." His kiss is more urgent now. "Deep down, I'm still a cold, heartless guard, and I'm not sure how to

151

shut that part of me off." I am lost in his kiss.

"You're not that person anymore, Cole." My breathing's heavy and fast.

"That's what I keep telling myself, but then, I killed that man—in cold blood. I know it would keep us safe, but I don't want to be a killer anymore." He pulls back and looks at me.

"You're not a killer," I say, taking his face in my hands.

"I am. I've been murdering people for years."

"You did your job like any soldier. No one could blame you for that. Isn't that what you are trained to do? What you were commanded to do? Neutralize the threat. Keep your people safe. That man was a threat. You took care of it."

"There's so much you don't know about me. And I'm afraid if you knew everything I've done, you'd hate me for it."

"Cole," I whisper against his mouth.

"Mmmm," he says, and then he's kissing me again, pulling me closer and holding me there.

I pull away long enough to say, "I'm in love with you, Cole. I don't care about the person you once were. I only care about the person you are today. Everything you have gone through helped shape the person you are now, and that man is my hero. And when you're ready to tell me everything about your past, I'm here. I will not judge you. There's nothing you could've done that will change the way I feel about you."

His body stiffens, and his eyes turn distant and cold.

"What's wrong?"

He drops his eyes to the floor. "I don't deserve you, Lexi."

"How can you say that after everything we've been through?"

"You have no idea," he says, and I watch as he clenches

his jaw and flares his nostrils. Something is eating him alive.

"Oh, but I do. Look at me, Cole. I'm a Sinner, branded forever." I pull his face toward me. "And you chose to love me still, despite this. You chose to see me for who I am, not for what or who my brand says I am. I am more than my brand, and you see that."

"Well, I hope you will be able to do the same for me. Because you don't know everything I've done."

"Of course I will. I love you."

His eyes rest firmly on mine as he takes my right hand in his. My lips part, and I close my eyes; I listen to the noise his lips make when he kisses my skin. It's a soft sound, almost like he's whispering.

"Hey, open your eyes for me," he says. "Look at me."

My lids open, and he kisses the corners of my mouth before slowly kissing his way down to my collarbone. I shudder.

"Are you cold?" he laughs.

"Not even close."

"Hmmm."

I let my fingers wander up his neck, through his hair, and travel back down to his broad shoulders. When my hands reach his face, I guide his mouth to mine. We kiss slow and soft until I feel his hand move to the small of my back. As he untucks my shirt, he deepens the kiss. I suck on his lower lip, and he grips me harder.

"Lexi," he says, shaking his head and huffing for oxygen.

I loop my arms around his neck and pull his head to my shoulder. His fingers find the flesh right above my pants, and I jump. The combination of nerves, adrenaline, desire, and fear is heady.

153

Cole chuckles lightly against my skin. I lift my arms toward the sky as he tries to pull my shirt off. But the damn thing's pretty much glued to me. He's kissing and touching and getting inpatient, about to rip it off. Then, somehow, he manages to peel the cloth off, get it over my head, and it drops to the floor like a drenched towel.

His eyes search mine for a minute, and then he smiles his crooked smile. "You have no idea how beautiful you are." He kisses my lips so softly, gently, sincerely. "I love you, Lexi."

I get lost in this moment, watching him, watching his emotions, watching his chest move with every breath. Taking the hem of his t-shirt in my fists, I tug it loose from his pants, yank it over his head, and toss it behind me. Zeus growls. I twist around to find the shirt has landed on Zeus's back. He whines and then lays his head back down, unwilling to toss Cole's shirt off. Up until now, I totally forgot he was even there.

Cole doesn't waste any time. His warm lips meet mine. He tangles his fingers in my hair as he pulls my head to the side, kissing every inch between my chin and shoulders. When his lips meet my ear, I listen to his heavy breathing, and a moan leaks out of my mouth.

"You're so warm," he says against my skin.

"Warm but filthy," I say.

"Isn't that the truth. But I think we're used to that by now."

I run my hands over his skin, his muscles rippling beneath them. Then, I slide my fingers across his hard shoulders and down his defined arms. But it's his chest, oh my lord his chest, that drives me wild. It looks like it was chiseled into perfection. Cole lies flat on his back, and I remain on top of him, sitting

154

just above his belt. My heart's beating so fast I couldn't count the beats even if I wanted to. A smile slowly stretches across his face. I relax my body and soak up the feel of him.

For a minute, I'm still, just staring down at him. When I move my hands again, his stomach starts to quiver. Emotion and pleasure overtakes him. I lean down to kiss his parted lips, and he wraps his hands around my head, crushing our lips together. Our mouths open together, and his tongue grazes mine, our kiss intensifying with each moment. He groans the second I pull away to catch my breath, sucking air into his lungs too.

Slowly I slide my hips down till I'm resting on his thighs, and just to make sure I'm not dreaming, I drop my ear to his heart and listen to his fast but steady heartbeat.

"I'm real," he says. "And I'm yours." He strokes my hair, and I feel my body flood with warmth, from top to bottom.

"Can you sit up for me?" he asks softly.

I do what he asks. Cole winks at me, and suddenly my knees loosen and I'm weak all over. He takes my head between his hands and brings my mouth back to his, and without breaking our kiss, I feel him unhook my bra. One by one, he brings the straps down to my wrists, and I allow him to remove it completely. I'm nervous, and I'm alive and terrified at the same time.

What if they find us, here, like this? What if we're seconds away from another spray of bullets? I tense up, trembling all over.

"Let me love you," he breaths into my mouth. His words make me lightheaded, and I close my eyes. He kisses the tip of my nose, my eyelids, and my forehead.

Cole gently rolls me onto my back, straddles my hips, and leans over on top of me. He lowers his head to mine, and I can't wait for him to kiss me again. But he suddenly stops an inch from my face and stares into my eyes. His eyes seem to shine, and I'm lost in their pools of darkness. His long, thick eyelashes are beautiful, and I watch them as he blinks.

"I'm out of my mind," he says.

"Me too. Come closer, and we can lose our minds together," I say. But he's already moving away from me, catching me off guard. "What's wrong?"

He shakes his head, his hands on either side of his face, and sits up and away from me. "I'm sorry, Lexi. I just ... don't know what's wrong with me." He won't look at me now.

I sit up, retrieve my shirt from Zeus's snoring figure, and cover myself with it while searching for my bra. "If this is about the past, I already told you, there's nothing you could've done to make me love you less."

"Don't say that. Not until you know *everything* I've done." He glances in my direction, his eyes glazed over. I feel myself go rigid.

"How am I supposed to take that?" I ask. He drags his shirt back on, his hands trembling and his expression unreadable. "Stop," I say while putting my hand on his arm, but he doesn't stop. "Please, just talk to me ... "

"I thought I could forget who I used to be. I thought I could atone for the past, but being here brings back a lot of memories." His once warm voice turns bitter. "The Sinners are right; I'll always be a guard, and they'll never let me forget it."

"What are you saying? You're not even close to the same person you were before." I can't help raising my voice as he stands up, and his hands ball into fists. I find my bra tangled on the floor and put it on, embarrassed.

"Lexi, I'm saying I will never, ever deserve you." His voice breaks.

"Stop, please, you're scaring me."

"Cole." Bruno's voice cuts through the tension before I have a chance to respond. He peeks through the thin curtain, and I scramble to put my shirt on.

"What?" Cole asks through gritted teeth, and I'm just as irritated as he is.

"Oh. Sorry, dude, but I need to talk to you."

"Can you give us ten?" I ask, my voice coming out harder than intended.

"Sorry, but this can't wait," Bruno says, ducking his head back out of the hut.

"You've got to be kidding me," I say to Cole. "We can't leave it like this. You have to tell me whatever it is you're afraid to."

"Not today," Cole says, his expression dark.

"Get your asses out here, lovebirds," Bruno says.

I step toward Cole, attempting to grab his arm, but when I do, he pulls out of my reach. "Cole," I plead.

He shakes his head and then walks away from me.

CHAPTER 13

"What's so important that it couldn't wait?" Cole asks. I snake my hands through my knotted hair and pull it back before going out. I shake as my emotions range from wanting to wrap Cole in my arms, to wanting to punch him in the face. I don't even understand what the hell just happened.

"We gotta get out of here," Bruno says, Grace at his side.

"That's it?" Cole asks.

"Yeah, dude, that's it." Bruno flicks his eyes between Cole and me and then cracks a knowing smile. "Did I cock block you, is that why you're mad?"

"Stop it," Grace says, smacking Bruno's arm.

"I totally did, didn't I?" He shakes his head, and Cole's face smolders. "I'd say I'm sorry, but I'm not."

Grace punches him in the arm this time, her face reddening. Bruno turns to her quickly and then back to us. "What? This place is dirty, diseased, and crawling with all kinds of insects and rodents. Just think of it as a favor, dude. My gift to both of you. And, you're welcome."

"So why the rush to leave the hut last night then?" Cole sounds annoyed.

"We can still have fun with our clothes on," he says. "And anyway, I'm dying of thirst, and I've got an idea."

Grace looks like she is waiting for the ground to open and swallow her up.

I'm so flustered I can barely speak. Stringy hairs hang in my face, and I straighten my shirt. I want to give Bruno a piece of my mind, but his smile is already gone. He stares upward, his gaze fixated elsewhere.

Screams echo above our heads, and I glance up at the sky. Turkey vultures circle around, six of them, like they're waiting to feed on us. Their bodies are dark against a sky sponged with silver and gray clouds. I run my tongue over my cracked lips just thinking about rain, but I know it's not coming. The artist in me longs to paint this scene. The fighter in me thinks it's a bad omen.

"Bruno, I'm thinking you're right. We should probably go. Even though I'd like to punch you right about now," Cole says. His voice breaks my fixation on the hungry scavengers. He's intense and broody.

Grace looks in my direction, but I refuse to meet her gaze. I don't want her to see the tension between Cole and me. And yet, maybe she's exactly the person I should talk to about it, since Bruno was also a guard. But now isn't the time.

Turning away from me, Grace asks, "Where are we headed?"

159

"The underground," Bruno says.

"Are you sure it's still there?" I ask.

"For our sake, I sure as hell hope so," Bruno says.

"And what exactly is down there?" Grace asks. She looks pale as she puts her hand against Bruno to steady herself.

"Supplies, I hope. It's the only place that might have what we need," Bruno says.

I nod my head, biting the inside of my cheek just thinking about it. The underground where Keegan trained me is full of dark passages and hidden entrances. It could be crawling with guards and completely booby-trapped by now. I lock eyes with Cole, and he furrows his brow, his lips sealing into a thin line. Despite our feelings toward each other at the moment, we both know we could be encountering a shitstorm walking in there, especially with the limited resources we have. But we don't have any other options left. Either we find water, food, ammo, and medical supplies, or we die out here.

"Bruno, can you take point?" Cole asks. "I'm running out of ammo." We're all running out of ammo, but there's something else going on with Cole.

"Yeah, sure ... that's why you want me to lead," Bruno says with sarcasm. I roll my eyes. "Let's send Bruno to the front line, because everyone knows the black guy in the movie always dies first."

We all laugh. I don't remember the last time I saw a movie. Watching surveillance cameras with Cole hardly counts as entertainment. It lightens the mood, but only for a moment. Only long enough for me to build up enough courage to follow Bruno into the place where I first connected with my brother.

"Let's take the route by the hospital, the way the van took

us," Cole offers. "Unless you know of another way to get there?"

"I'm afraid not," Bruno says.

"Are you sure it's abandoned?" Grace asks. "Like really sure?"

"According to Sutton it is." Bruno wipes his forehead. We're sweating out valuable fluids when we've got nothing to replace them with. "I thought about going there first, but once we got in, everything sorta just blew up and we ended up here." He rubs his temples as if he's trying to remember something. "I'd kill to get in and raid that training facility, have myself a weapon holiday."

"And we definitely could use some medicine and first-aid kits," I say. "Zeus's wounds need to be cleaned. He could probably use some antibiotics too."

"There you go again. Always thinking about that dog," Bruno says. Zeus growls at him and nudges him with his head. Hard. "Okay, okay, I'm just kidding, buddy."

"Right. So we avoid confrontation at all cost," Cole says with a scowl on his face. "Be smart. Get the basics, don't waste ammo or energy, and move fast. We got this."

There's a shrill squawking overhead. The vultures fight over something on the roof of a nearby building.

"Stupid birds," Bruno says. "I'm so tempted to shoot one."

"And do what? Eat it?" Grace asks.

"What else would I do with it? Use it as a weapon? Carry it around as my pet?" Bruno asks. He smacks his lips. "Beats starving to death."

"I'm not eating that," she says. "Those birds are foul."

Shooting a vulture and cooking it does sound tempting.

But anything sounds good right about now. I bite my lip, just thinking about the food I had in my pack before I lost it. Canned beans sound delicious right about now.

Bruno pulls his near-empty pack on and nods at Cole before moving out of the shadows. We all fall into a silent line behind him.

At one point, Grace turns to look at me. Her eyes search mine when our gazes meet, and she whispers, "Are you okay?" With Cole's eyes boring holes into my back, I shake my head at her.

Eventually, I fall into a rhythm, counting my steps, when I notice Zeus dragging his feet beside me. It worries me. His injuries need to be tended to, but we've got nothing to clean or bandage them with. I touch his head, prompting a swipe of his dry, rubbery tongue across his teeth. One of my worst fears is that his wound gets infected, and we have nothing to treat it with. But I can't think about that now.

We pass behind my old building. Memories come pouring back to me from when Bruno took me to see Sutton after Wilson pistol-whipped me in my quarters. My head aches just reliving it. He took me out the back way, and it was the first time I had ever laid eyes on the shantytown behind my building. It was a place of squalor then, but now, even my imagination can't think up anything more gruesome.

We stop against the familiar cement-block walls and duck away from the daylight. I let my eyes wander over the mass of huts, tents, and crudely made living areas. It's like a collage of colors, muted by dust and weathered by the constant beating of the sun.

The stench from a pile of rotting bodies invades my nose.

Flies buzz around my face. I swat them away, cringing and trying to keep my mouth closed. Swarms cover the corpses even as the turkey vultures swoop down to tear at the dead flesh. I cover my mouth to stem the feeling of nausea that sweeps over me. Too late. But there's nothing to throw up anymore. Just stomach bile. My retching must be loud, because everyone stops.

"Get us away from here," Grace says in Bruno's direction. She pats my back and holds my hair away from my face. I hear disgust and maybe even pity in her voice. Then she dry heaves, once.

"That right there is by far the sickest thing I've ever seen," Bruno says. I straighten my back and look at him as he covers his entire face. I guess he's never seen anyone throw up yellow stomach fluids before. But he's pointing to the vultures dining on the dead Sinners.

"Yet you want to eat one of those vultures?" Cole asks. It's a half-attempt at being funny. Maybe he will be back to his old self soon. Broody, sulky Cole isn't working.

He touches my shoulder. When I look into his eyes, pity's written all over his face, in the way his eyebrows gather in and his mouth turns down. I'm still unsure of what to think or say. His behavior makes me question what exactly he's hiding, and yet, I know he loves me.

"Ready?" Bruno asks me.

I nod.

Bruno clears his throat and runs down the alley filled with trash. He accidently kicks a can, and it rattles against the walls and between his feet. He jumps like it's a firecracker. I'm too nauseous to laugh at him, and I know that sound could give our location away to any guards in the area. He stops and holds

163

up his fist. So we all stop and wait for his next command.

It's quiet, which is abnormal for daytime. Before, the Hole was a constant chatter of noise. People would crowd into the streets, buying, selling, bartering, and surviving. Patrol was constant. Vehicles would rumble past, and prostitutes worked the streets, some as young as twelve years old. Guards were always detaining Sinners for this reason or that. Children of Sinners would play ball in the streets, yelling as kids do.

Where'd all the people go? Wilson couldn't have killed them all.

Bruno goes forward again, checking left and right, up and down. He signals for us to follow. Grace hops over the trash behind him, and Zeus stops to sniff and dribble urine every once in a while. I don't even know how he has any left. But at least he's still producing it.

I follow Grace. Zeus pees on the wall, just as a shadow moves to my right. I jump away, startled. Zeus lowers his leg and sniffs at the person. Satisfied, he walks away. A hand pulls back a dark hood, revealing a gaunt face. Cole and I draw on him. There's no way to tell his age because of how sickly he appears. His eyes rest in deep, hollowed sockets. His neck's branded orange for gluttony. He opens his mouth. I notice blisters around the edge of his lips in the creases, and his tongue's covered with them as well. I lower my weapon.

He tries to speak, but nothing but a hoarse whisper comes out. His bony hand reaches out for me, but I step back, unsure of what to do. He opens his mouth again, but nothing happens. He raises his shaky right hand to his mouth.

"Maybe he wants a drink," Grace says, hand on the weapon at her waist.

"Like the rest of us?" Bruno says, cocking his head to the right.

"Is that what you want? Water?" I ask. His eyes register what I'm saying, and he nods, barely able to hold up his own head. "We don't have any. I wish we did." His eyes close, and his head slumps back against the building. I look back at Cole, who still has his gun drawn. I wave my hand up and down so he will lower it. The guy isn't a threat. He can't tell anyone we've been here. He can't talk.

"Lexi, I'm sorry. But we can't help him," Cole says quietly, keeping his gun trained on the guy. I suck in my bottom lip and turn back to face the man. He doesn't bother opening his eyes this time. I turn back to Cole, sighing as I wait for him to tell me what I want to hear. He shakes his head, avoiding eye contact. I step forward toward the man, careful not to get too close.

"I wish we could help you," I say.

"Now the Hole has zombies? Awesome," Bruno says, under his breath but loud enough for everyone to hear.

"Let's go before I lose my mind," I say.

I start to feel weak. As I step away from the ill man, my knees wobble, and my hands feel limp.

At the end of the alley, Bruno checks both ways twice before crossing the street. The ground begins to rumble. Bruno holds up his fist, and everyone but Grace comes to a stop. I think the sun must be in her eyes. She's going to step out, in full view of an oncoming vehicle. Bruno's frantically waving his arms to get her attention. He can't yell for fear of giving away our position.

My stomach drops as panic creeps up my insides. *I have to*

stop her. Just before Grace takes her first step into the street, I jerk her shoulder to a stop. She stumbles backward, her body landing on top of me. Cole drags us both back into the shadows. At first, she flips over, giving me an angry glare.

Then she hears it too—the unmistakable sound of an engine sputtering along the street. Her shoulders tense. She stands and holds out her hand. It's clammy as I take it. We press ourselves against the building, willing ourselves to disappear into the cement blocks.

The vehicle, a big, black SUV, careens along the street. It zips past our position, leaving nothing but another cloud of dust to cover us as we finish crossing to the other side. Once there, Grace pulls me into a hug. When she releases me, her eyes are glassy, and her chin trembles.

"Thank you, Lexi," she says, exhaling a sigh of relief.

"You're welcome," I say. I know she'd do the same for me.

Bruno wraps his arms around Grace and pulls her into his chest and says, "Don't you ever scare me like that again, you hear?" He kisses the top of her head and takes a deep breath. "You should've gone home like I said." Grace elbows him and gives him a dirty look.

"I'll go home when you go home," she says, smiling and still breathing heavily from the scare and adrenaline.

"We're not moving fast enough," Cole says. Our heads all swing toward him in unison. "We've gone one block. One freaking block."

"Hey, Rome wasn't built in a day," Bruno says.

"Yeah, well this isn't Rome," Cole says with disdain.

"We need frequent breaks. None of us has had any water, and the heat is too much."

"True. Let's just try to make it before nightfall," Cole says.

"Let's keep going," Grace says, looking to Bruno to lead.

He treks onward between buildings, mountains of trash, and the searching eyes of the cameras mounted in the streets.

I exhale, attempting to let all the tension out of my body, but it's no use. Soon we will reach the hospital where I first met Sutton, where Alyssa died, and where I was almost raped.

I'll never forget riding in the blacked-out van to meet Keegan for the first time since he'd left home. The van was shot to hell by the time we arrived, but the joy and utter excitement of seeing my brother again made it all worth it. This time, there will be no happy reunion. He's gone forever. Now, the best I can hope for is water. If I allow myself to hope, maybe even food and first-aid supplies.

Bruno leads us down the alley where Cole helped me hop over the ledge so many times before. And just like then, Cole jumps over and reaches out to assist me. His hands tenderly wrap around my waist, pulling me down into his arms. He doesn't release me until my feet are steady. He lifts my face to his.

"You're angry with me, I can tell."

"I'm not mad at you; I'm hurt more than anything," I say. "You know how I feel about being lied to."

"We'll talk soon. Promise."

"Yeah."

He touches his forehead to mine and looks into my eyes. "Focus on my voice. We've overcome all this; and we'll do it again." He kisses my lips, and his are just as chapped as mine.

I nod.

"Okay, you good?"

167

"I'm good."

The stench of sewage hits me like yesterday, and no matter how many times I've walked through the narrow alley, breathing through my nose still isn't an option. I hear Grace suck in her breath in front of me. *At least I don't see any rats this time.*

The buildings squeeze us into a line. Bruno's elbows barely clear the high-reaching walls as he stops at the edge of the street across from the hospital. He checks both ways before turning right. Grace disappears around the corner after him.

And then it's my turn.

We're here.

The formerly clean façade of the hospital has aged seemingly overnight. The walls crumble in places. The glass is blown out in the majority of the windows. The main entrance is boarded up with wooden planks and red tape.

Zeus nudges me from behind, prodding me to move. I check both ways and glance up at the top of the hospital where the guards used to be stationed, but no one's there. *Here it goes* … I sprint around the corner with Zeus on my heels.

I tap Grace's shoulder when I catch up to her and Bruno. Cole taps mine. We move from building to building and house to house, in the shadows if we can find them, but otherwise, out in the open.

A bicycle lies on its side against a shack. I wonder who used to ride it. From the way it looks, it used to be blue, but the faded color has surrendered to the orange rust creeping up the metal bars.

Bruno stops to catch his breath, so I press my back against a building, and my eyes are drawn to the black entrance of a small house. There are torn yellow curtains hanging idly in the single front window. A weird sound, like a pot banging around inside, suddenly stops. I squint toward the house when I see the small face of a child peeking back at me.

The wide, hazel eyes of the child are striking against her dirt-caked cheeks. She blinks. Her long hair falls over her shoulders. She looks up and down the street and then returns her stare to me. I'm guessing she's about six years old. She shifts positions. Then she sees Zeus, and her lips part. Her hands cover her mouth in shock. *I remember that feeling. Oh please, little girl, please don't scream.*

I slowly raise my hand and wave at her, not wanting her to be afraid of us. She waits a few seconds before waving back. But she doesn't smile. Her eyes look far too mature for her heart-shaped face. I was starting to wonder if anyone had survived the revolt and lived here anymore.

Zeus's ears perk up, and a low, guttural growl escapes him. Cole grasps his collar. I don't want the girl to be afraid of him. I catch eyes with Cole, and sensing my panic, he makes Zeus sit. Then the sound of a car approaching interrupts us. My head snaps up. The little girl holds her pointer finger to her sealed lips. She flicks her head to the left and points in the direction of the car, which sounds like it could be about three blocks away, coming quickly. Its muffler makes a loud rattling noise.

Bruno leads us into the crevice of a building and hunkers down. As I take cover, I look back in the window for the girl, and she nods silently. Then she disappears.

The car comes closer, and we slink into the shadows. I hold my breath as it passes. It's black with tinted windows, like all the others, but I notice a loudspeaker mounted on top of it.

After it's gone, Bruno stands up. His knees crack. My mouth feels like cotton's been shoved inside. I'm starting to have a harder time focusing, and occasionally my boots catch on the ground and I trip. Cole grabs my shoulder, but judging by the weary lines on his face, he may be running out of energy too. *When are we going to get there?* It's nearly impossible to get my brain to think rationally.

Five blocks. Six blocks. Seven blocks pass in a blur of desolation. I tell myself to speed up, but my legs are heavy, like I'm dragging them through mud. Our stops become more frequent. Every time we start out again, Grace sighs. I'm irritable, and the sweltering heat doesn't help.

"Dude. I'm pissing brown," Bruno says after taking a quick break. *Come to think about it, I haven't peed all day.*

"Thanks for sharing that with the group, love," Grace says.

"Just keeping it real."

"So this is what it's like being around him twenty-four seven," I say to Grace.

"I'm afraid so. Sarcasm is Bruno's trademark. I've learned to roll with it."

My eyelids start to flutter, and my head begins to bob.

"Lexi, you still with me?" Cole asks, putting his hand on my waist. I lean against a wall, closing my eyes.

"Not so much; my head's spinning," I say.

"Hang in there; we're almost there," he says, sounding dehydrated too. I bring my hands to my face and rub my burning eyes, but the spinning won't stop. My body leans forward, and he catches me with both hands. "Whoa, there. I got you."

He hoists me over his shoulder.

"You don't have to carry me," I say. But it comes out sounding more like a long groan.

"Yes I do and I am. Where I go, you go. And you weren't moving." He grunts under my weight. His shoulder pushes through my stomach, but I don't have the strength to argue with him.

"Dear God in heaven, please say we're here," Grace says, holding on to Bruno's arm.

"Well I'm not God, but we're here," Bruno says.

CHAPTER 14

Cole lowers me to the ground and bends over to catch his breath. Zeus plops down next to him, his nearly dry tongue dangling from between his teeth.

"It's that building right over there." Bruno points.

"Hallelujah," Grace says, raising her hands in the air.

"One last push," Bruno says, wiping sweat from around his eyes, "and we're in." He straightens his back and lifts his chin.

Cole extends his hand to me and pulls me to my feet. "Do you think you can manage?"

"Sure." I twist the ring around my finger, drawing strength from its inscription.

Bruno sprints along the building, checks the timing of the cameras, and then shoves through the heavy metal door. Relief floods through me. *It's open.*

It's dark inside except for the light that spills through blown-out windows. The smell of feces and urine fill the air. My skin crawls at the sight of rats the size of small cats skittering across the floor in front of me. Empty water vials and cans of peas litter the floor.

"Lexi, come on," Cole says, and then I realize I've fallen behind.

We follow Bruno into the same monotone office space as last time, where chunks of drywall lie crumbled on the floor. Empty bookshelves and a desk covered in dust sits in front of a chair that has been turned over.

Bruno points to the open closet marking the entrance to the underground. Cole eagerly, but carefully, lifts the floorboard panels in the closet and then peeks into the empty space.

"I can't see a damn thing," he says.

"Hold up; I've got a flashlight," Bruno says, pulling it out of his pack. Bruno shines the light in front of Cole, making a pathway for him.

"That's better; I'll take Zeus down the ladder first," Cole says.

I remember how this went last time.

Sure enough, Zeus whines as he crushes Cole's face with his oversized paws. Cole curses the entire way down. Who knows how Cole has the strength to carry him after everything we've been through.

"Okay, Lexi, you're up," Bruno says, moving aside so I can make my way down the rickety ladder.

Stepping into the shaft, I use my right foot to feel for the next rung down. It's slippery and just as precarious as the first time I made this trek. I close my eyes, willing myself to concentrate on getting down without slipping off and hurting myself. The light from Bruno's flashlight is like a small candle to an abyss. It barely just reaches the bottom of the landing.

Soon, almost everyone is down, and Bruno replaces the board at the top. The ladder creaks as he climbs down. I hear a snapping sound.

"Oh shit!" Bruno says.

Six steps from the bottom, the whole thing gives out. Bruno lands, with a crash, on his back. The flashlight skitters across the floor, and for a minute, he doesn't move. His hulking figure lies on the hard floor with the flashlight spinning in circles, before I reach down and pick it up. Grace rushes over to him.

"Are you okay? Are you hurt?" she asks. He groans. "Move your toes." In the dim light, I watch him wiggle his toes. "Did you hit your head?"

He mumbles.

"What?" she asks in a panicked voice.

"No, but your shirt's in my face," he says as he pushes her back an inch. "Not that I'm complaining about your boobs but … "

"You're such an apple," she says, a chuckle coming out of her. Bruno laughs weakly and rolls onto his knees.

"First cracker … now apple?" Cole asks. "Grace, we're starving, and you're cursing with food?"

"I know, sorry. But it's a habit."

"Now I know how the giant felt when he came down the beanstalk." Bruno laughs at himself. I can't stop myself from snorting. Grace takes Bruno's hand and hugs him close, then she shoves him away and frowns at him.

"Guess we're not getting out the way we came in," she

muses over the broken ladder.

I flick the light down the tunnel, eyeing the weeping ceiling, the bars lining the walls, and the black hole at the end. This time, no firelight welcomes us. In fact, all you hear is the dripping of water and the echo of our voices against the pitch black.

"Where's Steven when we need him?" I ask, remembering the first time we arrived, when Steven escorted us underground. Now, it's Cole's turn to chuckle.

"I wonder if he got out," he says.

"He did," Bruno says. "He was in my group, remember?"

"Say, where's the dripping coming from? I'm about to start licking the walls," Grace says. She looks at Bruno, and the flashlight casts weird shadows beneath her eyes.

Zeus takes off ahead of us. He stops to whizz a few times, but nothing's coming out, and he raises his head to look at us while making a snuffing noise. In the darkness, his eyes shine an eerie green.

"Oh, don't worry … we see you, doofus," Cole says. "Your hose ran dry. It happens."

I shine the flashlight ahead, occasionally flicking it to our feet to make sure there's nothing for us to trip over. I still feel weak, but the drop in temperature wakes me up. My head's clearer. Or maybe I just have hope.

"Keegan lived down here, right?" Grace asks, lowering her voice into a whisper as we walk.

"Yes, he did." My voice trails off.

We enter the space where my brother Keegan and I reunited around the fire for the first time in years. *I was so happy to see him. God, how I miss him.* A charred, black spot stains

175

the floor where the fire had been. Blackened wooden planks used for seating look abandoned and sad. The heaviness in the air settles in. Zeus sniffs around and finally settles on an old t-shirt lying on the floor in front of him, dirty and forgotten. My feet freeze in place.

It's just ... empty, a disturbing reminder of what used to be. A hand touches the back of my neck and squeezes. It's Cole, of course. *If only Keegan were here now.* He'd know what to do. He'd have an answer, even if it wasn't the right one. He was passionate about what he believed and never backed down from anything or anyone. My brother had a heart of gold. I loved him. I love him still. *And someday, I'll bury him like he deserves.*

Zeus's head perks up. His ears stand up straight as he woofs at something.

"Zeus, what's there?" I ask as we all turn toward the hallway.

I point the flashlight down in the direction he's looking. *Was that a face I just saw?* I squint and step in that direction. By now, Cole's next to me, hand on his gun.

"Come out with your hands over your head," Bruno says in a firm voice. It echoes into nothingness.

Zeus continues to growl, each one getting louder. But no one answers, and the shadows play with my mind. If I think too hard, I see bodies moving in the darkness. The flashlight feels slick in my sweaty palms. I stop moving and listen intently for noise. Zeus's whole body points in the direction of whatever is out there. The drip, drip, dripping of water sliding off the pipes overhead makes the only identifiable noise.

"Show yourself," Cole says. I hear nothing in response.

Cole doesn't lower his gun. He's focused on the energy of his dog. He knows Zeus would not be acting this way if there wasn't anybody out there.

Zeus barks louder, making me jump in my own skin. His fur stands straight up on his back, and his tail moves in a measured manner, all while his posture remains tight. He cocks his head to the left.

"What the hell is his deal? He looks confused," Bruno says, sweat glistening as it rolls down his biceps.

"He's trying to get a sense of what he's hearing," I say.

"You're kidding, right?" Bruno asks.

"Nope. Zeus has the best intuition, especially when it comes to people we don't know. If he trusts them, Cole does. So that's enough proof for me."

"Come on, follow me," Cole says to Bruno. Cole takes the flashlight from me.

They move forward with their guns raised, the small light fading as they travel farther into the dank hallway. Zeus takes off after them, sniffing along the way.

My body shivers, and I wrap my arms around myself, but it doesn't help. My heart's palpitating so fast, I need to sit down. Without that little bit of light, the room gets darker and darker. All I can think about is the last time I was here with Keegan, as the only sound coming from the hallway is the drip of water.

The very thought of water makes me lick my lips. My throat's so dry, it feels raw.

Grace sits down next to me. It's so dark that if I didn't feel her warmth, I wouldn't even know she was there. I lean my head on her shoulder.

"Don't move," a voice says.

177

My breath catches in my throat. It's hard to make out where the voice comes from. Grace tenses up beside me.

"Why are you here?" the voice asks, in a demanding tone. "I didn't invite you, did I? I don't recall inviting anyone."

"Why are *you* here?" I ask right back.

"I live here. Well, I hide here," he says.

The man is in front of me, off to the right, and although I can't see him, I detect the slight smell of alcohol permeating his breath when he speaks. *Great, he's been drinking, and he's probably armed.* He shines a light in our faces. I blink my eyes and turn my face away as he cackles. Grace links her arm through mine.

"Well I'll be damned. If it isn't Lusty Lexi." He laughs a deep, throaty laugh.

"How do you know me?" I scrunch my forehead to protect my eyes, and he flicks off the light. *Lusty Lexi? Who used to call me that?*

Just then, Zeus barks, and I hear footsteps heading toward us. Cole's flashlight appears. The man puts his light back on and shines it toward Cole and Bruno. That's when I get a good look at him. The scraggly hair and missing teeth give him away immediately.

"Stop right there, or I'll smack them," he says. "Or should I say kick them? My legs are stronger."

Zeus parks his body at the edge of the light and ducks his head down. His butt goes straight into the air, like he wants to play. He dances around the man wildly.

Cole and Bruno stop dead in their tracks, pointing their guns at the man who points a gun at me and Grace. Cole's eyes track Zeus, looking for cues.

178

"If you so much as touch them, I'll blow your brains out," Bruno says.

The man laughs. "Lusty, your guard's alive; that's great," he says. "Or maybe it's not, depending on if you like him. Do you?"

"Former guard," Cole says with an edge in his voice. "And yes, she's with me, so I suggest you back away from her."

Zeus continues to pop up and down. He almost runs into the man, who attempts to push him away. Trying to follow Zeus while keeping track of the conversation isn't easy.

"Cole, you know him," I say. The man's eyes flick to me, a grin spreading across his face as I stare down his barrel.

Cole shakes his head.

"You don't recognize him? It's Bill," I say.

A look of recognition crosses Cole's face.

"Ah! You remember me?" Bill asks, clapping his hands and jumping up and down. I'm not sure why he's so excited; you would think he had just won the lottery or something.

"Yeah ... " I say.

"Bill? Crazy Bill?" Cole steps in closer with his gun pointed at him. "Of all people, how the hell did *you* manage to survive?"

"By eating and drinking, and I forget what else. Maybe breathing?"

"No, you moron. I meant the revolt, how on earth did you manage to survive?"

"I came down here."

"When?" Cole asks.

"Um. Give me a minute." We all stare while he counts using his fingers.

"Forget it. How did you know the underground even existed?" Cole asks impatiently.

"I'm a nosey person. I watch people. I watched them coming and going from the opening. I love secrets; they're so much fun. Don't you think?"

Cole's face has confusion and annoyance written all over it. Bruno inches closer, gun pointed at the man's head. So I decide to change the subject before Cole or Bruno punch him—or worse.

"Hey, Bill, do you have any water?" I ask.

He scrunches his eyes at me, looking me up and down, slowly lowering his gun and placing it in the waist of his pants.

"I do, I do. I'll get you guys some, and then you can leave?" He glances at Bruno and Cole, who haven't lowered their weapons.

Bruno jumps forward, holding Bill at gunpoint. "You'll give us water and food, but we're not leaving." Bill laughs, even as Bruno shoves the barrel into the side of his head.

"I like your style. Straight to the point. So now we're roommates? That's great, I love roommates. Okay, be right back."

"I believe Bill has fallen off his rocker," I say to Cole.

"Yeah … he's … crazy all right," Cole says, laughing and shaking his head.

"Or it's an act," Bruno says.

A while later, we sit in the old training room, in the middle of the floor, sharing water and snacks. Bruno stands over us, gulping down as much as he can handle. The lights are dim, only a few still work.

The feel of the hard mats under my hands reminds me of my training. All the times I wrestled with people in my group, ran sprints, and worked to build strength come back to me. But most of all, I feel Keegan's presence.

"For the main operation, we divided everyone into teams. I'm assigning you to mine. One, because I love you, and two, because you're that damn good," Keegan had said.

I close my eyes and remember the way he looked at me when he said it. He cracked his neck like it was no big deal. But it meant everything to me, my older brother believing in me that much.

"Lexi, water?" Cole's voice snaps me back to the present.

"What kind of question is that?" I have to shake away the memories, or I'll drown in them. I tip the bottle to my lips and concentrate on just hydrating myself. Keegan would want me to be strong.

If there's one positive thing about the Hole right now, it's this—the first taste of water I've had in days. In order to keep from getting sick, I sip it. But part of me just wants to dump the whole thing all over me like a shampoo commercial and sing out loud.

"Why're you keeping this all to yourself? Don't you have any friends?" I ask Bill, who sits to my left. "I don't get it."

"Lusty, you silly girl. If I shared this with the outside, you wouldn't have any right now. See what I mean?" He casually tips back a bottle of water and sips it. Then he pulls out another

181

container, a round one with a cap on it. He bites off the cap, and I smell the stinging burn of alcohol. He takes a long swig before putting it away.

"There's no one around up there to take the stuff, man," Bruno says. He shakes his head and squints his eyes.

"Things have been happening since you all … " He throws his hands in the air. "Left." He leans back, putting his hands behind him, and glares at Bruno. "Oh they're out there all right. Hiding. Oy vey, did you see that bug? That was a nasty one." We all turn to see what he's pointing at, but there's nothing there.

"Bill, why are they hiding?" I ask.

"So they don't get taken. Being taken never has a good outcome."

"Taken?" I ask, raising an eyebrow. "By who? Why?"

"You're so full of s—" Bruno starts.

"Help!" someone yells. It's a man's voice, but I don't recognize it.

I stop mid-drink and look around as everyone goes silent. Zeus's ears stand up, and he cocks his head sideways.

"Someone help me!" the voice yells.

"Who is that?" Bruno asks Bill.

Bill gives him a sheepish grin. "Oh, I totally forgot about that guy. I don't know him, so that makes me not like him," he says.

Bruno brings his gun up and shoves it against Bill's temple. His lips turn down, and he narrows his eyes. "I don't trust you, man," Bruno says.

"Who is it?" Cole asks. He's standing now, his shoulders tense and his eyes ablaze. Bill doesn't answer. He just gulps more of his pungent drink. "Tell us now."

"I think it's a guard, if I remember correctly … He's got a very nice uniform on."

"Tell me you didn't bring a guard down here," Cole says.

"I'm not the enemy!" the voice says. It echoes off the walls and around the large room.

We all look at one another, unsure of what to do next.

"Bill," I say. "Where is he?"

"I'll show you, but don't panic, because I don't know who he is."

"Let's go," Bruno says. "Now."

Bill reluctantly stands up with Bruno's gun centered on him. He pats his pants and shrugs his shoulders. When he begins walking, he stumbles and swerves.

"I'm about to confiscate your bottle, old man," Cole threatens.

"No, no, anything but that," Bill says. "I'll do anything you say."

He stands in front of the large metal door that leads into the hallway and past the women's communal shower area. If it weren't for the voice pleading to be free on the other side, the thought of a shower would thrill me.

"Please, let me out of here," the voice says.

Bruno stares at Bill. Bill stares at Bruno. It's a standoff.

Grace sighs, gun trained on the door, awaiting instructions from Bruno. Cole looks to Bruno, and the two exchange some kind of guy-guard-macho look. Bruno turns back to Bill and gives him the stare of death.

"We better not be walking into a trap, you drunk fool." Bruno pushes his weapon against Bill's head again.

Finally, Bill rolls his eyes and turns the knob. When Bruno pushes open the door, Zeus tears through it, disappearing into the hallway.

"Do you have no control over that dog at all?" Bruno asks Cole.

"You asked to see the captive. Remember that, if he's dangerous, it's not my fault," Bill says. He leans against the doorframe, his eyes rolling in his head. "So here goes nothing."

"Who's there?" the man asks in a shaky voice.

I flip on the light.

Oh my God.

Sitting in the hallway, duct-taped to a wooden chair, is a man. He's been blindfolded. Just looking at the large shiner on his head makes mine throb. His chin quivers. His knuckles are bloodied and dirty. I push Bill aside as I file into the hallway to get a better look at him. *That's no guard.* On his dark blue uniform is the United Powers emblem, right on the collar.

"What the hell, Bill! You're holding a monitor hostage?"

"A what?" he asks. He stumbles into the space to my right. "He's a computer monitor?"

"Oh hell." Cole lowers his gun, whips out his knife, and immediately begins cutting the blindfold and restraints away from the man.

"He came down here, and I don't know him. People I don't know make me very nervous and on edge."

"Bill, a monitor is a person the United Powers sent to help us," I say, pushing him aside. "He's not a guard."

As the man is freed, he flexes his wrists and fingers. He blinks several times, revealing dark blue eyes that if you weren't close enough, you'd think were black. He clenches his

184

jaw and stares at us, seemingly unsure of what to do.

"Were there any other monitors who came with you?" Bruno asks. The man seals his lips while evaluating Bruno, who's appearance would be enough to intimidate anyone.

"Hey, slow down a minute, give the man some water and a second to breathe before you jump down his throat," Grace says.

I hand her a bottle, and she gives it to the monitor, who hesitantly takes it. He drinks it slowly, never taking his eyes off us.

"Thank you," he says to Grace. His voice comes out raspy.

"Now ... answer my questions," Bruno says.

The man clears his throat. "How did you know there were others with me?" he asks, raising an eyebrow.

"We just assumed someone as important as you wouldn't have come to a place like this alone," I say. His eyes rest on me, on my brand, and then he focuses on my eyes.

"I'm not sure if anyone else made it," he says. "We were shot at, the lot of us. Somehow, I found a way down here."

"So that's it? You could very well be the only monitor that's left. And from the looks of things, if Wilson finds out you're still alive, he'll try to kill you too." Cole's words are harsh, but they about sum up what's happening. The little hope that sparked inside me when I saw this man's United Powers emblem vanishes.

185

CHAPTER 15

I'm suspicious and hopeful and scared as I stare at the monitor who survived the attack. There are a million things I want to ask him, but I don't know where to start. He could be the key to our future.

Before I can get my thoughts together, Grace asks, "So how on earth did *you* manage to survive?"

"As soon as the others around me started falling to gunfire, I fell to the ground and pretended to be dead. Once they had us in a pile, I slowly made my way out. When no one was watching, I took off down the nearest alley."

"Wow, that's brave of you," Grace says, despite the skeptical look on her face.

"I didn't have many options," he says, his lips forming a wry smile.

Bill starts pacing in circles, making my headache worse.

"So are you going to tell us what we need to know, or are we going to have to beat it out of you?" Bruno steps forward, his frame menacing the strange dignitary, who winces under Bruno's intense stare. "What's your connection to all of this? Why should we care you're alive or, better yet, why should we keep you that way?"

The man winces again, leans back, and then looks away.

"I suggest you start talking," Cole says.

The monitor looks to Cole. "My name is Roméo; I'm a monitor. After the revolt, Sutton managed to get some sensitive information to the United Powers. It was enough to grab their attention."

"What kind of information?" Grace asks.

"All I know is there were some images, documents, and a little video footage," Roméo says. He shifts positions. I can't tell if the questions or his bruises are causing his discomfort.

"So ... that's what was on the disk?" Bruno asks.

"What disk?" Cole asks, turning his attention to Bruno.

"During the revolt, Sutton told me he had to get to the control room, that he needed to download something. Huh, it all makes sense now," Bruno says. "Man, he's good."

"So they got the disk," Cole says. "Why'd it take them so damn long to send you here?"

"Because the United Powers are not about to put other countries at risk, or possibly spark another world war unless they have good reason to."

"You mean to tell me that wasn't enough for them?" Bruno asks.

"Unfortunately, no. But the United Powers have suspicions that something more's happening, something greater,

187

something that can change everything."

"Oh, great. Like what?" I ask, wrapping my arms around myself.

"Now that is exactly what we're hoping to figure out."

By now, a new anxiety is spreading through my veins. What is happening? And what could possibly be so bad that it could change everything?

"You know Wilson loves torture. He might be torturing Sutton," Bill says, suddenly stopping his frantic pacing.

Cole gets in Bill's face and practically spits as he says, "These comments of yours aren't helping matters, and you're really starting to piss me off."

"You don't like to hear the truth?"

"Oh, hell, I'm done." Cole spins around and walks back to his pack. He takes out some duct tape and heads toward Bill. "Don't make me tape your mouth shut."

"Hey, what's our next step?" Bruno interrupts. "This guy doesn't seem to know all that much of anything. A complete waste of energy." Bruno looks from Cole, to Grace, and then to me. He relaxes his stance.

"Lexi and I will gather supplies," Cole says. "Then we'll head back out."

"I'll keep an eye on Bill," Bruno says.

"And I'll make sure Roméo gets something to eat," Grace says. She gently touches her stomach and then gives me a smile.

"Okay, then let's gets started," I say. But before we can part ways, Bill stops us.

"I've stockpiled some of the good stuff in the closet of the training room."

"Got it," Cole says, moving quickly out of Bill's grasp.

Bill reaches for me, but Cole knocks his hand away and pulls me with him.

"But beware, not everything down here's safe and secure," Bill calls from behind us.

"Thanks," I say over my shoulder.

Cole picks up his pack, throws it on, and dusts his hands off on the sides of his pants. He takes my hand, and we intertwine our fingers. His skin, no matter how many times I feel it against mine, instantly causes my heart to jump.

In the hallway and out of view, we stop for a moment.

"Hey," Cole says. "You all right?"

"Yeah, I'm fine, just trying to wrap my head around everything." I stretch on my tiptoes and wrap my arms around his neck. Cole smiles before touching his lips to mine. He brushes my cheek with his thumb, and I close my eyes, soaking in the feeling.

"I'm sorry for the way I acted earlier," he says. I step away from him, taking in his earnest eyes and serious face.

"It's okay. We can talk about it as soon as we're done here."

He gives me a half smile and then opens the door to the training room. The smell of gun cleaner permeates the air as Cole opens the closet. Four rows of shelves wrap around the entire closet. I run my fingers over the cool, smooth black pistol closest to me. Picking it up, I release the magazine and place it on the table that stands in the center of the training room. Sliding back the chamber, I check to make sure there's no bullet inside. It's empty. I grip the pistol and wrap my fingers around it. Like a glove, it fits perfectly. It's strange to me how comfortable I've become handling guns. Of course,

Keegan taught me safety always comes first; you must treat every gun as if it's already loaded, otherwise accidents happen. Searching the closet, I manage to find four more magazines that go with the pistol.

Cole checks out the big guns. He finds one and gingerly pulls it off the rack. He runs his hands over it like it's a rarity.

"This'll do the job," he says with a slight smile.

"I don't think I've seen it before," I say.

"I'm surprised Bill has one; it's an M4." Cole carries it with such confidence, like it's a part of his body. He flips it over, slowly, checking every inch of the weapon, making sure there's nothing missing or any visible damage. I watch as his head nods with quiet admiration.

"Bill's done a pretty good job keeping the weapons in good condition."

"So it appears," I say.

While he examines my gun, I walk around the table and look for anything else we might need. In a container at the end of one shelf are two different kinds of hand grenades. I've never handled grenades before, but I carefully grab one of each and weigh them in my hands. One's heavy and slim. The other is rounder and weighs less. Either way, I can't help but wonder how something so small can cause such a large explosion.

"Do you think these are worth taking?" I ask.

Cole spins around, sets down my gun, and looks at me. His forehead scrunches up, and his eyes flicker. "I'm not sure I'm comfortable with you handling grenades. Have you used one before?"

"Well, no. But it can't be that complicated. You pull the pin … and throw it. Fast."

"Uh-huh, then what?"

I stop and think for a minute while chewing my bottom lip. "Run the other way?"

"Then yes, take some. But remember to protect them like you would your gun. If someone gets their hands on one, they can pull the pin, and blow you both to pieces."

"Won't happen."

"And what makes you think that?"

"Because Wilson wants me alive, and blowing me away defeats that purpose."

"True, but not every guard is going to follow orders, and the crazy Sinners won't always either."

I instinctively rub the brand around my neck and lower my eyes.

"Lexi, I'm sorry. I didn't mean … " His voice trails off, and he steps forward.

I put my hand out in front of me. "It's fine. Let's not lose focus." I swallow hard, blink back a tear, and continue examining weapons. "Is there really a difference between them?" I ask, pointing at the grenades.

Cole cocks his head to the right while picking one up. "One's offensive, meant to kill just by the concussion. The lighter one's more defensive, used to throw from a covering position."

"I'll take the lighter one. I think that's best, right?"

"It's your call. I trust your judgment."

"Wait, what? Did I hear you correctly?" I ask, cocking my head and smiling at him. "Seriously? You trust me now?"

"Yeah, but trusting and accepting are two very different things."

Cole's lips part as he moves toward me. He wraps his arms around my waist, hoisting me onto the table. He parts my legs and stands between them, rubbing his hands up my thighs toward my hipbones. I suck in my bottom lip and hold it down with my teeth. He's only inches away from me now, and he touches his forehead to mine. He takes my face between his hands and brings my mouth to his. His mouth trembles against mine as he kisses me. I lock my arms around his back, pulling him in closer. Cole's passionate and gentle. This moment feels different somehow from before in the tent. Still, my stomach flutters, and my pulse accelerates. I want him glued to me. Then, without warning, he stops. His eyes are closed, but his face is pained. He strokes my cheeks with the outside of his fingers and furrows his brow.

"Hey, what's wrong?"

He doesn't answer me.

"Okay, I think we need to talk now." Reaching up, I touch his face, and again, he freezes.

At first, he says nothing, and his eyes remain glued shut. He takes a long, loud, deep breath before releasing it. The air rushes past my face, moving my hair, and I twitch. I smell the mint on his breath from the leaves he puts in his water. My stomach's turning into knots. I'm lost, confused, and can't tell what he's thinking or feeling. My legs start shaking. What's he doing?

"Cole, say something ... You're scaring me."

He shakes his head and clenches his jaw before slowly opening his eyes. He stares at my legs for a moment before glancing up at my face.

"Now's not the time."

"If not now, then when?"

"I don't know."

"Whatever you're keeping from me isn't going to change the way I feel about you."

"I'm not so sure about that."

"It's from your past, before we even met. How could it possibly—"

"Because it will. Okay?" He glances at the floor and steps away from me.

"Do you know how hard it was for me to open up to you, to be vulnerable? I told you things I swore never to tell anyone. I was ashamed and humiliated. Yet, I still took the leap and let it all out there.

"Cole, if I've learned anything, it's that sometimes secrets hurt more than the truth. And right now you're really hurting me."

Just then, there's a knock on the door. Cole walks away from me to open it. Grace is there with her arms wrapped around herself, her lower lip trembling. The way she looks melts the smile off my face.

"Hey," I say. "Do you need me?"

"Actually, I do. Would you mind walking to the bathroom with me?"

"Sure. Let me grab my stuff." I put my gun in its holster.

"I'll get your extra magazines," Cole says.

"This isn't over," I say before walking into the hallway to meet Grace.

She's staring at the floor. Her shoulders are slumped, and she fiddles with her fingers. I loop my arm with hers and try to hide the burning pain deep in my chest. Grace needs me.

Whatever secret Cole has been keeping can certainly wait another few minutes.

"Come on, it's this way," I say.

Nothing much has changed down here in the underground. It still feels like a dungeon in some spots. Deep down, I keep hoping Keegan's just around the next corner. As we pass his room, I can still feel him. I hope he's proud of me.

I'm not a fan of dead silence, especially when there's tension in the air. And right now, between Grace and Cole, it's suffocating. I hum to myself to keep from focusing on the bad.

When we reach the bathroom, I open and hold the door for Grace. I release it, and it closes with a click. Grace jumps. I flick on the switch next to the door and hope the lights work properly. Everything seems a little more rundown without the maintenance people.

Grace doesn't walk to the bathroom stalls; she doesn't even look at the showers. *I could really use a shower right now.* All she does is cross her arms, uncross her arms, and cross them again. My mouth feels dry, and I have a strong sense that whatever's going on isn't good. But I can't take the static between us anymore.

"What's going on? What's wrong?"

She runs her hands through her hair, and tears spill over her eyes. She steps back, leaning against the wall for support.

"I'm scared. Really scared, and I don't know what to do." She stumbles over her words and shakes her head. Now she looks up and stares at the ceiling. She slowly lowers her head, as if it pains her to do so. "If I tell you something I need you to promise you won't say a word to Bruno about this."

"Okay."

"No, I mean it. Not a single word. If he finds out, there's no telling what he'll do. You have to promise me you won't tell him, or anyone else." There is fear and determination on her face. I have never heard her use that tone of voice.

"Whatever it is, it's your business to tell, not mine."

She covers her face with her hands and starts crying. "I'm … pregnant."

I feel the weight of my body drop to the floor, yet I remain standing. My knees lock, and my eyes open wide with shock.

"Oh dear Lord," I say. "Are you sure?" I move my legs forward and lean against the wall next to her. At the same time, we lower ourselves to the ground. I pull my knees into my chest and turn my head in her direction.

"I've never been late. Never. And I tried to push it aside and blame stress, but it's not. My boobs are killing me, and I mean *killing* me. I'm nauseous all the time, and my last period was two months ago. I want to be happy, but I'm petrified." She sits cross-legged and twiddles her thumbs. "We have to get out of here before he's born."

"He? How do you know it's a boy?"

"Let's just say it's an intuition. My mother has the same thing. She was always right when it came to guessing the sex of someone's child."

She can't be happy about being pregnant with the situation we're in right now. I weigh my words carefully.

"I'm sorry; I can only imagine how scared you must be, but it'll be all right. We'll keep you and the baby safe. We're going to get out of here. We will."

Grace grabs my hands. "You can't tell Bruno, okay? You have to promise me this stays between us."

195

"Grace, I'm not a liar. I've been lied to so many times I refuse to do the same to others."

"You're not lying; you're just not going to say anything to anyone. Okay?"

"Don't you think Bruno has the right to know his wife's pregnant?"

She shakes her head slowly, releasing her grip on my hands. It almost makes me dizzy. "No. You don't understand. We've been trying for years to get pregnant, and it never happened." She releases a loud exhale. "We both want to be parents in the worst way, and if he finds out now, it's going to ruin everything."

"What do you mean?"

"He'll only worry about me and the baby. He won't be able to focus on the mission. That would lessen our chances of helping Roméo, finding Sutton, and getting out of here. I'm telling you, this man will go berserk if he finds out. He loves me so much, and if he knew I was carrying our child, he would be too distracted to perform his duties. And I don't want to leave him, or any of you guys."

"I'm so sorry, Grace. I don't know what to say. A part of me wants to be happy for you because it's what you've always wanted, but another part of me is afraid for you and the baby."

"I know. It's okay. I'm not even sure what my feelings are anymore. Not telling him hurts because I feel so alone in this."

"So that's why you told me?"

"Yes, I had to tell someone or I was going to start freaking out. Zeus knows. But that's it."

I laugh out loud and so does she. "He's a great secret keeper … He knows all of mine too." I sigh. "Well, I'm glad you told me. This way I can think of things to keep you behind us and out of danger. Not all of us can go above ground, a few will always have to stay and protect what we have stored down here. In your condition, you can't throw yourself around and dodge bullets."

"I won't do that; plus, I have all of you to help protect me."

"Good point."

"So you promise this stays between the two of us?"

"I can promise I won't volunteer the information ... but I'm not going to lie if he asks me."

"Oh, he won't ... He's not that intuitive."

"Okay, stand up. I want to give you a hug."

We both get up onto our feet, and I hug her tight.

"Thank you," she says. "I really needed a friend."

"Me too, Grace. Me too."

CHAPTER 16

A monitor survived the attack.

Cole finishes washing his face, and I take a turn at the sink. We haven't said much to one another since discovering the monitor. The tension between us is thick and heavy. We move around like strangers, only speaking in please and thank yous.

My head's going to explode from all the secrets and information stored inside. I smooth my hair and tuck curls behind my ears. Staying alive, scavenging for food, and running is all I know. I have no idea what day or month it is. I don't even know if I've turned nineteen yet. The only thing I'm sure of is that the Hole is brutal and hot ... and tends to bring out things in people you'd rather not see.

Like Cole, for instance. I trust him and know he loves me, but since we got here, he hasn't been himself. Then again,

198

maybe I didn't really know him to begin with. Maybe the Cole I met here is the real Cole. I begin pacing as my doubt gets the best of me.

Cole steps in front of me and places his hands on my shoulders.

"Hey, what's going on with you?" he asks. *Finally.*

I shake my head. "I'm fine … just trying to wrap my head around everything. Does it make sense to you? We saw what they did to the motorcade. Who could have survived that? Who could survive that and then somehow find this place?"

"Look at me," he says.

I do.

"Okay, now take a deep breath." I inhale deeply and slowly exhale. "Good. Now listen to me. Okay?" I nod. "Whatever this monitor, Roméo, is about, we will figure it out. Right now, he's our best chance to get the drop on Wilson and to find Sutton. I know it's a huge risk and we're really throwing ourselves out there, but I think there's a good chance this guy could be our ticket out of here."

It makes a lot of sense, but something is nagging at me. "I don't know, Cole. Nothing has really been going our way, and now all of sudden we just happen to find the person we're looking for here?"

"You're starting to sound so cynical, like Bruno."

A slight smile plays on his lips and for a minute, I think he might kiss me. I want him to kiss me.

"Maybe Bruno's right," I say.

"Well, whatever that guy's hiding, Bruno will get it out of him. You can be sure of that." I look at him skeptically and frown.

"I can't sit around waiting for him to talk. We need to do something. Now."

"I know. Let's go above ground, do some recon. Someone has to know something. Someone has to have seen something."

"Yeah, but you know how it is in the Hole. You keep your mouth shut, don't make waves. Who is gonna tell us anything?" I don't need to tell him how intimidating he looks or how much Sinners hate guards.

"Well, we have to try, Lexi. Sutton needs us to get proof of what's been going on here, and that's what we have to do. OK?"

I inhale deeply, the weight of it all threatening to crush me.

"Okay," I say quietly.

"Now let's get ready." He kisses the top of my head, and my eyes flutter. I reach for him, but he steps away and straightens his shoulders. I notice the extra magazines he's stowed away in the tan vest he wears over his t-shirt.

"What? No handgun?" I ask.

He smiles and pats his thigh. "Doubting me, are you?"

"Of course not. Not when it comes to fighting." I didn't mean for it to come out that way.

Cole looks cross for a second. Then he turns to walk away. I follow him out of the bathroom and into the hallway where the light flickers above our heads three times. I glance at Cole, but he's looking up. A thundering noise pounds above us, and I wonder what it could be. I clasp my hands together and feel my palms already sweating.

We go through a series of hallways, each getting narrower with every turn. The cool air gives me goose bumps.

At first, it feels like we're wandering through an endless

maze, but the last turn leads to a hallway that opens into a wider tunnel. Immediately, I know where we are.

It takes everything within me to restrain my emotions. So much has changed since I stood here, praying we'd all survive the revolt against the Commander and his regime. In front of me were Sheldon and Keegan, brave and determined. I remember how hot it was in my full gear, hoping Cole was alive and trusting in Sutton's plan. I grit my teeth remembering my friends, some of them in their last moments of life, fighting to hold on.

Veronica lay bleeding out on the top of the wall, Sheldon fell over the edge, and Sutton was shot. And then, Keegan. *God, his death will forever be imprinted in my mind.*

"Lexi," Cole calls me out of my daze. From the expression on his face, I can tell he knows I'm reliving every inescapable and horrific moment of it.

He brings his first two fingers to his eyes and mouths the word "focus." I thrust out my chest and clench my jaw. I can't let the past cloud the future. After all, I still have him and Sutton. *Because we will get him back.*

The siren's wailing when we exit the underground. Its piercing scream rattles my nerve endings, and my hands shake just the slightest bit. It's early, but no one's going to work anymore, so I'm not sure why they even bother with the siren. Maybe it's just habit or maybe it's to keep the Sinners on edge. Either way, it has an unnerving effect.

Our mission has changed slightly. We didn't expect for things to go this way. We came here to get Sutton. However, now that all but one of the monitors is dead, we need to find a way to get the information that will put Wilson away.

Roméo, the monitor Bill captured in the underground, has quite a bit of interest in how things in the Hole work. I guess having your colleagues slaughtered on arrival will do that to a person. But, as optimistic as I am, I'm having a hard time believing that he survived and miraculously found his way to the underground.

Cole and I creep silently through the streets. Our objective is to figure out where the records are kept and do reconnaissance for Roméo. Deep down, I'm torn about doing anything that delays rescuing Sutton.

The siren stops, and I realize I haven't really been paying attention. Deafening silence permeates the air. Cole holds up his fist. I stop in my tracks. He kneels in place with Zeus at his side. I hunker down beside him with Zeus at my elbow, panting and slobbering all over my pants.

"Ew, thanks a lot Zeus."

Of course, he licks my hand, and I give him a quick hug and kiss the top of his head.

"Hey, do me a favor and don't get hurt, okay?" I say to him. His wounds, luckily, have healed nicely, and there's no puss or drainage anymore.

And then something strange happens. A blaring sound of feedback, like that from a microphone too close to a speaker, deafens my ears. A voice, high-pitched and sharp, strikes me immediately.

"Miss Hamilton," the high-pitched voice says.

I stop breathing and cringe. It's Wilson. My hands grasp my gun tighter as I contemplate what to do.

"I want to personally welcome you back," the voice continues.

I suck in air, pushing myself against the wall of the cement building, using it to hold me up while looking around, left, right, up, and back at Cole, whose face slowly turns red.

"That bastard ... " Cole says. His jugular vein bulges from his neck as he looks around, his finger tense above the trigger of his gun.

"You have a decision to make. But let's think about everyone at stake here, shall we?" Wilson pauses and breathes into the microphone. "There are a few people left in your life that I know you care deeply for, and if you want the opportunity to save their lives, you will turn yourself in by midnight tonight. But, if you refuse, I promise you this: you will be hunted down, and I will stop at nothing to find you." He clears his throat and coughs. "And your refusal to surrender won't only cost the lives of the ones you love, but it could very well cost the lives of hundreds, if not thousands of Sinners, as well. Do you want thousands of lives lost when you could spare them all? Think about all the blood you could shed, Lexi Hamilton. And to everyone listening, the person who delivers Miss Hamilton to me, alive, shall be set free." He laughs, but I hear the vicious edge to his tone. "Oh. I almost forgot. There's one last thing. Sutton's clock is ticking. Soon his body will rot for weeks in the burning sun, just like your brother Keegan's did." And then, the microphone shuts off with a loud banging noise.

I'm stunned. My jaw hurts from grinding my teeth, and I have to tell myself to breathe to keep from screaming obscenities.

So Clayton was telling the truth. Wilson did have Keegan's body on display for days after his death. I want to rip out Wilson's throat with my bare hands. But now that he's promised freedom to Sinners, we have to be much more careful. We can't afford to let anyone we encounter live. The thought makes me ill.

God, why can't I be as merciless as Wilson?

But I can't be that way. It's against everything I've been taught. I won't leave Sutton behind. I won't fall for Wilson's lies. He'd never let my friends, Cole, and Zeus walk away alive. And they'd never agree to hand me over to save themselves. We just have to figure out a way to beat him at his own game.

Cole places a supportive hand on my leg, and I catch eyes with him. He shakes his head, his mouth set in a firm line.

"Don't you dare believe a word of it," he says. "He won't get near you; I'm not going to let that happen." Cole holds his gun ready, his jaw set in place, determination in his eyes. If he's not afraid, then I'll be strong too.

Wilson's words echo in my ears. I try to concentrate on the sound of our feet thumping on the ground. Zeus keeps a steady pace along Cole's side. But a small voice in the back of my head has me second-guessing every move we make. It's only a matter of time before they find us. We are outnumbered, outgunned, and malnourished, we have everything to lose.

We come to the intersection where, during the revolt, one of the squads branched off to go to the hospital and my team went to breach the Commander's headquarters. Even now, the memories seem so vivid, so real. My heart drums. I look right, the way I went before, but then Cole turns left. We're heading toward the hospital.

When I swallow, dust gets caught in my throat. It makes me cough and soon, I'm gagging. Cole stops when he realizes I'm not following him. Zeus loops back around and nudges my leg with his giant head.

"Lexi. Breathe. I'll get you some water. Breathe, dammit," Cole says and begins rummaging through his pockets. His fingers move fast as my eyes tear. He brings a canteen of water to my lips. I struggle to get it down between coughs. The cool liquid runs down my throat and washes away the phlegm. He puts a hand on my face. There is so much unspoken between us in that moment, it weighs me down. He doesn't want to say it. He would never say it. But the truth is, we are going to die. We are going to die, and Sutton is too.

A tear runs down my cheek. Cole wipes it away. He looks like he is about to say something, but then he closes the canteen and returns it to his pocket.

Zeus circles, feeding off Cole's energy. My body tenses, and Cole's goes rigid. *What's happening?* Suddenly, he yanks me into the shaded part between two buildings, slamming my shoulder into the wall. *Oh my God. What is happening?*

"What the—"

Cole puts his finger to my lips. He quickly draws his gun and then pushes Zeus's head behind him. Footsteps approach.

Judging from the uneven rhythm, it sounds like a group of people. Zeus's ears perk up, and he sits at attention. His eyes hyper-focus on the street, small woofs coming from his mouth.

Cole slams himself against the wall, sneaking looks around the corner. His finger stays ready above the trigger. I cut my eyes toward the source of the noise, my breath coming in uneven bursts.

"No stopping," a voice commands.

I don't hear a reply and can't see past Cole's shoulder. His stiff posture and the way he slowly backs away from the entrance of the alleyway tell me he's just as worried as I am. Why can't he be honest about how he feels? Why must he always put on a brave face?

"No, sir, please!" someone screams.

"Get back in line, or I'll shoot you. Your choice," the guard says.

"I'd rather die," the voice says.

"As you wish."

There's a gunshot and more screams. *What in God's name is going on?* I cringe away from the sound as moaning and crying replace the screams. I picture another lifeless body in the street and want to throw up. No matter how many times I've seen it, it doesn't get easier.

With his back still flattened against the wall, Cole turns his head toward me. His eyes are wide with adrenaline as sweat trickles down his dirty face, like paint dripping down a wall. His lips are pressed thin, his jaw tight. Once again, he says nothing, but instead turns back toward the entrance just in time for the people to come into view.

I suck in air.

Guards parade a group of about fifty Sinners, like stray dogs, through the street. As the Sinners walk, they stumble. Their eyes look tired, and their bodies look weak from malnutrition and disease. They're dirty, and their clothes are in tatters. Some bleed. Some of them weep as they walk, and others wear blank stares, eyes glazed over. The first guard leads and instructs them while the others surround the group and make them move faster.

"When it's over, you go back to your homes," he says in a demanding tone. He turns around and leads the sad group down the road. "You hear me? Straight home."

A face in the crowd flicks in my direction.

No!

I jump back into the shadows, sure she's seen me. My pulse races. I can't breathe.

I think I know that woman. I've seen her before.

Amber. It's her. It's unmistakably her.

One of the nurses I used to work with in the hospital, she looks like a shell of her former self. Bulging eyes stare out from a shriveled face. Her once vibrant hair lies limp down her back in thin strands.

I hold my breath waiting for her to scream, "She's there!"

But minutes pass, and the group continues down the street.

That was close.

I slide down the cement wall, letting my gun dangle in my hands for a short moment. My chest feels like it's on fire. Cole squats next to me and puts his hand on my neck, and for the first time, his touch doesn't comfort me. I push my feelings aside and focus on what's happening.

"We should follow them. See where they're taking them," I say.

"Medical records ... that's what we're looking for," Cole says. "We can't afford to get sidetracked. Besides, Wilson just increased his army by thousands by offering freedom to the person who turns you in. Now, instead of just guards, every

Sinner able to stand will be trying to take you down."

And he killed the last Sinner who could identify us. *He can't go around just killing people who happen to lay eyes on us.* Neither of us say anything for a few seconds. Wilson has changed everything.

"Look," I say, pausing to gather my thoughts. "Most of those people looked really sick. Maybe they were being taken somewhere that could lead us to information that could help Roméo." I push myself up and brush off my pants.

Cole removes his hand from my neck.

"Okay, fine. But if it gets too risky we're turning around." In that moment, I know something between us has changed because Cole stands aside and motions for me to take the lead. And for the first time in forever, I feel like I might be in control of my destiny.

I slink along the walls of the surrounding buildings, keeping the tail end of the slow march within view. *It's no wonder I don't see anyone if this is what they're doing to those who come out during the day.* And then I think about Amber and how she almost saw me. She looked like crap. *I guess even her plan to bribe the guards eventually fell through.*

And then we're there.

The Commander's old headquarters, where the transformation center was moved after the revolt, looms overhead to the left of the main gate. The entrance to the video viewing room changed into thick, cement double doors with guards at attention on either side. Cattle chutes line the outside, forming two lines, where people get separated—spouses, children, parents, lovers, and friends—males on one side and females on the other. Then the guards force the Sinners into

208

the building. Creeping into the shadows, I point the entrance out for Cole as Zeus sits by my side.

Watching them separate the Sinners into categories infuriates me. Bile burns in my throat. My hands clench my gun, turning my knuckles white. This is a completely new kind of evil.

Amber's figure disappears on the right side and through the new, heavy doors. After the Sinners are inside, some of the guards light up cigarettes or laugh and talk together.

What are they doing to those people? What is this place?

It's like the guards aren't human. Like Cole said he was in the past—solid and hard, without a conscience. Cole exhales in disgust.

Before I can gather my senses, Zeus darts out of our hiding spot and runs straight across the street.

What the hell?

I'm about to dive after him when Cole practically rips me back into place, his eyes flashing a warning.

"What're you doing?" I say with anger before checking both ways, making sure the guards haven't spotted Zeus. They haven't. Zeus stands, staring at a teenage boy while holding a flat, red ball in his mouth. When the coast is clear, I sprint toward them, despite Cole's attempt to keep me in place.

The young man's eyes turn to quarters and his mouth drops open as he stares at Zeus.

"The ball's my brother's," he says in barely a whisper. "Please, don't hurt me."

Zeus approaches him and drops the ball at his feet, whining.

Relief washes over the boy's face as he picks up the ball, never taking his eyes off Zeus.

"Thank you," he says.

Zeus ambles forward as the boy holds his hand out and gives him a quick lick, and then he nudges him into a dark entryway.

"Okay, you stay safe," the boy says. He catches sight of me and gives a small smile. "I'm glad you're here to help us."

Before I can reply, footsteps come up behind me, and I flip around. I raise my hand to my gun, but it's only Cole. He curses under his breath, and his movements are rigid as he draws closer.

"Halt!" I hear someone say.

Oh crap.

My eyes meet Cole's. He gives a darting glance toward the voice and turns back to me. His finger moves to the trigger of his gun, and I know exactly what will happen next. I duck my head, and Zeus covers me with his body. Just then, Cole fires three times.

Cole dashes into the space behind me, using the wall as cover.

"Go!" he shouts.

Zeus and I run together.

More shots ring out. Small spits of dust kick up close to us. I race between buildings, turning left, and then turning right. Zeus trails me, and Cole follows.

"Halt!" the voice shouts again.

But Cole drowns it out with the sound of his gun.

I don't look back to see if he hit the person or if they're still following us. I go until my legs can't carry me anymore. I run until I know we're safe. Somehow, we end up in an alleyway, where laundry hangs from clotheslines. Patched clothes, old sheets, and faded underclothing are slung carelessly over the thin lines. I sprint underneath, my breathing becoming heavier. My blood pumps through my ears. I turn to check on Cole and Zeus.

Next thing, I'm lying on my back, staring at a light-blue checkered shirt slung over my face. At first, I can't move. Then, I begin to thrash with my hands and feet. The tangled line catches, wrapping around the shirt and my head at the same time. I gasp for air.

Someone rips the shirt off my face. The thin line of laundry trails behind it. I squint into the sun as a dark head comes into focus. Standing over me is Zeus, staring down with a shirt in his mouth.

"Your timing is impeccable," Cole says. He rips me off the ground and shoves me forward. I feel slightly humiliated.

"Where are they?" I ask, trying to catch my breath. My head spins just slightly.

"Not sure. We'll hide in there."

He helps me through a doorway and into a vacant room. It smells musty. The cement-block walls are covered with a thin film of mold. I see a staircase in the far left corner, snaking upward to the next floor.

Zeus runs up with the old shirt still in his mouth, shaking it left and right. *Seriously, Zeus, you think it's alive?*

Cole looks around. Glass crunches under our boots with each step we take.

"We need to get to higher ground to see where we're at." We reach the stairs, and he waves me up behind him, scanning our surroundings as he leads.

The staircase opens up, and sunshine pours through the

hallway. The room upstairs resembles an over-crowded dorm room. Dirt and dust streaks the windows, but the glass remains intact. Zeus makes his home on the dilapidated couch, tearing at the cushions. Fluff springs from the overstuffed pillows.

My feet stick to the floor, and I look down at the filth grabbing at my soles. *Yuck.* Bunk beds line the walls, and someone's written all over the cement in bold, black marker.

As I read the writing, Cole says, "Only you'd clothesline yourself during a gunfight."

I turn to him and smile. He's right. If Keegan were alive, I'm sure the two of them would be having a good laugh at my expense.

He smiles for the first time in days then says, "Are you all right?" He turns me to face him.

"My pride's a little bruised, that's for sure," I say. He looks at me for a minute before letting go.

"I don't doubt that." He leans against the wall, peeking out the window.

I collapse on the couch, next to Zeus, and listen as he growls. A spring pokes my butt, and I jump. Part of me wants him to be able to act like a pup for once. It has to get old, being serious and on guard all the time, even though that's what he's trained to do. I reach across, whipping the pillow out from under his paws, and he grabs it with his mouth.

"You did a good job back there, buddy," I say to him. He snarls at the pillow and proceeds ripping its guts out. "That boy could've gotten himself killed."

"Those guards would've killed them both," Cole says. As he speaks, I notice the red rims around his eyes and the dirt caked on his face.

"Did you know them?" I ask.

He shakes his head and averts his eyes. If he's trying to pretend his secret isn't eating at him, then he's doing a poor job of hiding it.

The silence emanating from him bothers me so much, I can barely sit still. I am on edge. Nervous. Sick to my stomach. Angry.

I need to do something to take my mind off of our relationship and Wilson's threats. I get up and walk to the wall on the opposite side of the bunk beds. As I read the black ink, I'm shocked.

"Cole?"

"Yeah."

"Come here. You need to see this ..."

CHAPTER 17

Cole peers through the cloudy glass one last time, his hands loosening on his gun. He sets his gun down on the corner of the couch, carefully moving around the furniture as he makes his way toward where I stand at the wall.

"Who are they?" he asks, placing his palm against the cement blocks.

"Sinners ... like me."

"You mean, like us," he says in a firm tone. I tilt my head toward him but his eyes are glued to the names on the wall.

Mollie Bayberry, Gluttony.

Sam Buckwalter, Wrath.

Kelsey Miller, labeled Lust. I'll never be who they say I am.

I can totally relate to that.

Naif Gwinn III, Greed. Midwest. I lived in a bomb

shelter underground for five years with my family. When we came out, we were all accused by people we didn't even know. When they came for us, my parents fought the guards and were shot in front of me. I lost everything. I ended up in hell. But I met others inside and have survived living here for two years. I don't know how some days. I wasn't greedy before, but I would kill others for food now if it meant I'd make it one more day.

Kimberley Drajogvic, Lust.

Ben V. Shunnemaker, Pride. It's who I am.

My fingers shake as I strain to read all the names. Some of them leave messages related to their sins, others write just their names and brands. I can hardly believe my eyes as I take it all in.

Jerry Piagentini. I was born here. I don't remember my parents. I grew up on the streets, working odd jobs for guards to make enough to eat. I'll probably die here. Life is hopeless.

Kristen Dayspring, Lust. From High Society, formerly known as NYC. I was accused the night of my 18th birthday by my best friend. I had a party while my parents were away, and she was jealous of the gift her boyfriend got me. I liked him, I'll even admit to wanting him ... but it wasn't worth it. I never got to say goodbye to my mom and dad. If you ever meet them, tell them I love them.

"Did you know her?" Cole asks.

"No, I don't recognize the name."

Cole lapses into silence, and I wonder what he's thinking.

"After Keegan left, I wasn't allowed out much. I think my mom was afraid of losing me too."

"Huh, isn't that ironic," he says quietly.

"Yeah, tell me about it. Keegan forgave her for everything before he died … Sometimes I wish I could do the same. But I'm still angry with her for sending me here. How can I not be?"

"Lexi, you can't hold on to that anger," he says. "Trust me. You might end up doing something that later on you'll deeply regret. Forgiving someone who hurt you is hard as hell to actually do, but in the end, it brings you the kind of relief you need to move on. Like when you close a book, so you can open up a new one. I have no clue where that weird metaphor just came from." He gives a small chuckle.

I laugh at him. "Well, I can't bring myself to do that just yet… but forgiving also applies to forgiving yourself."

Cole's jaw twitches as my words silence him. He looks away, swallowing hard.

Suddenly, my mind flashes to a quote from the book Alyssa read before her death, *The Last Silk Dress*. It's in one of the scenes where the daughter, Susan, tries to rationalize her tumultuous relationship with her mother. The words come back to me, hitting me like lightning.

"And it was too late for me to decide that I could forgive her for anything. Or hope that she would forgive me. She didn't want my forgiveness. She didn't want me."

"It's no wonder Alyssa thought of me when she read that book," I whisper to myself. I wish I knew where it was now. I shake my head and turn to watch Cole, but he's completely caught up in reading the various stories written on the wall, his hand stretching out to one in particular.

"Hey," I say. Cole's head snaps up as he drops his hand

from the wall.

"Yeah?"

"Do you think there's anything here to write with? There's something I need to do."

He presses his lips together for a moment. "Let me see what I can find."

Cole's eyes jump around the room. Zeus lifts his head from the couch as fluff topples from his head. Everything's a mess. Blankets and clothing are tangled on the floor. Zeus has shredded the pillows beyond use. One of the end tables is overturned, and crudely made silverware is scattered around the living space in front of the couch.

"Here, found something," Cole says. He strides over to the corner of the room, flicks a quick glance out the window, and picks up a black marker. "How about that, sucker?" He flings it to me.

"Perfect, thank you." I catch it, unscrew the cap, and then I reach up to my tiptoes to find space for my name. Out of the corner of my eye, I see Cole watching me closely. I lean my head back and begin writing.

Lexi Hamilton, Lust. In love with Cole Veneti, a former guard. Falsely accused, but it no longer matters to me who they think I am. Brands don't define who you are, you have the power to decide that on your own. I might be damaged, but I'm not broken. Believe me, you can overcome anything short of death.

When I finish, Cole's waiting, holding out his hand. His jaw's set, and his brown eyes focus with intensity. I hand over the marker and watch as he easily stretches up and begins to write.

Cole Veneti, unbranded, but I'll be damned if I don't deserve to be branded with every one of the seven sins. Former guard turned resistance member with Zeus, the best dog you've ever met. Lexi Hamilton rescued me from the hellish life I was living. I'm sorry for the past, but I hope to redeem myself this time around. If we manage to band together and stop hating each other, then we can beat the system. NEVER GIVE UP HOPE.

He stands back, rereading his words, and I take his hand in mine. We don't speak, but I feel stronger standing here, just holding his hand. Just having him by my side blows my mind. Evil brought us together, but love makes us whole.

Someone nudges our hands, and I look down to see Zeus gazing up at us. I can't help laughing. Cole and I let go of each other, and I squat to Zeus's level while taking his face in between my hands and allowing him to lick the side of my face.

"We didn't forget you, you're part of our family," I say. Then Zeus burps, and I cringe away from his mouth. It smells like fish. "For that, I might just disown you, though."

"How about we go downstairs and take a look around?" Cole suggests. He picks up his gun and focuses on the mission again. "If it's clear of guards we should head back to the underground. As soon as we can."

"Cole, before we go, I just want to say you've already redeemed yourself ... I think you should know that." He lifts his eyes to mine, and the pain that radiates through them takes me aback. "Whatever secret you're keeping from me, you need to get it out, otherwise it'll consume you ... and us."

His posture tightens, and his hand flexes at his side. "Soon ... I promise, okay?" His shoulders slump as soon as he says it.

218

I wipe my hands on my pants and straighten my shoulders. He's right, we should go, but I hate not knowing what's eating him. If something happens to us, I don't want anything left unsaid.

Cole traverses the steps lightly and slowly. Zeus scampers down behind him, and I bring up the rear. Cole turns around and raises his eyebrows at me, waiting on me to follow.

I take one last look at the wall where we told our stories. It's in permanent ink—our commitment to each other and to the resistance. I can't help wondering what Sutton would think about our small band of revolt members being in the Hole. Or how he's holding up. Or if he's okay. Then I feel the building shudder.

"Cole?"

"Yeah?"

"Did you feel that?"

"Feel what?" he asks half-heartedly, poking his head out the doorway.

"The walls; they're shaking." I hop down the last step and put my hand on the wall.

"Well, that's never a good thing." He leans out the door as he scans the alleyway. The air's stagnant and heavy with moisture. Sweat pours off my forehead. "It's clear," he says. "Let's go."

I hear a sound like a thunderclap. "What is that?" I ask in a shaky voice.

Zeus barks, sprinting across the room toward Cole as our eyes meet in a moment of panic.

"Get down!" Cole says as he dives to the floor.

Dust and ash billow around us. I fall to my knees, covering

my head with my arms, pressed against the wall. Crashing and banging echo all around. When I try to breathe, my lungs fill with particles and dust, making me cough. My body trembles, but I can't move.

I brace myself as the walls come down around me. A slab of concrete lands next to my head, and I begin yelling. "Make it stop!"

The earth shakes beneath me, and I press my fists against my head. When it stops, I'm still squeezing my eyes shut. All I hear is the sound of my heartbeat thrashing in my ears.

"Lexi!" a voice yells.

I cough, twice, three times, and raise my head. A layer of gray ash covers everything. I pull my shirt up over my nose and try to breathe.

"Lexi, answer me," Cole says with panic in his voice.

This time, I shake my head, and I hear him clearly.

"I'm here," I say. "I'm all right."

I cough again, wondering what the hell happened. Slabs of concrete encircle me like a cocoon. The wall I crowded against is still standing, miraculously. I thank my lucky stars Cole's alive. We're both alive.

"Where?" he asks in a panicked tone. "I don't see you."

"I'm ... " I don't finish. *Where am I? Trapped.* "Against the back wall. I think." When my eyes come into focus, I reach out and touch the concrete that surrounds me. My skin is clammy, and I clutch my throat. "Oh my God. Get me out, get me out... Cole, please get me out of here!" It feels like the walls are slowly moving closer to me and soon I'll be a pancake. My heart pounds as a sharp pain shoots across my chest.

"Don't worry; I'll get to you," he says.

"I'm going to have a heart attack." I dig my nails into the back of my neck and clench my teeth so hard, I'm afraid they might break.

"No you're not. Close your eyes and just keep talking to me."

Zeus starts scratching away at the concrete that surrounds me. He whines and whimpers, and he moves all around. I hear him digging and breathing hard, trying to get to me through the pieces of cement floor.

"Zeus, good boy. Let's find our girl," Cole says, as Zeus continues to tear away the debris.

I retreat into the fetal position and cover my face with my hands. I swallow hard, only to gag on the dust ball that's stuck in my throat. It's an awful feeling. Gagging, gasping for air, and fighting the panic filling your lungs. I want to be brave. I want to be found. I don't want to die.

"Okay, Lexi, you have to calm down," Cole says. "I need you to help me out here. I know this is difficult for you, but try to think about me and not your fear."

My lips and chin tremble. I am starting to hyperventilate. "Get me out." I scrape my hands against the floor, and debris cuts into my skin.

"Working on it," he says. "Listen to me. I need you ... to open your eyes just for a minute, and see if you're able to move anything."

"Are you serious?" I ask, but it sounds like I'm blubbering.

"Yes, focus on my voice and do it."

"But what if ... "

"I'm not going anywhere without you. Even though you can't see me, I'm right here."

Opening my eyes, I'm immediately lightheaded. The room spins, and I see black spots. "I'm going to pass out."

"Oh hell no. Don't do that. Breathe, deep breaths … slow deep breaths. You're strong; you can do this."

My arms shake when I try to move a piece of cement; my muscles feel like jelly. I try again but with no luck.

"It won't budge," I say.

"It's all right," he says in a not-so-calm voice this time. "Just give me a minute to think. There's no need to panic."

"Too late."

I run my hand down the wall, and sweat makes my fingers slip off. Ash covers my arms and hands, making a thick, filmy layer on my skin. I taste the thick, dry paste coating the inside of my mouth. *Yup, here we go. I'm going to puke.* I turn and heave, but only saliva-thickened ash comes out. *That's new.*

I pull my legs to my chest and rest my forehead on my knees. I hear Cole moving chunks of concrete. But then I hear someone or something moving around on the other side of the back wall. The movement stops.

"Cole," I say through my clenched jaw.

"Yeah?" he asks, slightly muffled.

"How long?"

"Not sure," he says.

Out of the corner of my eye, I notice some of the rubble moving in one little area, and then Zeus's paw breaks through.

"Zeus."

I scoot forward and reach out to touch him, wrapping my hands around his paw. His pads are rough, almost like sandpaper, and his nails are worn down to almost nothing. He whimpers, and he doesn't pull back his foot, almost like he knows I need a paw to hold on to.

"Not good." Cole grunts, and I hear something scrape across the floor. A giant crashing noise follows. "Damn it," Cole says.

"Now what?"

"I'm not gonna lie," he says. "This might take a while."

I say nothing in response. Zeus whimpers, and I hold on to him. On the other side of my prison, Cole's feet drag back and forth. I imagine he's working as fast as he can, but from my end, nothing looks like it's opening up. I close my eyes and hum a tune to calm my nerves.

Pretty soon, I notice it's getting darker. The sun is setting. *How long have we been here?* I try shifting my position, but my tiny cell doesn't allow me to stretch out my aching legs. I lick my lips, but my tongue's dry and scratchy.

"Cole?" My voice comes out raspy.

"What?"

"Can you hand me your water?"

"How?"

"Through the hole Zeus made."

"Huh? Zeus made a hole?"

"Um yeah, I've been holding his paw."

"What the heck? Why didn't you tell me?" He sounds exhausted. I'm furious with myself for needing to be rescued.

"I figured you knew."

"How would I … Never mind. Hold on. Zeus, move your paw." But Zeus growls at Cole as he pulls his paw out of my hand. "Geez, controlling much? She's mine too, you know."

I picture Zeus lowering his chin to his chest, but keeping his eyes on Cole. He does that when Cole annoys him.

Cole's bloody hand comes through the hole, and he grabs my fingers.

"Thank God," he says as he gives my hand a squeeze. I don't want to let go. "If you want water, I need my hand back."

"Sorry."

"Here." He shoves a small canteen through the slit. It's warm going down my throat, but it takes the pasty crap with it.

"Thank you." I push it back through the hole, and immediately Zeus sticks his paw back through so I can hold it. "Any progress?"

Cole's silent at first, and I bite my lip. "I'm going to die in here, aren't I?"

"No," he says.

"I'm gonna lose it soon." Sweat pours down my face, back, and chest. I feel warmth throughout my body, and my ears burn.

I rest my head back on the wall and wait for it.

"Look what's here," he says.

Keegan places his palms against the tall bureau and pushes it along the wall. The knobby legs wobble as it catches on the carpet in his bedroom. A small, wooden door appears out of nowhere.

"Wow, when did you find it?" I ask.

"Just last night," he says. Keegan bends over, putting his hands on his thighs, catching his breath. "The door's stubborn

as nails, but I eventually got it open. It takes you to the hallway, near the fire escape."

"You snuck out?" I ask, my voice squeaking at the end.

"Shhhhh," he says and quickly locks his bedroom door before returning to jam open the secret passageway. I peek inside, noting the thick cobwebs through the darkness.

"Are you going to tell Mom?" I ask.

"No," Keegan says. He shoves the door back into place and levels an intense look at me. "Don't tell anyone—Mom or him—no matter what. No one but you and I can know it's here. It's our secret, okay?"

"Okay," I say.

"Promise."

"Keegan, I promise I'm not going to say anything."

"Good." He runs his hands through his curly hair and takes a deep breath. "Look, if things get real bad, you can escape through here."

I lower my eyes and fiddle with my hands. The fact that Dad's gone and we moved to High Society is bad enough. But I can't even begin telling Keegan about the burning sensation in my arm or how our Stepdad shuts me away in the closet when Keegan's not around.

"Lexi, answer me!" I hear Cole's voice yelling at me, and I'm back in the cement trap.

"Sorry, I didn't hear you," I say. My arm tingles with pins and needles, and the memory lives fresh in my mind. I shift my legs as much as the space allows.

"What do you mean you didn't hear me? I was screaming," he says.

"I blacked out, and I had a flashback."

225

"Well, no more of that. You scared me."

"It's not like I can control them … "

"I know. I'm sorry. Okay, let's keep talking, maybe that'll help. What was the flashback about?"

"Nothing significant, just something from my past," I say, shrugging it off. I can't admit how the clarity of my memories seems to be coming back. Like I was in a fog for years. A shiver runs down my spine, and I grasp my arms.

"Such as?" he asks.

"Keegan showed me a way out of High Society." My voice catches.

"Really? Is that how he got away?"

"I guess so."

"Are you sure these flashbacks are real?"

"I'm not sure. Sometimes they're foggy, but this one I remember clear as day. I'm actually hoping one of them will give me a clue as to why Wilson wants me alive. Or maybe just help me understand how the hell I ended up here."

We're silent for a while. I think Cole has stopped digging. Zeus is panting.

"Mind if I ask you something?" I ask.

"It depends on what it is." Cole resumes throwing chunks of cement.

"Your parents. What happened to them?" I ask. Cole sighs, and then he's silent. "You don't have to tell me if you don't want to, I was just curious."

"No, it's all right," he says. "I don't mind telling you." His voice sounds serious. "My mom was a good woman." He breathes hard, and I can't imagine how tired he must be. "She worked hard and loved me and my father. But when I got older

226

and she didn't need to take care of me, she spent all her time with my dad. So that's when I started doing my own thing."

"Like what?"

"Wrestling. And not to brag, but I was really good. I kicked everyone's ass, hard-core."

"Oh my God. I'm picturing you wearing that lovely outfit right now, and I have to be honest … it's not really a turn-on." I laugh so hard my chest burns.

"I made that thing look sexy; all the girls who watched me wrestle never complained."

"Okay, trying to make me jealous isn't a good idea right now."

"I figure you can't punch me through the walls."

"Smart-ass," I say.

"Don't worry. I wasn't interested in girls back then. Wrestling was my life."

"I want to hear more about your parents."

"Well … my mom got really sick, and my father wouldn't leave her side."

"What was wrong with her?"

"Not sure. We couldn't afford to take her to the doctor," he says in a flat, monotone voice. "So when the guards recruited me, I joined without hesitation, because I knew the money could help my mom."

"Wow, really?"

"Yeah, why?"

"I don't know. I thought maybe you wanted to be a kick-ass killer or something."

He laughs wryly. "Not so much. Just wanted to compete in wrestling. That was as far as my aspirations went at the time. I

227

was not a diehard fan of the regime."

"But that's amazing, what you did for her, for your family," I say. "Did she get better?"

"No. It was too late. She passed away shortly after I joined." He clears his throat and takes a drink of water. "And then my father committed suicide."

I'm shocked into silence until I cannot hold back.

"Oh no, Cole." I reach my hand through the hole, and he grasps it, twisting the ring around on my finger. "I'm so sorry." I fight back tears, just imagining the pain he must have felt losing both his parents the way he did.

"So you see, when I read your ring's inscription, I believed it because I've lived it," Cole says. His voice breaks, and I hear him sniff.

"If she were alive, I have no doubt, she'd be really proud of the man you've become." I squeeze his fingers.

"I hope so ... because I wasn't always the man I should've been. When my parents died, I let anger consume me. I didn't care that what I was doing was wrong or that good people were getting hurt or killed."

"Making mistakes is part of growing up. You're a better man than you were before, and that's what matters," I say.

He laughs weakly from the other side of the wall. "Here you are, stuck in a partially collapsed building, giving me a pep talk." He locks his fingers with mine.

"What would you say to your dad if you could?" I ask, often wondering what I might say to mine if he were still alive.

Cole clears his throat. "I'm not angry with my dad anymore, because now I understand why he did it." Cole pauses for a minute and takes a deep breath. "When you love someone as

228

much as he loved my mom, you can't possibly go on living without them. And for all intents and purposes, I belonged to the regime, to the Commander. I was lost to him. I get that now."

"What made their love so strong?" I ask.

"I was just a kid myself, so I can't really say. But if I had to guess, it was that they always supported each other and talked about everything."

"So, they didn't keep secrets from each other?"

"No, and I know where you're headed with this … "

"Cole, come on. You know truth is the foundation for every relationship," I say. "And I remember when you were angry at me before for not telling you the entire truth about my stepdad." I hesitate, wondering if pushing Cole now is the right thing to do. "You said, 'What is a relationship if we can't trust each other?' And now, here I sit, waiting for you to open up to me."

"I'm afraid to tell you," he says, his voice breaking.

"Why?" I ask.

"Because it's going to break your heart."

All I want to do is look him in the eyes and read every expression on his face. Instead, I have only walls with soft moonlight filtering in through the cracks.

"Tell me. Please, I can handle it."

"Lexi, I—"

The sound of footsteps cuts him off. Zeus growls.

"What are you doing in my building?" a male voice hisses.

CHAPTER 18

I whip my head around too quickly at the sound of the voice. Dizziness sets in as I try to figure out what's going on based on what I hear. *"My building."* It's certainly not a guard. A guard would shoot first and ask questions later.

"We're stuck," Cole says.

Their footsteps circle each other. They must be eyeing each other up and down as they talk, evaluating whether or not it's safe. Zeus growls, planting himself near the small hole. I try to look through it, but his giant body blocks the view.

"Well, I guess I have you to blame for them bringing my building down." The man seems angry but pensive.

"Why are you wearing lab clothes?" Cole asks.

Lab clothes? Why would Cole be so worried about what the man is wearing? I'd be more worried about his weapons.

"What's it matter to you? And get that gun out of my face;

there's no need for it," the voice says. "And by the looks of it you're not stuck. So get out!"

"It's not me that's stuck," Cole says. "And I'll keep my gun where it is, for now."

"Then who is?"

"Do you work in the lab?" Cole asks.

"Why do you care?"

"It's not a tough question—yes or no?"

"I do."

"So you work for Wilson?"

"Not by choice," he says. "I despise that asshole."

"Can you tell me what's going on in there?"

"Why would I tell you anything? Talking to you can get me killed."

"Because I need ... we need your help."

"I'm not sure I can help you."

"I bet you can. I need to know about experiments being conducted there. Can you tell me about that?" Cole asks.

"Experiments?" The person sighs with frustration.

"Yes. I need to know what kind of experiments are being conducted on Sinners in the lab. The lab where you work," Cole demands.

"We give them shots. They take them. Some get sick. Others don't. That's all I know. You honestly think Wilson would expose his secrets to Sinners?"

"No, I guess not," Cole says.

"So would you mind explaining to me why you are in my house?"

"We needed somewhere to hide," Cole says.

"Look, I know who you are," the voice says.

I suck in a breath and bite my lip. All he'd have to do is call the guards, and we'd be screwed. There's no way I'm getting out of here without help.

"You can't stay here. Your presence has done enough damage." They're both silent for a few seconds. "But I'm willing to help you get her out. Now move so I can take a look at the wall."

I hear feet shuffling. Zeus barks. "Easy there, killer," the man says.

A few minutes pass, and I hear things being moved around. "Yeah, she's jammed in there all right. Let me see if I can round up a few buddies to help."

"No way," Cole says.

"Do you want her out or not?"

"Yes ... " Cole says. "But why do you? For the reward?"

"No," the voice says. "I do shit work all day, every day. It'd be nice to do something good for once."

"Why should I believe you?" Cole asks.

"All Wilson does is lie. He's not going to reward anyone for anything, and I'm not about to give the bastard what he wants."

"Do it," I say. "Get me out of here, please."

"Hello, Lexi," the person responds.

"Hi," I say to the man. Cole peeks through the hole, and I whisper, "God, I hope he's a man of his word."

"That makes two of us," Cole says.

A few minutes later, more feet enter the room, and Cole jumps up. From the sound of Zeus's nails on the floor, he's pacing and sniffing all around.

"Wow. You have a lot of friends," Cole says.

"Not everyone is loyal to that imbecile," the man says.

People begin moving chunks of cement and whatever else fell through the ceiling. Everyone talks in whispers as they shuffle around. I press my back to the wall as the dust rises again.

"Here goes nothing," a voice says.

I hear a collective grunting and then feel a breeze hit me in the face. Twelve pairs of eyes peer back at me as I count six men holding up the gigantic piece of cement that was covering me. I climb out of the space as they drop it on the floor. Dust poofs upward.

"Thanks, guys," I say hesitantly. Two of them smile, but the others frown. Their figures tower over me, and they're better fed than most Sinners in the Hole judging from their healthy coloring. All of them have facial hair with beards of varying lengths, but even that doesn't hide their brands. Three orange brands for gluttony, two black for sloth, one green for envy. The one branded green smiles shyly. It strikes me as interesting that the other smiling man has no brand at all.

"It was nothing," the unbranded man says, stepping forward. I recognize his voice as the man who first discovered us here, in his house.

I take a good look at him and offer to shake his hand. Cole instinctively steps to my side. I notice the man hasn't even removed his lab coat yet.

"It wasn't nothing to us," Cole says. "Thank you."

"What's your name?" I ask the man.

"Hank."

"Nice to meet you, Hank."

"And it's nice to meet you."

"Hey, by any chance have you heard anyone in the lab mention the name Sutton?"

"Yeah, actually I have. If I recall correctly, they have him working in the medical part of the lab. But I've never seen him."

"He's working? In the medical part?"

"I don't have a clue what goes on behind those doors, none of us do."

"Do you ever see any of them, coming or going?"

"They don't ever leave; they sleep there."

"But they have to let them out at some point, right?"

"No, they don't. We hand them cylinders via a pass-through, but we never get to actually see them."

"Oh, okay. What's in the cylinders?" I ask.

"Lexi, we need to go," Cole interrupts. "Thank you, Hank." He whistles to Zeus and signals for me to follow him, even as my legs feel like they are about to give out.

"You're welcome," Hank says.

"Wait," I say, limping along behind Cole. "If you see Sutton, tell him I'm here and that we're working with Roméo." Hank gives me a funny look. "He'll know what it means."

"I'll do my best, but I can't guarantee anything," he says.

"Thank you so much, and take care of yourself," I say.

"And you do the same. Whatever you do … don't let Wilson catch you."

Cole shakes Hank's hand. He practically shoves me through the doorway and into the alley before anyone can say another word. I have to rub my eyes to believe what I'm seeing.

In the darkness, I see the silhouettes of bodies moving about on the street. I guess the guards don't grab Sinners for the labs at night because I see more now than I ever did during the day. Cole rubs his chin and rocks on his feet at the crossway.

Do we go right or left? I'm unsure. I rub my arms as a chill shoots through me. The shadowy figures of Sinners moving about the street unnerves me in a way I can't explain. It's like watching skeletons wade past in a sea of death. The whites of their eyes gleam in the moonlight. I hear screaming and clasp my gun tight.

A woman streaks out of a doorway close to us, causing me to jump in my skin. She's lucky I don't shoot her. My hands shake, and my heart thumps in my ears. In her hands, I see a small piece of bread.

Cole jerks to a stop as another woman, slight of build, stalks down the first and punches her. A feral look covers her face as she bares her teeth and narrows her eyes. She lands a thundering punch, and the first woman goes down to the ground. The second one plucks the bread from her hand and shoves it into her ravenous mouth. Only then does she see us.

I freeze. She squints. Then she scampers back into the dark entrance of the house. I feel queasy. Moving around in the darkness will only get us so far. Pretty soon all of us, including Zeus, will be easy to identify.

Cole maneuvers through alleys and over trash, inside a concrete jungle of gutted houses and crumbling buildings.

The pungent smell of feces mixed with tepid water, sweat, and the burning stench of old blood seems to penetrate us everywhere we turn. I wrinkle my nose. No matter how many times I inhale it, it never seems natural.

It's taking longer to get back to the underground, and for a moment, I think we're lost. The timid light of the sun is creeping up toward the horizon when I tap Cole on the shoulder. He looks behind him and holds up his fist. Zeus's lips curl up, and he stands rigid. I freeze in place.

"Turn around," Cole says.

"What?" I ask.

He shoves me back behind him, but in my confusion, I stumble to the side. His hand catches me, and he looks me directly in the eyes. His voice comes out in a desperate, pleading whisper.

"You don't want to see this."

I wrinkle my forehead and push his hand off my shoulder.

Zeus's ears stand straight up, and his hair raises as he lets out a low growl. Something's not right. I glance around Cole.

The crude wooden stage's stark outline settles against the pink of the morning light, taking my breath away. I blink back the memory of Claire and Mac, executed for loving each other just a few months ago. This is the exact place where I witnessed their murder at Wilson's hands. Cole tried to protect me even then.

Now, the faces of the people gathering around the stage wear tightly pressed lips and fearful eyes. I can't stop myself from clenching my fists in anticipation. Outside of the staging area, even more Sinners congregate, and guards stand at the edges, patrolling with their weapons raised. As much as I want to run the other way, I'm more curious. I take a step toward them, but Cole's hand catches my elbow.

"No," he says. I yank myself away from him. "We're not chancing it."

"I have to see what's going on," I say.

I push my hair around my neck and face, and slowly

236

edge toward the crowd. Cole grunts behind me, but I can't stop myself from moving toward the large group of people. If something's happening, I want to know what it is.

I can't tell exactly how many people have shown up, maybe a hundred or more, but I find an opening at the rim and work my way in. No one seems to notice since their eyes are all glued to the stage. Their whispers carry though, and I can't ignore them.

"First execution since ... " a voice dies off.

"When they brought Keegan's body here, that was the last time he showed up in person," another voice says. I watch as the person leans over to her neighbor. "And they stripped him of his clothes; it was a sad sight."

"I hear he was bloated as a balloon by the time they ... "

"Wonder who they're bringin' in this time. Must be somebody important."

Bile burns its way up my throat, but I force it back down with a hard swallow. I attempt shuffling to the right. I don't want to hear anymore. But the words ring painful, dangling in my ears despite it. My heart feels like someone's ripped a hole through it.

Suddenly, an SUV pulls up in a cloud of dust. The brakes squeal to a halt. Every guard around the perimeter stands ramrod straight and salutes. Usually, a musical anthem would play, but not this time.

I press my lips together and feel my muscles stiffen. The crowd goes silent. The people seem to cower in place, lowering their eyes. It's hard to swallow the lump in my throat when I hear the loudspeaker on the SUV turn on.

With a bang and a groan, the driver jumps out and opens

the back door. A shorter man steps out, his face turned down and his posture rigid, while the driver drags a crumpled figure out of the backseat.

My heart stops.

A hand rests on my shoulder, but I cut my eyes toward the vehicle, noting the familiar gaits, the heights and temperaments of the people exiting. My hands feel clammy. I turn back to see who's touching me and find Cole off my right shoulder. He grits his teeth and stands completely stiff.

The shorter man climbs up onto the stage first. The sun rises behind him, forcing me to squint. I've been up for days, and the rims of my eyes burn like acid. The Sinners seem to inhale one collective breath as the crumpled figure is pulled across the stage and forced to kneel.

He looks up, and his green eyes catch the light. His gray hair is all but replaced by tufts of white. His hands are tied behind him. The bloodstained lab coat he wears hangs off his fragile figure, and his pants look five sizes too big.

Suddenly, I want to scream.

Sutton.

No. No. No. Please, God, no. I gasp. My feet move before it even registers. I push people aside and attempt to swim through the mass of bodies separating me from him. *He doesn't even know I'm here!* I'm breathless. My heart races as I try to push my way through.

Cole snatches me back, jerking me to a halt as Sinners glance my way. *What the hell?* I give him a dirty look and am tempted to pound him with my fists. I rip my wrist away as he grabs me back with his powerful grip, wrenching me to my senses.

238

"Hold still." His voice comes out in a hiss.

This is my only shot! He's right there! I have to save him!

Before anyone recognizes me, the loudspeaker blares to life. The shrill voice on stage steals my attention. Guards file in behind the short man.

"You all know this man, but you might not recognize him," Wilson says. He delivers a swift kick to Sutton's broken body, and it takes everything within me not to cry out. My hands cover my mouth, and I bite down on the skin of my palm, drawing blood.

Sutton's head snaps up as he absorbs the pain. He falls forward onto his hands. For a moment, I don't think he'll get back up. *God, please help him.* His jaw tightens before he pushes himself back up, the Adam's apple in his throat bobbing up and down.

My stomach wraps itself into knots. I step backward for a moment, clutching my core. This isn't the first time they've roughed him up by the look of the cuts and bruises all over his face and neck.

As the sun breaches the soulless, dark walls, Sutton's eyes wander up to the clouds, and I wonder who he's thinking of, or if he's praying like me. I glance around quickly, trying to come up with some sort of plan, but there are too many guards and they'd see me before I ever reached him. Unable to use my gun, I stand helpless in the face of pure evil.

"The mighty Dr. Sutton. The untouchable brother of the Commander," Wilson says. He gives a thin, wicked smile. His eyes turn into slits. "He led the revolt against his own brother, leading insurgents and ingrates to their death. But now he bows to me."

Wilson winds up and delivers another kick with the toe of his heavy boot to Sutton's side. Sutton grimaces as he collapses to his right, his hands flying to his ribs. The crowd is deathly silent as Sutton's rasping breaths fill the void. As the light flows across his face, I take note of the way his hands tremble.

"Ms. Hamilton, if you don't turn yourself in within forty-eight hours, I will kill your precious Sutton. Right here on this stage." Wilson spits on Sutton, who still grasps his ribs. I recoil with disgust and horror. "I will pluck out his eyes. I'll rip out every individual fingernail. You will watch as I make him suffer." Wilson's high-pitched threats draw me in. All I want is to kill him. I can't stop my hands from clenching and unclenching.

Then Sutton's head rises. His eyes meet mine, and they widen with shock or fear. He shakes his head back and forth ever so slightly. He's losing weight, and his hair has turned white seemingly overnight. But the very force of his stare makes me stop.

I need to save you.

"No," he mouths.

You're the only father I have now.

"Leave me," he says. He coughs, and I watch as he grimaces.

"I can't," I whisper.

He mouths something else.

"What?"

He peeks at Wilson, who drones on about ruling the Hole and bringing Sinners in for "check-ups." He's so caught up in himself that he doesn't notice Sutton communicating right in front of him. He paces to the far left of the stage.

240

But then a guard, who's staring at Sutton, stops to glance in my direction, squinting; I duck behind a man in front of me, and slowly, I look over his shoulder as the guard turns back to Sutton.

"Get … records," Sutton mouths.

The guard swings back around, and I duck again, praying he doesn't see who Sutton's trying to talk to.

I bite my lip. I know exactly what he said this time, and my shoulders slump. Even if I don't stand a chance at rescuing him with all these people around, I can't bear the thought of leaving him. Not like this. Not in the shape he's in.

"You work for me!" Wilson shouts.

He punches Sutton's face. Blood pours from the corner of Sutton's mouth as he lies on the platform, spitting and coughing. A squeal escapes from my mouth. Everyone looks at me. Wilson glances up. His eyes scan the crowd as he motions for his guards to search.

Sutton's sea-green eyes plead with me from afar. *Leave me*, he's begging, but I'm having a hard time breathing.

"Go!" he yells this time.

"Find her," Wilson orders loudly. "She's here."

It's a trap.

I shuffle backward, and then slowly attempt to phase out of the crowd. The guards push their way through as the people around me begin shoving and screaming. Their bodies block me from finding my way out. All my blood rushes to my ears. I pull my gun out from my waistband and grip it as I dive into the sea of arms and legs. I can't see Sutton anymore. Or Cole. Or Zeus.

Gunfire rakes the crowd, and I slam to the ground. Now,

everyone's clamoring, and people claw at the dirt to get away. I'm like an animal, covered in dust, on all fours, as bloody flesh scatters in bits around me. I feel the splatter of blood on my face, but I keep going.

Wilson's yelling over the banging of the gunfire. As I get to the edge, a guard turns toward me, pointing the muzzle of his gun at my chest. My hair hangs over my neck, but his eyes widen when they meet mine.

I'm screwed.

He reaches up to signal to his men, but before he can, blood pumps from his chest. He's been shot. I launch myself forward onto my feet and sprint away from the cacophony surrounding me.

Next thing, Cole's behind me, firing off shots. His M4 bangs away in bursts of three. With his support, I focus on what's in front of us, my nostrils flaring as we bolt down the street, through alleys, and push our way through shacks that topple onto each other like dominoes. Guns burst behind us, chewing up the dirt, but they don't follow for long.

Soon, all I hear is the faint sound of guns and screams. Everything within me wants to go back, to rescue Sutton and kill Wilson, but that's not what Sutton asked of me. I can't stop picturing the way he pleaded with me to go, the way his green eyes stood out against his swollen, broken skin. I stumble to the side and heave. When I begin running again, Cole's waiting for me, his face bloodied and tight.

I wonder where Zeus is, when he hops in front of me. His haunches appear out of nowhere, yet a bone dangles from his mouth. I slow to a jog and examine him. His fur's matted with blood, but he's not wounded. I squeeze my eyes closed and then stop. He sits and looks up at me, the bone hanging from his teeth.

I want to barf. Again.

Even Cole stops. He leans into a crevice in the walls, and I hear him getting sick.

The bone's not a ham bone at all. It's not even an animal bone. The bottom half has flesh hanging off of it. While I gag on my own spit, I reach out to him. He whines and dances in a circle. Bits fly off, landing in the dirt.

"Zeus, drop it," I say. My voice breaks.

He drops the bone on the ground, and my hands fly to my mouth. The bloodied flesh lands with a splat as the bone rolls inches away from my dirt-laden boots. I kick it away, afraid of losing my entire stomach if I look at it again.

"No!" I say. "Leave it!" Zeus hangs his head, and his tail droops. I watch as he backs into a wall and lies down with his head in his paws.

Cole's head pops up, and he looks slightly green. He glances toward Zeus and then back at me, but he says nothing. Judging from the creases on his forehead, he's worried. He fingers his trigger and looks eagerly at the street.

I'm too afraid to talk. Every muscle, tendon, and ligament in my body is wound so tight, I can barely flex. Yet I can't stand still. I bounce on my feet. I'm ready to get the hell out of here.

A movement catches my eye, and my insides twist. My hand automatically goes to my gun as the hairs on the back of my neck feel electric. A few feet away, a female in the street stops and stands up straight. I think she's looking at us, but I can't tell. Then she starts walking toward us.

Cole puts his hand on my wrist and shoves me behind him. Zeus bares his teeth, and I hear a slow, deep rumble from within his belly.

"Cole?" the voice asks.

No freaking way is this happening.

Her voice sounds familiar. It's coy, and as she comes closer, I see the auburn tint of her hair in the sunlight.

No way. Not now.

"Amber?"

"I knew it. I knew I saw you." She smiles, and some of her teeth are gone. Her stringy hair wafts in the breeze, and her bony hands stretch out to hug him. He shakes her hand awkwardly instead. I can tell by her eyes she's hiding something, and I don't like it. Zeus woofs at her, and she steps back, the smile fading from her hollowed cheeks.

"Looks like I've got my ticket out of here," she says.

CHAPTER 19

The siren blares. Amber won't stop staring at us with her gaunt eyes, a mischievous smile playing at her lips. If I wasn't in such a rush to get out of here, I'd smack it off her face.

Cole stands in place, not showing any emotion, and I wonder what he's thinking.

She's got us, and she knows it.

"It won't be long now; they're on their way," she says.

"Amber. You're insane if you believe Wilson, of all people, would actually let you leave here," Cole says.

She steps closer, smirking at him. She's so skinny, I could snap her in half. She's definitely not the girl I remember. And yet, she's bloated, her arms swollen, and she scratches at her skin.

I scrunch up my face, struggling between feeling pity and

swallowing down the bitter taste in my mouth that comes with seeing her. She's never been a friend of mine, not since I was assigned to the hospital and forced to work with her.

I guess not much has changed.

"Still looking for the easy way out, aren't you?" I ask.

"Whatever it takes," she says with a sneer.

"Won't work. Not this time," Cole says.

As his brows pull down and his tone lowers, I notice other people around us seem to disappear, scrambling for their hiding places. In the background, the sirens scream their warning.

Zeus woofs at my side, and I put my hand on his collar. If he pounces on Amber, she might scream and bring attention to us.

"Now, we run," I say to Cole.

But Amber steps in front of him, blocking our way. I narrow my eyes at her and clench Zeus's collar as he stands on his back legs. My grip's slipping. Amber's eyes are glazed over though, so she doesn't even flinch at his imposing posture.

"Oh, no … you're not going anywhere," she says. Her face is flushed, but she's not sweating.

"Right," Cole says. Just then, he swings the butt of his gun up and grunts with the impact.

His gun connects with her jaw, and she crumples to the ground. My mouth opens wide, but Cole's already on the ground, scooping Amber over his shoulder. He stands, and her arms flop around behind him.

"Let's move," he says.

I don't have time to ask him why he's taking her with us. Heaven knows we can't carry everyone that recognizes us. I pull Zeus along and sprint through the streets and alleyways.

246

Every time I check over my shoulder, Cole is right behind me with Amber, like a limp rag doll.

"Left," he says.

I check around us and turn left. "Clear!"

"The alley, four blocks up, on the right," he says.

By now, I hear him huffing slightly in between words. She can't weigh much, but then again, he's running with her over his shoulder, plus carrying all his equipment.

Zeus tags along beside me, his tongue hanging out, like it's the best thing in the world. Whenever Sinners see him, they back away, leaning back into the shadows. I can't really blame them.

The static from the loudspeakers fills the air again, the output making me cringe. We stop for a moment. I catch my breath as Cole hunkers down next to me, propping Amber's body against a wall. The siren stops abruptly. I hear Wilson's loud breathing, and it makes me shudder with disgust.

"Beginning today, Sinners will not receive rations," Wilson says.

Feeling the effects of shock, I turn toward Cole. His lips are curled, and his eyes hold a hardened, flinty expression. I can't stop myself from thinking about those poor people fighting over the small portions of water and food they had. *It's only going to get worse.*

"But of course there's one exception. If you capture any of the revolt members, you'll receive food for one month. If you deliver Lexi Hamilton, alive, you'll be given your freedom. Happy hunting, citizens." The speaker cuts off, but not before I hear his cruel laughter on the other end.

"He's going to starve them?" I ask.

247

"Yes. Wilson plays mind games. He knows you care about people. He's trying to find a way to break you."

I cannot wait for the day when I can push my knife right through his throat.

With those few words, Wilson just upped the ante. Zeus lets out a low whine, sensing my apprehension. He nudges my leg, and I pat his head.

"Stay strong. And run," Cole says as he hefts Amber over his shoulder once more. I don't know how he has the strength.

Now, my head's really on a swivel. I probe every darkened corner and every shadow. I take note of every possible exit for future reference. My muscles feel tense as I pass the next block. I hesitate, second-guessing each move, before crossing all entrances. My senses are on overload.

I hit the fourth block and turn right into the alley. I slow my pace and feel the burn in my lungs and the stickiness of my hair on my neck. My sweat beads on my shins and slides down my legs.

"Here," Cole says.

I stop, and Zeus sniffs around as Cole lowers Amber's body to the ground. He barges through a doorway and drags her inside. And we're back where we started.

"And you brought her, because?" I ask, stumbling around until he flips on his flashlight.

"She was in the lab today. Maybe she knows something." He picks up her body with a grunt and motions me forward. "When she wakes up, Roméo can interrogate her."

"Good thinking, but after that blow, we'll be lucky if she knows her name." I'd laugh, but my body's too uptight. The knots in my neck would take a rolling pin to push out.

248

He gives me the flashlight, and I shine it down the tunnel and back into the underground. With each step, my feet sting and my eyes burn. I don't feel safe until I see Grace's wide eyes and outstretched arms. She grabs me tight and hugs me like it's the last time she'll see me.

"Oh thank God, I thought something happened to you," she says. "When you didn't come back last night, we thought the worst." Her eyes drift to Cole with Amber draped over him. "Who is that?"

"A witch," I say.

"I second that," Cole says. He places her body on the floor. Her head flops awkwardly to the left and rests on her shoulder. He touches her forehead with the outside of his hand. "Her name's Amber. She worked with Lexi at the hospital." He looks at me. "Her head feels warm."

"Well, yeah, you did knock her out," I say.

"Why'd you do that?" Grace asks.

"Oh, just you wait. You'll want to knock her out yourself."

"Lexi, I'm being serious here," Cole says.

I walk over to Amber and touch her arm. It *is* warm. When I do the same thing as Cole, the heat from her skin radiates into mine. "She has a fever."

"Great to have you back, bro," Bruno says while running toward Cole and pulling him into a man hug. "I was about to call in the cavalry." He slaps Cole on the back and smiles.

"Welcome back. Did you manage to get any information?" Roméo asks. He appears from behind Bruno, his smaller stature hidden by Bruno's towering figure. His voice is quiet, but very serious.

"Actually, yes. Turns out Bill was right," I say.

"Ah-ha, yes, I knew it!" Bill says. "I'm awesome. Go on and say it. 'Bill, you're the most brilliant man alive.' Do it; go on."

"Bill, your wisdom has left me breathless," I say while rolling my eyes at him. "Anyway, they were escorting Sinners to the lab. After a few hours, they came out and were ordered to return home."

"When they left, did you notice anything different about them?"

"Not really, if anything … maybe a little confused?" I say.

"Amber"—Cole points to her lifeless body—"was part of the group. Thought maybe you'd want to question her," Cole says to Roméo with a nod in his direction.

"That, and she was trying to turn us in," I say with a frown. I watch as Roméo strokes the cleft in his chin and lowers his eyes for a moment.

"By the looks of it, she didn't come willingly," he says. I glance at Cole, and he shifts on his feet. "Unpleasant people are always a pleasure to work with," Roméo says. He grabs at his collar, pulling it away from his neck. "Lexi, is it too much to ask for you and Grace to stay with her? When she wakes up, let me know."

"Sure," I say. "Oh, wait." Their eyes turn back to me. "We saw Sutton." Everyone stops and stares at me.

"How?" Roméo asks, breaking the silence. "Was he all right?"

When I try to answer, nothing comes out.

"Definitely not," Cole says. "Wilson beat him publically, trying to lure Lexi in."

"Guess that means you didn't get to chat," Bruno says.

"He did … mouth to me … to get the records," I say.

"Are you sure that's what he mouthed, Lusty? Because reading lips isn't a skill we all have."

"Yes, I'm sure of it."

"Poor Sutton. Where was he?" Grace asks.

"The execution stage," Cole says. And I don't miss the look that passes between him and Bruno. Bruno's body tightens, his shoulders arching upward.

"Also … " Cole says.

"More good news?" Bruno asks, but he's not smiling. His fists clench at his sides.

"Wilson took away the daily rations."

"Here comes the zombie war," Bruno says.

"But on the bright side of things, we have food down here, so we aren't gonna starve." Bill seems pleased with himself as if he personally collected all the food.

"This mission just got a whole lot harder," Bruno says. "They all know what Lexi looks like. How are we going to hide her? It was bad enough that people outside the Hole were fed wanted posters and notices every hour. Now, people inside the Hole will be hunting her too."

"You're not hiding me anywhere. There's no way I'm staying down here while you guys are up there. Plus, it's not just me; they know all of us, except Roméo. And I doubt they know Bill's with us."

"Have you got anything good to tell us?" Bruno asks. "You're like the harbingers of death."

"Sorry, man, not a damn thing," Cole says.

"I'm going to grab some things; mind if I take Zeus with me?" Bill cuts in. I twist my head in his direction, confused.

251

"For what?" I ask.

"Company."

"If he'll go with you, sure," Cole says. "Just make sure he gets water and something to eat, please."

Zeus follows Bill down the dark hallway, and I turn around toward the others. Roméo leaves the room. Cole hands me a protein bar and water, but he says nothing. Whatever hovers between us isn't going away.

"Why don't you boys go get some sleep? Lexi and I can handle this," Grace says.

"No, you two rest first," Cole says.

"I can't ... too much on my mind," I say. "Really, please go sleep." Selfishly, I'm looking forward to some time alone with Grace.

"Okay. But only for a few hours."

"All right."

"Promise you'll come and get me if you need anything," he says to me.

"Of course."

Grace and Bruno hug and say they love each other, while Cole and I stand in awkward silence.

After they leave, Grace puts down two tan towels right next to each other, a good three feet away from Amber. She sits down and pats the other one for me to join her. I plop down, untie my boots, and place them behind me. The smell of soggy socks and wrinkled feet fills the air. I snort, but Grace says nothing about the aroma. For a few minutes, we sit in silence as I rub my throbbing feet and stretch my cramping muscles. Grace leaves for a few minutes before coming back with more water. She snacks on some nuts. It's deathly quiet except for her munching.

"This room's so uplifting, don't you think?" Grace asks, her attempt at humor.

"More like depressing." We both laugh.

The only light is from the propane lamp Bill somehow managed to find. It lets off an eerie glow, making Amber's hair almost bronze. My mind runs away with me. I wonder how much time we have left down here. How much time we have left at all. And then I think of Sutton. We are all on borrowed time.

"Maybe you should paint it."

"For her, not a chance. Besides, she is *not* staying."

"She's that bad, huh?"

"You have no idea."

"Well neither of us knows her story and what she's been through. Maybe we should give her the benefit of the doubt. Under her layer of hardness, she might be weak and hurt. I've come to realize cruel people are the ones who tend to hate themselves the most and treat others like dirt in order to make themselves feel better."

"Maybe you're right, but it's something I can't relate to."

"No, you, my girl, are an exception. I admire you," Grace says.

"Why?"

Amber begins to stir, and her head drops to the side as drool drips down her chin.

"Ew, I hope I don't do that in my sleep," Grace says.

"Zeus does."

I smile at her, and she puts her arm around me.

"With everything you've been through, you still carry

a heart of gold. It would be so much easier for you to be miserable and mean. But not you; you've taken the hardest route possible."

"Which is?"

"Forgiveness. It's one of the hardest things for us to do. To actually be able to completely forgive and move on, not many are capable of doing that."

"I'm not so sure I've done that."

"Oh, but you have, dear," she says. "Bruno told me about Keegan leaving you, and how much he hurt you, but you forgave him. Someone taught you how to forgive, no?"

"My father." I lean my head over and rest it on Grace's shoulder. She rests her cheek on me. "He always said, the stronger forgive those who hurt them. When you hold the anger in … all it does is tear you down and cause you to be vulnerable. And believe me, I still struggle with it every single day. Between my stepfather, my mother, and Keegan … I haven't fully wrapped my head around my mom and stepdad yet, so don't give me too much credit. Abandonment and torture aren't things you forget. But I find when I'm focusing on them, it takes me away from what I have today. Cole, and you guys. You're my family now." But I can't hide the way my voice quakes when I say Cole's name.

Grace pauses and then says, "Are you two all right?"

I shift uncomfortably. I'm not really sure. "We're okay, just working through some things."

"You don't sound convinced," she says. "If you haven't noticed, I'm pretty good at reading people, and I can sense the tension between you."

"That obvious, huh?" I sigh. "I know he loves me, but he's

keeping something from me, and I wish he would just spit it out."

"Patience, dear. When he's ready, he'll tell you. Try to understand we're not guards and we'll never be able to comprehend what they've been through. Plus, every relationship has its highs and lows. Bruno and I definitely have had our lows."

"Really?"

"Oh yeah." She laughs. "For a while, I thought I'd never meet a girl he hadn't dated. But that was my own insecurity I had to deal with. He's never given me any reason to doubt him. Not once. But we've definitely been through a lot in our two years together, and I have no doubt you and Cole will make it through this too."

Amber starts twitching, first her eyebrows, and her mouth, followed by her hands, and now almost her entire body. She flaps around like a fish on dry land. She moans but doesn't open her eyes.

I gasp.

"Help me, Grace; she's having a seizure. We have to protect her head and try to hold her down."

Grace does exactly what I ask her to do, and I kneel down, resting my butt on my heels so I can place Amber's head on my legs and hold it still. As soon as my hands touch her face, I yank them away.

"She's burning up," I say.

"What should we do?" Grace asks with panic in her voice.

"To the showers. If we don't get her temperature down, she'll keep seizing … and possibly die." And like a soldier carrying a wounded man, I get behind Amber, giving her a bear hug and locking my hands across her chest, as Grace grabs her legs.

We lift her up.

Amber's thrashing, and sweat drips down my neck. Her body's like a sauna. Her head rolls to the left and then to the right, then front and back. I tighten my hold on her because she's getting harder to control.

"I'll open the door with my back," I say. Luckily, it's not a door with a knob, or I'd have to drop her.

Grace nods, eyes wide.

Slamming my back into the door, it swings open, and my adrenaline races.

"Okay, open a stall, start the water, and let me know when it's lukewarm."

"Why not cold?"

"Cold water only cools the skin, and shivering would just cause her core body temperature to spike."

"How do you know that?"

"Luckily, I paid attention to the nurses when I worked in the hospital."

I kneel down as Grace lets go of Amber's legs. She goes into the closest stall and turns the knob. Brown water spits through, but eventually it starts dripping nearly clear water.

"While it's warming up, can you grab some towels? They're in the corner cabinet by the sinks."

"Got it," Grace says.

Amber's still seizing, so we have to work fast to remove her clothes and get a steady stream of water to lower her temperature.

Grace comes back with an armful of towels.

"Oh, that's perfect."

"All right, just tell me what to do."

"Okay, fold one, and when I lift her head, put the towel underneath." Grace follows my instructions.

Lowering Amber's head to the ground, I kneel down, sitting on my heels, and hold her head in between my thighs.

"Good, now sit on her hips, face me, and hold her arms down."

Grace breathes hard and her arms shake as she holds Amber down. I draw my knife and hold my breath as I begin to cut Amber's shirt down to her midsection.

"This time, sit on her shins facing away from me, and yank her shoes and socks off."

As Grace does this, I hear a gurgling sound. I look down, and Amber's about to heave. Scooting back, I hold her head with just my hands now and turn it to the side as she vomits. The smell of curdled milk sickens me. I force the bile burning in my throat back down and notice Grace gag.

"Breathe through your mouth and try to get her pants off."

Amber continues to puke. Grace sits on her thighs and unbuttons her pants, and then she moves backward, still sitting on her legs, pulling the pants further down with her.

"Amber, can you hear me? Open your eyes. I need you to open your eyes for me!" I say. But she doesn't.

"I'll check the water," Grace says.

Using my pointer fingers, I pull open Ambers eyelids and see her eyes have rolled back into her head. Using the towel next to me, I wipe the sweat off my face and neck. My tongue's dry, and my muscles ache.

"It's ready," Grace says. "I put towels down to cover the

257

floor, hopefully it'll be a good enough cushion."

"Good thinking." I smile a weak smile.

We pick her up the same way as before. I back into the shower, getting drenched, and slide down, leaning my back against the wall. I spread my legs apart, and Grace hands me the towel for under Amber's head. I allow her head to rest on my pelvic bone and hold it with my trembling hands. Grace sits on her legs and gets wet as well.

"I don't want you getting cold," I say.

"I'm fine; I'm just praying this works."

Suddenly, I hear a loud banging noise. Fearing the worst, I reach for my knife, but something streaks through the bathroom so fast, I don't have time to react. Not far behind, Bill follows, cursing up and down about something I don't understand.

"It's loose!" he says. "Take cover!"

CHAPTER 20

A huge, dark animal of some kind darts across the floor and hides behind the lockers. Its nails on the floor sound like nails on a chalkboard.

"Bill, what the hell was that?" I scream. Grace sits frozen in place, unsure what to do.

"Fantastic! It worked. I knew it!"

"What are you talking about?" I ask through gritted teeth.

"That there was Zeus," Bill says with the biggest smile painted across his face. "And you didn't even recognize him."

My jaw drops to the floor, and I'm about to get up to beat Bill's ass. Grace sits and stares, and Bill smiles like a lunatic. I want to slap him.

"What did you do to him? If you hurt him, I'll kill you, Bill. I swear on my life. I'll kill you."

"Oh, Lusty, relax yourself. He's fine, just a bit embarrassed,

I think."

"Zeus," I say. "Come here."

He pokes his head around the metal lockers with flattened ears and sad eyes.

Grace and I still hold on to Amber who seems to be doing a little better. Her body only twitches now, no more flailing.

Zeus slowly makes his way toward us with his head down and his tail between his legs. The darkness of his fur makes it hard to distinguish him from the shadows around him.

"Turn on another light," I say to Bill. "Now."

Grace quickly throws a towel over Amber to cover her.

"Geez, you're very demanding." He laughs as he walks to the light switch. "One. Two. Three. Here we go."

At first, the bright light causes me to squint, but after my eyes adjust, my nostrils flare in anger.

"He's gray! No wonder I can't see him." Zeus is so dark, it's hard to make out his black mask. My muscles tense, and I glare at Bill. "What'd you do to his fur?"

"Dyed it with hair coloring."

"You're unbelievable." I shake my head at him because there's not much else I can do at the moment.

Cole and Bruno storm into the bathroom with worry etched onto their faces. I'm sure they heard my blood-curdling scream.

"What happened? You all right?" Cole darts right past Bill and doesn't even notice Zeus. But Bruno does. He cocks his head to the right and to the left before he laughs. Cole's eyes lock on mine, and he scrunches his forehead waiting for my reply.

"No, I'm not all right." I point toward Zeus. "Look what Bill did to him."

Cole spins around; his back straightens as he makes his way toward Zeus. Zeus whines and runs back behind the lockers.

"He's black?" Cole asks.

"No, it's actually dark gray," Bill says. "But the lighting down here sucks, so he appears much darker."

"Bill dyed his fur," I say. "And now Zeus is embarrassed and keeps hiding."

"What did you do that for?" Cole spits at Bill. "He's not your dog."

"Camouflage."

"Come again?" Cole furrows his brows at Bill.

"Damn ... you're good," Bruno says to Bill.

"Stay out of this," Cole snaps at Bruno.

"You know, man, being darker could actually save his life," Bruno says. "Think about it. He doesn't stick out. He blends in."

"Bruno, sometimes I like you more when you keep your mouth shut," Cole says.

I open my mouth to say something, but nothing comes out. My words get stuck in my throat, my lips parted.

Cole glances at me while pointing at Amber. "I'll deal with Bill later. What's going on with her?"

"She started seizing because her temperature got really, really high."

He lifts his eyebrows at me. "Lexi, you're a good person. Do you realize that? That girl wasn't nice to you ... ever, yet here you are, taking care of her."

"She's still human, Cole. Besides, she was just jealous of us."

Cole smiles his crooked smile, and his dimples make my

heart ache for him, for the person I know he is.

"Would you mind turning the water off for us?"

"Sure, no problem." He turns the knobs, stopping the flow. "I'll grab towels and clothes for the two of you."

"Oh, that would be wonderful, thank you," Grace says.

"There are three of us," I remind him.

"Can't you cover her with a sheet or something?"

"Hey, try to be nice."

"That is being nice." He walks toward the lockers and goes around to the back to comfort Zeus. But the next thing I hear is Cole in hysterics.

"I'm sorry, Zeus. Really I am ... but you look ridiculous, buddy."

"He looks like he's been rolling around in a pile of ashes. He looks geriatric," I say.

"Even better. They won't expect his big bite," Bruno says.

"Okay, boys, would you mind leaving us alone so we can get dressed? Please?" I add.

Bruno and Bill leave, but Cole stays.

"I'll carry her back for you," he says.

"I'd appreciate that, because at this point, I'd be dragging her."

After I get dressed, I retrieve a red t-shirt that matches Amber's hair and meet Grace in the hallway. She looks tired, with dark circles forming under her eyes.

"You should get some rest," I say, walking back to where Amber lies. "Let's get Amber dressed quickly, and you can go lay down. Put her arms in the shirt first, and then we'll pull it over her head."

"Okay," Grace says.

First, I pull Amber's wrist through the arm hole, and then, in unison, we move up her arms. As they flop around, I can't help feeling bad for her. She doesn't make a sound, and her eyes remain closed as I manipulate her enough to center the hole of the shirt on her head. Then I glance down at her shoulder. My stomach plummets to the ground. I let out a cry.

"Cole, come quick," I demand.

"What?" He crouches next to me, and I point to what I just found.

Grace takes a quick look. "Please tell me that's a bruise," she says.

"Definitely not," I say. "It looks like she was injected with something; you can still make out the needle stick." I squint and examine the area around it.

"What's with the black ring around the injection site?" Cole asks.

"I don't know. Hurry up, we need to show Roméo."

Cole scoops Amber into his arms, I help Grace to her feet, and we take off down the hall.

"Zeus, let's go," I say. When he comes into the light, I chuckle because he really does look like he was rolled in soot.

"I better grab something to eat and drink," Grace says. "And I can get Roméo on the way if you want."

"Sure. Can you please grab something for me to eat too?" I ask.

She nods. "Of course."

After Cole puts Amber to bed, he sits next to me on the floor with his legs out straight. He pats his thighs, and I go to him. I sit sideways so I can bury my face in the crook of his neck. He wraps his arms around me and strokes my hair.

something. He sighs in obvious frustration.

"Would you like me to sketch it for you?" I ask.

"She's good," Cole says. "Really good."

"The United Powers needs to see what the injection site looks like. Make sure it's as detailed as possible. Can you do that?" He turns to me and scrunches his forehead. His eyes are bloodshot.

"Sure."

He hands me his pen, and it slips out of my hand. *He's sweating too. He's nervous.*

I hold the pad of paper with my left hand and bend over to pick up the pen. I step toward Amber. She's breathing fast, but her body's placid.

"Here's a chair." Cole places it right behind me, and I take a seat.

"Thanks."

"You're welcome."

"Oh, wait. Are there any pencils?" I ask Bill, who's leaning against the doorframe, looking as perplexed as the rest of us.

"Yes, I'm sure of it. I'll be right back," he says.

While I wait for Bill, I steal another look at Amber. Her sharp nose and narrow face look the same, but different, like years have passed since I last saw her, instead of months. Her coloring is tinted the yellow of a sunflower.

I touch her forearm. It's cool and dry. Taking a closer look at the mark on her arm, I try to figure out what causes the black ring. It can't be dried blood under her skin, and I'm not sure, but I doubt it's a hematoma. My mom had one once after she fell down the stairs of our High Society apartment. She was heavily medicated and slipped, causing her leg to turn variations of black, purple, and blue. It took weeks of rest and lots of ice for it to finally go away. But this doesn't remind me of that. It's too perfectly round to be anything unintentional. I wonder if it's safe to touch. I want to see if it changed the texture of her skin in any way, but I pull my arm back and decide it's smarter to wait and see what Roméo has to say.

"I even found colored pencils. How lucky is that?" Bill asks as he enters the room.

"Maybe if I was drawing a rainbow."

Bruno chuckles, and it's a welcome sound.

"Hey, maybe not right now, but you might want to later, so I figured you should have them."

"Thanks, Bill. That was nice of you."

"No problem."

Holding a pencil in my hand feels so familiar that it comforts me. I place the tip down on the paper and get to work. I look up frequently and study the area before working on the next piece, shading in the area and making sure it's precise. The ring is about the size of a silver dollar. I look from my drawing to Amber's skin and compare the two over and over. I decide it's perfect when I can't tell which one is real.

"Okay, I'm done." I hand the pad and pen back to Roméo, who inspects my rendition, lips pursed.

"Remarkable. I'm impressed."

"Thank you."

"She's about to throw up," Grace says.

"Grab a bucket or something—anything—towels," I say.

We're too late. Amber sits up and proceeds to vomit all over the sheet in front of her. Instantly, the smell reaches my nose, and I smash my hand over my face to prevent myself from getting sick as well.

Bill rushes in with a bucket and shoves it under Amber's face. She wraps her arms around it and continues to heave. I've never seen anyone throw up so much at one time. She's not even coming up for air, for breaks. Her face remains in the bucket, and I glance at Roméo, who's writing away in his notebook.

"I'm out of here," Cole says. "Your puke is one thing, hers is not."

"Go, I've got this." I stand and move from beside Amber so I can take Cole into a hug.

"Uh-huh."

"I'll see you in a bit."

"Please be careful around her. We don't know if what she has is contagious or not."

"I will." I pause, thinking about Amber possibly being contagious. "Do you think you can find something to change her into? I want to get rid of these vomit-soaked clothes."

"Okay." He touches my cheek and kisses my lips quickly, and I want nothing more than to curl up in his arms and sleep.

He breathes deep and lets me go. Cole motions to Bruno, and they both take off. Grace stays behind looking putrid herself.

When Cole's out of sight, I focus on Roméo. Amber's still throwing up, although I'm pretty sure she's just dry heaving at this point. I'm so grateful her fever's gone, enabling her to sit up on her own, because I don't want to get any closer to her. The copper tips of her hair look like they've been dipped in vomit. She tries to wipe her face but succumbs to another round of heaving. Her shoulder blades pop forward each time.

They look so thin and frail, devoid of the liveliness she used to possess.

"Why ... won't ... this ... stop?" she asks between heaving. I glance at Roméo, who drops his head and stares at the floor. His pad dangles at his side, and his fingers are clenched white around it.

"Amber, it's Lexi."

"I hate you," she says, pulling her head out of the bucket and turning toward me.

I raise an eyebrow. "What else is new?"

"Get away from me," she says. She sounds like she's been smoking for fifty years.

"Excuse me, Miss Pissy," Bill says, "but Lusty saved your life. So show some respect."

Our mouths fall open as we all turn toward Bill. He shrugs.

If Amber was strong enough to fight, I'm betting she'd jump out of bed in an instant.

"She's making me sick on purpose." Amber slams her head back onto her pillow, staring at the ceiling in exasperation.

"Amber, you're a piece of work," I say.

She picks her head up and wipes her mouth with her forearm. "What's wrong with me? Am I dying?"

My eyes wander toward Roméo, who's still taking notes.

"Maybe," he says without looking up.

Dang.

"Excuse me!" Amber says in her nasty tone. *Here she comes.* "What kind of shitty answer is that?"

Roméo glances at Amber and folds his hands in front of him. I admire his ability to maintain composure, because I already regret helping her.

269

"Hello?" Amber spits. "Are you deaf? I'm talking to you." Her face falls back down, and she proceeds to empty her gut.

"I see that," Roméo says.

Amber coughs before lifting her head. "So answer me."

"I already did."

Oh, I like him.

"'Maybe?' That's your answer?"

"Precisely."

"All of you get out."

"You don't give the orders here," Roméo says, towering over Amber. "It would be in your best interest to get rid of that attitude of yours. We're the only ones here who can help you. So take some time to process that."

"Jerk-off, who the hell are you?" Amber asks.

"All right, everyone out," Roméo orders. "Lock her door. She'll be screaming for help soon enough."

"No, I won't."

"We'll see."

Bruno and Cole arrive with the change of clothes and more towels just as Bill, Grace, Roméo, and I exit the room.

"Oh shit. She's dead?" Bruno looks disappointed.

Bill shuts her door and shakes his head. "She's fun."

"Told you," I say.

"You don't need the change of clothes?" Cole asks, as if he had to run a marathon and sacrifice his firstborn to get it.

"Not right now. Roméo here is letting the princess stew in her own juices. See how she likes it," Bills says with a snicker.

"Now we talk," Roméo says. "Let's go to my room."

Once inside Roméo's room, we stand nervously, waiting to hear his diagnosis.

None of us sit down. Instead, we lean against the wall, and Roméo sits on his bed with his head in his hands. He takes a few deep breaths and runs his hands through his slick, sweaty hair.

It feels like minutes pass while we wait for the monitor to speak, to tell us something. And then he opens his mouth.

"Before I tell you anything, I need to know I can trust you. All of you."

"Are you kidding me?" Bruno steps forward slightly. He looks like he is about to pounce on the guy.

"We're risking our lives by keeping you down here," Cole says. "We could have just delivered you to Wilson."

"Then why haven't you already?" Roméo's tone is sharp, surprising.

No one speaks at first.

"Because Sutton trusted you," I say, trying to push back tears. "He believed in you. He thinks you can put an end to ... all of this."

Roméo shakes his head. "Sutton. Sutton was a romantic, a fool."

"What did you just say?" I ask.

"How can you say that?" Grace adds. "You don't even know him."

"I know a fool when I see one."

Just like that, something snaps in me, and I go right for his throat.

CHAPTER 21

I'm in a rage, hot, sweaty, and determined to choke the life out of this bastard. Thoughts fly to a broken Sutton face-down on the stage as Wilson kicks him in the ribs. Sutton trusted him. He trusted that if he could just make the monitors see what was happening, that everything would change, that they would put an end to the regime. Sutton believed, and I will not allow this man to belittle him, to make him out to be some hopeless idiot.

"Whoa, whoa, whoa. Hang on a minute, Lexi." Cole pulls my left arm back as Bruno pulls my right. I'm off the ground, suspended in air, feet kicking in the direction of Roméo's head.

"What's wrong with you? Let me go!"

"If I let you go," Cole says, "you need to promise me that you are going to calm down."

My heavy breathing and racing heart bang in my ears. I am

all adrenaline, emotion, and limbs. Huffing, I charge toward Roméo again, my left arm somehow slipping from Cole's grasp.

"Oh, no you don't." Bruno grabs me around the waist and pushes me back toward Cole as the two of them hold me in place.

"We need to hear him out, Lexi," Cole says calmly in my ear, loud enough for everyone in the room to hear. "If he says or does one thing I don't like, I will personally take him out." Cole shoots a threatening look his way.

"And I'll help," Bruno adds. "In fact, it would be my pleasure." A smile crosses his face. I think Bruno truly enjoys messing with people.

"Okay. I promise. I will hear him out. But that's it. I don't owe him anything. His next breath is not promised to him." I have no idea where all this is leading, but I resolve to listen to what this stranger has to say. Unconvinced, Bruno and Cole keep a loose grip on my arms.

Roméo stands and begins to pace the room. He sighs heavily and then begins to open up. "Look, I understand this is personal for you, but I'm here to do my job, and it's not about saving Sutton." I grumble in response. "Let me explain," he says. "The United Powers has been monitoring activity in the Hole ever since Sutton first made contact. Apparently, years back, Wilson, under the direction of the Commander, had a strain of virus made that was undetectable and lethal. He's been working on it for some time now, trying to come up with just the right strain of the virus that will not only be contagious enough to infect others, but also so lethal that the human body doesn't have enough time to fight back or make antibodies. Sutton suspected he was testing it on Sinners."

"Oh my God," Grace says.

"Are you saying he's using them like human lab rats?" I ask, relaxing my arms against the strain of Cole and Bruno.

"That's exactly what I'm saying. He also mentioned the dark circle that forms around the injection site. So, yes, Amber has been infected with what could be the newest strain."

"But how do we know this is true?" Cole asks. "There have been rumors for years about a Sinner's sickness. No one really put much stock in it."

I look at him. He's never mentioned a Sinner's sickness before. I feel queasy.

"Let me be clear. When Sutton came to us, he clearly had humanitarian ideals in mind. But, from the outset, the United Powers' first and foremost concern was protecting ourselves and our allies from a biological weapons attack. Our goal is to stop the manufacturing of this virus. And, if we cannot do that, then to find a cure or a vaccine for the virus, without which millions of people could die."

"My God. You aren't here to save us. You aren't here to stop Wilson. You're here to save your own ass!" I lunge for him as Cole and Bruno pull me back again. I curse and scream at them. Don't they realize what is happening?

"So your mission was basically to get samples of the virus?" Bruno asks.

"Unfortunately, yes. But I'm told he hasn't perfected the virus. He was trying to make it airborne. It seems he is still injecting it into people. And, frankly, how contagious it is or isn't at this point is questionable."

"But we've seen people in the streets who look like they're on their last leg. We touched those people." Grace places a

274

hand on her stomach. She looks like she may hurl.

"Unless you exchanged bodily fluids, you are okay. And even then, it all depends on how long they've had it. They may no longer be contagious. From what I can tell, an infected is only contagious until the fever sets in. So if Amber had a fever when you brought her in, then I don't believe she is currently contagious."

"How do you know so much about contagious diseases?" Grace asks.

"I am the former head of Infectious Disease Control and Education for the United Powers."

"Oh that's great!" Grace sounds relieved. She comes to my side. "He's really smart. That's a good thing, don't you think?"

I nod.

"So now that you know it's happening, will the United Powers send in forces?" Bruno asks.

"Not yet. They won't send in any troops until they know for sure that's what's happening. They only have Sutton's theory to go off of, and unfortunately, that's not enough for them. They want solid proof. And frankly, they may hold off until news of a vaccine or cure is found. They won't risk more lives."

"But the lives of Sinners are okay to risk?" I ask, my chest puffing out again. "People are dying."

Roméo looks at the brand around my neck. Something I can't figure out crosses his face. Disgust maybe? "A few convicted criminals dying is of little consequence."

"Convicted? These people are merely accused. All it takes is for someone to say a person looked at them the wrong way, and that person ends up here, branded, like Lexi—falsely accused. There is no trial. No jury of peers. No conviction. Just

275

a brand and the worst kind of prison imaginable," Cole says.

No one speaks. Roméo hardly bats an eyelash. Oh no. He knows. He's known all along. The Hole and what happens here—he already knew and doesn't care one bit.

I slump backward into Cole's and Bruno's arms. I'm going to faint. My eyes move from side to side, my lashes flutter. I'm getting hot.

Cole, Bruno, Grace, and Bill speak to me at once. I can hear them, but it's muffled. Their words sound like drums beating against my ear. I'm weak and nauseous. I want to lie down.

Bill smiles at me, concern on his face. He places a cool, wet towel on my forehead and holds it there as Cole and Bruno bring me to a sitting position on the ground. I'm acutely aware of how embarrassed I am. As I settle against Cole's shoulder, everything goes black.

My lids flick open. They're still here. I glance around for some indication as to how long I've been out. Now, I'm lying down, wet cloths on my head and neck, and Grace holding my hand.

Bill, Cole, and Bruno are actively engaged in a conversation with Roméo that sounds even more heated than before I passed out.

"You okay?" Grace smiles down at me when she sees I'm awake.

I don't respond. Instead, I listen to the men talking.

"When the Commander first built the Hole, he funneled

276

every cent into the lab. Now we're seeing the results of years of that research and development. I suspect the first Commander had his reasons, mainly experimental, maybe even to gain some control over the Sinners. After all, there are far more Sinners than soldiers. But the second one, Sutton's brother? Judging from what I'm seeing here, his reasons are far more diabolical," Roméo says.

"One bad decision led to another," Bruno says.

"Lunatics," I say and slowly sit up. "But it makes sense." I mean, I remember tidbits of conversations between Father and others about lab experiments, but I never imagined it'd look like this. My stomach knots itself into a pretzel. I recall one conversation clearly now.

"There've been rumors of mass rapes and beatings," his friend had said. *"Keep your children inside. It's not safe out there anymore."*

"I know; I'm afraid it's only going to get worse," my father had replied. *"Yet somehow, they manage to cover up most of it. I'm not sure we'll ever know the full magnitude."*

"Have you heard anything about the lab testing—?"

"Shhh! That's enough. We need to take this conversation somewhere else," my father said.

I shake the memory away.

"So what prompted the United Powers to care? I mean, why now? Sutton is convincing and passionate, but there must be a reason you guys were sent here *now*," Bruno says.

Anger flashes through Roméo's eyes as he turns toward Bruno.

"About six months ago, a Sinner crossed the border into Canada. We're not sure if he was sent by Wilson or if the man escaped. But he was deathly ill by the time he was taken to the hospital. When he died, they performed an autopsy, and it confirmed he died from an unknown virus. Medical professionals have never seen anything like it before, and the only reason they know it came from the Hole is because the man had been branded. So when they heard Sutton's theory, it immediately caught their attention. But they're demanding solid evidence, and until they get it, the United Powers will watch from afar."

"Sinners don't escape," Bill says. "Before the rebellion, not a single person got out. So Wilson had to have sent him. Right?" It was the most intelligent thing Bill had said since I'd known him. We all stared at him in disbelief.

"It's certainly a possibility," Roméo says. "But we can't know for sure."

"Makes me wonder what the Sinners are being told when they're injected," Cole says.

"There's only one way to find out," I say. "I'll be right back." I stand, a bit shaky, and then steady myself before sprinting down the hall back to the room Amber's being held in. I unlock the bolt, open the door, and shut it behind me with a click.

Amber's curled into the fetal position at the top of her bed in the one spot not saturated with her vomit. The smell of rotten eggs, milk, and rancid meat swirls around the room, causing me to almost pass out again. I pull my shirt over my nose and move toward her.

"Wake up," I say.

"Get out," she replies.

"Not until you answer my questions."

"Go to hell."

"This is serious, Amber," I say through gritted teeth. "Why'd you get a shot today?"

"It's none of your business." She sits up and looks at me with bloodshot eyes. She swings her fists, but she's so weak it's like being hit with a feather. I grab her wrists with ease, holding her until she's too tired to fight me.

"Tell me."

"Let go of me!" she screams.

"Answer me." I grasp her wrists harder. My hands completely encircle them, she's so thin.

"Ahhhhh! A vaccine," she blurts out.

"For what?" I ease up just enough to let her know I'll stop if she keeps talking.

"For what's killing us. But you wouldn't know about that, would you? You're healthy. You look like you're one bagel away from High Society."

I don't look nearly as malnourished as she does, but still, I don't remember the last time I ate real food.

"You were told it was a vaccine?"

"Yes." Tears drip down her face.

"What else did they say?"

"That it was up to us if we wanted it or not, but they only had a hundred of them."

"Did everyone with you choose to get vaccinated?"

"Why wouldn't they? Who wants to die from that?"

"And you didn't know they'd force you to go get the shot either way?"

"No, why would I assume that?" she asks, her voice incredulous.

"Was there anything else they had you do?"

"No."

"How about your information—did they write your name down?"

"Yes." I release her wrists, and she flops back down to her pillow. "This is ridiculous."

The door opens, and Cole stands there, pinching his nose. "You get everything you need out of her?"

I nod in his direction and then turn back to her and say, "I'll be back to get you cleaned up."

"No, wait! You know something don't you?" Her voice dances on the edge of panic, and she speaks quickly, trying to grab my arm as I move back.

"I have to go."

"Bitch. I answered your questions." She narrows her eyes at me.

I leave the room and bolt the door, and Cole pulls me into his arms.

"Until we know everything about this virus, I'm not comfortable with you being around her."

"She's not contagious anymore; you heard Roméo."

"Still. She's evil."

"Evil or not, she's dying. And I'm not like Wilson. I won't leave her in there to rot away in her own filth."

"So let someone else take care of her."

"Yeah, like who? Bill?"

"Why not?"

"You're joking, right?" By the look on his face, I know he's not.

Back in his room, Roméo is writing with his right leg

crossed over his left, tapping his right foot in the air.

"They were told it was a vaccine, one that would keep them from getting the virus that's going around the Hole," I say, winded from my encounter with Amber. Roméo looks up at me as if I'm a distraction from important work. "They made them feel lucky, almost honored, that they were chosen."

All eyes rest on me.

"Wilson's a sick son of a bitch," Bruno says. His tucks his hands into his pockets. Grace sits at his feet with her head leaning against his legs.

"So now what?" I ask Roméo.

"We document everything: her symptoms, how long they last. We count the hours or days that she lives. And we need to find out where in the hospital Sutton's records are hidden. My guess is that Sutton could be the key to blowing this wide open."

"His office," I say with a shrug. "It's the only place he charted. But wouldn't Sutton have told us if he had anything to do with these experiments? If anything, he was trying to stop them."

"He's smarter than Wilson." Cole says. "I imagine he hid any records well."

I turn and rest my forehead against Cole's chest; the softness of his cotton shirt feels good against my skin. He encloses me with his arms and kisses the top of my head. Then he pushes me away for a second.

"Roméo, is it safe to be around Amber?" Cole asks what we're all thinking.

Roméo takes a second to consider the question before responding, "I don't think she is contagious any longer.

281

Otherwise, I wouldn't risk your lives or mine."

Zeus snores loudly from his spot in the far left corner of the room, and it draws our attention until Bruno speaks again.

"She may not be contagious anymore, but I'm pretty sure she's dying. That's not news anyone wants to hear."

"Should we tell her?" Grace asks.

"Not yet," Roméo says.

Cole shoves his hands into his pockets and shifts his weight from one foot to the other.

"Okay, Bill, you got nominated to help me clean up Amber. Shall we do this?" I look at Bill, whose bushy eyebrows raise up on his forehead. They almost blend in with his wild hair.

"Why do I always get stuck cleaning up bodily fluids?" He looks genuinely offended. I shoot him a "because-you're-crazy-as-hell" look, and he acquiesces. "I've got gloves, some bleach, and a few scrub brushes."

"All right."

Bill and I walk in unison, step for step. He fiddles with his fingers and counts quietly. He's strange. But for some reason, I like being around him. Maybe because as annoying as he is, he makes me laugh at times.

"Lusty?"

"Bill?"

"What?"

"I'm not sure, you said my name first."

"Oh right; I did. I hate to say it, but … I think this country's going down the poop shoot."

"I'm afraid you might be right."

"I need another drink."

"You're still drinking?"

282

"Yup, just not as often as I would like."

"How can you function, drinking all the time?"

"I don't get drunk. I drink just enough to calm my nerves."

He scratches the back of his head before picking a scab off his neck, and I smack his arm with the back of my hand. "Don't do that. The last thing you want are any open wounds around Amber. Not to mention that's completely gross."

"It's nice to know you care so much."

In the supply room, we grab everything we can. I carry towels, linens, clothes, and a bottle of bleach that I'm holding in place with my chin. Bill grabs buckets, trash bags, gloves, and face masks.

Standing outside her door, I hear nothing but our breathing, and I hope she's passed out. We place our things on the floor. Bill hands me my mask so I put it on, noticing the spearmint smell immediately.

"It helps with the smell." He points to the mask.

"Yeah, some of the nurses I worked with did the same thing. They claimed it worked."

"It does. Hot damn these gloves are tight." Bill puts on two pair of rubber gloves, and I decide double-gloving is a great idea.

"All right, you ready?" He nods. "Let's get this over with."

Bill crosses his eyes at me, and I smile under my mask. He unlocks the door, turns the knob, peeks in, and pops back out.

"Asleep," he says in a whisper.

"Good; let's hope she stays that way."

"If not, can't you punch her and knock her out again?"

"Believe me, it's crossed my mind."

The mask dulls the smell just enough that I don't have to

crinkle my nose as we approach Amber. Her clothes and sheets are caked in vomit. The floor seems clean at least. Her bucket sits next to her bed. When I glance inside, it's almost half full. I didn't know someone could produce that much at one time. I pick it up, carry it out the door, and place it on the floor. When I come back in, Bill's untucking the sheets at the corners of her bed.

"How are we going to do this?" he asks.

"Let's try rolling her onto her side, and I'll shove the old sheets underneath her, followed by the clean ones. Hold her until I have the clean sheets in place. When I say okay, roll her over the lump of sheets toward me, and I'll hold her while you grab the nasty ones out from under her and then pull the clean ones out and tuck them in."

"Good idea; I thought you were going to tell me to hold her."

"Oh no, that'd be a bad idea."

Amber groans now and then as we clean her bed. Her eyes stay closed, but her lips move, almost like she's trying to talk but nothing comes out.

"Did you grab clothes?" I ask.

"Oops." He runs out of the room, tears everything off, and then comes back, putting on new gloves. This time he holds a t-shirt and pants.

"I'll do it while you step out," I say.

"Won't you need help?"

"No, I'll be fine." I fight nausea just looking at her barf-stained clothes. Bills nods his head and clears the room, leaving me to dress Amber.

"Bill, I'm done."

284

He re-enters the room.

"Okay, what about the bleach?" I ask.

"To clean her?"

"No." I laugh at him and shake my head. "To help with the smell. And kill the germs."

"Right."

I see Amber stir out of the corner of my eye. I wave to Bill, and he looks in her direction.

"Maybe later?" Bill asks.

"I agree."

"Ahhhhhhhh!" she screams.

Amber bolts up to a sitting position in her bed. Her eyes practically bulge out of her head. Her hands and fingers tremble, and she doesn't even look at us. She stares at the opposite corner. "Get away from me!" she screams at the top of her lungs. "Get away!"

She picks up her pillow and hurls it across the room toward the empty corner and sweat drips from her forehead.

"Amber," I say. She doesn't respond to my voice so I try again. "Amber."

Nothing.

I move slowly toward her and feel my pulse quicken.

"Don't you dare come any closer." Her voice is deep with rage, but she almost chokes on her words. Bill steps back, scrunching up his face.

"What's she doing?" he asks.

"I'm not sure. Maybe she's having a nightmare. We have to wake her up."

"Wake up, Amber," Bill screams.

"Why are you here?" Amber asks. "You promised to leave

me alone. You promised." Her eyes still fixate on the empty corner, and her nostrils flare.

"Slap her," Bill says.

"No, she thinks someone's here to hurt her."

Amber screams some more. She's incoherent. No matter what Bill and I say to her, she doesn't acknowledge us. I place my hands on her shoulders and shake her. She jumps out of bed and retreats to a fetal position on the floor. *Great.* Then her head snaps up, and she starts swinging her arms.

"Maybe a bucket of cold water?" I ask Bill.

"Be right back."

When he's gone, I climb over her bed and stand between her and the imaginary person.

"Amber, it's Lexi."

She clutches her chest, and then her throat, choking herself.

"Don't do it," she begs through her tears. "Let go."

"Do what?"

Bill comes running in with a bucket of water that spills as he makes his way toward me.

"Allow me," he says. He stands above her and turns the bucket over, and the water pours onto Amber's head.

So much for the new clothing I worked so hard to get on her.

No response. Not even a shiver. Her eyes remain fixed on whatever she's seeing.

Damn, that's creepy.

I catch a glimpse of Bill's face as his eyes widen. Then he shrugs, still holding the empty bucket. "Well, that didn't go as planned," he says. "Now what?"

"Go get Roméo."

286

I feel so helpless, trying to come up with something that can snap her out of her hallucination.

Just then, Amber stands up and charges the wall opposite her bed. I leap toward her and wrap my arms around her waist, but she fights me with all her strength.

"Amber, wake up."

She doesn't hear me or respond to me. I don't exist to her at all. An eerie feeling comes over me, like when Zeus barks at something that isn't there. Her eyes are so intense; I wonder what or who she sees.

"Leave her alone," I yell at whoever she's seeing. "Get out of here, before I shoot." But nothing happens.

"Who are you talking to?" Cole yells over the noise as he and Zeus enter the room.

"I think she's hallucinating; I'm trying to snap her out of it."

"So, you just threatened to shoot … what, exactly?"

"Come hold her," I say.

"Are you serious?"

"Yes."

Zeus spots the pillow in the corner; he pounces on it and tears it to shreds.

"Why did you come for me?" Amber asks. "I no longer belong to you, don't you get it? We aren't married anymore. I left you."

She attempts to wrench away from me, so I quickly tighten my grip.

"She was married?" Cole asks. He takes her in his arms, and I start yelling at her ex-husband. I'm not a superstitious person, but at this point, I'll give anything a try.

"Leave her alone," I say to her husband.

"Lexi, have you lost your mind?" Cole looks concerned.

"No, I'm trying to make him go away."

"There's no one there."

"I know that."

"She can't hear or see any of us," Roméo says, appearing at the foot of the bed. "She only sees what she imagines in her mind. It's a hallucination."

"Somebody help me!" Amber screams so loud my ears ring. "Help me, please!"

"So what do we do?" I ask.

"Unfortunately, we can't do anything. The virus is attacking her brain and waking up her fears."

Amber stops screaming for a moment, and we all stop to stare. Cole releases her slowly. He comes up behind me and rubs my shoulders, but I remain tight as a drum.

Amber looks around the room, a glazed look in her eyes. I'm guessing she still doesn't see us.

"She looks a bit nuts," Bill says.

"Do you hear that?" Amber asks. Her voice comes out raspy and hoarse. Her entire body shakes nonstop. I find myself stepping back, bumping into Cole.

Something's happening again. I can feel it.

"Let's play a game," Bill says. "Who can guess what's coming next?" I give Bill a dirty look. Now isn't the time to play games.

"Oh shit, it's getting louder," Amber says. She shuts her eyes and covers her ears while rocking in the corner. "No, please, no. They're coming in through the holes."

Amber's legs begin kicking, her arms swinging, and she

288

shakes, sending chills down my spine. Her piercing screams rattle me. I clap my hands to my ears and cringe.

Roméo's eyes meet mine.

"Isn't there anything you can give her? Roméo, I can't watch her suffer like this."

"Then leave." His eyes are stone-cold.

His reaction shocks me and makes me remember how badly I wanted to choke him earlier.

Amber alternates between screaming, crying, and blubbering. She jumps to her feet and starts running but slams into the wall and falls backward, landing on her back. She gets back up and spins around while flailing her arms everywhere. Then she collapses.

It doesn't end there. She continues to yell, "Get these bats off of me!"

I make my way over to her, cautiously, and throw my body on top of hers to keep her from thrashing and banging her head on the floor. She fights me, scratching and clawing at my arms and hands. She bites the meaty flesh of my thumb, and I cry out, but don't give up. When I look at it, the skin's not punctured. I try to pin her down, anything to make it stop. She writhes below me though.

"Lexi, what the hell are you doing?" Cole asks.

I wrap my arms around her and hold her while she fights the demons in her head.

"Trying to keep her from hurting herself," I say in my best "you're-not-the-boss-of-me" voice.

Cole's pissed. But instead of arguing, he comes to my side and holds her legs.

After what feels like hours, Amber's screaming becomes

soft cries; her voice is shot to hell. Her breathing slows down, and then all at once her rigid muscles relax, and she finally goes limp.

A sigh of relief escapes me, and I look at Cole. He lifts Amber's slack body, places her gently in her bed, and covers her with the blanket.

I put my hands over my face as my shoulders slump. I feel so defeated.

"Lusty, please go get some sleep. I'll watch her," Bill says.

"For once, I agree with Bill," Cole says. "It's been over twenty-four hours since you've slept. You're coming back with me."

I answer without opening my eyes. "All right. Thank you, Bill."

"Sure thing."

"Roméo, what happens after the hallucinations?"

"Go rest. You're going to need it to deal with the next phase."

I nod my head and take a deep breath. Cole scoops me into his arms, and my head collapses on his shoulder. I'm spent in every possible way.

CHAPTER 22

When I open my eyes, the warmth of Cole's body surrounds me, enveloping me in safety. A dim light from the hallway shoots a sliver of light into the training room, barely illuminating our area. Around us, everyone sleeps with blankets piled over them. Zeus snores, and his nails tick against the floor as he dreams. Cole's hand grasps mine for a minute, and I place my hand over his, tracing the veins that spider over his fingers. Spinning my body around, I face him. When his eyes meet mine, they look pained.

"Hey," he says in a whisper.

"Hey."

He runs his hand over my face and breathes softly.

"So are you ready?" I ask. His forehead pinches together, causing me to feel dread. *He isn't ready.*

"Ready for what?" he asks.

I sigh.

He knows exactly what I'm talking about, and he's trying to think of a way to get out of it again.

"I don't want to talk," he says. His voice lowers with his eyes. "Right now."

"You don't have a choice."

"Fine ... but we should take this elsewhere." He flips the blanket off us, the chilly air hitting my body with a shock.

"The hallway?"

"Wherever. It doesn't matter."

We tiptoe through the room and into the hallway, and he stands with his body barely touching the wall, his hand running over his head, sweat coursing down his face.

"Telling you this is by far the most difficult thing I've ever had to do," he says. He slowly turns my way, and his eyes drop to the floor.

"Why?" I ask, my voice starting to rise. I don't know if I am ready to hear this. "What are you so afraid of?"

"Losing you."

"Cole, you're not going to lose me."

"I'm not so sure about that."

"How can you say that?" Adrenaline starts to flow, and suddenly my breathing is uneven.

"Because once you know, you'll never be able to look at me the same." He takes a shaky breath. "All I've ever wanted to do was protect you."

"Just say it, please."

"Only ... if you promise to stay and discuss this with me when I'm done." He looks up.

"I will."

"No. Promise me."

"All right. I promise."

A heavy silence weighs on us. We don't speak for minutes.

"Do you remember when I told you about the guards?" he finally says. "And following orders? If you don't follow, they'll kill you."

"Yeah, I remember," I whisper. *I don't want to hear this. I don't want to hear this.*

He takes a minute and stares at the ceiling before he says, "I was young when I joined the guards."

His expression is pain and anger and fear and desperation. I hate seeing him like this. I place a hand on his arm.

"It's okay, Cole. Just tell me. Please." I want to cry. I now know that what Cole has been keeping from me is so bad, he is about to collapse from the weight of carrying it this long.

He pulls his arm from me.

"My first assignment was to arrest a man the Commander wanted in custody. When I found him, he didn't fight me, and actually, he didn't say a word. He turned around, and I handcuffed him. I remember looking at him with amazement. His expression was blank; he showed no fear, no anger, nothing. I tried to imagine what this man could've done, what the Commander could want him for, what sin he could possibly have committed. It was something bigger." He covers his face with his hands for a second then leans against the wall. "When we arrived at the Commander's headquarters, the Commander stood at the door waiting for us."

"Asshole," I say.

"Please, Lexi, if you interrupt me, I won't be able to finish."

"Sorry. But he is."

293

"I know that," he says. "We took him straight to the interrogation room where I handcuffed him to the metal bar on top of the table. The room was dark except for one light above the table, giving me just enough light to see him and the Commander, who sat across from him, laughing. The interrogation went on for hours.

"Finally, the man said, 'Are you done?' His voice wasn't angry, but calm and direct, something I didn't expect.

"The Commander leaned forward and said, 'Yes, in fact, I am ... but I'd like to know what drove you, what motivated your mission. Did you honestly think it would work? That you, one man, could somehow influence the people of our society, and change the way our system works?'"

Cole stops, and I raise my eyebrows, urging him to go on. So far, nothing he's said seems horrible enough for him to be afraid to tell me. I start to relax a little, relieved.

"The man took a deep breath, folded his arms across his chest, stared right into the Commander's eyes, and said, 'Like I've always said: You can overcome anything, short of death.'"

I gasp. It feels like someone punched me in the stomach and then drop-kicked me in the head.

Did I really just hear that? I shake my head as tears sting my eyes like needles.

"No!" I cry out, slamming back into the wall.

"Lexi, I'm so sorry." Cole's voice cracks.

I don't want to believe it's true, but my ears ring with my father's words.

"You? It was you who ... arrested ... my father?" I spit out.

"Yes."

"Why? He did nothing wrong!" I say through gritted teeth,

tasting the salt from my tears.

"I didn't have a choice. You know that."

"Did you torture him?"

"Lexi, please ... "

"Answer me!"

"No ... please, you don't want to hear this."

"Oh my God, you did! I want to know every single detail, even if it kills you to say it."

"The Commander." Cole takes a step toward me. "That bastard ordered me to follow through with the interrogation. And Lexi, you know I didn't want to. It was a requirement of training, and I never had a choice."

A blood-curdling scream bounces off the bare halls. My scream.

"What exactly did you do? What did you do to my father? And don't lie to me, Cole! This is my *father* we're talking about! I need to know everything." Spit flies from my mouth, and my ears ring.

"Lexi, trust me, you don't want the nightmares, the visuals, the sounds. They will haunt you as they do me."

But I stand my ground, and by the look on his face, he's well aware I'm not letting this go. "Cole, the truth. Now."

"The Commander needed to know what your father knew, what his plans were, and he was willing to do whatever it took to get the answers." He pauses. "One by one, the Commander forced me to extract his fingernails. Your father grit his teeth, and even though I knew it was agonizing for him, he said nothing." Sweat pours down Cole's face, the vein pulsing in his forehead. "When that didn't work, I punched him in the face multiple times until there was blood gushing from his nose and he was practically gagging on his own blood. His teeth hit the floor, and his eyes were swollen shut." Cole takes a deep breath and clenches his fists.

"'Keep going,' the Commander ordered. So we waterboarded him several times, and I felt sick, sick to my stomach as he almost drowned every time. I remember trying to breathe for him as he was gasping for air. He was limp in my arms when I dragged him back to the chair under the lights.

"'Sir,' I said to the Commander. 'I think he's had enough.' But he said, 'You're only done when I say you're done, now continue, soldier.' He questioned your dad. 'Tell me who you're working with,' he commanded. But your dad didn't break. The Commander screamed at him, 'I know your family, I know your sexy, beautiful wife. I could take her for my own when you're dead.' Your father didn't flinch as the Commander went on describing your family in detail. 'Your oldest son, Keegan ...' Your father grimaced at the mention of his name. 'It'd be so easy to have him accused. I could even tell him you're the one who did it. And Lexi, sweet, pretty, young Lexi, with her turquoise eyes and her curly hair ... she'd make a great whore in the Hole.' That's when your dad finally started crying.

"But he still didn't slip, not once. Not even when the Commander tore off his shirt and made me handcuff him to the table. Your father kept his head down, and I remember hearing him pray. My hand shook as I held the leather handle of the whip. My palms were sweaty, making it harder to grip ... and there was a lump in my throat that I couldn't swallow. The Commander removed his chair, and then your father leaned onto the table for support, his hands still cuffed to the bar. I stood still, like stone. Looking at his scar-less back, knowing I was about to tear it to shreds.

"'Hamilton, are you ready to talk?' the Commander asked him.

"'I have nothing to say,' your dad replied in a calm tone.

"'You know I have the power to take everything away from you,' the Commander screamed in frustration. I could see the red flush crawling up his neck as his eyes bulged in that terrible way we both know so well.

"With blood spurting from his mouth, your dad said, 'Even if you kill me, my family will become stronger, more powerful than you can dream. So get on with it.'

"'Suit yourself.' The Commander smiled and searched for my eyes. 'Begin. And don't stop till you're told.'

"Instantly, my body froze. I don't know what came over me, but I turned to the Commander and said, 'I'm done, sir. He's made it quite clear he's not going to say anything.' He wasn't going to suffer by my hands any longer. All I knew was this was wrong. And I was done following through with this torture. The Commander said, 'Soldier, you're dismissed. I'll deal with you later.'

"I was taken back to my barracks and waited for my own punishment, but before I left, your father caught my gaze. His eyes, like yours, pierced my soul. He nodded at me, and even in his pain, he thanked me." Tears stream down Cole's face, and he crumples to his knees.

"He said to me, 'There's still hope for you yet.' After I closed the door, I heard his screams echoing down the hallway." Cole completely breaks down, his hands covering his face as he gasps for air, sobs wracking his shoulders. "I can't take it back, and I want so bad to erase the memory, to erase what your father had to endure. But, Lexi, I can't, and it's killing me." He looks up at me with bloodshot eyes and tries to grab my hand.

I hold up my hand to stop him. "Don't touch me. Don't come near me."

"I'm so sorry." He chokes on his words. "I would do anything to go back and change what happened. I don't want … your father's blood on my hands."

My cheeks are wet with tears, and I have to hold my fists at my sides to keep from attacking him. "How … Why didn't you tell me before? Didn't you think I had a right to know that you knew my father? That you *tortured* him? And to think, all the times I said to you that I wished you could've met him. And you already had. And yet, you still said nothing."

He lips part as he tries to catch his breath, and he closes his eyes. "I was trying to protect you."

"By lying to me?"

"By avoiding causing you pain."

"What the hell do you think you just did!"

"Lexi … "

"You took my father away from us—from me."

"And if it wasn't me, it would've been someone else. Either way, it was going to happen. Your father knew it. That's why he didn't fight me."

"How dare you! If he had any idea he was going to be arrested, he would've taken us and ran. He would have protected us. Protected *me*."

"No, he wouldn't have run."

"Oh. And you knew him better than me, huh? You think a couple of hours torturing an innocent man means you know it all."

"Your father was a smart man. He was well aware that if he didn't come willingly, we would've been ordered to kill his family. He was protecting you."

Of course he was. My father always put his family first; I know that. But that doesn't ease the burning anger building in my chest.

"I trusted you," I say, as I step away from Cole.

"I warned you I wasn't worthy of that honor," he says. He slumps against the wall, looking small and weak and broken.

"I can't believe I allowed myself to be so duped into thinking you were better than any other guard. You're no different than Wilson!"

"Please. Don't do this." His voice sounds defeated. I feel nothing but rage.

"Right now, you are the last person I want to be around."

"But ..." His voice cracks.

"Hey, guys, everything okay?" Bill asks, his voice slicing into the tense air between us.

"No, we're in the middle of something," Cole says.

I clench my fists. "Actually, we're quite done," I say in a shaky voice. With tears spilling down my face, I try to hide in the shadows. But judging from Bill's raised eyebrows, he already knows something's not right.

"I came for Lusty, but if you're busy—"

"I'm not."

"Lexi," Cole begs.

"What's going on?" I ask Bill.

"Amber's in a lot of pain, and I don't know what to do for her," Bill says.

"Okay, let's go," I say.

"I'll meet you there," Bill says. He practically runs away from me.

"I know it's selfish to ask, but please forgive me," Cole says.

I wipe tears away with my fists as I turn to Cole. "Forgive you for lying to me about my father? And what you did to him? He was everything to me, and the man I love was the man who took him away. I need time. I need time to process this, and I'm asking you to give me space."

He nods, the shadows dancing on the dark pits below his eyes. "All right. If that's what you need," he says, his voice weak. His Adam's apple bobs, and he rests his head in his hands.

I can't feel pity for him. I won't. "It is."

Clenching my jaw to keep from falling apart, I turn away from Cole and try to focus on Amber and her sickness. But in the back of my mind, I play out the scene of Cole beating my dad mercilessly as the Commander watches. I stop and dry heave in the hallway but don't feel any better afterward.

I want to punch the wall or kick something or scream. Right before I enter Amber's room, I stop and press my forehead against the wall, placing my hands next to my head as the tears freely fall. I practice breathing in an effort to calm my burning rage.

I hear Amber in her room, moaning and groaning. Straightening my shoulders, I walk through the door in time to see her flipping restlessly from one side to the other on her bed. She mutters to herself and then leaps out of bed and paces. Her head snaps in my direction. She looks like she's been crying. Her eyes are bloodshot and swollen almost completely shut.

"You must enjoy seeing me like this," she says.

"Amber, you know that's not true."

She laughs. "You're a terrible liar."

"Shut up," I say.

The corners of her mouth curl upward. "Well, look on the bright side: at least you're not dying like me."

I shake my head. "Who said you're dying?"

"Nobody has to tell me. I already know."

"You can't give up hope—"

"You're joking, right?" she says with anger and sarcasm. "It's not a vaccine. You think I'm too stupid to know that?"

"Why would you say that?"

"Because Wilson wouldn't waste money to save Sinners. Wilson only cares about Wilson and what he can take from whomever he thinks has more than him. Sinners have nothing. We are useless to him."

Amber clutches her stomach and doubles over, wailing in pain as she falls to the floor. She clenches her teeth and screams. I drop to my knees and put my hand on her back.

"Amber, what can I do? Believe it or not, I want to help you."

She turns her face toward me, and her eyes dart to mine. "Shoot me," she says with desperation. Her voice comes out in a low groan edged with misery.

"No. I'm not going to kill you."

"I'm not asking. I'm telling," she says.

I shake my head.

"The pain's unbearable, it feels like someone's burning me with a torch."

"All the time?" I ask.

"No, but … soon … it'll be constant." She writhes forward, screaming between words. She pants, and her mouth opens, her lips pulling back with each scream. Her hands fly from her stomach to her hair. Strands become entangled with her fingers, and thin pieces fall to the floor in patches. Her eyes are as wide as quarters as she opens them again. She collapses forward onto all fours. I grab her arm, trying my best to stay composed while my skin's crawling.

"I'm begging you to shoot me."

"And I already said no. If you want to go ahead and shoot yourself … that's your decision."

"I can't," she says.

"Why not?"

"I'm not strong enough to pull the trigger. Emotionally, I can't do it. But you are. I know you are, because you hate watching people suffer."

"You're right, Amber, I do. But you could still live through this."

Amber sits up and shoves my arm away from her. She's on my level now, and we sit face to face. The hair on the back of my neck stands up.

"I'm not going to survive. No one ever does."

"Don't say that."

"And why not? It's the damn truth. But lucky for me, I'm dying quickly. So I won't linger like Alyssa did."

Hearing her name knocks the wind right out of me. I gasp and put my hand out to steady myself against the wall. Suddenly, my mouth's as dry as sand. I shake my head.

"What?" I ask. "For a minute, I thought you said 'Alyssa.'"

She narrows her eyes. "I did."

302

"No. No way. She didn't have the virus you have," I manage to say as I feel a sudden cold freeze my core.

Amber cocks her head at me. "The only difference between us is that her death was peaceful. She had morphine. You have nothing to give me, and so, what? You're just going to sit there and watch me while I suffer, listen to me scream? Are you gonna watch me waste away while the virus eats my insides? I've seen what this thing does to people. Without pain medication, I'm going to be in excruciating pain … 'til the end."

"Amber … "

"Lexi, try to understand. I don't want the virus to be what actually kills me. The last thing I want is for Wilson to have that kind of power over me. And you of all people … should understand that."

I shake my head, drawing my arms into myself. "Alyssa didn't have this virus."

Amber's face tightens, and for a moment, her eyes look almost sad, but then she closes them for a second and clears her throat.

"When Alyssa arrived at the hospital her temperature was so high, she was seizing. The uncontrollable vomiting came next, followed by hallucinations. And when the hallucinations finally stopped, that's when the crippling, unbearable pain began."

"You're lying." My voice comes out angry and strained.

"Lexi, I might not like you, but I've never lied to you."

"Alyssa didn't have this virus!" I say with a trembling voice.

"By the time you arrived, the black ring on her arm had

already faded. So, yes, Lexi. She did."

"No," I spit at her. I stand, and the room spins as I try to steady myself. "She couldn't have." I shake my head in disbelief.

"She was one of Wilson's lab rats," Amber says. "Just like me. Only she didn't have a choice, and I was stupid enough to think I did."

Suddenly, my ears pound. Rage runs through my body, and I take off running.

I don't see or hear anything but myself breathing hard and fast. I focus on sprinting to the restrooms. When I reach the door, I kick it open and flick the lights on. Taking a quick look around, I dart to the stalls and begin kicking the doors repeatedly, listening to them slam into the walls. Metallic banging echoes all around me, but I don't care.

"Son of a bitch!" I scream, as I rear up to plant my foot in the door. The muscles in my arms strain as I grasp the metal framework. Nothing compares to the pain that's ripping my heart apart, shredding it like a blender. I drive my foot into the door until I'm exhausted. I hunch over, trying to catch my breath. The door hangs off one hinge. My body's spent. I'm sweating and breathing hard, and my mind's still running a marathon. The hows and whys of the last two conversations are weighing on me. How could I have been so blind? Cole has been lying to me since the day we met. And Sutton lied to me about Alyssa.

Someone grabs my arm, and I turn my head. Cole's there, with Zeus by his side.

"Lexi, calm down." Cole's voice drips with pain.

"Leave me alone!" I shout.

He grabs me and slams me into his chest as I bang on him with my fists. I crumble against him, hating him and loving

304

him all at once.

It's like someone took a knife and split me open. Grabbing fists of his shirt, I convulse, tears pouring down my face.

Cole's arms tighten around me as he scoops me up and lowers himself to the ground. He sits against the wall and holds on to me like he's never done before. He's trying, but nothing will lessen the pain I feel.

"Lexi, you might hate me right now. But when you're hurting like this, all I know is … I need to hold you."

My shoulders shudder at his words. I'm too defeated and broken to break free from his arms. All I see is Alyssa's face, all I smell is Alyssa's hair, and all I hear is her saying … "Don't let me die. I don't want to die a Sinner. Don't let me die."

But she did die, and I let her down.

Why not me? Why her? Why my dad? I would've taken their places. She was only a child. How could anyone but the devil himself experiment on an innocent child, knowing it would kill her?

I flashback to the smile she wore when Cole arrived for her date. I see her gasping in pain and hear her call out my name. Her call bell sounds, and I sprint to her side. I'm in her bed, holding her broken body. I cry, wishing I could remain strong for her. I tell her it's okay to go to her mom. She slips away from me, her body going limp as the last breaths escape her tiny mouth. Her heart no longer beats. Her voice doesn't answer me. I've lost my friend all over again. I've lost my father all over again.

"Wilson killed her," I say between gasps for air.

"Why do you care so much about whether Amber lives or dies?"

"No, Alyssa! He did this to Alyssa," I say. Cole's body

305

stiffens. "She was thirteen years old! Only thirteen. And he picked her."

"What?" His voice cracks.

"Amber told me. He injected her with the virus," I say through gritted teeth. "He killed her."

"No way," he says. I feel his body shake against mine, and he sniffles. Zeus nudges my arm, and I let him into our hug. He licks my face, which only makes me cry harder because I know he feels this too.

"She never should've died." Snot runs out of my nose. "She should be here with us right now." My throat burns, and I have difficulty swallowing.

"I know," Cole tells me. "God, Lexi, I'm so sorry."

"This isn't your fault."

"No, but I've hurt you, and now you have this on top of everything." He reaches up, pulls a strip of toilet paper off the rack, and hands me some.

"I will never forgive myself."

"There wasn't anything you or anyone else could've done to save her."

"Cole." I hesitate. "We have to kill him before he murders hundreds or thousands more."

"And that's exactly what we're going to do."

I don't have an ounce of energy left in me. I haven't moved from the floor in the bathroom in what feels like hours, struggling between composing myself and breaking down into tears. I push Cole away, and he sits helpless to stop the growing tension that fills the empty spaces between us.

Bruno and Grace come in and sit down on the floor. Cole fills them in on Alyssa and Amber. I cover my ears because I don't want to listen. I'm still battling the reality of the truth about Cole and the cause of Alyssa's death. Then I hear her voice in my head.

"It's okay, Lexi. I'm safe now. You can do this; use your love for me to get up and do what must be done. You have the strength of your father, Keegan, and myself. We're with you. Someone needs you right now. Help her come to us."

I blink several times then rub the back of my neck. Grace's voice echoes around me.

"Poor Amber," she says. "She's clawing at herself and scratching her skin off. She won't stop screaming. I can't stomach it anymore. Wish there was something we could do for her."

Straightening up, I stand on wobbly legs and clear my throat.

"There is," I say. "She asked me to end it for her. She begged me, but I refused."

Cole's pained eyes raise to meet mine. "Lexi. I'm not sure now's the best time for you to make that kind of decision."

"She doesn't deserve this," I say. He flinches. "And if I was in her position, I'd hope you'd do the same for me."

"Lexi, why don't you let me do it?" Bruno asks, hopping to his feet.

"No." I tighten my fists at my sides, forcing myself to stay composed. "I'll do it. She asked me, and now I am going to

307

give her what she asked for."

"Wait, you're going to kill her?" Grace asks.

"No, Grace. It's the virus that's killing her, and I'm going to stop it."

"Lexi, it's murder."

"It's not, Grace. It's assisted suicide. And, Grace, *she* wants this … not me. But what I do want for her is peace. She deserves that at least." I can't even believe the words that come out of my mouth. I feel like I'm constantly riding the space between being a savior and being a demon. And now I know the delicate balance my father walked. *That Sutton still walks.*

Grace stands, takes my hand in hers, and leads me forward. "Come on, let's help Amber."

She doesn't let go of my hand as I drag my legs to the doorway. Cole and Bruno follow.

When we arrive, Amber's eyes catch mine, and she smiles gratefully. I run my hands through my hair, hesitating, wondering if I can go through with it.

Cole removes the sheet on the bed and scoops Amber up into it. He carries her into the bathroom.

Bruno grabs a chair and drags it into one of the shower stalls, carefully making sure it's level before nodding and stepping back.

I can't believe I'm going to do this.

"Thank you, Lexi," Amber says through her quivering lips. "I knew you'd understand."

Cole places Amber gently down on the chair. "Goodbye, Amber," he says.

She smiles at him. "Take care of Lexi."

He nods. "You know I will."

"Amber, I'm so sorry this happened to you," I say once he moves.

"I know you are. But don't you dare feel guilty. This, this is my decision, not yours. And I apologize for how I've treated you."

"It's okay, I forgive you."

"All right, good. Let's do this. I'm ready to go home."

"Do you believe in heaven?"

"Because of you, yes, I do."

"Well, then please tell God I'm sorry." I don't want to cry, so I clench my jaw. Shooting someone like this feels completely against my nature, even if it is merciful in the long run.

Bruno, Grace, and Zeus say their goodbyes. Suddenly my heart's in my throat, and I bite down on my lower lip as I approach her. She looks tiny compared to the chair she sits on, the stall swallowing her body whole in its white mildewed prison. Yet, Amber looks at peace. She takes a deep breath.

"Are you scared?" I ask.

"No, I'm ready to leave this hell." Even as she says it, she scratches at her arms, picking open more wounds, and drawing more fresh blood. It trickles down and drips onto the floor.

"I understand." I breathe deep. "Close your eyes."

I look up at the cement ceiling, say a silent prayer, and reach for my gun. I focus on Amber and steady my hands, locking my feet in place. I ignore how her fingers shake as she awaits her execution.

I aim right between her eyes and pull the trigger.

CHAPTER 23

It's done. At some point, Cole pulls the gun out of my hand. Everything looks blurry. Hands, I don't know whose, pull me away from the spatters of blood and brain matter that used to be Amber. The sound of voices is drowned out by ringing in my ears from the blast of the gun. I glance down at my shaking fingers and twist them together. But I can't make them stop. I cover my ears, as if blocking out the noise.

I killed her. *God, forgive me.*

I close my eyes but still see the droplets of blood sprayed all over the wall tiles and the way her body bolted backward with the shot, and then slumped off the chair into a heap on the floor. My stomach lurches. The expression on her face is crystal clear in my mind—the sunken eyes, the hollowed cheeks, and the raspy whisper in which she pleaded with me to end her miserable existence. *God, what have we become when we kill people to make their pain bearable?* My breath catches in my throat.

"You okay?" a voice asks.

It's not okay.

"Not really." That's the thing about emotions. You can't control them. The only thing you can do is hope you'll find a way to somehow keep your head above water.

Immediately, I want to be alone. No one tries to stop me as I shove through the door and skid into the dimly lit hallway. My bloodied boots stick to the floor as I bolt. My eyes flood with tears, and a moan escapes my lips. I hear myself, but it doesn't sound like me. No words can describe how I feel or what is going through my mind. I'm passing several blackened doorways when it hits me.

My old room.

I screech to a stop. The door's wide open, but it's dimly lit. Inside, I can barely make out the wall I painted so many months ago. My bed's still on the right side with rumpled covers. I go in, sit down, put my head in my hands, and let myself cry.

The tears cascade down my face, and my stomach muscles clench from the force of my grief. I try to wipe the tears away, but to no avail. They just keep coming. I feel pressure on the bed and turn to find Zeus, who snuggles up against me. He pushes my arm so that I have to put it around his head.

I'm relieved to see him, but I can't find the words to tell him what I've done. I know Amber wasn't the nicest person; in fact, I didn't even like her. And I know she asked me to do it. But it's still unnatural to kill someone in cold blood, no matter how much you dislike them and no matter how much they beg.

I constantly find myself in the position of having to weigh the consequences of my actions. If I didn't do it, she would've suffered and endured a very painful death. If I hadn't killed so many guards, my friends and I would've died instead. If we don't rescue Sutton, Wilson will kill him. If I don't kill Wilson, this will never end.

It's just too much for my head. I swallow my tears for a moment and let my eyes drift to the painting on the wall.

Cole's eyes stare back at me through the red and black paint. *I can't even trust him, and yet I love him, maybe more than anything.* And then, I see Lexington Bay, with my father and Alyssa, sitting together. Maybe Amber's with them now, pain-free. Maybe, in another life, she wouldn't be so hateful of others because she'd have a chance to start over.

Last, I focus on the Hole getting blown to pieces in the painting. This is the one part of the painting I want to come true so bad that it hurts. Just thinking about how amazing it would be to live a life free of brands, free of hatred and corruption, pains me. I want it all and want it to happen without costing everything and everyone I love. I wipe my tears with tightened fists.

I miss my dad. I miss Alyssa. I miss Keegan, standing here with me and telling me he loves me. I wish he'd walk in without knocking like he used to. I hated it then, but I'd give anything, *anything,* to see him again. And Sutton, being beaten in front of my eyes. *God, it's too much.* I groan from the depths of my soul, unable to control my emotions as they spill out. I struggle to breathe. And what of Cole? Will I ever be able to trust him again? I never dreamed he could keep a secret like that from me, that he would lie to me.

My hands continue to tremble. Before I know it, I'm down on my knees, my hands against the wall, praying in broken whispers.

"Please, give me the strength to fight evil with good. Give me the wisdom to know the difference. Help me to never lose myself in all this hatred, lies, chaos, and sickness ... " I stop as a tear trickles down my cheek, and my voice cracks. "Please protect Grace and the baby growing within her. And please, *please,* help us save Sutton before it's too late. I can't bear to lose him."

I sit back on my heels, allowing Zeus to scamper down beside me. I turn my head and kiss his waiting face. I sniffle and bury my face in his warm neck. He allows me to cry into his fur, sitting patiently as I grasp him like a scared child with a huge teddy bear. I pull away, catching my breath and letting him settle half on my lap. I can't help but laugh through my tears. A gentle peace comes over me, and I straighten my back.

"What would I do without you?" I ask. His ears perk up just as I hear steps behind me.

"Is it all right if I come in?" Cole's voice reverberates through my small room, and I flip my body around.

"It depends on why you're here."

"I know you need space," he says with his hands out in front of him as if to say, *Hold on a second.* "But I had to make sure you're all right."

I stand up and wipe my wet palms on my pants. He walks in, eyes immediately drawn to the wall.

"You did what she needed from you," he says, not stepping any closer. "And it was more than anyone's ever done for her."

I want to throw myself into his arms and inhale his sweat-soaked shirt, but I stop myself. Part of me feels guilty when I notice he's changed clothes. I'm guessing he helped clean up Amber's body after I ran out. But I can't quite forgive him for lying, no matter how much I want to. "It still hurts."

He's quiet as he sits down on the bed and puts his hands on his knees. I listen to his breathing as he stares at the painting.

"I say it's time to retrieve those records and show the world who Wilson really is," he says. "What he's made us all do in order to survive."

"Do you think the world cares?"

"Deep down, I do. And if we show them that their lives are in jeopardy, they'll step up to the plate," he says. I stare at him, squinting, and he levels his gaze at me. "I know I don't deserve you, or your forgiveness. But ... that doesn't change why I came."

"Cole, I ... "

"You don't have to say a word. But I need to tell you that I love you and nothing's going to change that. Not ever."

I turn my head and stare at the wall I painted. The faces, the memories, all flash through my mind. I flick my eyes back to Cole's. He raises his eyebrows, his black eyes boring holes through my soul.

"So ... are you ready for this?" he asks. I clench my fists and nod my head.

"I've never been more ready in my life."

CHAPTER 24

I try my best to pay attention as Bruno and Cole go back and forth over how they should get into the hospital. They stand, pointing at a homemade diagram sitting on a table in the training room. Since there are no chairs left, the rest of us sprawl on the floor, subjected to their constant discussion of tactics, as the lights flicker overhead, giving me a headache.

"I need to use the restroom; I'll be right back," Grace says.

Bruno nods without looking up. I don't know how he hasn't suspected her secret yet. This is the second time she's left the room to pee, and we've only been sitting here for one hour.

She gets up from her position along the wall and saunters to the doorway, glancing over her shoulder at me. When she returns a few minutes later, she slides down into place, resting her hands over her abdomen. Her face glows, and her mouth turns upward. The secret weighs on me like an anvil dragging me under the waves with her. *Is it better this way?* It's not my place to make that decision. I pull my eyes away from her.

Bill drinks from his small bottle. I don't know how he can drink so much and still understand anything we're talking about. But somehow, he's found himself an endless supply of vodka, and he doesn't think waiting until we're free to celebrate is good enough. He belches loudly, but the guys don't even stop to notice. He looks at me with his gap-toothed smile, and I roll my eyes.

"Want some?"

"No, thanks, you go right ahead and enjoy that," I say.

"Have to while I can."

Zeus moans as he lies on his belly, supporting his head between his two front paws, eyes sorrowful. I can understand that. I fidget with my fingers, wondering when Cole and Bruno will reach a decision.

"How about the basement windows?" Bruno asks.

"No way, too close to the training center," Cole says.

"Oh come on, man. If we get in there, we're right at the main staircase which goes straight to the eighth floor." Bruno leans over the papers and points to a location with his index finger. "It's perfect."

"Yeah, but impossible."

"Actually, it isn't," Bill says from the shadows. "The guards rotate every four hours. Hit them on a shift change, and you got them." The eyes in the room all move in his direction. Under the flickering light, Cole's forehead wrinkles up as he lifts his right eyebrow. "The guards on the roof of the hospital take smoke breaks together. You'll see the burning light of their cigarettes. This leaves their posts ... well, let's just say, 'unguarded.'" Bill laughs as Bruno stands up straight. "What? I enjoy observing people, even a bunch of slime balls."

"Old man, your intelligence is kicking my ass right about now," Bruno says. "How about helping us out here."

"Bruno, just because he drinks doesn't make him unintelligent," Grace says.

"Who said anything about him drinking?" Bruno asks with his hands in the air.

"Grace, it's fine. It doesn't bother me," Bill says. "Because now my problem can be used for the good."

"And how is that exactly?" Cole asks, turning fully to face Bill.

"Think about it. Who's gonna pay any attention to a drunk? I'm not a threat."

"Huh, never thought about that," Cole says. "I must admit, we're very lucky to have you."

"I appreciate that. I've always wanted to be some kind of hero." He stumbles to the table and pulls the drawings in front of himself. "Okay. So check this out: guards are positioned here and here." He points them out. "At shift change, they rotate this way, and then some go for a joyride, if you catch my drift." His voice drones on, and Bruno and Cole soak it all in.

"Okay, so say everything goes as planned, and we get the records," Cole says. "Then what? How're we getting them out? And how many files are we taking?"

"Let me worry about that," Roméo says, entering the room. "But I'll need time to go through them. If we don't get the right ones, it won't matter to the United Powers. Even though I've documented Amber's course with the virus, they'll want more. Without proof that there are and were others, they'll step back. I must acquire the most accurate information possible, so the United Powers can see the full scope of what's happening here."

"And you're sure telling them what you know won't be enough? I mean, we will back you up," Grace says.

"I wish it could be that simple. Only hard-core proof will open their eyes to the danger here. They like to stay neutral unless given a very solid reason to intervene. Besides, no one will believe the word of a Sinner whose father was killed by the current regime, two ex-guards with an axe to grind, a drunk, and a woman who … I'm sorry. What do you do again?"

"Okay, okay. We get it. No need to insult the people keeping you alive," Bruno says. "Back to the files. How will we carry them out?"

"How about a backpack?" I ask.

"That should work just fine," Roméo says.

"I'll carry it. The drunk guy, remember?" Bill says.

"What about me?" Grace asks, her voice eager. "What can I do?"

I flash her a pleading look. I worry she's taking on too much, risking too much. But she shrugs me off. I want to make an excuse for her, but I don't get the chance.

"I could use your help going through the files," Roméo says.

"Oh, that's perfect," she says. "Just tell me what you're looking for, and I'll do my best."

"I can give cover or lead," I say. "I know my way around the hospital and Sutton's office."

"All right; that's all settled," Bruno says. His hand slaps the table, and his voice turns monotone. "After we get these

318

files, our next course of action will be to get them out of the Hole with Roméo and Bill." He stares at Grace, lingering on her face for a while before turning to the rest of us. "Once we make it back here safely, we'll work on the escape plan." He exhales.

"We got this," Cole says.

I'm more than awake now. I scoot forward, pushing myself up to stand, and look over the drawings on the table. I examine the rough diagrams they made of the hospital and training center. I see the entrance to the basement they're talking about, and it gives me chills. It's the exact area where some of the guards cornered me months ago and Cole and Zeus came and rescued me before they could finish what they'd started. *Thank God.*

"This plan, it's going to work," I say, not making eye contact with Cole. "No matter what happens, our main objective is the get the records out of the Hole." I glance quickly at Cole, noticing his clenched fists. "Even if it means lives lost." He opens his mouth and then closes it.

"So I guess it's 'til death do we all part," Bruno says with a laugh. Grace shoots him a look. He wraps his arm around her, pulling her body closer to his.

"Okay, guys, it's time for the fun part," Bill says.

I raise an eyebrow in his direction. "Which is?"

"Stocking the weapons. But I have to clean all the ammo first to ensure our guns don't jam, because a jammed gun isn't gonna do us any good." He swigs his bottle and tries to shove it back in his pants. He misses three times before getting it in.

"When will you sleep?" Grace asks.

"Sleep is so overrated," he says. "I prefer catnaps." He

319

shrugs and walks toward the closet where the weapons are stored.

"I'll stock the food and water," Grace says.

"Want me to come with you?" I ask.

"No, sweetie," she says and then winks. "Bill needs your help, not me."

I know what it's like inside the hospital. Aside from being on top of the most heavily armed training center, it's probably going to be dark, and those long hallways and patient rooms could hold anything. So I hope the weapons we have are sufficient for the task.

When Bill enters the weapons closet, he sits down and begins cleaning guns. The potent smell of lubricant fills my nostrils. I join him, watching as he carefully wipes each part down and then, when satisfied, puts them all back together. The entire time, he's quiet. His eyes focus on his work.

My hands are greasy and black by the time we finish. We set the guns to the side and then begin cleaning rounds of ammunition. The copper tone gleams in the light as I rotate it between my fingers. I don't usually carry an M4, but Cole seemed pleased to find one here, so I want to make sure it works. My mind wanders aimlessly while wiping down each one.

Keegan probably sat in this very same room and divvied out weapons before the first revolt. He might've cleaned his gun. He might've said some prayers. He might've felt Dad's presence, guiding him through each step of the planning. I'll never forget his green eyes greeting mine the morning of the main assault. I imagine him with me now. I need his strength.

I can't go without you, Keegan.

320

But you can, and you will, Lexi.

Would Dad want us both to die for this?

Our destinies were decided long before we were able to choose. I think, even if you knew you'd die tomorrow, you'd still fight. Because your conscience, like Dad's, would never allow you to be at peace if you didn't.

But what if my courage fails? What if Sutton doesn't make it? I feel like we're wasting precious time.

You won't fail because you're my sister. And our blood runs the same ... vulnerable but steady, not fearless, but courageous under fire despite our fears. Sutton has already made his choice. He's courageous enough to die. That, alone, should be your inspiration.

I can't bear the thought of losing my friends.

You've got to let that go. Our lives are grains of salt filtered by one large hand. Who we love and what we do doesn't matter if we forget why we're here in the first place.

Bill snorts, wrenching me from my thoughts. I jerk upward, dropping the ammo in my hands. It clatters to the floor. Bill gives me a weird look.

"Lusty, you all right?"

"Yeah ... " I wrinkle my forehead and gather up the ammo. My hands shake, and my heart beats fast.

I know Keegan's right. I've got to let it all go—the painful losses of my family, Alyssa's death from the virus, Sutton's capture, Grace's pregnancy, Cole lying about his past, and shooting Amber. All of these things battle for my energy, my attention. But I can't let them have it. I can't let the past cloud the task ahead of me.

"No you're not. I can see it in your eyes."

"Then why'd you ask?"

"Because I care about you. Not in the way you would hope though."

"Ha! Thanks, Bill," I say, giving him a warm smile. "I care about you as well, so please don't get yourself killed out there, all right?"

"Aw, Lusty, I told you, I wanna be a hero … I'll die with honor to get this done, if it's what I need to do."

"Me too. And by the way … I'm glad you're here with us."

"Thank ya. That means a lot to hear you say that. And you know, I might fight you for Zeus when we get out of here."

"Not a chance in hell, Bill. But we can find you a dog of your own."

"Now that right there sounds good to me. I've always wanted a companion that would put up with my craziness." He rubs his hands together and then picks up a gun. "Now we've got to load these in."

I place the magazine charger onto the magazine, and with my other hand, I pick up a ten-round clip. Using some force, I push the rounds into place, until the magazine is full. Then I take the extra clips and push them into a belt with seven pockets, each pouch holding two clips. Bill and I fill four belts.

When I'm finished, I whistle through my teeth. "That's a lot of ammo."

"And we're not done yet," Bill says. He goes to the wall and picks out grenades. We put them on the table, dividing them up for each person.

I grab some magazines for Cole's handgun and fill them up, just in case he has space to store them in his pants. I pack myself some too. It looks like there are only two pairs of night-vision goggles, so I pull them off the shelf. I'm sure Bruno and Cole will want them for inside.

"How in the world will you be able to run, carrying all this?" I ask.

"Not too worried about the running part." His admission takes me by surprise, and I step back, surveying the weapons. "The surviving part, now that's a tad worrisome," Bill says. I snort.

The door swings open, and Grace enters in a rush. Her forehead glistens with sweat, and her eyes turn to saucers as she lays her gaze on the weaponry we've stacked and loaded. She stops and holds out her arms.

"What you got there?" Bill asks.

"I know I said I'd pack food, and I was, but then I found these and thought they'd be helpful … just in case." She puts three kits on the floor and then kneels and opens one up for us to see inside. "See? They're blow-out kits … in case someone's injured."

"Wonderful," Bill says.

"What's in them?" I ask.

"Bandages, one tourniquet each, Quick Clot for helping blood clot faster, gauze … " she says as she shows me each one. I pick up one package and turn it over in my hands.

"The label says it's a chest decompression needle," I say. "I don't even know what you do with it."

"Me either, but hey, we at least we have one," she says. I put the needle back in the sack and see shears, a glow stick, and exam gloves. Afterward, she puts it all back inside the brown pouch and gives it to me.

She stands up and brushes off her pants. "Taking them

leaves less room for food and water, but weapons and medical kits are more important."

"Don't worry about it." Bill comes around me and gives her a hard look. "We'll even out the weight between the five of us. We'll each have enough to snack on and drink."

"Hey, Lexi?" Grace says. "C. Hamilton, that's your father right?"

"Yeah, why?"

"The message on the wall, I read it on my way over, and I didn't want to just assume it was him."

"It's my dad."

"What's his first name? If you don't mind me asking."

"Of course not. It was Christopher."

"I've always loved that name; it's strong."

"Thanks. Me too."

"Well, if you guys are all right here, I'll be on my way," she says. "See you in a bit." She glances at me, then leaves as fast as she entered.

"Brain break time," Bill says.

"What?"

"I'm going to take fifteen."

"Okay."

Bill slumps against the wall and closes his eyes. Next thing I know, he's snoring and smacking his lips in his sleep.

I put the medical kits beside the stacks of weapons. My eyes burn, and I feel zapped of all my energy. I flick the light off and am about to head into the training room, when I see Bruno and Cole, quietly going over plans for the hospital. I decide to stop next to the doorway and listen.

They sit on the floor, papers laid out between them. Their

324

hushed voices bounce off the low ceiling. Zeus sits loyally at Cole's side, and Roméo sleeps under a sweatshirt against the wall. The blinking overhead light shows dark hollows beneath Cole's eyes. Yet, he's still awake.

"I guess that's it." Cole sighs. He folds up a paper. "Our fate rests on tomorrow."

They gather the remaining papers and tuck them into their clothes. When only one's left lying between them, Bruno clears his throat. I watch as Cole's head snaps up.

"Listen, man," Bruno says, "all joking aside, if something happens to me—"

"Stop. Nothing's going to happen, all right?" Cole says.

"But if it does, promise me you'll get Grace the hell out of here. I came into this mess willingly, but her ... she's here because of me. So please ... don't let them ... " Bruno can't even finish.

I twist the ring around my finger and feel my heart catching in my throat. I've never heard Bruno's voice sound so broken and vulnerable before. *And he doesn't even know the worst part.* Cole leans over and puts a hand on Bruno's shoulder.

"You're the best damn combat fighter I know. We're smarter than them," Cole says. He pulls his hand back, and they lock eyes for a moment. "We are all getting out of here alive."

I think about their friendship. I can't even imagine the fire that's tested it so many times before this. They know each other's moves, and effortlessly work in small spaces together. They trust each other with their families and lives, like brothers.

"Okay, no more mushy crap," Bruno says. He laughs and punches Cole in the shoulder, breaking the tension. Zeus's head perks up.

I laugh to myself until a clatter outside the training room drives my attention away. Grace cusses. She carries a huge backpack and a box of canned goods. I rush out of the weapons room to help her.

"Grace, you're holding too much weight," I say, as I pick a few cans off the floor.

"Shhhh," she says. She rests the box on one knee while reorganizing the cans to balance better. "Don't baby me in front of him."

"You really should tell him."

"No way, not now," she says.

"Grace, he has a right to know, even if it's painful."

"You're right. He does, and once we're done with this, I'll tell him. Timing's everything with Bruno."

"By coming with us, you're putting you and your baby at risk."

Cole's jaw drops open, and I realize he must have followed us out, and obviously overheard some things. I put a finger to my lips, telling him to keep his mouth shut. "Please ... stay here," I say to Grace.

"No. I'm coming with you." Grace's face dissolves into a perfect smile as Bruno arrives and takes the box from her. "Thank you, darling. There's no room in my backpack."

"Looks like we're set," he says in his booming voice. "When wifey brings food, I know it's game time." He puts his arm around her and pulls her in for a kiss on the head.

I give a strained smile before taking a seat next to Zeus. He rolls over, all paws and fur, almost scratching me in the face with his nails. His tongue hangs out sideways, and I run my fingers over his belly.

After a while, I lie down on the floor and stare at the ceiling. Once, I trained in here. I even danced in here. And now, I wonder if I might die in here. I close my eyes and picture Alyssa in her last hours of life.

I feel Cole's presence. I open my eyes and then turn to face him, even though I don't have the energy to talk.

"How long have you known?" Cole asks in a whisper.

"A few days."

"And she hasn't told Bruno?"

"No, and it's not our place to tell him."

"He has a right to know."

"Dammit, Cole. I had a right to know. Don't be a hypocrite."

"So it's okay for her to keep a secret from her husband?"

"It's between them. We should stay out of it. And no, I don't agree with what she's doing, but it's none of our business."

"His wife's pregnant. If it were you, and you told others before me, that'd destroy me." He sounds wounded, lost.

I find myself scooting away from him.

"You're right. Secrets have a way of destroying relationships."

He sucks in air and swallows hard. "You're right. I was wrong for not telling you." He pauses. "I made a huge mistake, and I'd do anything to go back and make the right choice, but I can't."

"Cole, I love you. That hasn't changed." Someone hits the lights, and the room goes completely black. "But I won't be able to forgive you just like that, just overnight."

"I hope you do," he whispers, "before it's too late."

CHAPTER 25

Zeus paces back and forth. I throw a blanket at him, trying to distract him from whatever got him worked up. He lets out a low, gruff growl. Finally, I push myself up on my elbows.

"What's wrong?"

He woofs and then nudges my hand. "Grrrrrrrrrrr." He lets out a very unpleasant noise.

I sit up completely, tossing my thin cover. Reaching over, I shake Cole's shoulder. He moans as I tug him awake. His covers rustle as he sits up and flicks on a small flashlight.

"What time is it?" he asks. He rubs his eyes with one hand and squints at me.

"I don't know. Look." I point to Zeus.

"How long has he been doing that?"

"A couple minutes, at least," I say.

Zeus's hair stands straight up the entire way down his

spine. He's fixated on the entrance to the training room, and his eyes glow green against the flashlight. He bares his teeth and keeps woofing. It sends all my senses into overdrive. My body tingles the way it does when something's awry, and my heart picks up pace.

"I'll wake Bruno," Cole says in a tight voice.

But everyone is already awake.

Grace immediately makes for the restroom, but Bruno grabs her elbow. "Something's happening. You can't go out there right now." He pulls out and turns on his flashlight, checking the room for signs of an intruder.

Roméo stares, bewildered by the bright lights flashing in his face. He struggles to his feet.

"What's going on?" he asks.

"Where's Bill?" Bruno asks, putting his boots on and gathering his belongings. "Stay here," he says to Grace. She looks over at me, then Cole, and then takes a seated position against the wall.

A crashing sound reverberates throughout the training room. Cole's light flicks in the direction of the entrance. We see Bill on all fours, wading through trash. *Crazy drunk.*

"Here," Bill says.

My eyes quickly focus on the hallway behind him as Zeus's woofs grow ever louder. His ears point in the direction of the hallway, his tail stands up, moving back and forth in a rigid motion.

I pull on my boots, hastily lacing them together over my sweaty socks and barely keeping my fingers steady enough to pull the final knot tight. I can't seem to clamp down on the fluttering sensation going on in my stomach.

"Everyone to the weapons closet. Run!" Bruno says while practically shoving us toward it.

Cole flicks his flashlight onto a lower setting as we scamper across the training room floor toward the weapons closet. Once inside, he shuts the door and stands in front of it. He then instructs Zeus to block it with his massive body.

Something is definitely wrong.

"Load 'em up!" Bruno says.

"Everything?" Grace asks. A quizzical expression crosses her face.

"All of it," he says. "And do it fast."

He begins pulling on a vest and shoving grenades inside. Every pocket, every possible inch of his clothing is filled with something lethal. He has to be carrying close to one hundred pounds, if not more, by the time he's done. And that's before he picks up an M4 and two knives from the table.

After Bruno gets his gear on, he takes Cole's place, and they rotate getting ready, arming themselves and packing medical supplies and food.

I pack extra magazines for the new handgun I choose and shove them into my pockets and then throw on a vest. It's a little too big, but it makes it easier to carry everything I need. My hands shake as I shove as much in as possible. *This is it.* Finally, I push the medical kit into my backpack along with extra food, hoping it doesn't burst.

When I finish, sweat drips down my nose. I pull at the collar of my t-shirt, but the vest and backpack hold in the heat like a sauna. I examine Cole. He wears a helmet strapped under his chin with night-vision goggles mounted on top. His biceps pop out as he handles his M4, sweat rolling in slick paths down his forearms. He catches me staring at him. I see his Adam's apple bob for a slight second before he turns his head away, sealing his lips.

My attention's drawn back to Zeus as his ears shift directions. Cole cracks the door open barely an inch, and then we hear it. Quick thuds move in our direction, so Cole flips the lights off.

"Oh, shit," he says. "They've found us."

"Let them come," I say, mostly to myself.

The darkness makes me feel like I'm staring into a black hole. I can't see any shadows. I clench my gun, but I've got no line of sight, just darkness. My mind forms a mental checklist of everything I packed. *I'm ready.*

More thumping.

Zeus's growling is constant now. He's also pacing, ready to attack whatever is out there. But his steps are quiet, like a predator stalking prey, sneaking about undetected.

Cautious whispers echo in my ears. My feet freeze in place. I roll my stiff neck and take deep breaths. If they were friendlies, I imagine they'd want us to know who they are, and they'd be introducing themselves loudly instead of sneaking around in the darkness.

"Move out," Cole says. "Now."

Adrenaline rushes through my body like electricity through a live wire. My heart jumps in my chest as my pulse beats loudly in my ears. A hand pushes me forward, and I extend mine outward, connecting with Cole's backpack.

We move out of the training room, each connected by a hand to prevent from getting lost in the labyrinth of the underground.

A crashing sound splits the highly charged silence.

My skin is on fire. We need to escape. Now.

Cole picks up the pace and turns left. My legs feel heavier under all the equipment I carry, but I do my best to keep up with him. Every second counts.

I don't hear Zeus growling as much, so I hope that means we're going unnoticed despite our gear rattling around. But then I see little red dots marking the walls around us, and I know the worst has happened.

"Get down!" I yell.

Cole makes a fast right turn, and I stumble behind him.

A barrage lights up the darkness. Green and red tracers zip past, shattering the quiet, and illuminating the space around us. Bullets lace the wall, sending rock fragments everywhere. Grace screams, and my ears vibrate with Cole's M4 return fire. He bangs out three bursts and then repeats. Only he and Bruno have night-vision scopes, so they are the only ones who are able to shoot. The rest of us hobble along in the dark, trying not to get shot.

"Hurry, follow me," Cole orders over the commotion.

I don't know where Cole's taking us at first. I'm too busy ducking my head and following him in the eerie lighting. It takes me back to when my parents took Keegan and me to see fireworks when we were children. I remember sitting on a blanket with my family and sharing laughs and food together. I remember my mom's face as my dad popped open a bottle of champagne and poured her some. They clinked glasses right before the fireworks began.

Keegan was never as silent as when the first one exploded over our heads. Green, and red, and blue, and shapes of hearts and smiley faces lit the night sky. I couldn't believe fireworks

332

came in so many variations. My favorites were the glittery ones that descended like stars. I remember looking back at my parents as they sat together. Dad's arm was around Mom, and they looked so happy with the light of the fireworks reflecting off their faces. But it was Keegan's smile I loved most.

Remembering my family like that, together and happy, hits me square in the gut. I'm pulled back to now. But now, it's not fireworks, it's bullets spraying us.

I step through rubble. A haze of smoke and dust thickens the air, and I inhale the ashes. My nose burns with the smell of lead. As we run, I try to clear my throat, which feels as though it's coated with paste.

Cole makes more turns. The hallways seem to narrow the farther out we go. Bruno lights the guards up from the tail end of the line, his gun steadily barking. I glance over my shoulder.

Roméo's chin quivers, and he winces with every boom and crack. His hands fumble along the wall as Grace follows behind, hunching under the weight of her backpack. She ducks her head, keeping it low. Her eyes lift to mine, her expression sad and fearful. *No, stay focused.*

All I hear is the pop, pop, popping and the bang, bang, banging of rapid gunfire. I clench my gun with clammy hands as my backpack straps cut into my tense shoulders.

Cole quickly opens the main hatch as the hammering of the guns behind us grows louder. He wrenches the bolts open and slams the door outward. It bangs against the ground. A small cloud of dust shakes upward.

He turns toward us and waves us forward as moonlight creeps into the tunnel. I step out behind him, ready for anything, and sprint across the street. The others trail behind me, each

333

one of them gently tapping the one in front to let them know they're safe. I exhale with relief when everyone shows up in one piece. We sit in a position half-sheltered by darkness, across the street from the entrance. I smash my back against a wall as Zeus sits obediently beside me, twitching with a thirst for more action.

Bruno pulls a grenade from his belt. He glances at Cole, who nods.

"Man, if I throw this ... we're never getting back down there," Bruno says.

"Toss it," Cole says in a low voice.

If we can't go back inside, then where'll we go? And if we get the medical records, then what? I catch Roméo's face and wonder if he's thinking the same thing.

The firing ceases. But my head still thrums with the echo of bursting guns. I squint to see inside the dark entrance. The hatch has been pushed to the right by Cole. It's gray and well camouflaged, tucked between two cement block buildings. A dark green metal awning of some sort connects them, sagging overhead. It's a wonder it hasn't collapsed yet. It casts just enough shadow over the entrance that most wouldn't suspect its presence. Bruno stands outside the hatch, waiting with steady hands.

They should be approaching the narrow hallway leading into the wider berth of the tunnel. My finger tightens on the trigger of my gun. My breathing's ragged, my vision focused. They must know they're vulnerable, that, for once, we have the upper hand.

In a split second, Bruno pulls the tape off the spoon, slips the pin out, and throws it into the tunnel. I hear it tumble through the hallway. Voices echo into the street as they scream and scramble to get away.

"Cover!" Bruno shouts. His hulking form races across the street as we all dive for positions of safety. I yank Zeus against me, cowering against the building.

The grenade explodes. A puff of ash and smoke and dust spirals above the entrance. Bruno grabs another grenade and lobs that one in too.

The hatch is almost blown off, hanging by one hinge and punctured with little chunks of cement. Slowly, the metal awning hanging between both buildings drops down with a crash. The brittle edges of it slice into the ground. Anyone within a few block's radius had to have heard that.

I hold my breath, waiting. Bruno jumps out from his position of cover and holds his gun at the ready. He approaches the hatch. He carefully lifts the sharp metal edge of the awning so he can peer inside. Thick, gray clouds of smoke billow out, and he waves Cole to come closer for a look.

Cole follows him, holding his gun tight to his shoulder, as Bruno steps down into the tunnel. Their bodies disappear. I grit my teeth. I feel so helpless, but I know if anyone's going to get it done, it'll be Bruno and Cole.

Gunshots split the humid, moonlit night. I jump to my feet, exposing myself, but not caring. Zeus barks, and we both sprint across the street.

Not Cole, please. Not anyone.

In the midst of the trailing smoke, I watch as Bruno and then Cole exit the tunnel. Paths of sweat form light streaks on their grimy faces. Relief washes over me, and my shoulders relax. They're alive, uninjured. Cole's eyes meet mine, but his posture doesn't ease a bit. Even in the moonlight, I see his forearms flexing.

"All clear," Bruno says.

"Who was that?" Roméo asks.

"Guards, an entire squad," Cole says in a strained voice. "And there'll be more."

I turn around, and see Grace struggling under the heavy load she carries. I run to her and offer to help her off her knees, but she shrugs me off.

"Can I carry something for you?" I ask as I reach out my arm.

"No, dear," she says too quickly. "I can do this, but thank you."

That's when I notice numerous people standing in the street. They come silently, and their eyes follow our every move. I swallow hard and put a sweaty hand on Zeus's back. He seems as uneasy out here as he did underground. He won't sit, and he woofs at every sound.

"Oh my," Bill says. "Follow me."

His voice sounds steady and sure. The way he carries himself stuns me, not what I'd expect after witnessing all the drinking he does on a daily basis.

"Lexi, stay within arm's length," Cole says. "I'll shield you with my body if it comes to that."

"They're not going to shoot me."

"And what if they do? Even by accident? I'm sorry, but I'm not willing to take that chance."

Bill leads us through alleyways and streets. He moves quickly, like a fox. Now I know why I never paid him much attention before. Though always drunk and obnoxious, he's adept at keeping under the radar.

He avoids wide, open areas, so we dredge through trash in the murkiest alleyways, and then he stops, lifting the lid of a sewer. *You've got to be kidding me.* He raises an eyebrow, sensing my thoughts.

"Want to hide from them?" he asks. I nod. "You first."

I carefully step onto the first slippery rung. My hands slide down the wet ladder as I struggle to hold on with all my equipment. The farther we travel downward, the lower the temperature drops. I wrinkle my face as the stench of decaying bodies, garbage, and stale water hits me. This is worse than I thought.

"And how come we weren't informed this existed?" Cole asks as everyone reaches the bottom.

"Don't know, man, but I'm not complaining," Bruno says.

"Well, good thing I know about it, huh?" Bill says in whisper. Even then, his voice carries.

"Let's not forget there are cameras everywhere in the Hole." Bruno says. "They might be following us."

"Let them try," Bill says. He begins cutting a path down the dark tunnel.

My boots make a sucking sound with each step, and water trickles from somewhere. Luckily, I can't see what I'm stepping in.

"This tunnel runs about one hundred yards," Bill says. He cautiously peeks around the corner. "The first Commander began construction on it, but after a while, it was abandoned."

"Really? I can't imagine why," I say, almost gagging.

It's quiet, except for our feet sloshing through inches of liquid. Then something brushes against my leg.

"Zeus, please tell me that was you," I say. My voice comes out shaky. But I already know it wasn't Zeus because his tail whips my knee from in front of me.

"Something run along your foot?" Bill asks. "Probably just a rat." He flips on a light, and the hairy bodies skitter across the floor, through the muck.

"Ahhh, I hate rats," I say.

"Would you prefer bullets flying around your head?" Bill asks.

"Smart-ass."

"I'm going to throw up," Grace says. She stops, her bag slides to the side of her back, and I catch it. She heaves violently and then stands up straight.

"Are you okay?" Bruno asks as he pats her back.

She swallows and gives a thin smile. "I'm fine; it's the smell."

"Yeah, tell me about it," Bruno says. But his tone falls flat compared to the usual jokes he tells.

Bill stays close to the wall on the left side, stopping occasionally to make sure all of us follow. Every noise carries, especially the jangling of our equipment.

"What in the world … is that?" Grace asks.

Cole flips his flashlight across the tunnel, and I find myself groaning with disgust. My hands fly to my mouth.

A body lies there half decomposed, its clothing stretched across bloated, green-tinted skin, liquid dripping from its nose and mouth. As soon as the stench reaches my nose, I don't know if I will be able to keep from puking.

"Don't look," Cole says, trying to redirect me with his body.

But I've already seen the maggots crawling through the

nose of the body. My breath catches, and I turn my head away. *This isn't real. This isn't the closet with the dead cat and the maggots weaving in and out and all over me. I'm not being tortured by my stepfather anymore.* But my arm begins burning to the point that I tear at it with my hands.

"Lexi, you'll all right, I'm right here," Cole says. I realize I've left claw marks on my arm and have to shake my head free of the nightmarish memories. "You're bleeding." He sounds breathless.

"I am?"

"Not a lot," he says, wiping my arm with his bare, rough hand. Sure enough, when he pulls it away, blood stains his fingers.

"Poor person probably came down here to die," Bill says.

"What a terrible way to go," Bruno says. "Smelling like crap."

"Bruno!" Grace says, then she turns to Bill. "Please, I'm begging you to hurry up."

"Only a few more … " Bill stops and then tugs on a ladder hanging from a black-stained cement wall. "Ah, here it is." He smiles. "Going up?"

"Oh, for the love of God, yes," Grace says.

Bill climbs up the ladder, carefully removing the lid of the sewer with a scraping sound.

"All clear," he says.

With the delicate balance of tightrope walkers, we somehow manage to get back up the ladder and enter the street without being seen. Strangely, the sewer comes out into an alley between two shacks.

"It's no wonder you survived here so long," I say in a whisper.

Bill grins at me, light gleaming off his teeth. "Being crazy has its advantages."

"You're not that crazy," I say. "Just different, but it's a good different."

"Lusty, I must say, you're my favorite person here." We smile at each other, and he pats my shoulder.

When I turn around, Grace holds onto the wall and stumbles out of the sewer. Her skin has a chalky undertone as she turns and throws up on her own shoes. My stomach drops. I put a hand on the back of her neck and give her a squeeze as she finishes. When she comes up, her eyes are watering, and she purses her lips to keep from crying. But there's no time to rest. And even if there was, she motions us forward, not wanting to make us wait on her account.

Bill leads us toward the hospital, the tall, dark outline of it just a few blocks away. I notice there are no stars, just a velvet blanket of navy blue laid over us and the large moon glowing white as it hangs suspended above.

Mosquitoes and flies crawl all over us. I instinctively whack and shoo them away from my face.

We get through one block, discreetly staying in alleyways packed with broken furniture, trash, bodies, and countless other obstacles. But the next block is a street. Already, my heart beats in my ears, and my legs feel numb beneath my knees. The Sinners have to be hungry, and here we are, running around, with food packed onto our backs. *God save us.* If I were them, I'd want to hunt me down too.

Cole taps my shoulder, letting me know he's behind me, and I move ahead. I keep my head on a swivel and scan in patterns. I check rooftops, houses, and especially dark doorways and windows. All of my senses work together, keeping me tense and alert.

I hear screaming and pause, flicking my eyes in the direction of the noise. Two Sinners fight each other in the street as a small crowd surrounds them. Children are pushed to the back of the crowd, an attempt to shield them from whoever's making the grunting and moaning noises.

Bill stops and points to a doorway. I follow him inside. He peers through the single window in front with a frown on his face.

"We can't move until they're done," he says.

A hand rests on my arm. I turn, and it's Grace. She nods her head left. I follow her gaze as the street noise grows louder.

"They're fighting over food," she says in a low voice.

Bill shakes his head. "It's heartbreaking," he says.

"But there are children," she says. Her mouth's set, and her hands rest on her hips.

"Grace, we can't help them right now," Bill says. Before he can finish, Grace opens the door and stoops in the entryway.

"Pssst," she says.

"What are you doing?" Bruno asks.

"Psst," she says again. A young boy glances in her direction. His filthy face and sad eyes fill my heart with compassion. I know exactly what she's doing, and it makes me love her more.

"Come here," she says.

"Grace, you can't. You're risking exposure," Bill says. I put my hand on his shoulder, and he grunts, exhaling a frustrated sigh.

The young, dark-haired boy wanders over. He wears a t-shirt that's too small for him by about three sizes, tattered jeans, and no shoes. At first, he seems afraid. His eyes widen, and his mouth parts in awe as he takes in the sight of our group and all our equipment.

Grace gives me a beckoning look. With trembling hands, I unzip part of her backpack and pull out a protein bar.

He jumps back, hands flying in front of his dirtied face.

"It's okay, I'm not going to hurt you," I say. He slowly drops his hands.

He reaches out. I notice the dirt under his fingernails and the creases of his small hands as I place the bar in his palm, giving him a tentative smile. It's not much, but it's better than nothing. The boy rips open the wrapper and shoves the entire bar into his mouth, eyes warily scanning us.

The crowd begins breaking up. I hear Bill's impatient foot tapping beside me as the boy swallows his last bite and licks his lips.

"Do you have any more? My sister's starving too," he says in a quiet voice.

"Yes," I say, before Bill can answer. I give him two more bars and then zip Grace's sack back up.

"Dahlia," he whispers. A little girl standing in the street alone, staring at the group of Sinners, raises her head, trying to locate him. "Dahlia, come here."

"Now this is just great," Bill mumbles. But I don't pay him any mind when I see her.

A head of bouncy, scraggly curls frame an almost luminescent complexion with large, almond-shaped eyes and full lashes. She reminds me of a china doll. The boy waves her over quietly.

At first, she seems frozen. Her eyes move nervously between the dispersing crowd of Sinners and us.

"Hurry up," the boy says. I see the hesitance in her eyes as she slowly steps toward us. She twists her fingers around in front of her. When she gets to the doorway, the boy pulls her inside. "Look, they have food!" He holds out the protein bar, and her eyes light up.

"And we can eat it?"

"Yes," her brother says.

He hands her the protein bar, and she shoves it into her mouth. Her cheeks puff out like a chipmunk as she chews.

"We haven't had anything to eat for two days," he says. His hands go to his stomach, and he rubs it as his eyes fall to the floor. He kicks dirt around with his bare feet.

My eyes water, but I blink back the tears. *How many more children are starving in the Hole?* Then the little girl grabs her brother, and he hands her the last protein bar. As she stretches out, her torn sleeve slides up her thin, pale arm.

My heart breaks into pieces when I see the perfect, dark circle marking her. My chest tightens, and my hands ball into fists. *Oh my God. She's younger than Alyssa.*

"When did you get that?" I blurt. I point at her arm, and she retracts it as quickly as she extended it. Her eyes flash a warning, and her brother puts his arm around her protectively.

"Lexi," Cole says. I fight the urge to wrap her in my arms as Cole pulls me back. He gives me a warning look.

She can't be saved.

"I'm sorry," I say. "I … "

The boy squints. He examines me for a minute and then drops his arm from around his sister.

"She got that vaccine thing this morning," he says. "At least she won't get sick."

343

I want to die when he says those words. Because that's what they told Amber. Part of me wants to scream out loud. I do my best to mask my emotions, but my facial muscles twitch as I try to keep from crying.

Oh my God, please let us get these records out ... He's still killing children.

"It's time," Bill says.

The boy pulls his sister's hand, their faces instantly turning grim and serious. Dahlia coughs, and I see her cringe.

I know what she's about to go through, and I fight the images of her screaming in pain like Amber.

"Take your sister and go straight home; it's not safe out here," Bruno says. His voice cracks a little. He bends down with all his equipment on. "Be brave, okay? And don't tell anyone what happened here. It's our little secret."

The boy nods. "Okay. I won't tell anyone."

Outside, someone calls their names. The boy flips his head to the side, his shaggy hair lying across his forehead, then he runs down the street, holding Dahlia's hand. She looks back once, and we catch eyes, but then I tear mine away. I can't breathe. My heart can't take much more; soon, it's going to combust.

Bruno helps Grace get up, and I see tears in her eyes. She wipes her hands on her pants and gives me a weak smile. I can only guess what she's thinking. *These could be her children. This could be their future, if we don't stop it.*

"Come," Bill says. He runs his hand through his wild hair.

I'm thankful for the interruption because I don't want to go to pieces right here. It's time to focus on finding the medical records.

Bill steps out of the building, checks around, and runs down the street, stopping and waiting for the rest of us to catch up. My equipment feels like a load of boulders on my back, and I lean to compensate for the weight. The dark silhouette of the hospital grows closer with each step. Dahlia's small face flashes before me, but I put her in a tiny compartment of my brain and push it away for now.

I concentrate on steadying my breathing and staying alert. The faint fingertips of the sun stretch over the horizon, and things become clearer with the pink of early morning. I see the dilapidated structures people live in, the cement and faded fabric decoupage that makes up so much of the Hole. The gray buildings, dirt streets, and the abandoned and burned-out cars along the road remind me of the people who still live here. Most of the cars have blown-out windows, missing rims, and black, bare-tread tires with scuff marks.

It's not long before the siren wails loud and clear. I look up, staring into the sky, and see birds sitting on the loudspeakers mounted on the walls of the buildings. They don't bother moving. In fact, they fight over spots to perch. *Probably looking for fresh pickings after last night's fights.*

Four blocks from the hospital, Bill leads us into a tiny, one-room shack. He scans it and then says, "Clear."

My shoulders throb, and every muscle in my back aches. Following his cue, I pull off my backpack and relax my shoulders. He puts a finger over his mouth and sits down.

As we settle down, our knees and legs bump into each other, and our equipment bangs together. I pray no one hears it. Then Zeus sits in my lap, completely obstructing my view of everyone else. I groan as his paws dig into my thighs. His

345

head sits way above mine; he's so darn big.

"We wait here," Bill says. "Tonight, we'll enter the hospital."

"How do you know someone doesn't live here?" Bruno asks.

"I don't, so we'll take turns guarding it," Bill says. "Meanwhile, I say we rest some."

Outside, occasional engines growl in the street, whispers of voices travel, and feet scamper past. Birds caw and scream in the sky. The flies fester on my flesh and buzz about my head. And in the distance, I hear the marching of boots and the scuffling feet of Sinners.

I lean my head back against the wall and close my eyes.

Tonight will change everything, forever.

CHAPTER 26

It's dark, but I'm awake. My eyes quickly adjust to the darkness. Bill stands, wide awake, staring outside the hut. His head moves from left to right, scanning for trouble. He holds his gun in front of his midsection.

"Fifteen minutes until go time," Bill says, not even glancing my direction. "Rise 'n shine sluttastic," he adds, even though he sees I'm already up.

"Sluttastic? That's a new one." I crack my neck.

Cole slowly wakes, blinking and sitting up straight. When he lowers his dirty fists from his eyes, he resembles a raccoon.

"Where's the fire?" Cole asks. I snort, not looking at him.

"There's no fire, dipshit, just the normal world exploding. Nothing new and exciting," Bruno says.

"Explosions cause fires," Cole says.

"Always gotta be a smart-ass, don't you?" Bruno asks. He

takes Grace's hand and pulls it to his lips. She smiles at him as he kisses it, his fingers interlocking with hers.

Cole watches them too, but if he thinks I'm going to allow him to do that to me, he's wrong. He looks at me, and I glance in the opposite direction.

I remember the conversation Grace and I had in the shower room. I asked her about the female guard who helped us get into the Hole. I felt there was a connection there that Cole and Bruno weren't willing to talk about and couldn't resist sticking my nose in it. But, as usual, Grace lived up to her name when answering me. She explained that Bruno had dated lots of other women before, some quite beautiful. But, she said, she didn't play his games. And because of that, he chased her and practically begged her to be his wife. The other women were his past. She was confident she was his future. And when I see the gentle way he handles her, I can tell she's right.

"Pack it up; it's game time boys. Oh, and ladies, sorry," Bill says. The corner of his mouth lifts up, giving away a sly smile as if he's enjoying this.

A combination of groaning and equipment clunking around fills the shack as we jostle about. My muscles feel stiff, and my tendons crack when I straighten my knees. I'd stretch, but our elbows are already knocking into each other as it is.

"Okay, listen up, here's the plan," Bill says. From one of his pockets, he pulls out his bottle and tosses the liquid down his throat. "We're going to split up, taking two different routes to the hospital, and meet up in the basement. Hopefully." He shoves the bottle back into his pants.

"And why are we separating, exactly?" Cole asks.

"It'll better our chances," Bill says.

"And by that you mean one of us making it there alive?"

"Precisely."

Not one of us seems fazed by the fact that he's giving instructions while swigging alcohol. In fact, Bruno and Cole both nod.

"Grace and Bill, you're with me," Bruno says. "Roméo, you go with Lexi and Cole." Zeus woofs. "Seriously, dog? Go with your twosome."

Grace and Bill line up behind Bruno as he stands in the doorway. He glances all around, then disappears into the night, followed by Grace. Bill squints his eyes, taking one good look at Cole and me, before moving out through the narrow doorway, his footsteps fading away.

Cole's posture is strong and his face relaxed as he straps on his helmet and pulls the night vision over his eyes. He exudes calm while double-checking everything, including us, before squatting in the doorway. His head swivels left, right, up, and down. His jaw twitches, and he runs outside, pausing in the alley between buildings for me to catch up with him. But instead, I push Roméo in front of me.

"What're you doing?" he asks.

"Putting you in the middle. Zeus and I will hold up the back," I say. "It's easier to protect you this way."

"Okay, good. Just tell me what to do because this is way out of my comfort zone."

"Don't worry. I'll do my best to keep you alive."

"Thank you."

Roméo rubs his chin and exhales nervously. He looks smaller with his equipment on, less confident carrying a gun, and it's obvious he's not used to combat. After all, he wasn't

349

sent here for that. He peeks his head out the door and runs.

Last, it's Zeus and me. I look down and pat him on the head. *This is it.* The moonlight reflects in his shiny brown eyes and his tail stills. His ears stand up like antennae. I give him a weak smile and then move with him galloping at my side.

I inhale a fresh cloud of dust and feel the growing stickiness of my clothes against my skin. When I reach Roméo, I tap his shoulder. We hunch down between buildings.

I squint, hearing only our steps and my breaths leaving through my teeth. Behind us, the alley opens into another street with small huts stacked up like decks of cards. In front of us looms a busy intersection where rusted cars and boarded-up buildings sit. I hear voices echoing throughout the street in front of us and lean around Cole's wide shoulders to get a better look.

People gather at the intersection, standing in a circle while trading jokes and talking. At first, I see only males, but then a small female joins them.

Even if they're harmless, we still have to act as if they're our enemies. *And they very well might be if they see us.*

The female laughs and smacks one of the males on the back. One of the others shakes his head. None of them have noticed us so far, but my hands stay tense around my gun. We take very slow, cautious steps.

Cole goes first, loose stones crunching under his boots. He turns left, around a corner, and out of the alley. They still haven't given us any reason to believe they've seen us.

One foot in front of the other. I press my lips together and keep my gun ready. We sidestep along the building.

A barrage of gunfire opens up. The Sinners all freeze.

Bullets ricochet above them, chipping and scattering pieces of cement through the air. Sinners dive for cover, yelling and directing each other where to go.

My heart pounds in my chest like a drum on steroids. Cole picks up the pace, but Roméo has a harder time keeping up as he gasps for air. Doors slam, curtains close, and people disappear into huts and doorways. I can't help wondering where the others are and pray they're okay. The sporadic shooting continues. It comes from the direction of the hospital, getting louder and then slowing. Then I hear the thundering of something bigger.

I scan the perimeter for the source of the noise. Zeus lets out a bark, baring his teeth, but when I glance again, there's nothing.

Just then, Cole yanks Roméo into the doorway of a building. I follow without question. After clearing the room, Cole ducks down and pulls all of us away from the door. My backpack and I stumble sideways.

"What the—"

"Shhh," he says, a finger to his lips. He peeks up over the windowsill and then slams his back into the wall below it. His hands turn pale gripping his gun.

A vehicle roars past. I close my eyes and hold my breath. When the vehicle's out of hearing distance, I open my eyes. Roméo's shaking, hands white in his lap.

I get up, dusting the dirt off my pants. I share a water from my backpack with Roméo, who guzzles it down, struggling to catch his breath in between gulps. When finished, he tosses the empty bottle aside. He jumps out of his skin when the popping of the guns start up in the distance.

351

Where are the others?

We head back out into the cacophony. The street's littered with poorly made cement blocks that have crumbled. My feet are on fire, as if someone's rubbed the skin off. Glass litters the ground and crunches under my boots.

The hospital is only three blocks away now. Time's moving in slow motion, yet it's a blur to me. I swat flies away from my face with clammy hands. I don't see Bruno, Grace, or Bill anywhere. Every shadow could be one of them, or a guard. I just hope I know which it is when the time comes.

Throughout it all, though, Cole never waivers. He's quick and decisive. Just the way he runs, directs, and observes makes me feel confident in him, even when I can't trust my own instincts.

We're on the last street before the main intersection in front of the hospital. Cole abruptly turns, weaving through an alleyway filled with trash. Papers, bones, and torn material line the walkway from wall to wall. Something sticks to my feet, but I keep moving.

Up ahead lies another connecting alleyway, reminding me of a maze. When Keegan and I were younger, we'd sometimes make forts in cornfields near our house. The farmer would show up on my parents' porch yelling, but he could never prove it had been us trampling down his corn, making bedrooms and bathrooms and weapons rooms. That farmer was eventually accused of gluttony and taken away.

I blink, and the memory dissipates. Cole stops at the edge of the street. He holds up his fist. He hunches down, so all of us follow, except for Zeus. His ears perk up, and his tail goes stiff.

The ground rumbles beneath us. A shot of terror explodes

352

within me, sending fear through my brain. The clanking and shaking is unmistakable. That sound so familiar. It chokes me up as my thoughts race.

A large tank, silhouetted by the moon, thunders past the front of the hospital. Its turret faces forward, and a man sits inside, his hands rotating the fifty-caliber machine gun on top.

Oh man. We're screwed.

Just then, the gun opens up with a barrage. The building to our right takes the hits, cement and dust sputtering up everywhere. My ears rattle. They fire again, stopping in place, blocking our way into the hospital.

What is this? Target practice? It's too loud to ask Cole what they're doing. The wall begins buckling as the guards unload more rounds into it. I hear the gunner shouting while reloading his machine gun. He tosses shells out the side of his compartment and continues firing at the building, set on destroying it.

My insides twist, and my muscles ache, tense and waiting. Zeus paces, and I pull him to my side, worried he'll take off if we have to sit here too much longer.

Then I hear it. The wall of the building he's shooting at is thoroughly punctured. It begins to crumble. The upper floor comes down with a crash. The tank revs forward, the gunner screaming as he celebrates his victory over the scrappily constructed building.

Any other time, I'd roll my eyes at his lunacy, but right now, I'm ready to go. Cole waits until the tank rolls farther down the street. He glances up, checking for guards on the rooftops. When we move across the intersection, we'll be completely exposed.

He waves us forward, giving us support while we bolt across the street, coming alongside the hospital. I inhale deeply through my nose, then exhale through my mouth. My quads burn from squatting so long.

Three bodies in typical dark uniforms lie in a pile near the entrance of the hospital. I smell cigarette smoke and notice their cigarettes still burning, the ashes tender and red beside their lifeless forms. One of them looks like he's staring right at me. My breath catches in my throat. I slow my roll, hugging the wall, and focus on where to step next. Cole stops to examine them.

"Ahhhhh!" A figure comes bounding out of the darkness, yelling something unintelligible.

At first, my body freezes, unsure if he's friendly. His hands wave in the air. Instinctively, I point my gun at him. He doesn't slow down. Now, he's so close I can actually see his guard uniform and the light shade of his eyes. He's not stopping. I focus on the object in his hand and see the sharp outline of a gun, now pointed at me.

I squeeze the trigger and shoot him. He doesn't stop. Shells pop off to my side as I unload on him. His body slows, but he still stumbles forward. *This guy won't give up.* My pulse races in my throat. *How many rounds did I shoot?* His eyes lock onto mine, and his gun dangles from his hands. I finish him.

He falls forward. Blood flows from beneath him. I nudge the body with my shoe before firing off one more round into his head to make sure he doesn't get up this time. I feel a tap on my shoulder and see Cole's panicked eyes, his night-vision goggles off.

He shoves me forward. But I stop quickly and pick up the

dead guard's gun, shoving it into my pants.

Zeus howls. Another figure darts out of the shadows. I raise my gun, hands steady, finger stretching for the trigger.

"Don't shoot!" Bill shouts. His outline becomes clearer. "It's me." I relax my finger and bring my gun down, shoulders sagging with relief.

"Where the hell have you been?" Cole asks.

"Getting us in," Bill says. "The guards at the front? Yup, that was me." So that's why they were lying there with still-burning cigarettes.

"Are there more?"

"There's always more, and the ruckus you just made won't exactly help things." Bill turns, and we follow him.

"He was going to kill us," I say. "I didn't have a choice."

"The tank completely threw us off," Cole says.

"See? I told you they'd go for a ride," Bill says over his shoulder. "Remember?"

"You forgot to mention it was a tank," I say. "Slightly different than an SUV."

"Jeep? Tank? They decide that, not me. Besides, usually they take the jeep," Bill says. He runs past the side doors and we see Bruno and Grace just as Bruno swings the butt of his gun into a window alongside the hospital. The crashing of glass splits the air. He lowers his equipment in and slides through afterward, waiting for the rest of us to do the same. Cole is through next, then Roméo.

Zeus sprints in front of me, corralling Grace and dancing around her. *Zeus knows.* I hurry to her side, relieved to see her. Her face is coated with sweat, and her shirt's stained around the collar. We push our equipment through first, buying time so we can talk.

"Hey, how are you holding up?"

"Almost peed myself about a thousand times, but otherwise, peachy," she says. She steps back and clasps her hands over her belly. Her eyes drift downward quickly and then we both jump through the opening. Zeus follows and then Bill.

Once we're all inside the basement, chills chase up my spine, causing goose bumps on my arms. I let my feet settle beneath me before grabbing my flashlight and looking around. It's still a mess. Boxes are piled up in heaps. The tables, beds, and chairs are in the same places I remember. I feel Cole's eyes on me as I walk a few feet away from everyone.

This is where it was, this very spot.

I stand in the exact area where guards dragged me just a few months before. If it weren't for Cole and Zeus, they would've raped me right here. *And probably murdered me afterward.* I clear my throat and take a deep breath, feeling a twinge of guilt for being angry at Cole. He grabs my arm, and my hands reflexively come up.

"I'm right here," he says.

"Thank you," I say.

"Come on, faster people," Bruno says.

I straighten my shoulders, put the flashlight away, and focus. "The stairs are that way."

Cole leads, flipping on his night-vision goggles as we get further in. He steps over things we can't see and tries to lead us safely away from them. He stops. He's maneuvering in the darkness, and I wonder what he's doing. Then a flashlight flips on, and I notice he's pulled off his night-vision goggles He points the light toward the wall and nods for me to follow it.

356

The doorway to the staircase. Next to it is a sign that reads *STAIRCASE/8 WEST*. An eerie feeling washes over me. The morgue is only next door. It's too bad we can't take the elevator, but I know the cameras would probably pick us up immediately.

"This is it," I say in a flat voice.

He jiggles the handle, which doesn't budge. He slams his shoulder into the door, but it won't open. Another flashlight flicks on, and Bruno comes to the front of the line.

"Never get lucky," he says. "Everyone back up."

"Seriously?" I ask.

"Yeah, I'm going to blow this sucker."

"Oh, hell," I say, covering my ears.

Cole pushes us away from the door and holds the flashlight as Bruno fires at the lock. Next thing I know, the handle's dangling from the door. When Bruno pushes the door open, it squeals in protest.

They have to know we're in the building now.

"Run, Forest!" Bill says. But I have no idea what he's talking about.

Cole flashes his light up the dark stairwell. "Follow me."

We move in procession up the first flight. I do my best to be quiet, even as Zeus's nails tap along the floor.

Two flights. Roméo stops to catch his breath. He gasps and coughs.

"Come on, we're almost there," Bruno says. He pulls Roméo forward.

Three flights. Grace bends over, placing her hands on her knees. I run to her side and put my hand on the back of her backpack.

"What do you need?"

357

"Water, please." She sounds raspy, so I grab her water and let her drink some before putting it away.

Four flights. My lungs are on fire. My legs ache. I hope I don't start cramping up.

Five flights. Even Cole is breathing heavier now. He's not running so much as jogging up the steps now. His flashlight bounces, and he checks every door along the way. So far, all of them are locked.

Six flights. I'm pretty sure my backpack has completely stripped the skin off my shoulders. I glance back into the shadows. Roméo and Grace look worse. Bruno, on the other hand, looks like he could take another twenty flights carrying Grace and all her equipment on his shoulders.

Seven flights. Bill chugs from his flask, then chucks it away. It clanks on the way down the stairs, making me want to punch him for being so thoughtless.

Eighth and final floor—where Sutton's office is. Once again, the door's bolted shut. I feel all jumpy as Bruno and Cole try to get through it without using their guns. It's no use. Cole shakes his head. Bruno aims his gun.

"Stop," Bill says from the back. "Let me try."

Bruno pulls his finger away from the trigger and allows Bill to step in front of him. In his hands, Bill holds two tools that look like small bobby pins, except one of them is curved. First, he sticks one in the hole and jiggles it up and down, pulling it back out. Then he puts the curved end of the other one at the bottom while shoving the first tool back in. He pulls the bottom tool left, while flicking the other up.

With a click, he pulls the door handle, and it opens.

"What the hell was that?" Bruno asks. "Why didn't you

tell me you could do that?"

"You didn't ask."

Bruno slowly opens the door an inch. Nothing happens. He slides in, Cole moving in behind him. I give cover as the others enter, following shortly after. I can tell the sun's rising because the hallway's a strange hue of light blue. The doors to the patient rooms hang open, but I don't hear a sound.

This seems too easy.

Bruno moves toward the first room, clearing it. Cole moves to the next.

"Clear," Cole says.

"Clear," Bruno says.

They head into the next rooms as Grace, Bill, and I move farther down. I kick in a door and shove inside with my gun raised. I scan the room. My nerves are taut, but my hands are steady. The bed's undone, sheets half on the floor. The chairs are overturned, and the bathroom's dark. I slowly walk to the bathroom door and push it open. Nothing.

"Clear," I say, turning and walking out.

Bill's in the room next door, and Grace goes into the one beyond that. Four more rooms to go, and then we'll head to the office to raid it.

Suddenly, Zeus howls. The hair on my neck stands straight up.

I hear it. There's no mistaking the sound of a gun banging away. I sprint down the hallway, trying to find where it's coming from. Then I hear more shots, and my throat constricts. Bruno stumbles backward into the hallway with a man on top of him. In the guard's hand is a knife.

"No!" I scream.

But Cole comes to his aid, shooting the guy in the torso. His body jerks, and his hands slip, so Bruno shoves him off. More guards pile into the hallway from another room.

Oh my God, it's an ambush.

Hell rains down in the form of bullets. Zeus barks, snarls, and rips at the guard lying on the floor. Drywall from the ceiling begins collapsing in chunks around me. The clatter of quick rounds sounding off deafens my ears. *Pop, pop, pop! Bang! Bang!*

My ears ring. My heart sprints. I dive into the doorway of a previously cleared room and fire from there. I can barely see the white tiles of the floor anymore as men go down.

Zeus and Cole hop into the room with me. I squat so Cole can fire off more rounds from above me. He empties a mag and slams in another. We can't keep firing at this rate, or we'll run out of ammo.

As Roméo and Bruno sprint by, I grab Roméo. The melee is so loud that I have to scream in his face.

"Find Sutton's office now!" He gives me a blank look. "Sutton's office!"

Bruno grabs Roméo's shoulder and drags him down the hallway, past the elevators and in the direction of the office. A few guards close in, but we give cover fire, pushing them back down the hall. Pretty soon, they're imbedded in rooms, trying to take shots at our heads. I'd throw a grenade, but I don't think it'd go off fast enough before they'd toss it back at us.

The inside of the hallway's gutted and smells of sulfur. Dust peppers the air, making visibility almost zero. I cough and then shoot, cough more, and then shoot. Pretty soon, no one fires back. All I hear is the crunch of boots on debris and coughing from the other side. *Hurry up, Roméo.*

At this point, I'm not sure how we're going to get out now that the guards know we're here. We could be surrounded, for all we know. I slide back into the room and watch as Cole slams in another mag. He glances at me, puts his hand on my knee, and beckons me with his eyes.

"I'm okay," I mouth. He nods, strokes my cheek, and then his dark eyes move back to the doorway.

Sunlight filters in, magnifying the thick, white cloud in the hallway. Adrenaline explodes through me, despite the fact I've slept only four hours in the past two days. I'm keyed up, waiting in the doorway.

Someone stumbles over a pile of crumbling tiles. He curses as he falls forward, landing on his hands about five feet from our room. He wrangles himself up and into position faster than I expect. Suddenly, he points his gun in my direction, and I wonder why Cole hasn't yet taken this guy down. Fear ripples through me.

"Don't move," I think he says. But a flash of dark fur knocks him sideways.

Thank you, Zeus.

I take aim and shoot the man in the side. Blood bubbles out in a slow trickle at first, but I don't have time to stop. I flick my head around as another guard charges Cole with a knife. Pure panic erupts in me like a volcano. I grit my teeth. Before I even think of the consequences, I throw myself in front of him.

"No!" I say.

The figure screeches to a halt. He squints at me. His knife's leveled at my chest. Another inch closer, and it'd be through my sternum.

361

"Go ahead!" I scream at him.

"Wish I could," he says with slanted eyes. He pulls the knife away from my chest and tries to slash my face.

I sidestep him, using his own arm's momentum to shove him off balance as Cole plows bullets into his torso. Zeus tears into him, and when he's sure he's dead, he looks up. Blood stains his muzzle.

I suck in oxygen, trying to catch my breath. The air is thick with dust and death. Despite my muffled hearing, I think I hear my name being called. I glance at Cole. He points with two fingers down the hallway and fires off some rounds to discourage more guards from sneaking up on him.

"Go," he mouths. "Stay, Zeus," he says aloud. Zeus parks himself next to Cole like a good watchdog. Then I turn on my heel and run down the hallway.

"Lusty!"

Bill calls me, and this time I know I'm not imagining it. *Where is that coming from?* I hop over debris, steadying myself along the wall, and look around for familiar faces.

"Lusty!" He sounds desperate.

I ground to a stop, my feet sliding on the dust. My hands shoot out, and I catch myself before my face meets the floor. It's like a bloody jungle gym. A trail of blood leads into a room on my left. I peek in. My hearing's starting to clear up when I see his face.

Bill kneels on the floor near the entrance. He shakes his head, his hands trembling. His eyes bulge, and when he motions me to come in farther, I notice his hand's covered in blood. My heart stops.

I don't want to see.

362

I hear more shooting in Cole's direction, and the urge to run comes over me.

"No! Don't leave," Bill says sharply. His rigid posture and trembling lips tell me something more is going on in the room. "You gotta help me." Locking my eyes onto his face, I step in.

At first, I only see a foot.

A hand.

Oh my God.

No.

With each step, I get a clearer image of what's going on.

My throat tightens.

I cover my mouth with one hand to crush the scream that burns inside my throat.

No, please, God. No. No. No.

Grace lies on the floor, blood slowly amassing around her tiny frame.

My legs give out, and I fall to her side, dropping my gun beside me.

She whimpers with each breath, tears streaming from her eyes.

"Oh my God. Grace, no." I shake my head fast. *This is not happening.* I fling my backpack off and unzip the top zipper. My hands fumble until I find the medical kit. I'm shaking so much Bill has to open it for me.

"Lusty, what do we do?" he asks. His face radiates pain. "You're gonna help her, right?"

I nod my head and use the scissors to cut away her bloodstained shirt. There's a bullet hole on the right side of her chest right below her bra. Blood's bubbling out of it. *Oh, Grace.* I pause. *Hold on. Please. Just hold on.*

My eyes snap to Bill, who is blinking rapidly, holding back tears. My mind spins; I don't know what to do for her, other than pack the wound with gauze. But what good would that do? Using the stethoscope, I listen to her injured lung. Nothing. No air moving in or out. I'm guessing her lung's collapsed. Without medical intervention, she's going to die, and we have nothing here to help her. No doctor. Nothing.

My heart races so fast, it pounds in my ears. A shooting pain runs down between my shoulder blades, and I bite down on my tongue. My shoulders slump forward, and I look into Grace's eyes.

"How bad?" she asks. "It doesn't hurt; it just burns."

The words stick in my throat. I can't cough them out. The last thing I want is to tell her the truth, but what choice do I have? I glance down at my hands quickly, noting the blood covering my fingertips, and attempt to steady my breathing.

"I'm not going to die, am I?" She takes a deep breath and coughs a few times. "Lexi, say something!" Her question stabs my core, smashing it with a hammer. "Lexi?"

"Grace ... I think the bullet ... went through your lung." My chest shakes because I can't hold back my emotions. My friend is dying, and once again, I can't do anything about it. "It's collapsed."

Hopeless.

Worthless.

That's what I am right now.

Her breathing picks up pace, and she asks, "What does that mean?"

"It's not working."

Why her? It should be me, not her. She has everything to

live for. A baby. A new life.

I wipe tears with my forearm.

"Hey, it's okay, I still have another one … right?" Her eyes search mine, flitting back and forth between them. She's making jokes, trying to cheer me up even now.

"Yes, but … "

"Oh, dear God in heaven … I'm dying, aren't I?"

I swallow hard and choke out, "No! You're not!" I gently hug her. "Just hang in there, you hear me?"

She rubs the back of my head and says, "Okay."

"I'm sorry, Grace; this is all my fault," Bill says, his voice cracking.

"No." She gasps. Tears spill over her eyes as she takes a few more gasps of air. "This wasn't your fault."

Bill looks frantically through the medical supplies as I hold pressure to her wound.

"What about this needle thing?" he asks, holding it in front of me.

"I don't know … I'm not a doctor, Bill."

Useless.

Failure.

Taking Grace's wrist into my hand, I feel her clammy skin and take her pulse, but it's so rapid, I don't even bother trying to count, and that's when she starts the dry, hacking cough.

Her chest rises and falls faster each passing minute. *Oh my God, please help her. Help me. I don't have time to find help. She doesn't have much time.*

"Grace, look at me." I take her hands in mine, and her chin trembles. She bites her lip and shakes her head. There's no holding back my tears. I'm losing her. I gag on my words,

365

bury my face in her hand for a second, and kiss her cold skin. I swallow hard, clear my throat, and glance at her. Already the skin around her lips is turning bluish.

"I need to get you to Bruno, right now. And you need to tell him."

"I can't ... "

"Yes, you can. You're a strong woman, Grace."

"Lexi, whatever you do, protect my baby. I don't want to lose him."

Bill's eyes widen, and he slams his back against the wall. "What? No." He throws his hands in the air. "Why didn't they shoot me?"

I reach for his hands, and he lowers them into his lap. They're trembling, and I put a hand on his forearm for a second, silencing him with the shake of my head. We don't have time for him to grieve just yet. She needs us to be strong.

"Bill, listen to me. I need you to carry my stuff and cover me."

"Okay."

"Grace, I'm going to have to pick you up."

She nods.

"Wait, let me take her," Bill says, touching my arm.

"No. I'm carrying her." I pick her up, my right arm under her legs and my left arm cradling her back. She rests her head against my chest. Somehow, I get my legs moving and turn down the hall. My eyes fix on the doorway I need to reach. I pick up my pace and call out his name in a desperate tone.

"Cole!"

His footsteps echo behind me, and Zeus pants beside me before I have to say it again. My arms burn with her weight.

Her head bobs against my chest.

"Grace, stay awake," I say. She moans in response.

Cole's breath catches when he sees me.

"Shit," he says. "How bad?"

My eyes meet his briefly, and that's all it takes. He closes his eyes, because he *knows*. I don't need to say it out loud. He curses and then prays under his breath before saying, "How can I help?"

"Open … the door," I say breathlessly. I hook a right, and Sutton's office looms in front of me. I step over the carnage of the hallway and stop at the door, panting and sweating.

Grace is slipping away even as I hold her.

Cole bangs on the door, pushing it open. At first, we don't see anyone. But then I hear the rummaging of papers and boxes and know they must be in the closet.

"Bruno?" I ask in a shaky voice.

"Over here," Bruno says. He's in the closet, out of our view.

Cole stops me for a second. He leans over and kisses Grace on the forehead. "Love you, girl."

"Love you," Grace says back.

Roméo leans out, and his face turns white. He drops the papers in his hands, but he doesn't move an inch.

My arms go weak. I start losing my grip, and Cole takes her from me, carrying her in to Bruno who's rounding the corner of the closet into the main office. I lean against the doorframe to keep from falling. Bruno looks up and sees her. His eyes go wide as his mouth falls open.

The world freezes.

"Grace!" He darts to her, takes her from Cole, and collapses to the ground, holding her like a little child. And she looks like one, curled in his arms. Her skin's developed a greenish undertone to its rich ebony, and her eyes flick open when she hears his voice. He pulls her shirt over and sees where she was shot. With a groan, he rocks back and forth as he shivers. He doesn't even care that blood's pouring over his arms and chest. "You're going to be okay," he says.

"Honey—"

"Stop. You're not gonna die."

"I'm so sorry," Grace says. Her voice comes out in a whisper, and I have to strain to hear what she says.

"Cole, go find help!" Bruno says. Cole stands there and puts his hands on his head. "Now!" Bruno demands. Cole gives Bruno a slight head shake, his jaw twitching and his eyes glazed over.

"There isn't anyone," I say through my ugly cry, stuck in the doorway, unable to move.

"I'm begging you."

"Bruno, please … " I say. "She needs you right now."

Bruno shakes his head, clenches his jaw, and looks down at Grace.

Bill wraps his arms around me and guides me into the room. Then he turns around with his gun pointed toward the hallway in case guards decide to come. Even as he keeps watch, tears leak down his face. His gun shakes in his hands.

Cole meets me and pulls me into him. I sob tears and snot all over his shirt. He holds me up as all my strength leaves me. I turn my head to the side to watch Bruno and Grace's last minutes together.

"Grace, don't leave me." Bruno's voice cracks. "Not now,

not like this."

Grace coughs for a few seconds before gaining enough oxygen to speak. "Bruno, there's something ... "

My stomach clenches. Cole's labored breathing makes his chest shake. I brace myself for the words that are about to tear Bruno's world apart.

Grace lifts her hand and rests it on Bruno's cheek. She strokes it with her thumb, and she blinks fast, her breathing increasing as the seconds speed by.

"I didn't tell you," she whispers. "Because I didn't want you to worry."

Bruno scrunches his forehead. "Tell me what?"

Grace sobs, and tears spill over her face. "We're having a son."

A gasp.

Then stunned silence.

Nothing could have prepared me for the sound that comes out of Bruno next. A heart-wrenching scream that can surely be heard miles away. The kind that slices you like a knife, creating a wound that will never completely heal. His shoulders shake uncontrollably, and I grip Cole's shirt and cry so hard it feels like someone stuck a torch down my throat.

There's something about watching a man, a man with such physical strength, a man that has been nothing but a rock in all our lives, completely crumble before our eyes. Unhindered tears cascade down his defined cheekbones, over his jaw, and onto his clothes. He leans over her face, putting a hand on each side, opening and closing his mouth. Everything comes out as a groan.

"I'm sorry," Grace says.

"You're pregnant?" His voice breaks.

"Yes." Her breathing changes, and her voice weakens, getting softer with each word.

He sits back and slams his teeth together while looking up at the ceiling. His muscles all tense in his face as he lets out an excruciating scream. Then he bends back over, sobbing.

"This isn't fair! I'm holding everything I've always wanted, and I … " His tears fall onto Grace's shirt and snot pours out of his nose. He gags on his words, unable to speak. He kisses her face, then lifts her hands to his lips and kisses them too. In between kisses, he cries and rocks on his knees. When he notices her silence, he hunches forward.

"Don't you give up on me, Grace. Don't you dare do it. Fight, fight harder. For us, for our son."

But there's no fight left.

Grace's eyes roll into the back of her head. I run toward her and fall to my knees on the opposite side of Bruno.

"Grace," I say. "Look at me." She blinks a few times, and her tired eyes, her pained eyes, look into mine. "I'll be back. I'm going to get help."

Desperate.

I stand and turn around to sprint out the door, but Cole catches me before I make it two feet.

"Let me go," I say.

"Lexi," Cole says into my ear. "You know I can't."

"Please." I'm pounding on his chest, but he just squeezes me harder.

"I'm sorry, but I won't let you die, too," he whispers.

"She's not dying." But I know she is, and I cry into his shirt and almost suffocate myself. I have to turn my head to the side, and that's when all hope melts away from Bruno's face.

"Lexi," Grace says.

I take a deep breath, and Cole holds my arm as I make my way back to her.

When I'm with her, she takes my hand in hers. It feels like ice.

No. No. No. No.

"I'm here," I tell her.

"I want to tell you his name." She coughs and gasps and coughs again.

"Who?" I ask.

"My son," she says with her beautiful smile. "Christopher, after your father."

Stabbing pain in my chest.

Wrenching pain in my heart.

"Oh, Grace, thank you," is all I manage to say as my shoulders shake like an earthquake. I crumble like a building being blown to bits. My head falls into the crook of her neck. I don't want to let her go. "I love you."

"Love you, too," she says in a raspy voice. I lift my head and watch her fade.

"Christopher … it's perfect," Bruno says before throwing his head back and sucking in air. He drops his head back to hers. "Baby, until I can join you, please tell that boy of mine how much I love him and that one day … when his dad's work is done, we'll all be together again."

"I will," Grace says. "I love you, so much."

"Oh God, Grace, not yet. I'm not ready. Please hold on."

"I'm trying," she says. "But sometimes we don't get to choose."

371

I stroke her hair as her eyes glaze over. I lean down and whisper in her ear, "Thank you for being my friend."

She gasps and gasps some more.

I sit back on my heels and let her husband spend her last minutes with her.

Bruno's head hangs over her, and he kisses her blue lips. She lifts her arm around his neck.

"See you soon," she says to Bruno and then her arm slides off his neck and falls to her side.

Her entire body goes limp, and Bruno curls her body into his as he repeatedly tells her he loves her and he's so sorry he couldn't save her. He sobs and moans, breaking into shattered pieces.

"No! Oh, God, no," he says. "I'm supposed to save you!" His voice breaks, and he cries out, "Why did I let you come here?" Tears streak down his face as he clenches every muscle in his body. "Wake up, Grace. Grace, wake up, please. Don't leave me."

I couldn't save her either.

Cole opens his arms, and I press myself into him as we cry together. I grasp Cole so tight, I'm sure my fingers leave permanent marks in his sides.

Zeus nudges my leg and whines, reminding me he's still here.

An unbearable pain suffocates us. It'd be too easy to give up. It'd be too easy to lie down and surrender.

But I'm done losing people I love.

CHAPTER 27

I press my head into Cole's shirt, completely oblivious to anything and everything around me but the smell of lead, blood, and his sweat all mixed together. Grace is gone, and our small group doesn't even have time to think straight, let alone regroup.

The moment we need the most privacy and peace is the moment everything blows up. Bullets hammer the walls, and everyone drops down in a single motion. I jump in my skin, as if being woken from my worst nightmare. But it's not a dream. My hands release Cole's shirt, knuckles white from grasping. We both fumble for our guns. My attention turns toward the doorway to the office, now riddled with puncture holes. Bill fires back even as tears streak his face.

Bruno hovers over Grace's body and doesn't move an inch. I watch as the tendons flex in his jaw and his grip tightens on her. He doesn't seem to notice the outbreak of hell around him or even care. I meet Cole's red eyes. We're both thinking the same thing.

We can't count on Bruno to make the decisions right now.

I swallow my tears, laying aside my broken heart, and flick my attention toward Roméo. As the sounds of metallic bangs grow closer, Cole joins Bill in the doorframe, ducking in and out to fire.

"The files!" I shout over the noise. "Did you find them?"

"No," Roméo says. He blinks back his tears, and I quickly shove past him.

"Okay, I'll look."

I don't wait for him to react before ransacking the closet. I toss everything useless aside. The gunfire becomes more intense, and my hands shake as I dig down into each box, pushing away old books and relics. Dust poofs up around me, and panic rises in my chest when I find nothing.

Finally, after the third box, I find files inside, nestled at the bottom. My hands work furiously through them. I can barely read through my blurred vision.

Holy crap.

At the top of each file it says: Name, brand, age at the time of entrance into the Hole, diagnosis, and date of death. Underneath each of these, in Sutton's own handwriting, is a list of symptoms and possibilities.

God, why didn't he tell me?

"Roméo," I say. "Check these out."

Finally, he rushes in beside me, his lips quivering and his skin pale with fear. He scans the paperwork. At first, he says nothing.

"Please tell me these're the right ones!" My voice comes out scratchy and angry.

"Yes. Yes," he says. He kneels down and begins shoving handfuls of files into his backpack.

"We're losing ground!" I hear Cole shout. "Do you have them?"

"Yes!" I scream back at him. "Bill, I need you."

Bill shows up in the closet, his face coated with tears, sweat, and ash. Dark rings puff out from his eyes, and he gives me a despondent look.

"Your pack," I say. He stands there, frozen. "Bill, your pack!" He jumps to action and hands me his backpack.

I begin shoving files in, scanning as I go. Then I land on the one I want to find—Alyssa Jenkins.

Amber was right.

"No," I say, my cheeks heating.

"Lusty, you all right?"

I don't answer.

"I'll take that as a no. I'll get the rest of them." He immediately kneels and picks up where I left off.

Outside, there's constant gunfire. Cole returns it. Zeus's bark is hoarse. Bruno sobs over Grace's lifeless body. I quickly scan the handwritten record in front of me. I do my best to concentrate, just keep it together.

Alyssa Jenkins, Yellow for Greed, eight years old, virus: unknown, thirteen years.

My heart stops in my chest; my breathing slows. My hands shake even though I will them to be steady. Down below, her symptoms are written in plain language along with Sutton's facts about her condition, but I don't have time to read them.

I skim down to the last part, where it says the date of her death.

Alyssa Jenkins: Exact cause of death unknown. My professional opinion: Unknown Virus.

"We've gotta get out of here!" Cole shouts. He shoots, and the sound brings me back to reality. I shove the paper into Bill's backpack along with the others and zip it closed.

"Ready!" I shout. "Let's go."

Bill slings the sack over his shoulders and groans. Roméo does the same, sagging under the weight. There's no time to talk or lament our losses, only to run.

I come out of the closet after the others. My eyes meet Bruno's. He's still holding Grace, but his expression has changed. He sets his jaw, pushes his shoulders back, and stands with her in his arms. Other than the tears streaking down his face, he shows no expression.

"Bruno," I say to him. "They're coming; we have to go."

"She goes where I go," he says. His voice holds no compromise.

"Okay," I say.

I turn away from him, forcing my own emotions down. I can barely stand the sight of him carrying my beloved friend, but dwelling on it won't help us get out of here.

In front of me, Cole fires back at the oncoming guards. It's only a matter of time before they surround us completely.

"Move out," Cole says.

I'm not sure where to go. The firepower of the guards consumes the hallway leading to the back staircase, eliminating that as a way out.

I hesitate, thinking for a second before deciding on our

376

route. If the back staircase is taken and the elevators are useless, then we have no choice but the front stairs. With a quick prayer and a plea for luck, I motion for the others to follow me.

Here goes nothing.

With each step, I clench my gun and duck for cover. The blistering amount of shooting echoing behind us makes my insides quake with fear and adrenaline. My eyes are wide open, alert. I clamp down on images of Grace by focusing on the stairwell entrance.

Next to the entrance, on the right side, is a patient room. After checking it, I wave the others on. First Bill, then Roméo, and Cole. Zeus stays with me, his face a mask of teeth and unbridled ferocity. Next, Bruno, with Grace's body in his arms, runs past me, into the staircase. *If I could've carried Keegan out, I would've.*

"Go, boy," I say. But Zeus looks at me, his tail pointed. "Zeus, go, go, go!" He plants himself next to me. *Stubborn ass.* I move my eyes back and forth, making sure the way's clear. *I don't have time for this.* Then I wrap my fingers into his collar and push him across the hallway on skittering nails. He practically slides through the doorway and into Cole.

Just as Zeus's butt hits the threshold, a shot rings out from close by. I freeze and scan the perimeter, trying to figure out where it came from since the gunfire somewhere behind us has tapered off. Whoever it was knew where we were heading to make our escape. I bite my lip and squint while holding my gun, determined not to miss any detail. Then I see it. A blip of sunlight reflects from the metal of a gun.

Bingo.

There's a monster in the room.

The door to the patient room bursts open, and the guard comes flying out toward me. I raise my gun. My blood feels electric. I fire off a few rounds and then have to change my magazine. I slam a new one in, but in that split second, he slinks away, using the door as cover. On the other side of it, I hear him talking.

"You're coming with me." His voice is low and flat. *Creepy as anything.*

"Dream on," I say evenly.

He sticks his gun out and takes a shot at me. It spins high above my head, but I duck down anyway. I swallow my guts and poke my barrel out firing back at him. It's just enough to keep him behind the doorway. I can almost smell him from here, the mix of body odor, gun powder, and filth. The sunlight perfectly illuminates his shadow dancing across the door.

"You and your friends don't stand a chance," he says. He shoots at me, this time going off to my right. "Everyone's hunting you down."

"You leave them out of this," I say. "It's me Wilson wants, not them."

Just keep him talking.

My heart flutters. My breathing's ragged. I look across the hallway and see Cole's eyes as he stands in the entrance to the staircase, staring back at me. His white hands grip the doorframe. He's helpless. If he steps out, the shooter would just kill him on the spot.

"Don't," I mouth to Cole.

I see the frustration and agony painted on his face, but I don't have time to dwell on it before the guard emasculates

378

the walls with firepower. I slink down, curling my body into itself to avoid the ricocheting bullets. When I look up, Cole stares, narrowing his eyes and curling his lips. He glances out the door, but the gunman fires at him until he's forced to jump back, rendering me alone. Veins bulge from both sides of his neck.

"Go," I say.

"No," he says. He won't leave without me.

"You stupid whore, you've got nowhere to go." The guard's snide voice comes across muffled and low. He's pissing me off.

"Go to hell." I shoot at the door to the room he's hiding in.

He's silent for a minute, and I wonder if I got him, but then his shadow moves under the door again.

Just hold steady.

If I stay here any longer, I'm a sitting duck for the next wave of attacks. I can't withstand them all. This delay is eating up time for all of us. My blood rushes in my ears, and I grit my teeth.

In that split second, I make a choice.

I sprint forward, rushing the doorway. The guard rustles on the other side, but I don't stop. As he reaches around the door with his gun, I slam the door as hard as I can.

He screams out in pain. His body stumbles on the other side. Breathless, I step around the door and fire the entire contents of my gun at him. He scoots back with eyes wide as his body jerks with each bullet. Somehow, he manages to hold on to his gun. His eyes stare through me as his finger reaches the trigger.

My magazine's empty. *Crap.* I reach into my waist for another one, when he lifts his gun.

I dive out of the way as a round of bullets skitter past my shoulders, smashing into the wall behind me. I hear the piercing sound of shots and cement and screams. A bullet grazes my thigh, and instantly, I let out a scream from the burning pain.

I'm going to die.

Pulling myself into the hallway, the pain burns through my thigh, and I push through the doors to the stairs, relieved to be alive. Cole greets me, but I can barely look him in the face knowing I didn't finish the job. I stand up, limp around, and see Bruno resting with Grace, Bill standing guard, and Roméo chewing on the inside of his cheek. All of them think I've protected the rear.

I can't lead them without knowing that guy and his buddies aren't following us.

"Run," Cole says.

I shake my head. "Not yet." I pull a grenade from my pocket, and his eyes grow large. "Hurry, take the others downstairs."

"No way. Not without you," he says. But I shove him away.

"I have to do this." With that said, I push past him back into the hallway.

"Lexi, no!"

The guy's not dead. I hear his raspy breathing and the sound of him slamming a new magazine home.

He's waiting for me. He knows I'll be back to take care of him.

The thought makes my nerves jump and causes a rush of blood through my veins. I pull the tape like Bruno did, slip the spoon, and then toss the grenade into the room. It clatters across the floor.

"Shit!" The guy's scream runs up my spine.

I threw it hard enough that, with his injuries, he won't reach it in time to throw it back. I turn and sprint back through the doors. I'm practically flying down the staircase. My heart races. My hair sticks to my neck. I'm just about to second-guess my decision when I hear the grenade go off.

In the next moment, I'm tumbling down the stairs. My backpack slings over my head and carries me forward. I throw my arms up in a feeble attempt to protect myself. My elbows collide with cement; my hair splays everywhere. I can't focus. The walls seem to uproot and tiles drop from the ceiling.

I hit the landing with a thump and then roll into a fetal position. I try to breathe, but my chest's tight. *Is that gasping sound coming from me?* Pain rocks my body, like I've shattered every single bone.

A face with a big black nose and four brown eyes appears through my cloudy vision. *Or maybe it's two?* Something cool and wet hits my cheek and brings me into focus. I stretch out my fingers and feel Zeus prodding me to my feet. Around him, the carnage continues raining down. The walls groan.

"Come on, Lexi, get up," Cole says in a muffled voice. He links his arm through mine, pulling me up.

Mother of God. Burning pain shoots through my leg. It looks like a god of destruction swooped down and took a hammer to the building, breaking everything into pieces and turning it ashen and gray. I blink away the particles on my lashes. Bill's shadowy figure sprints down two landings ahead of me.

"Don't you ever pull that stunt again, you hear me?" Cole says as he drags me through the wreckage. "Even though it was the ballsiest thing I've seen you do." He mutters some other things under his breath that I can't decipher. "I know you're pissed and hurt and so am I, but you can't be that reckless."

The staircase seems to take forever. Every step leads to shooting agony in my leg, sending stars across my vision. I lean on Cole to help me get through it, his body solid and his grip like iron. Flashes of the past wreak havoc in my head. The weirdest memories, forgotten long before, resurface. Like the time I sprained my ankle in the woods with Keegan, and he carried me home. He wasn't that much bigger than me at the time, but he did it anyway. I'll never forget how he gritted his teeth and the tendons in his neck popped with every step. He was breathless when we got home, and he fell on the front stairs to the porch, dropping me on my behind.

Saved me and then dropped me on my ass.

I'd give anything for him to be here with me. He'd know what to do. He'd know where to go. He was always so sure of his decisions even if they weren't always right, but now I know, it's time for me to make mine and be confident like he was.

"Lexi, you got to keep up with me," Cole says. I turn my head to meet his gaze, but he's already focused on the next flight.

"I will." My throat's thick with tension.

Three more flights to go. *If I survived five, I can do this.*

More gunfire echoes in the distance. I don't know where it comes from, but the distinctive popping sounds tell me that we're not out of the thick of it yet. Ahead of me, the others finish their last flight of stairs.

The guards watching the cameras must love this.

Two more to go. I wriggle free from Cole even though the

pain's enough to make me want to scream. I have to do this for myself, push through it, and help the others. In truth, we're all fighting some kind of battle, physically and mentally. It's up to me to be strong.

Last flight. I bump down the stairs, clenching my jaw, and focus on the bottom. Bill flicks on a small light to break the darkness as they wait for us. When we're assembled, we stop to catch our breath before moving on.

I glance at their sweaty, dusty faces. Tracks from tears stain everyone's cheeks, whether from grief or from the thick particles in the air. Bruno's eyes water as they meet mine. Still holding Grace, he looks away.

There will be time to mourn later, I hope.

"Move," Cole says with impatience.

He takes lead and runs straight down a dim hallway. I glance up and see a camera mounted in the corner as we hook a right, so I shoot off a round at it, shattering the lens and hopefully disabling it.

Cole bangs open a door. I see the word *Morgue* in dark letters on the gray metal as we cross into the cool and eerie room. All of the supplies that were stored in here before have been stripped, leaving nothing but the metal tables. Bill's flashlight hits the refrigerators, sending weird shadows flitting across the numbers. I don't have time to look for the one Alyssa's body was stored in, but I can't escape the memory of zipping her body bag and saying goodbye to her. *Just breathe and focus.*

Cole pushes through the doorway at the opposite end of the room, and we're back by the entrance to the unmonitored staircase. We pass the elevator and then shove through the basement door and into the room where we began our journey. Goose bumps raise on my arms in response to the cooler air. A small ray of sunshine spills through the window and across the room, giving me a clear path through the mess.

I cover Cole until we're close to the window. Without asking, Bill pulls up a wooden table and moves it against the wall.

"Who's first?" Roméo asks. I can tell from his white face that he doesn't want to volunteer.

"Me," Bill says.

"No, Bill, you don't have to do that," I say.

"If anyone's going to get us out of here, it'll be me." He steps onto the table and turns back to look at me. "Cover me once you're out." With those words, Bill maneuvers through the shattered window.

More light filters in, and I squint. Particles float aimlessly through my vision. Then a rustle at the back of the room grabs my attention.

"Go, Roméo," I say. I turn around, pointing my gun behind us, expecting to see guards already standing there. But to my surprise, no one has found us ... yet.

Roméo doesn't hesitate as he climbs up and disappears through the opening after Bill. Then Cole goes. Bruno lowers Grace's body to help bolster Zeus through the window. Then Cole waits for Bruno to pass Grace's body through next.

A crashing noise echoes through the room just as Bruno's halfway through the window. *They found us.* Focusing my sights, I fire off a few rounds, sending the dark uniforms diving for cover. I keep shooting until I've got nothing left, forcing them to keep their heads down.

Then I jump onto the table and pull myself up onto the ledge. My hands are slippery, and Cole locks onto my wrists.

"You got this," he says. "I got you."

My foot slips. I hang for a split second. I hear footsteps gaining on me, and my mind fills with panic.

"Cole!" I scream. "They're here."

Cole's hands keep slipping from my wrists because of our combined sweat. I'm desperate. Behind me, voices shout.

"Grab her!" Brusque hands wrap around my ankles, and I thrash my legs to catch them off guard.

"They have my legs."

Cole's eyes widen in his beet-red face. "Get your hands off her!" he yells.

"My hands are slipping."

Then another pair of hands, strong and taut, latch on to my forearms and together, they yank hard. With a collective grunt, Cole and Bruno pull me through the window. I land on my stomach in the street beside the hospital, my hands grinding into shattered glass.

Bruno barely breaks stride before picking up Grace and taking off. I don't know how he functions, but I'm thankful he does. I push myself up, grabbing a grenade from a pocket in my vest.

A guard's fingers already grip the windowsill, attempting to follow me out. He stops when he sees me standing in front of him, my fingers grasping the frag. His eyes widen. *Is that fear I see?*

"Get back here," another guard says. "Come with us, and it'll all be over." I shake my head, locking my jaw. One of them squints at me. "Fine, have it your way. But your precious

Sutton will be punished for this one."

I turn it over in my head, those words. They make me sick, and my stomach roils.

With quick hands, I toss the grenade in and run. Behind me, they scream. The grenade explodes, silencing their voices and blowing more glass into the street with a shattering sound. I don't bother glancing back.

Up ahead, the others begin crossing the open street in front of the hospital. I pass the bodies of the guards in front of the main entrance and then freeze.

The bright daylight and vulnerability of being out in the open makes my heart skip beats. If the tank rolls up, we're really screwed. But already, Bill and Roméo have made it into the winding alley across from me, and Bruno carries Grace after them.

My breath catches in my throat when I meet eyes with Cole, who waits for me. He says nothing, but his eyes hold relief and fear.

"I'm okay," I say firmly.

He nods then checks both ways, while I scan rooftops. In the distance, the sound of rumbling metal grabs my attention. Cole's eyes flick to mine as I point toward the source of the commotion.

Here comes that tank again.

His jaw twitches, and he yanks me forward. Zeus joins us out of nowhere, his tongue hanging out the side of his mouth, his ears flopping around.

"Oh. Now you come," Cole says under his breath.

I look left and get a visual on the tank as it heads toward us. The slow pace at which it lumbers along makes me think they have no idea what we've just done at the hospital or they'd be firing at us by now.

My leg burns, and my feet ache, but with twenty-five yards left to cross, we can't stop. My force of will is the only thing holding me together.

To my left, the clanking sound moves closer, and behind us voices shout. I glance over my shoulder and see guards filtering into the street from the training center.

"She's over there," they shout.

Just then, a huge explosion rocks us, tumbling us forward. Smoke and debris cloud my vision as I crawl on all fours, coughing and gasping for air. My head pounds. Zeus's tail is the only thing I see, and I follow it, running into Cole, who pulls me into the alleyway between the buildings.

"They're right behind us," he yells, but it sounds like a whisper.

He doesn't need to repeat himself before Bill leads us away from the hospital and into the jungle gym of concrete with guards on our heels.

The siren sounds, screaming into my brain. The loudspeaker switches on, and the feedback crackles loudly. But even as I hear his breaths in the microphone, we keep running for our lives. Up, down, and around trash. Over piles of old tires, past decaying bodies. We've got to get the hell out of here with those records.

"Peekaboo, Lexi, I see you," Wilson says over the loudspeaker, his voicing arching into a screech. "If you think you're getting out, you're wrong. If you think you're getting away this time, think again."

If he thinks he can make me bow to him, he's wrong.

"Sutton's going to receive a lash for every guard you killed today. And from here on out."

Breathe, Lexi. He's just threatening you because he has no power to stop what's happening.

"Turn yourself in, and he won't suffer any longer."

But there's no guarantee you'd let him go. It's like Wilson's repeatedly punching me in the stomach and trying to rip out my heart piece by piece.

"I'll be seeing you soon," he says. The microphone slams down. The siren picks up where it left off, and I'm left to fight an inner battle.

"Over my dead body," I say under my breath.

Bill's eyes narrow into slits, determination written on his face. He waves us onward, through shacks, past wide-eyed Sinners, and farther away from the hospital, all while holding his backpack of precious records.

My old building rises into view from the depths of carnage. The sun glints off what's left of the windows, turning it into a brilliant orange, contrasting to the gray of the Hole. Bill leads us through the remnants of the checkpoint, past burned-out cars, and behind the building. Bodies are piled higher than the last time we were here. Mounds of them, reaching upward, arms and legs limply dangling over each other. It's enough to make me want to hurl.

The stench hits me, and I turn my face away. Tears prick at the corner of my eyes, but I never falter in my movements.

A hand touches my back, and I turn to face Cole. He's covered in dirt. He purses his lips and holds his M4 with confidence.

"Don't let him break you," he says.

I grab him and pull him close, inhaling his sweat, the ashen dirt, and blood-soaked clothing he wears, because I've got nothing to say back.

Cole should already know I'm not the same girl who came into the Hole months ago. I was innocent then, but I've since shed blood. I've watched people die, people that I love. I've learned more about the world in one year than most ever learn in their lives.

It'll take more than Wilson talking to break me.

When I push Cole back, he swallows hard, gripping my shoulders and clenching his jaw. Then he lets go, and we run and run until we're lost in the middle of the shantytown. Its perimeter spills out beyond where my eyes can see.

Our appearance garners suspicious stares, but we don't have time to hide.

Bruno collapses first. He falls to his knees, bending his head over Grace, his back wracking with sobs. When Cole tries to console him, Bruno puts out his arm, pushing Cole away.

"He needs space, don't take it personally," Roméo says.

So Cole stands up and walks over to me. When his eyes lock onto mine, my heart tumbles. They're full of love, anger, and desperation. He pulls me in for a tight hug and then releases me. His head turns away, but not before I see the tears.

Don't fall apart on me yet.

Roméo lies down, keeping his backpack of files close to his side. He cries, pants, and looks dehydrated. I quickly fish out water from my sack and give him some, passing it around until finally, Zeus finishes it off with loud slurps. I rub his side, then sit on the ground pressing my back against the wall of a tin shack.

Everyone's physically and emotionally tapped. My trembling hands inspect my leg where the bullet grazed me. I pour water on it, washing away the blood and dirt, and breathe a sigh of relief when I realize it's just a superficial skin wound.

Cole kneels beside me. "I'm so sorry. For everything ... I never meant to hurt you," he says.

I nod.

He leans down and kisses me with such desperation we cry between our kisses. "God, I love you." He chews on his top lip, his eyes so full of love and grief.

"I don't doubt that. I know you still love me, and of course, I still love you. Because if there's one thing I learned today, it's how precious life is," I say. He wipes the tears from my cheeks. "I don't know what I'd do if ... if I lost you." My voice breaks.

His shoulders slump, and he leans into me, pressing his forehead to mine.

"Hey, you're not going to lose me," he says, holding my face between his hands. I close my eyes for a second and take a cleansing breath.

I place my hands over his and say, "I need you to understand, I'm trying my hardest to move past what happened, but my father meant everything to me, and right now ... I'm in all kinds of pain."

He exhales before he clears his throat. "And it tears me apart that I'm part of that," he says.

When I glance up, Sinners have surrounded us. My stomach drops.

CHAPTER 28

Immediately, I reach for my gun.

"Stay back," I say, pointing it at the gathering crowd. I back up to Cole, who's already aiming his gun in their direction. Beside me is Bill, his gun raised. Inside the triangle formed by the three of us is Bruno, holding onto Grace, Zeus, and Roméo. "Don't move an inch, or I'll shoot."

But they encircle us, eyes locking onto our faces. Some of them squint, while others lick their lips. Very few smile or nod in acknowledgement. It's like a pack of wolves, testing their prey for weaknesses. They're probably so hungry, they'd eat Zeus at this point.

"Here we are starving, and she's got a pack full of food," a female voice says.

"Gimme the water," a man says while stepping toward me.

I point my gun at him.

"I said don't move," I repeat.

"I'm going to die either way, girl, so you'll just expedite the process."

"Come on, guys ... look at them ... they're not guards, you idiots." A girl pulls back on the man's shoulders. He stops and gives her a nasty look. He cracks his knuckles and raises a hand to hit her when someone yells.

"Hold on a minute!" Everyone turns to look at the person, and he points at me. "I recognize you."

"Oh yeah?" I ask. "Why am I not surprised?"

"Yeah, I recognize her too, from my dreams last night," another mane chimes in. "You're that girl. The one Wilson's offering the reward for. Lexi, isn't it?"

Cole steps forward a little, aiming right at the man with the smart mouth.

I don't like the direction this conversation's going. My muscles tense, ready for a fight if need be. Next to me, Zeus growls and inches toward them. Only then do some of them backpedal.

"Now hold up, let's all calm down here," a man with a black brand says. He steps forward. I flick my eyes to his, and he raises his hands up, palms facing me. "I've got a proposition to make here."

"You're joking, right?" Cole asks.

"I'm afraid not; we need each other, plain and simple. So let's say if you help us, we'll help you."

My shoulders relax some, but I don't lower my gun. "And why would we do that?" I ask.

"Look, girl, we're not interested in your reward."

"We're not that trusting," Cole says.

"And you can't possibly care about us," I say.

"Actually, you're wrong," a lady says. "There's not a single person standing in front of you that is happy with the way things are."

"All we want is to get the hell out of here," the man finishes. "We're well aware Wilson's a liar."

"Okay. So, say we believe you. How can you help us?" Cole asks. He has his sights trained on them still, sweat gliding down his face and arms.

The man with scraggly hair and the black brand exhales. "Now that part's simple. We'll assault the main gate while you get your people out."

"You might be crazier than me," Bill says. "And that's saying a lot." I snort.

"That doesn't make any sense. Why would you risk your lives … to help us?" I ask.

"We're starving, thirsty … dying," the man with the black brand says. "And you're the only hope we've got to end this, once and for all." I pause for a moment as his words swim around in my head.

"That's it?" I ask.

He chuckles. "That's it."

"Well, hang on a minute," the girl interrupts. "I think we need to ask for a guarantee, don't you?" She looks over at the man who was about to hit her and then to the man with the black brand.

The man with the black brand clears his throat. "Yes. One more thing."

"What?" I ask.

"The packs stay here with us. After all, once you're outta here, you won't need them." He smiles, looking satisfied.

"Deal," Bill says in a scratchy voice before any of us has a chance to respond. "Here's everything I've got." He opens his backpack, pushing aside files, and holds out his water, food, and some spare ammunition.

"Line up," the black-branded man says. He takes the supplies and divvies it out to the others as they fall into a thin line. "Make sure the children are fed first."

I like this guy.

They pass cans of food and water down the line. At the end of it, I watch as the older Sinners summon the young children from their nearby huts. Hesitantly, the children peek out. Their potbellies and sunken eyes bleed my heart. They've been living in filth for how long, and now they don't even have the basic necessities of food and water. The adults give them small servings, tenderly making sure they don't eat or drink too fast. My stomach drops. The Sinners handle each item with care, never letting the sight of the food make them crazy.

Bill finishes handing out his food. He nods his head toward me. "Well, are you in?" he asks.

Cole and I lock glances. Bruno hasn't acknowledged anyone yet. He stares into space with dead eyes. No more tears drop down over his cheekbones, and his hands lie limp at his sides, Grace's body lying beside him.

"What're you thinking?" Cole asks.

"I don't think we have a choice." I take a deep breath and open my backpack, emptying the remains of the food and water. "I'm in."

"Then so am I."

One hour later.

"Here's the plan," the black-branded man says. "We've managed to repair a car so that it runs. We'll distract the guards while your assets drive to the entrance. As soon as we get it open, you drive through."

"How will you make that happen?" Roméo asks. He swipes at a fly buzzing near his face.

"I've created a trusting relationship with a guard who works the gate, and she's willing to help us," the man answers.

It's my turn to raise an eyebrow. "A guard?" I repeat.

"You've trusted a few, right?" The man gives me a weak smile.

"Very few," I say.

Cole grasps my hand and squeezes it. "What's your name?"

"Levi."

"All right, Levi. Let's get started."

Two hours later.

I'm running on pure adrenaline. But we can't wait any longer or we'll lose the element of surprise we so desperately need. Before I know it, Bill's wrapping his arms around me with a long sigh.

"Stay with Roméo, and whatever happens, you have to get those files out," I say. "Oh, and Bill, thank you, for everything. Without you, we'd be dead."

A slow blush creeps up his cheeks, and he shrugs. "Shucks, Lusty, I only hope to make you proud." He smiles and salutes me.

My throat tightens, but I hold back my emotions. "You already have," I tell him.

"Take care of yourself, and that nutty gray dog," he adds.

This won't be the last time we see each other, right?

"Goodbye, Roméo," I say. He holds out his hand to shake mine, but I step in and give him an awkward hug. His one hand catches me around my back, and he steps away quickly when our bodies touch.

"Thank you for helping me," he says. His reddened eyes and thin body look nothing like the person I met the first time. "I'll make sure these reach the United Powers as soon as possible. Once they see the files, they'll have all the evidence they need. They'll have no choice but to intervene."

"Here's hoping," I say. "And thank you."

"There's no need to thank me; nobody deserves this life, and we can't let this virus get out into the general population," he says. "Now, go rescue Sutton, and I'll do my part."

Before I reply, he shakes hands with Cole, says an encouraging word to Bruno, and even pats Zeus on the head. He loads the files into the car and gets into the passenger seat next to Bill. They'll wait until they receive the signal to go through the doors.

It's going to be a long day.

396

Three hours later.

I wait in the shadows with Cole, Zeus, and some Sinners. I've given them the extra gun I confiscated from the dead guard during the night. We've spread out the remaining grenades along with Roméo's gun, since he won't be shooting much from the car. It's a risk we take in order to give these people a fighting chance.

I taste sweat as it rolls over my lip and into my mouth. Flies zip around my face, even landing on my nose, but I can't whisk them away with my gun in my hand and my body poised for attack.

I think of Bruno, who chose to stay behind. He refused to respond when we begged him to come. It didn't seem right to force him if he wasn't ready to leave Grace. *And he wasn't ready at all.* Bruno is in no condition for this mission and, in his state of mind, would probably end up getting himself killed. I don't know if he even cares about anything anymore, including his own life.

I don't want to do this without him and his expertise, but I know it's more important for him to be where he can focus on his grief. *Grace. Christopher.* Sometimes, mourning what you never had is just as heart-wrenching as mourning what you did.

Cole taps my shoulder and points ahead. Four guards stand at the ready while the gate opens with the sound of metal grinding metal. A black SUV prepares to roll inside. The guards salute the driver. The vehicle lumbers in as the doors bang closed behind it.

Across from us is the new lab where people were marched for their injections and the building where I first saw the projection about the history of the Hole. I blink, straining against the glare of the sun. A few minutes ago, ten people were herded inside. It was painful to watch. But knowing we're about to fight back makes it slightly more bearable.

Behind me, Sinners are getting antsy. Feet move, dust spirals upward in small tornadoes, and equipment bangs together. They're not the most battle-disciplined group, but they're willing to give their lives to help us.

In five minutes, we'll unload everything we've got at the lab to distract the guards from the entrance.

One minute passes. Two minutes.

A fly lands on my forehead. I scrunch it up, but the fly stays, skittering around on tiny feet. I shake my head, but it won't budge.

Three minutes. Four minutes.

"Mom, let me in!" I say, banging on the door to the study.

I hear something crash, and feet moving furniture around. Chairs or tables scrape against the hardwood flooring.

"Coming," she says in a breathless voice.

The thick door separates the study from the foyer. Inside, my mom keeps books and a computer. Sometimes she works on projects in there, and when she does, the door is kept closed for hours. After we moved into our High Society condo, she remarried. Then Keegan left, and Mom's distanced herself from me. Yet I keep trying to bring her back into my world.

Feet thump in my direction. "What's wrong?" she says as

she opens the door. Her eyes look tired and glassy.

"I need help with my homework," I say.

"Right now?"

"Yes." I try to shove my way in, but she holds the door with an iron grip. "What are you doing in there?"

"Nothing that concerns you," she says. She looks around nervously.

I sigh with impatience. "Mom, you're always in there."

"Some things are better kept behind closed doors, just don't tell your father about this," she says. Her forehead crinkles up.

"How would I do that? Dad's dead," I say.

She cringes and looks around. "No, your stepdad."

"He's not my stepdad. He's a monster."

Five minutes.

A barrage of staccato gunfire opens up, shattering the windows of the lab. The guards at the entrance scramble into a defensive position. Bullets spit at the dust.

"Fire!" Cole says, jerking me back into focus.

We spill out of the alleyway, firing off rounds at the guards as more appear on the top of the wall. The guards begin picking off our people. Bodies fall around me. I strip them of their guns and keep moving. Sinners burst through the doors of the lab and spill into the street. They trample over the cattle chutes, flipping some of them onto their sides. It's chaos.

It's exactly what we want.

Levi and his people spread out on rooftops and in the streets, and we move toward the lab, drawing more heavy fire. Down here, they can't tell me apart from anyone else. I feel a shot burn past my cheek. *Too close.* Still, I move and react because it's what I've been conditioned to do.

The four guards at the entrance barricade themselves behind a large SUV while the ones on the wall light us up. The popping of guns, screaming of voices, and the curses of those closest to me all fade into the background as I focus on our mission.

Cole runs in front of me, attempting to give me protection. Zeus stays right by my side, following every move I make.

This is it. I'm going to get Bill and Roméo out, even if it costs me everything.

My boots are covered in dust. My mouth is dry. My body follows every command my mind gives. I'm terrified, and yet, I feel no fear.

Cole jumps the barricades and pushes himself up against the doors of the lab, making himself a scarce target. I follow, and the rest of the group that's managed not to get shot slams into place behind us. My lungs burst in and out as I check my ammo.

Two guards come out from inside the lab, but we pick them off with easy double taps. After them, Sinners in white lab coats come out with their hands raised.

"Don't shoot!" they scream at us.

I recognize one of them. He puts his hands above his head, and his eyes almost pop out when he sees me. *It's Hank, the guy who helped Cole in the collapsed building.*

"Sutton knows it's you out here," he shouts over the noise.

I want to ask him if Sutton's okay, if he knows where he's being held, but I don't have the time. Instead, I nod at him, lowering my gun, and decide to pay it forward since he helped me.

"Go! Get out of here!" I shout at him.

"Hell no," he says. He picks up the nearest weapon, pushes himself against the wall, and joins us with a wicked grin.

I acknowledge him and turn back toward Cole, who's focused on the main entrance. The guards on the wall can't see us, but the guys hiding behind the SUV have us pinned down. Their fire ricochets off the walls around us. Behind me, someone grunts.

A fierce burning hits me like a hammer. I glance down. My arm's bleeding. Cole hears me gasp and examines me quickly, his jaw setting in place. He uses one hand, already covered in grime, to pluck a piece of shrapnel from my arm. I grit my teeth.

If we survive, it'll be a miracle.

Anger flashes through his eyes, and a vein in the middle of his forehead bulges. He reaches into his vest, pulls a grenade, and with an *umph* lobs it over the SUV.

The glass shatters with the explosion, and the automobile bounces. Limbs and equipment mark the area around it. The guns on the wall turn their fury in our direction, but I can't seem to get a good shot.

Cole darts forward.

This wasn't part of the plan. I scream, but he doesn't hear me. Once he reaches the corner, he's in full view of a fifty-caliber gun on the wall. Yet, somehow, he makes it to the vehicle. He butts up against the SUV, checking around it.

The big gun cough out bullets.

What the hell's he doing?

He turns back, diving for cover. Dust flicks up behind him where bullets trace his steps, and Cole hits the earth, taking me with him.

Next thing I know, his body covers mine like a shield. He's

coughing. I'm coughing. My chest burns, and my body aches in the places where he smashed me into the ground. His sweat drips onto me, and his arms feel solid around me.

When he realizes the gun can't reach him, Cole rocks back, pulling me up with him. In his eyes, fear remains. In my heart, I know he'd die a thousand deaths if it meant saving me. And I trust him with my life, with everything.

Courage, like an explosion, rocks me. He believes in me, Sutton trusts me, and my father knew I could lead. The Sinners I just met believe in me. I reach into my vest while Cole watches. I pull out the orange and black flare gun. He nods. I point it up to the sky and squeeze the trigger, which makes a whooshing sound.

The red glare of the signal slashes across the sky. In my mind, everything's paused around me, except for that flare. I stare upward as it fizzles out. *Bill and Roméo have to see that.*

In the background, the gate begins to open, and the guards up top scramble around. Some of them appear to be fighting one another. Their figures look black against the blue sky and piercing light of day. Then a flash of blond hair in a dark uniform catches my eye.

That must be Levi's connection. God help her.

I train my gun on the entrance as it opens, each inch bringing us closer to our goal. The car carrying Bill and Roméo is in sight now. Dust kicks up behind it, and the sun reflects off the glass. Bill drives like a wild man, speeding and swerving to avoid getting hit. *Please let the doors stay open long enough for him to blaze through.*

A body falls over the walls. The figure hits the ground with a thump.

Gunfire persists, riddling everything in its wake. Bodies lie dead or dying in the street. Bill rolls over one of them, and it sounds like his car is bottoming out. I hold my breath, but it keeps going.

Through the windshield, Bill's smiling. Inside, he looks as if he's yelling bloody murder and a few choice expletives. *He's freaking crazy, but I love him.* Roméo looks terrified, his hands gripping the side of the car as it flies.

Just a little bit farther, guys.

I step on shell casings everywhere I turn. My ammo's almost gone. The pain in my arm is dull compared to the fear coursing through me.

"Bruno!" Cole yells. His face lights up.

I turn around, and Bruno sprints toward us, gun poised, eyes focused. He lifts his head to acknowledge Cole but then focuses on where he's going. He fires off rounds at the wall, quickly stepping in with us alongside the lab.

"You came!" I shout, keeping my eyes on Bill's oncoming vehicle.

"Grace wanted me to fight with my family," he yells back. Cole smacks Bruno's shoulder and then trains his sights back on the car. "Let's do this."

A guard crawls out from behind the SUV and points his gun at the car. I can barely get the words out. My throat's on fire.

"Twelve o'clock!" I shout.

Cole's face scrunches up, his eyes becoming slits. "Shit!"

But Bruno fires, and his aim is true. The figure doubles over, and his gun rolls from his limp fingers.

"Nice shot," I say.

Just then, the faded blue car with rusty edges enters the opening of the gate. I raise a fist as Bill's eyes meet mine. The guns on the wall pour fire down like rain, puncturing the metal of the car with bullets.

Oh my God.

Roméo's head slumps over.

Oh my God, no.

Bill's no longer looking at me. He grips the steering wheel with tight knuckles and screams profanities as he passes through the opening. Roméo's chin bobs on his chest, his hands sliding off the sides of the car and out of sight. I feel sick to my stomach.

They're through.

But I can't celebrate. They're not in the clear yet. The men on the wall turn their attention outward. The glint of blond hair I saw earlier has disappeared from sight, and the gates begin closing. With most of the guards' attention diverted toward the car, I sprint out into the open. Zeus pants beside me. Cole and Bruno follow close behind, firing off rounds to cover me.

As we stand in the open, our guns pointed in various directions, I watch the blue car rumble over the railroad tracks and past the guard checkpoint.

Almost there.

My hopes arc upward. My breath comes faster, and my heart's going to explode with hope. If Bill can just get a bit farther out …

Please, please make it. For the dying people in here. For Sutton. For all of us.

"Oh, shit!" Cole yells. He aims his gun toward a figure on the wall. One of the guards stands with something mounted on his shoulder.

"RPG!" Bruno shouts. They both begin firing, but it doesn't seem to have any effect.

The guard quickly loads the rocket into the front and points it in the direction of Bill.

I look back through the gate. There's a few feet of sight left between both doors. Blue sky stretches before them. I can almost taste the rolling green hills that mean freedom beyond the Hole. The dust from the car picks up behind it as it thunders over a bump in the road.

Go, Bill, go! I realize I'm screaming at the top of my lungs. But then I hear an exhale of air from above, trailed by wispy, gray smoke.

I follow it toward the car.

And then my heart stops.

A huge explosion of grinding metal and fiery sparks is emitted into the sky. The car spins right, settling in the dust, smoke billowing upward. I don't see any movement in the windows.

The guards on the wall cheer loudly with their hands in the air. The gate finally slams shut, sealing Bill and Roméo and our chances away, forever.

"Noooooooo!" I scream as Cole grabs me. He yanks me away even as I cuss. I fight him, tears spilling from my face as the guards notice us for the first time.

"It's her!" they shout. "Get her!"

Bruno begins shooting as Cole pulls me away, sprinting for cover. Zeus trails behind us, staying with Bruno.

I want to fight Cole. I want to fight the guards, but my hopes crash to the floor. I've got nothing left.

"Don't you dare quit on me," Cole says in a strained voice.

I bite my lip and let him lead me away from the wall and the lab. The shooting continues behind us. I can't breathe. A weird sound comes from my throat when I try, like someone's sitting on my chest. My legs weigh a thousand pounds as I take each labored step.

Everything's a blur. I keep seeing the car explode in front of me. I was so sure they'd make it, so hopeful something would go right. Now all of this has been for nothing. Grace's death. Amber's death. Bill's death. Roméo's death. Death. Death. Death. For nothing. A moan escapes me. This isn't how Sutton wanted it. This isn't what I envisioned. This can't be why my father and brother died.

How could we have failed?

Next thing, Levi's standing in front of us. His hair is flying all over, and his face is covered in grit. He holds a bloody comrade. His eyes have lost all their hope, but I imagine mine look the same.

"Hurry, follow me," he says with urgency. He half-carries his comrade with him as he navigates the maze of the Hole, back to the shantytown. Gaunt faces greet us. As soon as they meet our eyes, they wander away, knowing we failed.

Levi places his friend on the ground and lets him rest on his back. Levi's chest moves up and down as he tries to catch his breath. He checks his friend's pulse and, feeling nothing, lets the man's hand drop from his own. When he turns to face us, his eyes are red and constricted.

"I'm so sorry," Cole says.

"We need to regroup and make another plan," Levi says, but his voice trails off at the end.

We have no other plans.

"Look, I just need ... time, okay?" Levi says. "We lost a lot of people, in just a few minutes." He puts his hands on his head as his lips tremble. "I didn't ... I thought ... "

Cole puts his hand on Levi's shoulder. "We'll hide over there."

We head into the nearest shack and try to catch our breath. Bruno joins us, not saying a word. Zeus follows on his heels, his tongue dripping saliva onto the ground. I watch as his ribcage moves up and down rhythmically. But nothing can take my mind off the memory of Roméo slumped over and Bill's eyes the last time they met mine.

I don't feel anything, not pain from my arm, not hope, just nothingness. It's all gone, all our chances.

We'll never get Sutton out now.

Cole settles beside me, pushing his back against a crude wall, and puts his arms around me. He doesn't cry, but I feel his desperation in the way he grips me tightly. Zeus settles at our feet, whimpering with his head in his paws.

I close my eyes and take it all in. We've got nothing left to hope for. The records are gone and everything else with them. I try to think of any other way of getting out, but we've spent all our resources in the last thirty-six hours. I let my head fall back against Cole in defeat.

"It's over," I say.

CHAPTER 29

You can overcome anything, short of death. You can overcome anything, short of death. I repeat it over and over in my head. *Dad … now what should I do, because I'm not sure I've got anything left …*

I curl into Cole's lap, and he holds me so close, I can barely breathe. His heart beats against my cheek, and I'm grateful we both survived, for that one small miracle. He attempts to soothe me by stroking my hair, but I hear his broken breaths. I feel shattered, severed in every way possible. If a heart could stop beating simply by breaking, mine would be silent now.

"Say something," Cole says.

"What's there to say? Except that I feel completely dead inside. We failed everyone today; there's no hope anymore for any of us." I press my face into his chest. "We lost Grace, Bill, and Roméo in a matter of hours today, and for what?"

"For something we all believed in, for something we all wanted to see succeed."

"But it didn't."

"Not today, but another day we will."

"How? The files are gone, the United Powers will never come, and eventually we're all going to die in here."

"Look at me."

"I can't."

"Look at me, please," he says. I shift my body around, and my eyes meet his. "Why did we come back to the Hole in the first place?"

"You know why."

"No, I want to hear you say it."

"To rescue Sutton. I know that, but how?"

"We will run, hide, and do everything we can to survive. And we'll figure out a way to get to Sutton, I promise you that. It might take time, but we're going to save him. And like you said before ... you'd rather be here with Sutton than outside the Hole knowing he's stuck in here. Am I right?"

"Yes," I say. "But we're short on time. God only knows what Wilson's going to put him through now. We can't wait, Cole; he needs us now."

"We'll go back for him, I promise. But not right now. We need to regroup first."

"Do you think just the two of us can do this?"

"Give Bruno his space ... He'll come around, and when he does, we'll be able to figure out what our next move's going to be. But for now, we have to do whatever it takes to stay under the radar."

I lower my face to his. We kiss, and it's the only thing that reminds me I'm still alive.

He pulls his mouth away but rests his forehead on mine. "Every single day, I'll do everything within my power to keep you safe," he says.

"I know, and I love you for that."

"Lexi?" someone whispers.

I pull away from Cole. "Did you hear that?

"Hear what?"

"My stupid mind is messing with me."

But then I hear it again. "Lexi?" A female voice echoes through my ears. My body stiffens, and I grab Cole's arm.

"That," I say to Cole. "You didn't hear that?"

"No."

"I swear I heard someone calling out my name."

"Nobody said your name."

"Lexi." This time I know Cole hears it because his eyes widen, and he turns his head in the direction of the voice.

"Give me your flashlight," I say.

Cole hands it to me, and I slowly rise to my feet. My hands shake as I inch my way toward her.

Cole grabs my arm, stopping me. "Let me go first," he says in a whisper. He steps in front of me, holding me back with one hand while searching with the other. He opens the flap of the tent and crosses into an adjacent area shrouded in darkness. On the far side, a lump of blankets rests in the corner.

"Lexi," the voice creaks.

My heart pounds in my ears as anger begins to strangle my chest. *I know that voice.* Something about it sends shivers up my spine.

Cole stops in his tracks, facing the blankets. He lifts his gun.

Slowly, I raise the flashlight, flicking it toward the voice. Movement from under the blanket startles me, and I drop the flashlight. A gasp escapes me when I see her unmistakable curly hair.

There's no way.

"What's wrong? Who is it?" Cole asks.

"It's no one; let's get out of here," I whisper in a shaky voice.

"Lexi, please," the woman says.

"Then why does that woman keep saying your name?"

"Oh, it is you." Her voice is so soft and weak. "I knew it."

"Because everyone here knows my name," I say to Cole. "Now put the gun down, and let's get out of here, now."

"My name is Katherine," the woman says to Cole.

I draw in a sharp breath.

"I'm Lexi's mother."

"Wait, what?" Cole asks, taking his eyes off the sights and partially lowering his gun.

"I'm serious, Cole, now," I say, attempting to pull him away. But he doesn't budge. "What are you doing?"

"Is that woman your mother?"

"No. She's not. Please come with me, or I'll go without you."

"Now hold up, if she's messing with you … "

"Shine the light my way," the woman says. "Let her see my face."

"Don't," I say to Cole in a demanding tone as I bend to pick up the flashlight. "I've been through enough today; I don't need to see her. I just want to leave."

Cole's eyes narrow at me, and I can tell he's not going to

411

let this go. But I don't want to do this, not now; there's nothing but bitterness in my mouth when I think about her. And as much as I thought I'd forgiven her ... there's a part of me that wants to tell her how I really feel. Because being betrayed by your own flesh and blood is a wound that might scar over, but the damaged tissue still remains. I was sent here because of her. All of this is her fault.

Every muscle in my body tightens, and my free hand clenches into a fist of rage.

"Give me the flashlight," Cole says.

"I'd rather not."

In a low voice, he says, "I'm not asking anymore." He snatches the flashlight from me and shines the light toward her face. She blinks away from it.

My nostrils flare as I raise my gun toward her head. My hands shake, and my blood rushes through my ears, as the realization dawns on me. She's really here, lying underneath blankets, in front of me. Her curly hair's matted and gray down the middle. She pulls herself up onto her elbows and faces me. I gasp when I see the black brand snaking around her neck. *Sloth ... how ironic.*

"Is that her?" Cole asks.

I swallow hard, and my body stiffens.

"Lexi?" Cole asks.

My breathing increases. I try to calm myself, but with one glance, Cole knows the answer to his question.

"Lower your gun," Cole says to me. "She's no threat to you now."

"I never was," my mother says.

"Shut up," I say to her.

412

"Lexi, it's not what you think," she says. "Can we talk ... alone?"

"No we cannot. I have nothing nice to say to you, and I'm not going to waste my breath or my time."

"You need to hear this."

"I don't need to hear, nor do I want to listen, to anything you have to say."

"I understand why you're angry with me, but—"

"No. There are not buts," I say, raising my voice. "You turned on me, your own daughter ... and instead of protecting me, you accused me, of something you knew for a fact never happened. You sent me to the most dangerous place in the country. And for what? What did I ever do to you? What did I do that was so wrong?"

"I love you," she says.

"Don't you dare say that to me." All my muscles tighten, and I clench my jaw so hard it sends pain to my ears.

In the back of my mind, I hear Keegan's words. *"I don't think she accused you for the reason you think she did."* But I'm exhausted and can't think straight. Seeing her in the flesh takes everything I have left.

I lower my gun and shake my head, too confounded to speak for a moment.

"Lexi, I'm begging you," she says.

"I don't owe you anything." I narrow my eyes at her.

"Your stepfather figured out what was going on," she says.

"Stop. That's enough."

"He broke into the study and found everything."

"I don't care."

"He figured it out; he realized what was going on."

413

"What was going on? Are you kidding me? That man was torturing me, and you just stood there and did nothing to stop him. Nothing!"

I spin on my heels and swallow the bile in my throat, pulling a shocked Cole with me. I need to get out of here before I shoot her.

"He never did those things to you," she says. I turn back toward her.

"You're insane."

"No, Lexi, I'm not."

"What? You don't think I remember? I know exactly what he did to me. I lived it. And he drugged you. So go right ahead and believe whatever you want to believe. I don't care anymore; I'm no longer your daughter ... You know nothing about me. I'm with the people who love and care about me, and I want nothing to do with you. Stay away from me, I don't ever want to see or hear from you again."

I'm practically running away from her when she says one last thing.

"He didn't torture you," she says loudly. "I did."

THE END

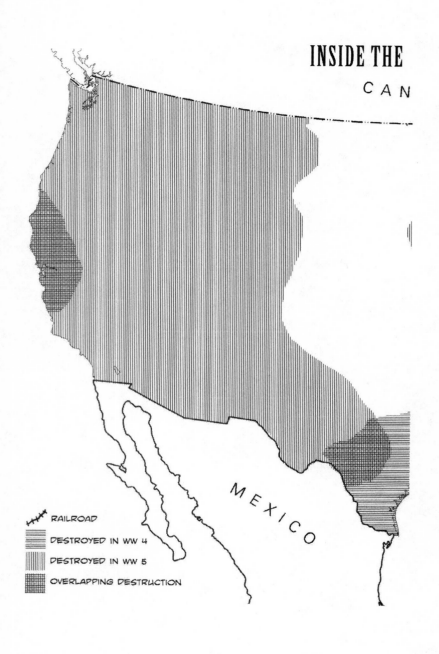

INSIDE THE

C A N

M E X I C O

RAILROAD

DESTROYED IN WW 4

DESTROYED IN WW 5

OVERLAPPING DESTRUCTION

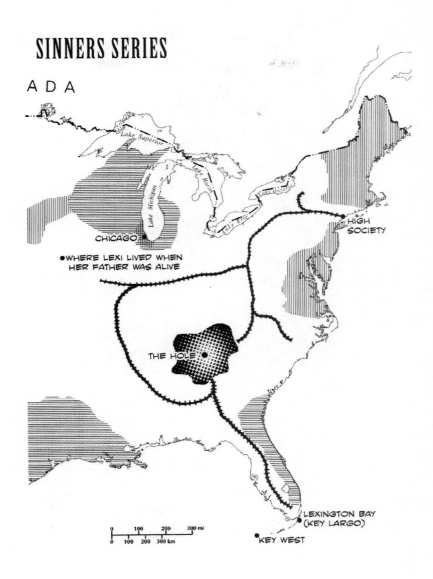

SINNERS SERIES

A D A

Abi Ketner

Abi Ketner Is a registered nurse with a passion for novels, the beaches of St. John, and her Philadelphia Phillies. A talented singer, Abi loves to go running and spend lots of time with her family. She currently resides in Lancaster, Pennsylvania with her husband, triplet daughters and two very spoiled dogs.

Melissa Kalicicki

Melissa Kalicicki received her bachelor's degree from Millersville University in 2003. She married, had two boys and currently lives in Lancaster, Pennsylvania. Aside from reading and writing, her interests include running and mixed martial arts. She also remains an avid Cleveland sports fan.

READ BRANDED CHAPTER ONE

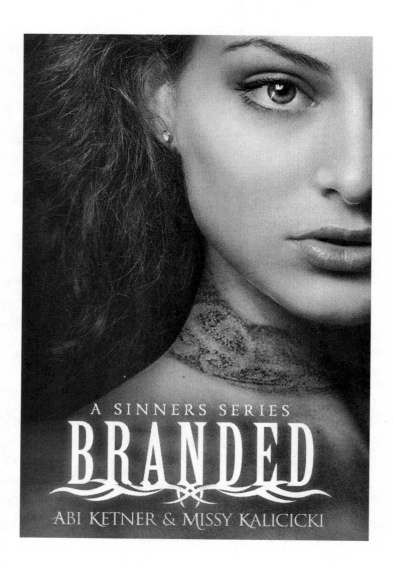

A SINNERS SERIES

BRANDED

ABI KETNER & MISSY KALICICKI

CHAPTER 1

I'm buried six feet under, and no one hears my screams.

The rope chafes as I loop it around my neck. I pull down, making sure the knot is secure. It seems sturdy enough. My legs shake. My heart beats heavy in my throat. Sweat pours down my back.

Death and I glare at each other through my tears.

I take one last look at the crystal chandelier, the foyer outlined with mirrors, and the flawless decorations. No photographs adorn the walls. No happy memories here.

I'm ready to go. *On the count of three.*

I inhale, preparing myself for the finality of it all. Dropping my hands, a glimmer catches my eye. It's my ring, the last precious gift my father gave me. I twist it around to read the inscription. Picturing his face forces me to reconsider my choice. He'd be heartbroken if he could see me now.

A door slams in the hallway, almost causing me to lose my balance. My thoughts already muddled, I stand waiting with the rope hanging around my neck. Voices I don't recognize creep through the walls.

Curiosity overshadows my current thoughts. It's late at night, and this is a secure building in High Society. No one disturbs the peace here—ever. I tug on the noose and pull it back over my head.

Peering through the eyehole in our doorway, I see a large group of armed guards banging on my neighbors' door. A heated conversation ensues, and my neighbors point toward my family's home.

It hits me. I've been accused and they're here to arrest me.

My father would want me to run, and in that split second, I decide to listen to his voice within me. Flinging myself forward in fear, I scramble up the marble staircase and into my brother's old bedroom. The door is partially covered, but it exists. Pushing his dresser aside, my fingers claw at the opening. Breathing hard, I lodge myself against it. Nothing. I step back and kick it with all my strength. The wood splinters open, and my foot gets caught. I wrench it backward, scraping my calf, but adrenaline pushes me forward. The voices at the front door shout my name.

On hands and knees, I squeeze through the jagged opening. My brother left through this passage, and now it's my escape too. Cobwebs entangle my face, hands, and hair. At the end, I feel for the knob, twisting it clockwise. It swings open, creaking from disuse. I sprint into the hallway and smash through the large fire escape doors at the end. A burst of cool air strikes me in the face as I jump down the ladder.

Reaching the fifth floor, I knock on a friend's window. The lights flicker on, and I see the curtains move, but no one answers. I bang on the window harder.

"Let me in! Please!" I say, but the lights darken. They know I've been accused and refuse to help me. Fear and adrenaline rush through my veins as I keep running, knocking on more windows along the way. No one has mercy. They all know what happens to sinners.

Another flight of stairs passes in a blur when I hear the guards' heavy footfalls from above. I can't hide, but I don't want to go without trying.

Help me, Daddy. I need your strength now.

My previous desolation evolves into a will to survive. I have to keep running, but I tremble and gasp for air. I steel my nerves and force my body to keep moving. In a matter of minutes, my legs cramp and my chest burns. I plunge to the ground, scraping my knee and elbow. A moan escapes from my chest.

Gotta keep going.

"Stop!" Their voices bounce off the buildings. "Lexi Hamilton, surrender yourself," they command. They're gaining on me.

I resist the urge to glance back, running into what I assume is an alley. I'm far from our high-rise in High Society as I plunge into a poorer section of the city where the streets all look the same and the darkness prevents me from recognizing anything. I'm lost.

My first instinct is to leap into a dumpster, but I retain enough sense to stay still. I crouch and peek around it, watching them dash by. The abhorrent smell leaves me vomiting until nothing remains in my stomach. Desperation overtakes me, as I know my retching was anything but silent. My last few seconds tick away before they find me. Everyone knows about their special means of tracking sinners.

I push myself to my feet and look left, right, and left again. Their batons click against their black leather belts, and their boots stomp the cement on both sides of me. I shrink into myself. Their heavy steps mock my fear, growing closer and closer until I know I'm trapped.

Never did I imagine they'd come for me. Never did I imagine all those nights I heard them dragging someone else away that I'd join them.

"You're a sinner," they say. "Time to leave."

I stand defiant. I refuse to bend or break before them, even as I shiver with fear.

"There's no reason to make this difficult. The more you cooperate, the smoother this will be for everyone," a guard says.

I cringe into the blackness along the wall. I'm innocent, but they won't believe me or care.

The next instant, my face slams into the pavement as one guard plants a knee in my back and another handcuffs me. A warm liquid trails into my mouth. Blood. Their fingers grip my arms like steel traps as they peel me off the cement. The tops of my shoes scrape along the ground as I'm dragged behind them until they discard me into the back of a black vehicle. The doors slam in unison with one guard stationed on each side of me, my shoulders digging into their arms.

Swallowing hard, I stare ahead to avoid their eyes. My dignity is all I have left. The handcuffs dig into my wrists, so I clasp them together hard behind me and press my back into the seat, unwilling to admit how much it hurts.

Did they need so many guards to capture me?

I'm not carrying any weapons, nor do I own any. I don't even know self-defense. High Society frowns on activities like that.

The driver jerks the vehicle around, and I try to keep my bearings, but it's dark and the scenery changes too fast. Hours pass, and the air grows warmer, more humid the farther we drive. The landscape mutates from city to rolling hills. They don't bother blindfolding me because they escort all the sinners to the same place—the Hole. Twenty-foot cement walls encase the chaos within. There's no way out and no way in unless they transport you. They say the Hole is a prison with no rules. We learned about it last year in twelfth grade.

To the outside, I'm filth now. I'll never be allowed to return to the life I knew. No one ever does.

"All sinners go through a transformation," one of the guards says to me. His smirk infuriates me. "I'm sure you've heard all kinds of stories." I don't respond. I don't want to think about the things I've been told.

"You won't last too long, though. Young girls like you get eaten alive." He pulls a strand of my hair up to his face.

Get your hands off me, you pig. I want to lash out, but resist. The punishment for disobeying authority is severe, and I'm not positioned to defy him.

They're the Guards of the Commander. They're chosen from a young age and trained in combat. They keep the order of society by using violent methods of intimidation. No one befriends a guard. Relationships with them are forbidden inside the Hole.

Few have seen the Commander. His identity remains hidden. His own paranoia and desire to stay pure drove him to live this way. He controls our depraved society and believes sinners make the human race unforgivable. His power is a crushing fist, rendering all beneath him helpless. So much so, even family members turn on each other when an accusation surfaces. Just an accusation. No trial, no evidence, nothing but an accusation.

I lose myself in thoughts of my father.

"Never show fear, Lexi," my father said to me before he was taken. "They'll use it against you." His compassionate eyes filled with warning as he commanded me to be strong. That was many years ago, but I remember it clearly. My father. My rock. The one person in my life who provided unconditional love.

"Get out," the guard says while pulling me to my feet. The vehicle stops, and I'm jerked back to reality. The doors slide open and the two guards lift me up and out into the night. A windowless cement building looms in front of us, looking barren in the darkness.

The coolness of the air sends a shiver up my spine. This is really happening. I've been labeled a sinner. My lip starts to quiver, but I bite it before anyone sees. They shove me in line, and I realize I'm not alone. Women and men stand with faces frozen white with fear. Some are hardened criminals; others, like me, are innocent. A guard grabs my finger, pricks it, and dabs my blood on a tiny microchip.

I follow the man in front of me into the next room where we're lined up facing the wall. Glancing right, I see one of the men crying.

"I didn't mean to hit the guard. I swear it!" he pleads.

I turn my head when I see a guard whip out his baton. The thumping sounds of his beating unnerve me.

"Spread your legs," one of the guards says icily.

They remove my outer layers and their hands roam up and down my body.

What do they think I can possibly be hiding? I press my head into the wall, trying to block out what they're doing to me.

"MOVE!" a guard commands. So I shuffle across the room, trying to cover up.

One.

Two.

Three.

Four.

Five of us sit in the holding room. A woman clings to a man sitting next to her. She grips his arm and I can see the whitening of her knuckles. Her eyes meet mine and then she quickly turns away. He's bent over his hands, defeated.

"I'm not the criminal they say I am," he whispers. His voice breaks.

One by one, they pull people into the next room, forcing the rest of us to wonder what torture we'll endure. I hear screaming from somewhere inside. An agonizing amount of time passes. I lean my head back and try to imagine a place far away. The door opens.

"Lexi Hamilton."

A guard escorts me out of the room, and I don't have time to look back. The first thing I see is a large photo of a regal-looking man on the wall. His frame is wide and he has cobalt blue eyes and a shock of black hair. He's handsome, middle-aged, and wears the uniform of the Commander. My jaw drops open. *It can't be...*

Then the door slams closed. Strong arms pick me up and place me on a table. It's cold and my skin sticks to it slightly, like wet fingers on an ice cube. They exit in procession, and I lie on the table with a doctor standing over me. His hands are busy as he speaks.

"Don't move. This will only take a few minutes. It's time for you to be branded."

A wet cloth that smells like rubbing alcohol is used to clean my skin. Then he places a metal collar around my neck. *Click. Click. Click.*

The collar locks into place, and I struggle to breathe. The doctor loosens it some as I focus on the painted black words above me.

THE SEVEN DEADLY SINS:

LUST — BLUE
GLUTTONY — ORANGE
GREED — YELLOW
SLOTH — BLACK
WRATH — RED
ENVY — GREEN
PRIDE — PURPLE

"Memorize it. Might keep you alive longer if you know who to stay away from." He opens my mouth, placing a bit inside. "Bite this."

Within seconds, the collar heats from hot to scorching. The smell of flesh sizzling makes my head spin. I bite down so hard a tooth cracks.

"GRRRRRRRRR," escapes from deep within my chest. Just when I'm about to pass out, the temperature drops, and the doctor loosens the collar.

He removes it and sits me up. Excruciating pain rips through me, and I'm on the verge of a mental and physical breakdown. *Focus. Don't pass out.*

Stainless steel counters and boring white walls press in on me. And that large, gilded photo stares at me like it's watching. A guard laughs at me from an observation room above and yells, "Blue. It's a great color for a pretty young thing like yourself." His eyes dance with suggestion. The others meander around like it's business as usual.

I finally find my voice and turn to the doctor.

"Are you going to give me clothes?" A burning pain spreads like fire up from my neck to my jaw, making me wince.

He shrugs and points to a set of folded grey scrubs on a chair. I cover myself as much as I can and scurry sideways. Grabbing my clothes and pulling the shirt over my head, I try to avoid the raw meat around my throat. I quickly knot the cord of my pants around my waist and slide my feet into the hospital-issue slippers as the doctor observes. He hands me a bag labeled with my name.

"Nothing is allowed through the door but what we've given you," he says.

I hide my right hand behind me, hoping no one notices. A guard scans my body and opens his fist.

"Give it to me." His eyes turn to slits. "Don't make me rip off your finger." He crouches down and I turn to stone. I don't know what to do, so I beg.

"My father gave this to me. Please, let me keep it." I smash my eyes shut and think of the moment my father handed the golden ring to me.

"It was my mother's ring," he'd said. "She's the strongest woman I ever knew." With tears in his eyes, he reached for my hand and said, "Lexi, you're exactly like her. She'd want you to wear this. No matter how this world changes, you can survive." I turned the gold band over in my palm and read the engraving.

YOU CAN OVERCOME ANYTHING...SHORT OF DEATH.

"You're going to take the one thing that matters the most to me?" I say, glaring into the guard's emotionless eyes. "Isn't it enough taking my life, dignity, and respect?"

A hard blow falls upon my back. As I fall, my hands shoot out to stop me from smashing into the wall in front of me. The guard bends down and grabs my chin with his meaty fist.

"Look at me," he commands. I look up and he smiles with arrogance.

"What the hell?" He staggers a step backward. "What's wrong with you? What's wrong with your eyes?"

"Nothing," I respond, confused.

"What color are they?"

"Turquoise." I glower at him.

"Interesting," he says, regaining his composure. "Now those'll get you in trouble."

Reality slaps me across the face. I have my father's eyes. They can't take them from me. I twist the ring off my finger and drop it in his hand.

"Take the damn ring," I say. I walk to the door. He swipes a card and the massive door slides open to the outside.

"You have to wear your hair back at all times, so everyone knows what you are." He hands me a tie, so I pull my frizzy hair away from my face and secure it into a ponytail. My neck burns and itches as my hand traces the scabs that have already begun to form. Squinting ahead in the darkness, I almost run into a guard standing on the sidewalk.

"Watch where you're going," he says, shoving me backward. His stiff figure stands tall, and I cringe at the sharpness of his voice.

"Cole, this is your new assignment, Lexi Hamilton. See to it she feels welcome in her new home." The guard departs with a salute.

"Let's move," Cole says.

I take two steps and collapse, my knees giving out. The unforgiving pavement reopens the scrapes from earlier and I struggle to stand. A powerful arm snatches me up, and I see his face for the first time.

OTHER MONTH9BOOKS TITLES YOU MIGHT LIKE

FIRE IN THE WOODS by Jennifer M. Eaton
THE ARTISANS by Julie Reece
PRAEFATIO by Georgia McBride
LIFER by Beck Nicholas
THE NIGHT HOUSE by Rachel Tafoya

Find more awesome Teen books at Month9Books.com

Facebook: www.Facebook.com/Month9Books
Twitter: https://twitter.com/Month9Books
You Tube: www.youtube.com/user/Month9Books
Blog: www.month9booksblog.com
Instagram: https://instagram.com/month9books
Request review copies via publicity@month9books.com

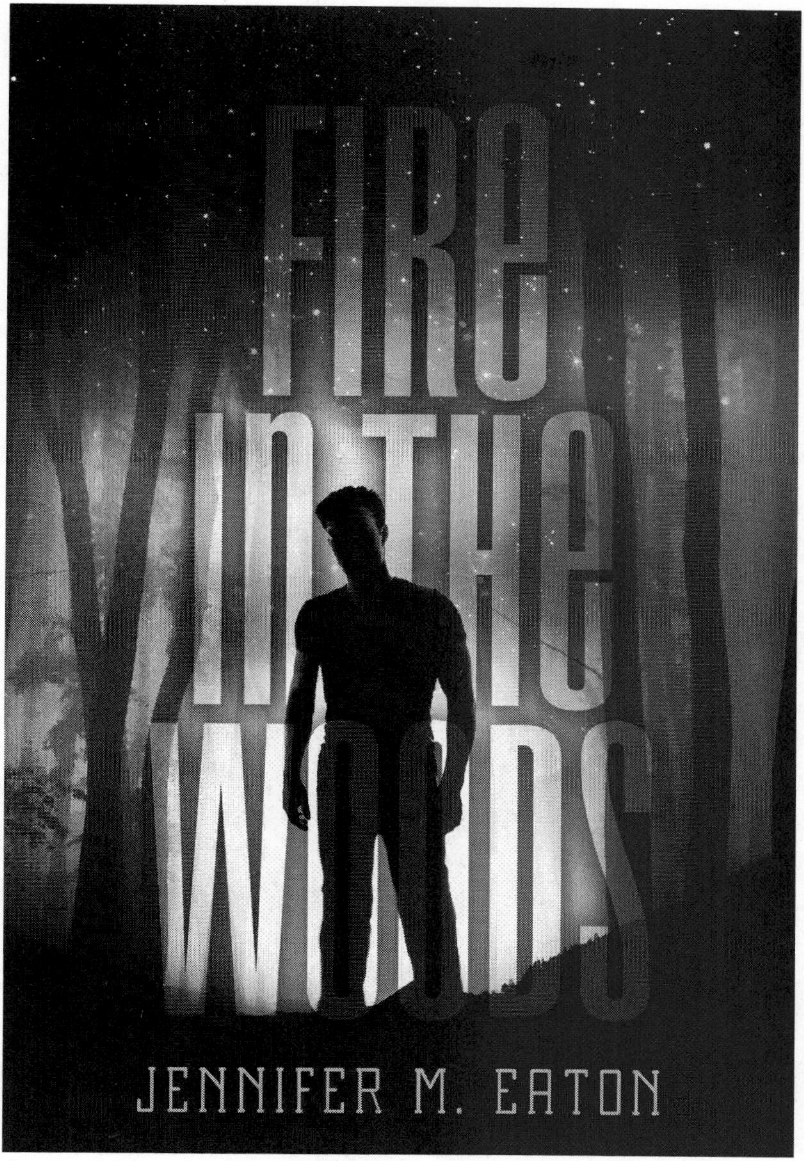
FIRE
IN THE
WOODS
JENNIFER M. EATON

The Artisans

"The Artisans has all the elements I love - spooky intrigue,
strong friendships, and a romantic tension to be savored."
~ Wendy Higgins, *New York Times* **bestselling author**
of *the Sweet Evil* **trilogy.**

JULIE REECE

BOOK 1 IN THE PRAEFATIO SERIES

PRAEFATIO

A NOVEL

"This is teen fantasy at its most entertaining, most heartbreaking, most compelling. Highly recommended." –Jonathan Maberry, New York Times bestselling author of ROT & RUIN and FIRE & ASH

GEORGIA McBRIDE

One slave girl will lead a rebellion.
One nameless boy will discover the truth.
When their paths collide, everything changes.

LIFER

BECK NICHOLAS